Tobsha Learner was
and has lived in both
well-known in Australia as a playwright and her
first collection of short stories, *Quiver*, has sold
over 150,000 copies internationally. Her third
book — the bestselling *The Witch of Cologne* —
was her first work of historical fiction and was
followed by another collection of short stories,
*Tremble* and her fifth book, *Soul*. Tobsha divides
her time between London, Sydney and California.

Visit Tobsha Learner at her website:
www.tobshalearner.com

Other books by Tobsha Learner

*Quiver*
*Madonna Mars*
*The Witch of Cologne*
*Tremble*
*Soul*

# Tobsha Learner
# SPHINX

HarperCollins*Publishers*

**HarperCollins***Publishers*

First published in Australia in 2009
by HarperCollins*Publishers* Australia Pty Limited
ABN 36 009 913 517
www.harpercollins.com.au

Copyright © Tobsha Learner 2009

The right of Tobsha Learner to be identified as the author of this
work has been asserted by her under the *Copyright Amendment
(Moral Rights) Act 2000*.

This work is copyright. Apart from any use as permitted under the
*Copyright Act 1968*, no part may be reproduced, copied, scanned, stored
in a retrieval system, recorded or transmitted, in any form or by any
means, without the prior written permission of the publisher.

**HarperCollins***Publishers*
25 Ryde Road, Pymble, Sydney, NSW 2073, Australia
31 View Road, Glenfield, Auckland 0627, New Zealand
1–A, Hamilton House, Connaught Place, New Delhi – 110 001, India
77–85 Fulham Palace Road, London, W6 8JB, United Kingdom
2 Bloor Street East, 20th floor, Toronto, Ontario M4W 1A8, Canada
10 East 53rd Street, New York NY 10022, USA

National Library of Australia Cataloguing-in-Publication data:

Tobsha, Learner.
 Sphinx/Tobsha Learner.
 ISBN 978 0 7322 8673 6 (pbk.)
 Bibliography.
A823.3

Cover and internal design by Darren Holt, HarperCollins Design Studio
Cover photograph by Zena Holloway
Cover background images and internal illustrations © Shutterstock.com
Typeset in 11.5/16 Sabon by Kirby Jones
Printed and bound in Australia by Griffin Press
70gsm Bulky Book Ivory used by HarperCollins*Publishers* is a natural, recyclable
product made from wood grown in sustainable forests. The manufacturing processes
conform to the environmental regulations in the country of origin, New Zealand.

5 4 3 2 1    09 10 11 12

In memory of Troy Davies

1959–2007

Maverick, muse and emotional anarchist

# Author's Note

This is a work of fiction written to entertain, inspire and intrigue and should be read as such. Any similarity to a living person or actual institution is entirely coincidental.

Many of the historical characters and their back stories are factual. For example, Nectanebo II did disappear mysteriously at the end of his reign. The character of Banafrit, however, is a literary device. The Antikythera mechanism — the oldest piece of machinery in existence, dating back two thousand years — is authentic, therefore the hypothesis that it might have had predecessors is logical.

Finally, the author would like to make it clear to her readers that she strongly condemns the illegal removal of antiquities from Egypt and any unauthorised exploration, commercial or otherwise.

# Prelude

Now, when I look at the desert, I am reminded of the year I spent in Egypt — the most definitive of my life. I never fail to be amazed by how sand resembles granules of glass, orbs made by grains colliding with each other as they shift, trickle and blow in invisible clouds across the horizon.

And I am reminded of how, if I'd had the eye of God that year, if I'd had some omnipresent aerial vision that could have wrapped itself around all the deserts of the world, I would have seen that when sandstorms settle they settle in patterns and those patterns make a cipher — a hidden prophecy.

# I

## Abu Rudeis oilfield, Western Sinai, Egypt, 1977

In the distance a dust devil skimmed along the horizon, its trajectory zigzagging with uncanny intelligence. The Bedouin believed such dust storms to be the restless spirits of those who lay unburied, bone-naked, lost in the harsh desert. Was this a bad omen? Worried the roughnecks might think so, I glanced over. The fieldworkers, big fearless men, overalls blackened with grime and oil, were paused, tools in hand staring at the phenomenon.

This landscape was second nature to me, a place where my soul sprang into thirsty agitation. I read terrain like the blind read Braille. Known as the Diviner, I had the reputation of being the best geophysicist in the industry, famous for my ability to discover oil. But the moniker made me uncomfortable: it seemed to suggest I had some mystical talent. In reality, I was meticulous in my scientific research but also prepared to take the extra gamble many others were frightened to.

The rumble of the generators rolled out over the sand like the growling of some colossal animal. To my left stood the pump jacks and rigs of the Abu Rudeis oilfield, the derricks sentries against the bleached sky. Captured by Israel in the

1967 war, the oilfield had been returned to Egyptian control in November 1975 and army tanks still patrolled its perimeters. This was border country, the atmosphere a tinderbox. It felt as if any sudden movement — a jeep careering off course, a bout of careless yelling — might trigger another bone-jarring exchange of fire.

Over at the control tower, the rest of the crew were hovering, waiting for me to give the final command to start drilling. A jeep was parked nearby, its door open, the driver tuning his car radio, the bulge of his pistol rippling under his jacket as he moved. Country and western music collided with the melancholic voice of singer Mohamed Abdel Wahab, the plaintive Arabic ballad blasting out with the heat across the blindingly white plains.

'Mr Warnock!' the driver shouted, pointing to the fake Rolex watch that had appeared from under the sleeve of his jellaba. I nodded and swung around to face the newly constructed rig. The derrick hung suspended over the rocky ground; the crew gathered by the control panel stared at me, tense with anticipation, watching for the thumbs down: the signal to begin drilling. My assistant, Moustafa Saheer, catching my eye, grinned and nodded.

In the instant I lifted my hand there was a huge explosion. I threw myself to the ground, a burst of gunfire followed.

Convinced I was about to die, an image of Isabella, my wife, shot through my mind — she was stepping out of the shower, her wet hair streaking down to her waist, her smile enticing, wry. It was a memory from eight weeks earlier — the last time I'd seen her.

I glanced over my shoulder — one of the wells had been transformed into a single blazing pillar. 'Blowout!' I shouted, but already the crew were clambering down, frantic, limbs tumbling over limbs. Nearby, a panicked soldier sprinted towards the inferno firing his automatic rifle uselessly into the air.

'Get in! Get in!' the driver screamed to me. Running like a burning man, I bolted for the jeep.

\* \* \*

We drove back to the camp in silence as black smoke billowed alongside the road. Moustafa stared out of the back window at the blazing oilwell now a flaming tower receding into the distance.

My assistant had trained in Budapest and spoke perfect English with a private school accent, but it had been his methodical analysis and easy-going camaraderie with the roughnecks — an asset in politically anxious times — that had impressed me. This was the third project I'd hired him on, and we had developed a concise communication based on an understanding of each other's personalities and boundaries; essential out in the field where it was often too noisy to hear anyone speak.

'All those months of calculation gone.' Moustafa's expression was lugubrious.

'C'mon, it's not our well burning. The company will cap the fire and we'll start our drilling a few weeks late.'

'A few weeks is still a great deal of money. This is bad for my country.'

After Nasser nationalised the Egyptian oil industry, he insisted that local men replace the mainly Italian, French and Greek field workers. But when Nasser died of a sudden heart attack in 1970, his heir, Anwar El Sadat, had introduced an open-door policy. The consultancy company I worked for — GeoConsultancy — was part of that policy. I'd been brought in by the Alexandrian Oil Company to assess whether they should drill south of the existing oilfield and develop a deeper, as yet untested, reservoir. After six months, with the help of Moustafa, we'd finally convinced them it was worth the risk.

The sound of the explosion still rang in my ears. I turned back towards the skyline; dusk had reduced the sea to an inky charcoal, the rippling waves glittered randomly. The sky was a burnt orange; the offshore oilrigs silhouetted on the horizon like marooned ships with bizarrely oversized masks, islands of industry. It was a sight that never failed to inspire me. I sniffed my fingers; they smelled of smoke and burning oil. The blowout had thrown everything into perspective. Suddenly, I was convinced that I would never get the chance to reconcile with Isabella. I hadn't spoken to her since our fight and the thought that I might never see her again had been terrifying.

Oil geologists spend a lot of time by themselves, analysing seismic data or studying core samples on site. You develop a certain self-sufficiency, the roar of your own blood filling your head until you find yourself deaf to other people. But after five years of marriage I had become welded to Isabella. We were the same animal, both of us fascinated by the way history folded itself into the ground, the trail of clues left by previous civilisations.

As a marine archaeologist, Isabella's hunting fields were the valleys and cliffs of the sea floor. Now, driving along the coast road that hugged the eastern edge of the Suez, I wondered whether she'd ignored my advice and had continued with her underwater exploration after our argument. She was searching for an ancient object, an astrarium, which she believed was a prototype of the Antikythera mechanism found off the coast of Rhodes in 1901. Although most experts believed nothing as mechanically sophisticated could have existed for thousands of years before or after it, Isabella was convinced it must have had predecessors. My wife was a maverick in her field, famous for making discoveries based on a few facts and an intuitive sense of where a site might lie. Her hunches were often uncannily correct — a fact that unnerved many of her contemporaries. She had been researching the astrarium for years, and now believed she was in the last months of her quest, having narrowed her search to Aboukir Bay near Alexandria — where the drowned Ptolemaic suburb of Herakleion lay, destroyed by a tsunami twelve hundred years earlier. Against my wishes she'd recently embarked on a series of illegal dives. There was a new desperation to Isabella's obsession and it frightened me.

\* \* \*

By the time we arrived at the field camp and pulled up beside the cluster of corrugated-iron worker cabins, I'd decided that regardless of whatever the company demanded, I would fly back to Alexandria early the next morning.

\* \* \*

Eight hours later, the well was still burning, despite the efforts of a ground crew working continuously. The sand berms that the tractors had pushed up around the well had contained the blaze, but thousands of dollars of precious oil continued to go up in smoke.

'It is impossible to put the fire out, my friend.' Mohamed, the manager of the oilfield, a usually cheerful man in his forties, appeared defeated. His large moon-shaped face seemed to have deflated around the collar of his stained boiler suit and his eyes glared out from below a soot-smeared brow. 'Forty men, their equipment and who knows how many gallons of expensive foam and the bastard is still burning. Any minute now the rest will go up and I will have an even greater catastrophe on my hands. A curse on the Israelis.'

Egypt had been given back the oilfields in 1975, after eight years of Israeli management.

'This wasn't sabotage,' I said. 'This was bad luck and maybe some negligence.'

'Negligence! We do what we can with the equipment available, but we are still catching up after the Israelis ruined the wells. Is that my fault?'

'Maybe it's time to look for some outside help?' I suggested.

'Never! Our roustabouts will get it under control eventually.'

'Eventually will be too late.'

I tried to contain the anger in my voice. Mohamed was quite capable of compromising the machinery to avoid losing face.

Moustafa stepped forward. I didn't stop him. Both of us knew he had the temperament and diplomacy to deal with the site manager's bursts of grievance, usually aimed indiscriminately at both government and private enterprise. Such tantrums had got three of my best field hands fired already.

Moustafa's tone was conciliatory. 'Mr Warnock did not mean to insult your professionalism, Mohamed. It is a major fire and it's going to take the best team around to extinguish the blaze. He merely meant to suggest that perhaps you might consider bringing in outside expertise.'

I glanced out the office window. A pernicious fog billowed above the blaze, snaking out across the landscape and staining everything in its path.

'I know a firefighting company run by a Texan called Bill Anderson,' I said. 'He's not cheap but he's the guy. He could be here within forty-eight hours.'

I'd first met Bill Anderson in Angola. After an abortive negotiation with a rebel leader and self-appointed oil tycoon failed to manifest, my company had hired a small plane to fly me quickly out of the country. Bill had been in nearby Nigeria, putting out a government oilwell that had been sabotaged by the same rebel leader, and had about as much affection for the region as I did. Between us we'd managed to persuade the manager of the local airfield to let us hide in his cellar until the next available Cessna arrived. We'd had nothing except a bucket, a crate of whisky and a pack of playing cards. By the end of the second night, we were violently disagreeing over philosophy, religion and politics. By the morning, we were lifelong friends.

'Forty-eight hours! I haven't got forty-eight hours!' Mohamed slammed his desk in frustration.

'You still have thirty intact wells, plus a brand-new drilling rig just waiting to go. You have forty-eight hours.' I scribbled down Anderson's telephone number. 'I'm going back to Alex until this is fixed. I can't open a potential new reservoir with this going on above ground — it's too dangerous.'

'The company won't like it.'

'That, my friend, is your problem.'

Mohamed sighed. 'One week, Oliver, then I promise the fire will be out, all the wells will be pumping again and you can start your drilling, *inshallah*.'

'God willing indeed.' I tucked the phone number into his breast pocket. 'You know where to find me.'

\* \* \*

It was about five in the morning by the time I got back to Alexandria. In those days, telephones were rare in Egypt and most people had to go to the post office to book a call. There was no phone in the company villa we were living in and so I had been unable to warn Isabella of my return. I would risk surprising her — she knew nothing about the explosion and I didn't intend to tell her about it. All I wanted was a truce and to have her back in my arms.

I hauled my luggage as quietly as possible across the cobbled back lane towards the old colonial villa. The security guard was just finishing his nightshift and let me in through the wrought-iron back gate; the enclosed garden, a sanctuary against the storm now buffeting the palm trees. Tinnin, the Alsatian guard dog, began to bark at my footfall. I murmured his name and he dropped to the ground whimpering, ears flattened.

As I pulled my key out I watched the window of the housekeeper's flat carefully. Ibrihim was a cautious, taciturn man. I didn't want to risk waking him. Shutting the heavy door behind me I slipped into the large entrance hall. The canaries in their large old-fashioned wire cage twittered wildly as the wind rattled the shutters of the French windows. After closing the windows I calmed the birds.

The house had been built in the 1920s and was an idiosyncratic blend of cubism with Islamic architectural overtones. The villa itself once housed the representative of the original British-owned Bell Oil Company, as it was known before Nasser nationalised the company. A photograph of Nasser now hung where the portrait of the original owner had once been. One evening, smiling furtively, Ibrihim had shown me the usurped and now hidden portrait — with a fez perched on top of his jowly Edwardian face the old patriarch looked like the ultimate colonial pasha — a dethroned prince exiled by revolution.

In the political chaos much of the original furniture had also been abandoned. Like many Alexandrian Europeans during the Suez Crisis in 1956, the plant manager had fled overnight but the Art Deco furniture, sofas and wall hangings remained; mementos of obscene wealth, all lovingly maintained by Ibrihim.

The bedroom door was ajar. The curtains were drawn and it was dark inside; I almost stumbled over an oxygen cylinder abandoned on the floor next to a wetsuit and mask. In the dim light I could just make out Isabella's sleeping form sprawled on top of the bedcovers.

I switched on a side lamp. There were maps spread out over the rugs — the spidery cartography of the sea floor, a parallel subterranean landscape, seductive in its mystery. In the middle of this pile lay a sheet of paper showing a drawing of a metal contraption; a fantastical device of dials and cogs held together in a wooden casing. The dials were engraved with a series of marks or symbols, like clock faces. I knew this was a fictional depiction of the astrarium drawn by my art student brother, Gareth. Isabella was close to Gareth, closer than I was in fact, and had commissioned the illustration, after briefing him from snippets of visual research she had amassed over the years. And now here it was — my nemesis, the one thing we always argued about — placed like a shrine in the centre of the floor.

Oblivious to the outside world Isabella had fallen asleep with her clothes on. Picking my way across the scattered papers it was easy to imagine her exhausted, falling across the bed after a day of diving. I didn't have the heart to wake her.

Instead, I sat in a battered leather armchair and watched her. The moonlight filtering in illuminated her strong face.

Isabella wasn't a beautiful woman in any conventional sense of the word. Her profile was just a little too angular to be considered feminine, her lips a little too thin. She had no breasts to speak of, I could almost span the width of her hips with one hand, and there was a constant hunger in the way she held her body, a tipping forward as if she was always ready to run. But her eyes were exquisite. Her irises were black; a kind of ebony that changed to violet if you stared long enough. They were the most startling aspect to her face; disproportionately large the rest of her features seemed to fall away from them. Then there were her hands — beautiful working hands with long fingers — tanned and worn, showing the hours immersed in water or spent painstakingly piecing together ancient objects.

Outside the villa, a nightjar cried out. Isabella stirred, groaned and rolled onto her side. I watched her lovingly, regretting our argument and ensuing estrangement. Isabella was how I anchored myself: to culture, to emotion, to place. And I was a man who craved place. I had grown up in a mining village in Cumbria and even now in my dreams I looked for the sweeping plains of Ordovician limestone, the landscape of my childhood. I was naturally drawn to solidity, to the slower evolving manifestations of nature. If I were to describe myself, it would be as a listener, a man of few words. Isabella was different. She used language to define herself, to ambush the moment and talk it into history. Nevertheless, she was able to read stillness, especially my stillness. That was the second reason why I'd fallen in love with her.

Isabella did not move. Finally I couldn't help myself. I leaned over and she woke, consciousness travelling slowly across her face to finally form a smile. Without saying anything she reached up and wrapped her arms around me. We sank down onto the bed.

Isabella's sexuality was an organic part of her nature; a spontaneous wildness that kept us both excited. We made love in exotic places: a telephone booth, beneath the tarpaulin of a boat in full view of the busy Indian port of Kochi, on the Scottish moors. But whatever the context, Isabella liked to stay in control. With her eyelashes brushing my cheeks, we kissed and I caressed her. Soon it felt as if there was nothing but the flame of her irises, her hardening nipples, her wetness.

She pulled away then took my sex into her mouth, staring intensely at me as she read my mounting arousal. Closing my eyes, I steadied myself against the base of the bed, then, knowing I was close to coming, pressed her back against the mattress. Pushing her knees apart, I buried my face between her thighs, losing myself in her scent, her taste. I brought her to the very brink then paused again, playing out the pleasure, watching her flushed face straining against the pillow. Then I entered her and the wonderful familiarity of us together sounded through me as I strived to hear her cry, her particular scream of orgasm.

I lay there afterwards, curled around her as she slipped back into sleep. Staring across the room, I listened to the sound of the rain lashing the windows. My last thought was one of thanks — for my marriage, for my life, for surviving. One of those moments of clarity one has in the dead of night: a quiet realisation that this might be happiness.

## 2

Two hours later, I woke to find Isabella standing by the open balcony door; hair streaming, naked against the early morning. The silk curtains swirling dervishes propelled by the wind.

'Isabella, it's freezing!'

Ignoring me, she stared out at the thunderous clouds low over the trees. I got out of bed, grabbed a dressing gown and wrapped her in it, then shut the doors.

'Please, can we get some sleep?'

'I can't. Oliver, how many years have I worked towards finding this astrarium? Ten? Fifteen, and it will be today, I know it!'

I glanced back at the window — the sky was as dark as it had been yesterday. 'That's not diving weather.'

'I'm diving anyway.'

'I'm assuming you have back-up with you — some of the French archaeologists, the Italians?'

Apart from an English archaeologist Amelia Lynhurst and a new young French academic who had just set up offices near the Stadium, marine archaeology was virtually unheard of in

Alexandria despite rumours of Cleopatra's sunken palace in the bay. Up until recently the political situation, dealing with poverty and the needs of Alexandria's citizens, had taken precedence.

Isabella smiled wryly. 'I'm afraid it's only me and Faakhir.'

Faakhir Alsayla was a young diver Isabella had been working with over the past few months. Although he was trustworthy and enthusiastic as well as a great diver, the young Arab was not an archaeologist.

'Christ, Isabella.' I would have preferred her to be part of an authorised team. Famous for making intuitive guesses — usually based on a few facts and just an obsessive sense of where a new site might lie — Isabella was a rebel in her own field and not liked for it. Her hunches were often uncannily correct — a fact that unnerved many of her contemporaries. We seemed to share this gift of divination, something I'd refused to discuss, not willing to acknowledge I had any talent other than good science.

'Let's talk about it later.' I tried to pull her back towards the bed, with no success.

'Oliver, I have to dive today! It's all planned. We've found the site of a Ra shipwreck I'm sure dates from the Battle of Actium. The astrarium could have been on board — the Greek historian Siculus mentions such an object being given to Cleopatra at her coronation.'

'What's the rush? You've waited years. Surely it can wait a few days?'

'I don't have a few days.'

I stared at her, a kernel of remembrance uncoiling in the back of my mind. 'This isn't about that prediction, is it? Isabella, you know it's complete bullshit.'

She angrily broke away from me. 'You just don't understand how I think, do you? That Newtonian you carry around inside you refuses to believe that there might be other principles, perhaps less conventional but just as valid, at play … At least I'm honest about my methodology.'

I tried to dismiss a creeping defensiveness. Sensing my shift in attitude, Isabella turned toward me.

'Come on, I've seen you out there on the oilfield, in your bare feet, sniffing the air. It's not just science you rely on, but you just won't admit it!'

'Sweetheart, the whole area's a military zone.' I slipped an arm around her waist.

'I've made provisions. There'll be an official on the boat.'

'Really? Or is this some dubious character you've bribed?'

She shrugged off my arm. 'I'm making that dive, no matter what!'

Under the anger I thought she looked apprehensive. At the time I thought it might be concern about us, the marriage, our careers, but now I know it was fear.

'So you really believe the astrarium was aboard this ship? Why would Cleopatra take it into the middle of a raging sea battle?'

'She was desperate. She knew her lover was delusional about his military power. She also knew that if Octavian won, he would murder Mark Antony and sacrifice their children. This was a woman who had staked all on winning. Siculus described the astrarium as a powerful weapon that could predict when to sail and when to attack.'

I struggled to keep my expression neutral. I believed in a world of cause and effect: crushed carbon made diamonds; crushed limestone, marble; compressed organic material, oil. This was my world: palpable, exploitable. Isabella's world was far more spiritual, things happened for a reason: there was a karmic logic to the outcome of events; the personal had an immediate impact on the political, the micro on the macro. I thought this a misinformed perception; an anthropocentric outlook that bred complacency; the determinist's investment in the notion of meaningful destiny.

'If Cleopatra had the astrarium and it was able to influence the outcome of the battle, why did she flee and abandon Mark Antony to Octavian?' I asked.

'I don't know, but if it had been me, I would have fought to change my fate right up to the last minute. The astrarium would have saved her, I know it.' Her obsessive tone worried me. Again, the desire to protect her shot through me.

There was a huge clap of thunder outside. A violent gust of wind threw open the French doors and pushed over a cane chair.

'That's cyclone weather,' I told her as I secured the doors. 'You are not diving today!'

'It's too dangerous for me not to dive!' she yelled.

She was almost hysterical by now and I knew it was pointless to continue to argue.

'You can dive tomorrow, first light,' I said, pulling her into an embrace. 'I'll go with you, okay? But this day is for us. We'll do something nice, maybe visit your grandmother. By tomorrow morning the storm will have cleared and visibility is going to be so much better.'

'You don't understand,' she murmured into my chest. But she let me guide her back to bed.

Back then, I thought we had all the time in the world.

\* \* \*

Already the salty tang of the sea air was discernible above the exhaust fumes, the wafting scent of incense billowing from jars placed outside night stalls tainted by the ubiquitous but faint odour of sewage. Isabella wound up the taxi window; we were driving down the Corniche — the long seafront path that swung around the glittering curve of the Eastern harbour. We stopped at a red light and I glanced across at the cafés on the sidewalk. Huddled around small tables were groups of men, some dressed in the pale brown jellaba and blue turban — the traditional dress of the fellahin — others in western clothes, sharing the large hookah pipes with their colourful corded stems snaking out into the mouth of the smoker. Inside one of the cafés a black-and-white television blared out to a small argumentative knot of men and youths. A football game was playing. A penalty was being taken and a sudden cheer catapulted through the men, reminding me oddly of England and the long afternoons of watching football with my father and brother.

I turned back to the Mediterranean. The emptiness of the panorama in stark contrast to the frenetic metropolis nestled up beside it. Liberating the eye, this elemental minimalism was always a comfort to me. It took me away from humanity, from the mistakes we make, the noisiness of life. In Alexandria, as in the rest of Egypt, this polarity was exaggerated, the desert touched the sea, just as the green fecundity of the delta surrounding the Nile and its canals butted right up against the sand. It was said that Alexandria had a front door and a back door and little else.

Northwest of the bay, out there under the waves lay Isabella's archaeological site. Looking out of the car window I remembered stories she told about growing up around myths of Cleopatra's subterranean city, how family friends would tell stories of swimming amongst strange sunken statues, ruins of palaces. Tales that buried themselves deep in her psyche, drawing her irredeemably to their mystery. I couldn't help being proud of the explorer within her regardless of how it impacted on our relationship. I reached across and took her hand as the taxi continued down towards her grandmother's villa.

\* \* \*

The wealthy suburb of Bulkely still retained some of its original mansions, wrought-iron gates still enclosed gardens of tumbling bougainvillea, Lotus trees and blossoming cacti as well as the palms. The Brambillas had once been one of the key dynasties within the large and influential Italian–Alexandrian community. Isabella's father, Paolo, had died shortly after the Suez Crisis in 1956 when, in reaction, Nasser nationalised all of the foreign-owned companies. President of the Italian Rowing Club, the Rotary Club and owner of a large and highly successful cotton-ginning mill, Paolo had been transformed from owner to manager overnight and the factory that processed the cottonseed had been handed over to the fellahin who had worked the cotton fields for centuries. The humiliation had been too much for the Don and he had died of a heart attack several weeks later. Cecilia, his young wife, remarried within the year, and moved back to Italy leaving her eight-year-old daughter with her in-laws to be brought up.

Isabella had barely talked to her mother over the years. Her grandfather Giovanni Brambilla, a broken man, retreated into the two passions that had always preoccupied him — hunting and Egyptology until his death ten years ago. Now his widow Francesca Brambrilla, was forced to rent out the top floor of her villa and had been pawning her jewellery for decades. Nevertheless, she retained her loyal Sudanese housekeeper, Aadeel, who had come with her as part of her trousseau. Although Aadeel was an official tenant of the villa these days and not an indentured employee, he still wore the uniform of the pre-Revolution servant — a red turban and traditional Egyptian male attire. It was the last act in a drama both were determined to play out: obsolete roles from a bygone era.

The Brambilla villa, although dilapidated, was still impressive. A familiar sense of intimidation rose in me as the taxi pulled up in front of its marble-pillared entrance. Isabella's background was one of assumed wealth, even when most of the money had been lost. But I came from nothing. I'd grown up with a miner for a father and a mother who was deeply religious. As a child, I'd concluded that if there was a God he'd certainly abandoned my parents to their hardships. It seemed to me that the poorer you were the more religious you were likely to be — this abdication of taking responsibility of one's fate — and it had led to my abandonment of Catholicism, my socialist tendencies at university and finally to my material aspirations.

As we both climbed out of the taxi we noticed a yellow Fiat sports car. 'That's Hermes' car,' Isabella commented. 'That'll make it an interesting encounter.'

'I thought Francesca hated him?'

'Exactly, but today is my grandfather's birthday and Hermes always visits, as he did when my grandfather was still alive. Nonna is too well-bred to refuse him.'

Hermes Hemiedes, an Egyptologist, had been an old friend of Isabella's grandfather. When Giovanni Brambilla died, Hermes had formed a relationship with the granddaughter. A very reputable interpreter, he and Isabella spent hours together poring over hieroglyphs that she needed translated. Although I didn't approve of Hermes' influence over Isabella in mystical matters, he had a dry wit that I found appealing.

\* \* \*

We had finished our lunch and were now drinking coffee in the conservatory waiting for the traditional dish of marmalade that completed the meal. Francesca and Hermes sat opposite, Francesca in a chair that was reminiscent of some eighteenth-century wooden Baroque throne — one of the antiques she hadn't been forced to sell. At eighty years old the matriarch still had the upright stance of a dancer and was the embodiment of classical European grace. She made me think of Rome of the 1930s — her dyed black hair sculpted into a short crisp wave, the creased olive skin suckered against the bones of a lineage bred for power and beauty.

In contrast Hermes lounged in a leather armchair. His hair was long, its silver roots merging into dyed purple-red locks that descended to his shoulders. He could almost have passed for an elderly woman, an illusion helped by a remarkable lack of facial hair. His eyes were golden brown with a tinge of yellow in the irises, indicating a curious ethnic mix somewhere in his lineage. The shape of his face suggested the Sudan while the thinness of his lips gave him a European look. His hands, gnarled by arthritis, bore witness to his true age, which Isabella had told me was around seventy.

A silver dish filled with marmalade was placed on the table, ten matching silver spoons curving out of the thick golden paste like swan's necks. They represented the members of the family, most of whom were long dead. Aadeel placed four glasses of water on the pearl and wood inlaid table. Quickly, I washed the bittersweet taste of the marmalade down with the water then reached for the small cup of viscous coffee.

Isabella could not relax. She stood up and walked to the window and pulled open the shutters. Her agitation seemed a conductor for the lightning that flashed across the sky. The distant boom of thunder sounded out a moment later.

Francesca sighed in exasperation. 'You think you can wish away the weather, Isabella? Sit down. You are making me nervous with all this pent-up energy.'

'Your granddaughter needs to be out there fighting the elements to find her holy grail,' Hermes said with theatrical relish. 'Archaeology is a noble calling. It defines the pioneer within us.'

'Please, Hermes, don't encourage her,' I said. 'At least not in this god awful weather.'

'Barry Douglas has dived in worse weather,' Isabella said, still staring out at the darkened sky.

'Barry Douglas is a self-confessed risk taker,' I retorted. 'He's not interested in anything unless it's highly illegal and involves sexual conquest.'

Isabella stifled a laugh while Francesca glared at me disapprovingly.

Barry Douglas was a mutual friend of ours, a flamboyant Australian who had lived in Alexandria for years. He restored archaeological artefacts — his speciality was anything made of bronze. When he wasn't working, he could be found in the bars, where I often joined him. His irreverent humour and earthiness was a respite from the frenetic pace of the city.

Francesca turned to me. 'You must tell my granddaughter to abandon this ridiculous quest of hers. Such obsessions destroyed my husband.'

'Nationalisation destroyed Giovanni, Francesca,' Hermes murmured.

Francesca glanced nervously towards Aadeel. Even I knew Hermes had transgressed; it was dangerous to voice such opinions. 'Shhh! I will not tolerate such radical beliefs in my house! I have the safety of my family to think about,' she hissed.

There was now open hostility between the two old associates. Isabella intervened.

'*Basta*! Nonna, this discovery is going to establish my reputation, you wait and see.'

'It will finish you,' Francesca replied ominously. 'We should never have let you go to university.'

I sensed an argument looming. Isabella had delighted her grandfather but appalled her grandmother by getting into Oxford to study Archaeology at Lady Margaret's Hall; Francesca was traditional and had envisaged a prestigious marriage for Isabella, instead she'd got me.

'So you would have been proud of me if I'd hooked a billionaire like my mother?' Isabella snapped back.

Francesca made a small spitting motion in her palm. She hated her daughter-in-law. 'I suppose I should be thankful that at least you are married,' she said. 'The fact that he is English does not make me so happy.'

She turned to me and said sharply, 'You know the English interned my husband in a concentration camp out here in the desert during the war.'

'Grandfather was a card-carrying member of the Fascist party,' Isabella interjected before I had a chance to respond.

'He was a nationalist, he loved Italy, and, yes, he wore Mussolini's shirt until Il Duce introduced those ridiculous race laws. They were the finish for the party here in Alex. We all knew each other then — Jews, Copts, Catholics, Greeks. It wasn't a problem in those days.' Francesca sighed deeply and visibly restrained herself from making the sign of the cross. 'You are a non-believer, Oliver, are you not? Isabella tells me you abandoned your Catholicism as a young man.'

'He is a scientist, of course he is an atheist, Francesca,' Hermes cut in.

'It was a conscious choice,' I told her. 'I was a bitter disappointment to my Irish-Catholic mother.' Despite myself, I couldn't keep the defensiveness out of my voice.

'Science cannot explain everything, Oliver. There are many mysteries in life.' Francesca spoke with an intensity I had never witnessed in her before.

'For once, Francesca is right.' Hermes smiled at me — a charmingly open smile, almost like that of a child.

'So this is where you inherited your mysticism from,' I said to Isabella.

The old woman leaned forward and gripped my arm with a surprising strength. 'You are wrong. She inherited it from my husband. Giovanni was the mystic. I keep what little faith I have left for my postcard collection of saints.'

She released me; her sharp nails leaving an echo in my flesh.

'He was the magus, a visionary,' Hermes added with a sigh, and for a moment a curious truce was drawn between the two old people, almost as if Giovanni himself had stepped into the room.

Isabella returned to the table. 'Careful, Nonna, I have sheltered Oliver from our darker family secrets. I don't want him to think we are all crazy.'

'But you all are,' Hermes concluded, and they both broke into laughter.

Ignorning them Francesca turned back to me. 'Oliver, this is Egypt. There are gods out there and there is sorcery. And sometimes the most rational people find themselves caught up in the inexplicable. Like my granddaughter and this quest for the impossible.'

'She will find the astrarium, I know it,' Hermes concluded.

The statement was delivered with a prophetic smugness that irritated me. It seemed to have a similar effect on Francesca.

'On the other hand maybe Isabella's search itself is a metaphor,' I replied.

'A metaphor for what?' Francesca smiled wryly.

'For her to find where she truly belongs.'

There was an awkward silence during which I realised I'd stumbled upon a truism that resonated for everyone in the room. Suddenly Isabella sprung up again.

'None of you understand how important this is!' Furious, she began pacing, 'Say they prove that the Antikythera mechanism was able to track the orbits of the planets including the Sun. Do you realise this will prove the ancient Greeks knew that the Earth wasn't the centre of the universe? Now imagine if I discovered an earlier prototype — say Babylonian or even Egyptian — that had the same function. My discovery would entirely change our view of antiquity! Not only would it force a complete revision of our understanding of ancient engineering, the existence of such a device would also change our notions of ancient navigation, and radically push back the date of our understanding of the first machine. I could prove that the Dark Ages were in fact far darker than we imagine.'

'Discovery or no, Isabella, you are a fool to keep diving in the bay. We are all watched everywhere we go — by the military, the secret police, the friend you thought you could confide in.'

'Your granddaughter is experienced, she will be safe.' Hermes put out a hand to reassure the elderly woman.

Pointedly she ignored it. 'No one is safe. Everyone suspects everyone else of being a spy. We publicly welcome Sadat's open-door policy but inflation has made us all desperate. There were food riots in January. Overnight, ration cards were worth nothing, you couldn't buy rice, bread, gas to cook with, the people revolted.

'Remember when people look at us, they still see the old order. Be on your guard, granddaughter. Don't delude yourself — they are all watching, waiting for you to make one mistake.'

'I know how to look after myself,' Isabella replied. 'Besides my big strong husband is coming with me on the dive.'

Isabella reached out and curled her fingers into my hand, a small fist of heat. An amnesty.

I turned to smile at Francesca, but she stared back in hostile indifference. 'Oliver, you are a fool if you think your oil money will protect you.'

# 3

Back at the villa I lay on the bed watching Isabella undress brusquely with that characteristic efficiency of hers, as if clothes were an irritant she needed to rid herself of: it was both amusing and erotic at the same time, and I loved the way she seemed to battle her own femininity.

I reached over and picked up a thrown stocking and handed it back to her. 'Where did you meet this official you're taking on the dive?'

She sat down at the dresser. 'At a lecture at the French Archaeology Society.'

'He could be working for anyone. Why can't you let yourself be supported by a proper team of archaeologists?'

'Right, and let them steal ten years of research from under my nose? Amelia Lynhurst already suspects I'm diving for the astrarium. I've heard a rumour that she knows I'm close to finding it. She would kill to get her hands on it,' she replied, now in bra and pants.

Amelia Lynhurst, Isabella's mentor when she began at Oxford, had lost a great deal of credibility after the publication of a controversial paper about a mysterious priestess of Isis who she claimed lived during the reign of the Pharaoh Nectanebo II during the Thirtieth Dynasty. Despite this, Isabella had remained close to the Englishwoman until they'd had an irreparable falling-out during Isabella's second year of university. She had never told me why they had argued.

'Will you stop worrying,' Isabella went on. 'Faakhir's cousin, who owns the boat, has got friends who work for the coastguard.'

'Sweetheart, if you're caught, it'll be prison for Faakhir and his cousin and the end of your career here.'

'We're not going to be caught. I'm not hauling up a huge statue, just a very small bronze artefact. Besides, your work is far more dangerous than mine.'

'My work is authorised exploration.'

'Bravo, but you're still blasé about the risks you take.'

She was right — I was being hypocritical. The locations my company sent me to were invariably dangerous terrain or in a state of political upheaval. Nevertheless, I still didn't like the idea of Isabella transgressing the perfidious labyrinth of Egyptian bureaucracy. It could endanger both our careers.

'Why not cancel for a few days,' I suggested. 'I could try to get some extra sonar equipment through GeoConsultancy—'

'Oliver,' Isabella replied. 'This is non-negotiable. The boat's been arranged. It has to be tomorrow! There's no more time.'

'There's always time!'

'No!' Now naked Isabella threw herself down onto the bed beside me. She was frantic in a way I didn't understand, and was shaking with anxiety. 'Tomorrow is the day Ahmos Khafre predicted I would die.'

Horrified, I pulled her into my arms. 'You are not going to die. It's all just superstitious nonsense, Isabella. And if you're really worried we'll dive the next day.'

She stared up at me, thinking.

'No, you're right,' she finally replied. 'I'm going to face my fear. We will dive tomorrow.'

We'd had this debate many times before, dating right back to our very first meeting in Goa. Isabella had just come from seeing a mystic who, amongst other things, had given her her astrological chart, which included not only the time of her birth but also the date of her death. She remained convinced of its accuracy, despite all my arguments to the contrary.

'I'm coming with you,' I said. 'And I promise you I'm not going to allow anything to happen.'

She rolled on top of me, her slim body pressed against mine as she stared solemnly into my eyes. I tried smiling but her face stayed serious, her gaze boring through any pretence, as if she were trying to look beyond the banter that had become the veneer of our relationship. I knew I had no option but to support her. Isabella did not believe in compromise, emotional or otherwise. For her, this would have been surrendering to mediocrity. She threw herself recklessly from one experience into another. This impulsiveness was one of the reasons I was first attracted to her. A characteristic so opposite to my own controlling nature, it had always provided a healthy counterbalance. But recently it had become something I couldn't protect her from, as much as I longed to.

'Is something else wrong?' I asked.

She appeared to be on the brink of speaking, but then hesitated before kissing me instead, her long hair falling either side of my face in a wave of musk.

I always wanted Isabella. I never understood why that was — maybe the differences between us created a space, a place I could eroticise. I couldn't tell you how; it just worked. The touch of her lips, her fingers, the scent of her neck, made me stiffen. She was the first woman with whom I truly understood the notion of desire, a thirst that was intensely emotional, not just physical. She was home to me; we made our own nation.

I pulled her down and we made love.

\* \* \*

I was woken an hour later by Isabella thrashing about in the bed. I shook her and she woke up — her heart racing against my chest; her face veiled with sweat.

'The same nightmare?' I asked.

'Yes, except I don't know if it's a nightmare or a memory. This time it was clearer, more specific …'

She faltered, staring into the distance as she forced herself to remember. I waited, knowing that, for her, part of the exorcism was in the telling.

'There's a platform,' she said slowly, 'with a group of people standing on it. They're dressed bizarrely, like animals.'

'Maybe they are animals?' I said.

She waved the suggestion away. 'No, they are humans, real people. There's a man with the head of a jackal crouching by a large set of scales. Then a tall figure with the head of an ibis holding a quill, and a man dressed in white — he looks terrified. There's blood on his robe. Another figure's holding him — this one has the head of a falcon — and they're in front of a throne. There's a figure sitting on the throne — maybe the god Osiris … '

'A ritual perhaps?'

She clutched at my hand. 'Incredible! I've just worked out what it is, after all these years. It's the weighting of the heart ceremony, Oliver! I've shown you the pictures, remember?'

The Ancient Egyptians believed that after a person died, their heart was weighed by Osiris. Depending on the purity of the heart, the deceased was either allowed to pass into the afterlife or was denied entry — a terrifying concept for them. The idea of the ritual disturbed me; partly because of its sheer grotesqueness, but also because it reminded me of my mother's attempts to indoctrinate me with a notion of sin.

'Why would I dream such a thing,' Isabella said, sounding distressed. 'Over and over?'

'It's probably a motif you return to when you're stressed — maybe a fear of being judged by your peers.'

'But it's so clear — the detail of Osiris's headdress, his eyes, the terror of the man waiting to be judged, the heat of the flaming torches on the walls … I'm telling you, it's like I have lived this. I just can't remember …'

'Buried memory?'

'If it is, maybe it should stay buried.' Restless, she got out of bed and went over to her desk.

'Isabella, you need sleep.'

'Not now. Besides going over the plans for tomorrow will help relax me.'

Naked, she put on her reading glasses and switched on a desk lamp, illuminating several maps of the bay and the sea bed. I knew she referred to two sources of expertise on the geography of the harbour's sea bed. One was Kamel Abdou el Sadat who had campaigned tirelessly to try and get the Egyptian authorities to fund exploration. The other was an earlier enthusiast — Prince Thosson, who had created early twentieth-century aerial maps of the bay. And it was these two men's own hand-drawn maps that now lay before her. She picked up a ruler and pencil and began to retrace her route for the dive: the defencelessness of her bare shoulders an innocent contrast to the intense expression on her face. My gaze moved down her body, to her legs curled together under the table, and then the tattoo on her ankle — a sparrowhawk with a human face turned in profile. It was her Ba, the Egyptian representation of the soul after death.

As I stood and walked over to the desk I noticed her slip a small envelope under the ink blotter: a tiny movement that she blocked by turning her back to me. I was still hazy with sleep and it didn't occur to me to ask her about it. She swung back around and smiled. 'Recognise this?' she said, and held up the drawing of the astrarium I'd seen on the floor the night before. 'It's a great rendering, I really think it's going to look like this, Gareth's a genius.'

'Oh, I don't know about that,' I replied gruffly; I couldn't help thinking about my brother's complete inability to look after himself both physically and financially — genius or otherwise. I took the drawing from her and peered at it. The diagram was an elegant ink drawing of a curious mechanism: the jagged teeth of cogs were set against more cogs, another perspective showed how the interior workings fitted within a wooden frame. Beneath the diagram was a series of six symbols or letters of an ancient script. I hadn't noticed them before. 'What's this? It doesn't look like Greek to me, isn't it meant to be Ptolemaic?' I asked.

'It is, but this is a cipher made of hieroglyphs. The Ptolemaic rulers took every opportunity to link themselves to Ancient Egyptian beliefs to legitimise themselves. I've found evidence that this cipher may be written on the mechanism itself. It's a phrase from a temple wall, an Isis temple, only recently discovered. I had Gareth write it down, he's good at riddles.'

'Have you solved it?'

'I have an idea, but I'll wait until I have the astrarium before I reveal my theory to a cynic like yourself.'

'Be careful of anything Gareth suggests,' I said. 'He's such a conspiracist.'

She threw her hands up in mock exasperation. 'You see? No wonder I don't confide in you. I'm too frightened of being ridiculed.'

'Come back to bed, please?' I begged, smiling.

Dawn was creeping under the blinds but by my calculations there was at least an hour before we had to get up for the dive. Sighing, Isabella switched off the desk lamp and skipped across the room. As she slipped in beside me, the familiar fragrance of her body was an immediate comfort.

'You'll always look after Gareth, won't you? He needs you, even if he'll never admit it.' Again, she seemed unnaturally fatalistic.

'Of course I will,' I answered, perplexed.

My brother Gareth, born sixteen years after me, was an unexpected menopausal baby adored by my mother but regarded as a late financial burden by my father. I had hardly known Gareth when he was a child, but, when I did visit, I would take him out for long walks across the moors describing the rock formations in the hope it would instil some greater ambition than my parents' aspirations. It must have worked for at the age of twelve he'd announced he intended to become a landscape painter. Later, when he hit adolescence, we stopped relating to each other. I assumed it was normal rebellion but part of me was secretly saddened by the alienation.

Isabella curled up against me. 'If anything should happen to me, Faakhir will know what to do with the astrarium.'

I pulled her closer, her leg over my torso, my arm slipped under her waist. 'Nothing's going to happen.'

'Promise?'

I nodded and reaching down kissed her deeply, and there it was — a simple pledge given simply. With hindsight I wonder that if I had argued with her, had made the case that perhaps sometimes it's good to leave some treasures undiscovered, old hurts and dramas dormant, unanalysed never to be returned to — would I have persuaded her not to have taken that dive?

Maybe, maybe not, but I wasn't that kind of man in those days. Then, with all the arrogance of a young gun who'd achieved a certain status and who believed Nature favoured the hardworking, I assumed our lives would go on forever.

* * *

The boat — a small fishing vessel aptly named Ra Five, with an old rusting cabin and a pile of mended fishing nets on board — chugged determinedly against the incoming tide, ploughing through the great webs of seaweed the storm had thrown up in the days before. Faakhir's cousin Jamal, a short muscular man in his late fifties with the calloused and scarred hands of a working fisherman, guided us out towards the bobbing red buoy that marked the dive site. He was the owner of the boat and, as Isabella had again reassured me, part of the coastguard and had therefore secured official permission for her to make the dive. I wasn't sure whether to believe her or not. Jamal's incessant smile was betrayed by a nervousness in his eyes and I suspected bribery had played its part, but I knew better than to ask.

Hanging over the cabin controls was a miniature Michelin man, and a plastic hula-hoop girl with a painted green grass skirt clinked against the eye of Horus as I steadied myself against the chipped wooden panelling.

'Careful, you might fall overboard.' Omar, the official Isabella had told me about the night before, joked. He was a plump man with a badly fixed broken nose and a thin white scar running vertically across one heavy eyelid down to his cheek. He wore a fluorescent pink life jacket strapped over his clothes and appeared to be taking little interest in the proceedings. After suffering two centuries of the illegal excavation and export of its ancient statues and artefacts,

Egypt had finally established a policing system that required all archaeological sites to have at least one of their officers present. If Omar was really such an officer and not just moonlighting, I strongly suspected Isabella had deliberately underplayed the significance of the astrarium.

Faakhir stood in the doorway of the cabin. He had a clumsiness on land that completely belied his grace when in the water. When I first dived with him I had been astounded not only by the fluidity of his movements but also his uncanny ability to locate objects on the sea bed, even in the murky waters of Alexandria's harbour. The fishing hut in Al Gomrok he'd grown up in had a number of small Ptolemaic objects placed casually next to a radio or an old family photograph. Objects his father and grandfather had either caught in their nets or hauled up from the sea bed over the decades. Faakhir himself had seen submerged statues and pillars many of which had become reefs over the centuries attracting schools of fish: the reason why the fishermen fished there in the first place. But there were levels of Faakhir's diving expertise that were unfathomable to Isabella and he was always strangely vague about where he'd trained.

'The Mediterranean makes brothers of us all,' he'd once said to me. 'She is like a language — you either speak her or you don't.'

'Are you going to venture in, my friend?' Faakhir asked me now.

'Maybe later. I'm happy to watch for the time being.'

'Oliver, wait until you see the shipwreck for yourself,' he said to me now. 'The royal boat is a skeleton but you can still see its shape. To imagine, Cleopatra herself might have sailed in it!'

Isabella appeared, an oxygen tank slung over her shoulder. 'Ready, Faakhir?'

Faakhir smiled. 'I have studied the map so many times I could swim to the site blind.'

'With the amount of sand that's shifted in the last few nights you will be swimming it blind. You know the drill. Let's cover the area evenly, side by side, until something registers on the metal detectors.'

Isabella's voice had the clipped authoritative tone she adopted when she was nervous, and again I felt apprehensive about the dive.

'How long will you be?' I asked.

'We've narrowed the location down to a few feet with the help of side-scan sonar, we have a window of opportunity of about three hours.'

'A mystery thousands of years old! We are going to make history, I know it.'

Faakhir's excitement was infectious and I couldn't help smiling. 'Just stay safe,' I told them both.

'Don't worry, we're very professional.' Isabella handed an oxygen tank to Faakhir.

Two metal detectors — clumsy Soviet-designed devices the navy used for detecting underwater bombs — lay on the wooden deck. Isabella and Faakhir placed the attached headphones over their ears and tested for sound. Both of them sat concentrating, eyes shut as they strained to hear the dull bleeping, already lost to the concentration of the task at hand. There was a strange intimacy to the act, and, momentarily I found myself irrationally jealous.

The plan was that they would swim along the sea bed at a distance of about half a metre from the bottom. As soon as they heard anything, they would signal me and I'd lower a steel tube, which they'd then sink around the bronze artefact. The tube would be lifted off the sea bed with the artefact preserved in the mud packed around it. Later, they would desalinate the artefact, first in a bath of salt water and then in fresh water.

Opening her eyes, Isabella checked her watch then stood decisively. Faakhir followed and solemnly they pulled on their diving masks. Sitting on the side of the boat, Isabella threw herself backwards into the sea. A moment later, Faakhir — flippers kicking like black fins — disappeared into the blue. We carefully lowered the metal detectors after them. Within minutes the only evidence we could see of their presence underwater was the movement of the rope leading down to them and the dull torchlight that rapidly vanished in the rippling depths.

Omar was sitting on an upturned lobster cage, his head tilted towards the sun as if he were sunbathing. I was convinced his indifference was disingenuous.

He leaned towards me. 'Mr Warnock, we are very pleased with your wife's work. We think she has much talent. But maybe a little crazy too, *non*?'

Hiding my instinctive distrust of the man, I smiled and nodded.

I took my own seat on the deck and stared back at the Alexandrian skyline, its hotels and apartment buildings broken by the occasional distinctive minaret of a mosque. It was hard to believe that Isabella might finally locate her holy grail.

I sat back remembering the first time Isabella had told me about the astrarium, sitting there at that bar in Goa. The establishment was a small bamboo and brick structure run by a German hippy and her Hindu husband, incense burnt in the corner and the Rolling Stones played incessantly through a small tinny speaker. Appropriately named Marlene Chakrabuty's Sanctuary from Hell they were famous for their Bloody Marys — my favourite cocktail. The air was constantly filled with the treacly aroma of hashish and an autographed cover of the Abbey Road album hung proudly above the bar.

I had just finished a job with Shell and was consumed by the ennui I always experienced after a successful exploration. Then I lived solely for the elation of the chase, the feeling of using all my senses, the intellectual rigour of the geological calculations involved as well as the emotional groping — the blind intuitive flash that always came to me standing out there in the field, sniffing the air — feeling the vibration of the rock beneath my bare feet; the roustabouts joking nervously amongst themselves as they watched me take off my shoes and socks to stand there in silence, eyes shut, reading the land under my naked soles.

In those days I was always running to the next job as quickly as I could to starve off any introspection. In truth it was the exhilarating rush of the next potential new oil reservoir and not the money that kept me running. From what, I never really knew, not back then, I just knew there was some part of myself I had been denying for as long as I could remember. I was thirty-three, a dangerous age for a man, a craggy lump of graceless Anglo-Saxon masculinity drooped over his barstool — not the most attractive proposition and I knew it.

I'd grown up in Cumbria, between the Lake District and the Irish Sea. Out there your body forms an island, a wind-battered automaton of pounding legs and flaying arms. Hot breath warming icy cheeks in the folds of a scarf as you tear jagged through the antediluvian landscape. This self-sufficiency, the dogged struggle against the elements, starts to define you and before you know it, you have become a curmudgeon — bristling, impenetrable and ready to deal with a hostile world. None of these characteristics had deterred Isabella.

She'd introduced herself by dropping a necklace of amber beads into my Bloody Mary. I looked up and was startled by the vivid energy that seemed to dance around her face — the ferocious intelligence that sharpened her features. I pulled out the amber beads, sucked the vodka off them, and, after holding them up to the light guessed that the amber came from Yantarny, Russia. To my surprise she seemed to find the fact that I was a geophysicist intriguing and, determined to engage me in conversation, she'd sat down next to me and demanded that I buy her a drink. I remember noticing how she seemed a little wild and reckless as if she were determined to shake off some recent trauma, but back then India was full of lost souls.

Three whiskies later she was telling me about her visit to the mystic who her grandfather had sent her to. My seduction plans were momentarily derailed. I had a strong aversion to mysticism and disliked the dispossessed westerners I often came across floating aimlessly, with their long hair and loose mock-native clothes, through the same geography as myself. However, I found myself suspending disbelief when Isabella went on to tell me she was a marine archaeologist, having trained at Oxford.

'It's a kind of portable astrarium — a mechanised model of the universe that doesn't just tell mean time and sidereal time but also incorporates a calendar for movable feasts, and has dials illustrating the movements of the sun, moon and the five planets known to the ancients. Leonardo da Vinci saw one that was built during the Renaissance — he described it as "a work of divine speculation, a work unattainable by human genius … axles within axles". Another was found in 1901 — the Antikythera mechanism. My hypothesis is that an earlier prototype existed.'

'And your mystic?'

'Ahmos Khafre, you should meet him. He's a really serious archaeologist as well as a world-famous astrologer.'

'Before you go on, I better warn you I'm a complete sceptic.'

'I don't believe you.' She hiccupped and I guessed she might be drunker than she realised. 'A sceptic does not use sorcery to tell me the exact place my amber came from.'

'That wasn't sorcery, that was just training, extremely good detective work and a tiny bit of guesswork. Plus …' I held the beads up again, 'I recognise the fossilised insect in this piece as the rare Slavic wasp.' It was a ruse I often applied to cover guesswork — the trickster covering his tracks with a pseudo-fact.

She stared at me her huge black eyes widening.

'I think, Oliver, that you are a man who is not entirely integrated with both his intellect and intuition. But that's okay we will be good for each other — I can make you whole and you can protect me.'

Her quaint use of English and her Italian accent had me hooked, but her uncanny observation made me uncomfortable. I decided if I was to bed her it would be sensible to steer her away from any further analysis of my personality.

'So let me guess, your mystic told you about a wonderful but deeply cynical Englishman with an interesting Northern accent …'

'Not if you intend to ridicule me.'

'I promise to suspend any disbelief.'

'Really?' Her lack of guile was utterly disarming.

'Cross my Newtonian heart and hope to die.'

She smiled, then, after finishing her drink, moved closer.

'Years ago, a mystic, Ahmos Khafre, was given a letter rumoured to be written by Sonnini de Manoncour, a naturalist who had travelled with Napoleon's troops. He wrote that he had come across information that a ship carrying Cleopatra, sunk during the Battle of Actium, had also been carrying a famous astrarium. One day I'll find that astrarium, I know I will. I have to.' She hesitated as if she were about to tell me something else, something of greater importance. Then in the next instance she looked pensive. I remember, even to this day, that intensity. Her narrow triangular face collapsing into vulnerability and, to my great surprise, I instantly wanted to rescue her, a sensation that only fuelled my desire.

'Can I be with you tonight?'

I could barely hear her over the noise of the revellers behind us and, for a moment, I thought I misheard. It was only after our lovemaking later the same night that she told me about how Ahmos Khafre had also insisted upon giving her a birth chart that predicted the date of her death. Furious at the culpability of such an action I'd sat up in bed and had tried, unsuccessfully, to persuade her that it was all superstitious nonsense. I failed. We were married three months later.

I stared down at the water, a little incredulous that now Isabella had actually carried out her quest.

My reverie was broken by Jamal's shout — the rope was twitching. I tugged it, the signal to Isabella that I was ready, and she replied with four twitches. I fastened the steel clip attached to the thick tube to the cable and lowered it into the water; in seconds it had disappeared, sliding down to the divers below.

Jamal reached into the back pocket of his jeans and pulled out a battered packet of Lucky Strike cigarettes, which he offered to both Omar and me. I'd given up a year before because I'd noticed it was affecting my sense of smell — an essential asset for my oil hunting — but that morning I lit up.

'Now we wait,' Jamal announced ponderously, then began to hum 'Stayin' Alive' by the Bee Gees under his breath while Omar stared fixedly out at the horizon. It was as if our thoughts drifted up with the cigarette smoke — independent patterns curling around each other then merging in a secret shared anxiety: what if we get caught?

A speedboat roared past, seemingly out of nowhere. Startled, my stomach tightened as I steeled myself for a raid by the coastguard. But Omar leapt to his feet and waved. A man on board waved back and the boat continued its trajectory.

Omar smiled, reading my expression. 'Don't worry, he is a friend. Besides we have nothing to hide.'

I had the distinct impression he was enjoying my discomfort.

Just then a flock of pigeons flew overhead. Both men looked up at the sight of the wheeling birds.

Jamal cursed under his breath and glanced nervously at the shoreline. 'That is not good,' he muttered.

'A bad omen,' Omar confirmed grimly, his gaze following the swooping mass.

'It's just pigeons,' I said, wondering why they were so agitated.

'Look again, my friend,' Jamal said, and pointed. 'These are land birds flying away from the land.'

'Perhaps they're flying towards an island.'

'What island? There is no island — just Cyprus, too far for pigeons. No, something is not right. Maybe the storm is returning, or perhaps something more dangerous.'

I was relieved when Isabella and Faakhir surfaced in a great rush of silver bubbles. Pushing her mask up to her forehead, Isabella appeared to be ecstatic.

'We found it, Oliver! Isn't that amazing? We have it! The tube's sunk and fitted — all we have to do now is lift it out! I've found the astrarium!'

# 4

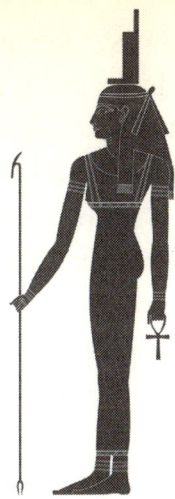

Isabella handed the metal detector up to me and hauled herself back onto the boat. Faakhir, smiling, climbed up after her while the others hung back, inexplicably tentative.

'We should go back now, make the final dive tomorrow,' Jamal announced, glancing at the horizon.

'Absolutely not! The site will be covered again by tomorrow. We have to retrieve it in the next hour, before the tide comes through!'

Isabella's tone was demanding and urgent. I glanced at the men and saw an expression cross Jamal's face, so fast I think I was probably the only one who noticed. I'd seen it before on some of the Arab oil workers: resentment. It was difficult for them to take orders from a woman no matter how much they respected her.

Faakhir, sensing potential conflict, put his hand on his cousin's shoulder. 'Please, we are so close, and if we dive tomorrow we'll have to start all over again.'

Jamal glanced up at the flock of pigeons — now barely a speck on the horizon. A particularly high wave lifted the boat and a couple of dull thuds sounded as the floats lashed to the sides bumped against the hull.

'Okay. But be as quick as you can.'

I picked up a spare mask, 'I'm coming with …'

'Oliver, I don't need …' Isabella began, but Faakhir put a hand on her shoulder. 'Isabella, we could do with the extra help.'

Isabella glanced back at me. 'Okay, but you'll have to follow orders, understand?'

I nodded; there was no way I was going to allow Isabella to take any extra risk by being understaffed.

\* \* \*

The site was illuminated by an underwater floodlight suspended by a rope. It was eerie swimming down towards the light — I had the strange sensation of an inverted world in which the sun lay beneath us. The water was cloudy, but as we neared the sea bed the site came into view — a suspended oasis surrounded by darkness. Clouds of fish hovered like a swarm of moths attracted by the floodlight.

At first the ship looked like some kind of unusual reef, a sudden manifestation of coral and molluscs jutting out from the sea bed, but the hazy outline of what appeared to be a sphinx's head and shoulders stood out from the base. Closer, the features of the statue took shape. Algae had covered everything but her face, which, unlike many of the images I'd seen in the past, had a human asymmetry about it. The arched nose and large eyes were surprisingly naturalistic and seemed to hold a wry humour. The creature stared back at me through the cloudy water with a beauty that was palpably and jarringly real. Was it a relic from the now submerged island of Antirhodos, which had once housed Cleopatra's palace?

Isabella swam into view, gesturing towards the rest of the site. Pivoting slowly, I saw how the sea bed had taken on the impression of the hull of a ship, with only the basic ribs of construction still imprinted on the mud. Isabella hovered over the site, indicating the rim and handles of the steel tube, which now held the bronze artefact.

She unhooked the floodlight and shone it onto the tube. Faakhir clipped a hook onto one of the handles so the tube could be winched to the surface once we'd freed it from the sea bed. He gave me the thumbs-up sign and we each took one of the handles and began to slowly pull the tube out of the mud. It wasn't easy, and I felt the muscles in my arms tighten and my mask began to steam up from perspiration. Through the clouds of dislodged sand I could just make out Faakhir's straining face.

Unexpectedly, the mud released its grip and the tube began to lift away, and finally a foot and a half of steel dimly gleamed through the greenish water. After waving her hands in excitement, Isabella tugged on the cable to alert the crew on the surface. The steel tube began its ascent.

As it moved, I thought I heard a distant thud, a dull echo underwater. Then the water itself seemed to shift in transparent planes. The fish shot away in panic, breaking the natural patterns of their shoals. Just as I turned towards Isabella, the whole area was plunged into darkness. The claustrophobia was intense. Panicking, I struck out wildly, hoping to touch the others. My fingers became entangled in seaweed and my chest heaved with blind dread. The darkness stretched ahead into a bewildering void.

After what seemed an eternity, the floodlight spluttered back on, but now the beam was pointing away from the site at an extreme angle, illuminating the descending clouds of stirred-up sand.

An earthquake, I thought, and looked up for the supply line. It arched above me, intact, but where were the others?

I peered through the thick fog of disturbed mud, but nothing was visible. I had the disorientating sensation of suddenly being entirely alone. Spinning around, I looked for Isabella — nothing, not even the glimmer of a diving mask. Then I caught sight of a small white hand curling upwards through the clouds of sand. I lunged towards her, my heart banging wildly against my ribs.

The sphinx had slipped sideways and pinned Isabella's leg against the sea floor. A silver cascade of bubbles gushed out from the oxygen tank pipe where it had torn away from her mask.

The gravity of the situation didn't hit me immediately; I suppose it was a combination of shock and disbelief. As I hovered there in the drifting cloud of mud I was thrown out of the moment, I was an observer. I hesitated — a fatal mistake.

Then, almost magically, Faakhir was beside me and both of us were swimming frantically towards Isabella. A cloud of pink blood now threaded its way through the water; her loosened hair floating like delicate seaweed.

I tore away my mouthpiece and tried to place it in her mouth while Faakhir prised the statue off her leg. But her mouth lolled open and she was already unconscious. Faakhir and I placed our shoulders against the sphinx and pushed. As it lifted from the sea bed, I pulled Isabella's crushed leg free. Holding her limp body to mine, I swam full pelt towards the light filtering down from above.

\* \* \*

We burst through the water's surface to the sound of shouting. Frantic, I pushed Isabella up towards the outstretched arms, then clambered into the boat myself and crouched over her body where it lay on the deck. My hands seemed like huge clumsy paws as I tried to pump the water out of her chest; the shock of her cold lips as I gave her mouth-to-mouth. Pump, breathe, pump, breathe; it seemed like hours.

The others stood by dumbly, silenced by the horror of the scene. The terrible, almost unbelievable images seared into my memory: the water trickling from the edge of her mouth, Faakhir's blanched face as finally he pulled me away from the lifeless body, her limp hands. All the while, the steel tube containing the astrarium stood on the deck, glinting in the sun.

'Isabella? Isabella!' In disbelief I shook her, my whole body trembling uncontrollably. Then I collapsed on the deck alongside her, cradling her to me.

Above me, as if at a great distance, I heard Faakhir suddenly shout. I glanced up to see Omar standing over us, a small revolver in his hand. He looked almost embarrassed.

'*Ana asif, ana asif.* I'm sorry this is necessary.'

The sight of him pointing the gun while apologising profusely was so incongruous, the three of us could only watch in frozen surprise as he tucked the mud-packed cylinder containing the astrarium under his arm.

'What are you doing? Are you crazy?' Jamal shouted.

'Excuse me for resorting to such extreme measures, but this object is infinitely more valuable than you imagine,' Omar's voice was clipped and bizarrely polite. He then aimed the gun upwards, as if about to shoot a warning signal into the air.

A blind anger roared through me. Not caring whether I lived or died, I sprang towards Omar and punched him on the jaw. He fell to the deck, dropping the cylinder containing the astrarium. It rolled to the side of the boat and lodged against the railing.

Dazed by my own action, I stared down at Omar's unconscious body. 'Who is he?' I asked.

Faakhir lifted one of Omar's arms and shook it, as if testing that he was really out cold.

'A nobody. A middleman,' he said. 'He doesn't worry me. It's who he might be working for that is the real concern.'

Faakhir's calmness and professional control was staggering. Somehow, in the midst of my shock, I registered that he too wasn't quite what he appeared.

I dropped to the deck and took Isabella in my arms again, caring only about the impossibility of bringing her back to life; the sky and the deck appeared to be receding from me. I was in shock.

Jamal picked up the fallen gun and aimed it at Omar. Faakhir grabbed his cousin's wrist. 'Stop! Kill him and we're all finished!' He took the gun, then squatted beside me, gripping my hand. 'Oliver, you must listen! You must let me go now so I can keep the astrarium safe. But I promise I will return it to you.'

Water seeped from Isabella's wetsuit, forming a pool around my knees. Her hand lay outstretched on the deck, the fingernails already bluish.

Faakhir shook me. 'Oliver, concentrate. For Isabella!'

I nodded now, unable to speak.

He turned to Jamal and said something in his own dialect. Immediately they hoisted Omar's unconscious body into the small life raft hanging from the side of the boat, then lowered it into the sea. Finally the reality of the moment came rushing painfully back,

'What are you doing?' I asked. My voice sounded oddly emotionless.

'Don't worry,' Faakhir said, 'he will be found alive within hours. But this way I have more time.'

He picked up the cylinder containing the astrarium and then sat on the edge of the boat. 'Oliver, when you get back to shore the police will be waiting for you. When they interrogate you, it is important that you don't mention I was on this boat. You have never heard of the astrarium. You and Isabella were on an innocent tourist dive. Understand? Isabella planned for all outcomes.' Faakhir's face was grim. 'Oliver, do you understand?'

'I understand.'

Behind him, the outline of the coastguard's speedboat was already visible. Faakhir took my hand.

'I will see you in a few days, my friend,' he said. 'I will come to you.'

Before I had a chance to answer, he'd slipped backwards into the water and with a ripple of his black flippers, disappeared from sight.

\* \* \*

The coastguard escorted our boat back to shore. I stepped onto the jetty carrying Isabella's body wrapped in a blanket. I remember talking to her, telling her everything was all right, I was there to protect her and everything was going to work out; my voice sounding curiously distant. Behind me, I was vaguely aware of Jamal arguing with the harbourmaster.

Minutes later, a police car and an ambulance screeched up to the kerb. Before I'd even reached the Corniche, an ambulance officer was guiding me towards the waiting stretcher. I laid Isabella's body gently onto it, arranging a limp hand that had fallen loose, tucking her hair carefully around her face, still murmuring to her; part of me refusing to understand the reality of her death.

Two police officers stepped up and, apologising, politely asked me to go with them. Ignoring them, I continued to stroke Isabella's cold face, her fingers that were stiff beneath my own.

'Mr Warnock, we are sorry to inform you that you have broken the law. You must accompany us to the police station. Please, we do not want to arrest you ...' Slipping an arm through each of mine, they pulled me away and marched me towards the police car.

Over my shoulder I watched my wife's body being loaded into the white van. It was the last time I ever saw her.

# 5

The police held me for over a day, convinced that Isabella had drowned planting sea mines and that I was a spy. They also interrogated me about Faakhir and his involvement with Isabella, even claiming he was my wife's lover in an attempt to break me down.

In a monosyllabic voice, I repeated the same story like a mantra: we had wanted to see the ancient underwater sights for ourselves, we hadn't realised we needed official permission, nor that the bay was a military zone; and I'd never heard of anyone called Faakhir. Over and over, they emphasised the fact that Isabella, as an archaeologist, would have known she needed permission to dive in the bay. I felt as if I was still underwater, mouthing words that floated on the other side of a glass wall separating me from an outside world.

At dawn I was freed, apparently due to a phone call from Henries, the British consul. I couldn't face going back to the villa; instead, I found myself stumbling through the streets towards the Brambilla family home. Time had stopped for me, refusing to spill over into the tragedy that had now become my life. I found myself standing under the stone arch of the entrance, too petrified to ring the bell. When I did, and Aadeel opened the door, my unshaved face, sullied clothes and violent trembling told him everything.

'Mr Warnock, we thought they would never let you go,' he murmured, ashen with grief.

'What have they done with the body?' I asked.

'She is already in her coffin. We bury her tomorrow afternoon.' Aadeel's face crumpled. 'I have known her all her life. She was the only reason my mistress still lives,' he whispered, his large frame now folding in on itself, squeezing grief tight.

I reached out to him, his shoulders heaving. But I, the Englishman, could not weep. Grief had me locked up like a safe, one whose code felt irredeemably lost.

* * *

'Oh Lord, take this soul, torn from us before her time, and transport her into heaven,' the priest intoned in Italian.

I stared at the coffin standing beside the freshly dug grave, the darkened recess as intriguing as a secret chamber. I wanted to smash open the wood and rescue my wife. Sudden bereavement is illogical, irrational. It refuses to believe the obvious; the scent, the physical warmth of skin, the weight of her head on your shoulder — the memory of these sensations stays suspended, waiting for the departed to return and confirm the internal illogical truth that beats on relentlessly — one that tells you that they haven't really died at all but are only hiding.

The priest began a Latin chant; his incomprehensible words emerging in a solemn murmur and I found myself furious — at a God that had allowed such a futile death, at the world, even at Francesca for hijacking the funeral arrangements.

It was a family tradition for the Brambillas to bury their dead within two days and because Francesca couldn't reach me during my interrogation at the police station, she had taken it upon herself to organise everything, from the funeral parlour through to the Catholic service at St Catherine's Cathedral. The whole event appeared brutally fast to me, as if Isabella had been drawing breath only moments before we were putting her into the ground.

The only thing left to me was the grim task of breaking the news to my family. I had called my father first, his reaction had been one of initial disbelief then an irrational insistence I return to England immediately as if my own life might be in danger. Dialling my brother's number had been more difficult. I was frightened the news might set off one of Gareth's lapses into addiction, but it had to be done. I'd been blunt and to the point; anything else felt evasive. Afterwards he had fallen into a long silence, then, to my annoyance, he launched into a Buddhism-inspired soliloquy about reincarnation. I knew his emotional clumsiness was unintentional but it still distressed me. The rant finished in weeping. That was Gareth, always oscillating between bravado and fragility.

The Valium the company doctor had prescribed made my head swim. The sun danced in streamers, catching the shimmering feathers on the more ornate hats of the women — a second of visual distraction, a brief respite from the crushing emotion that overlay everything. I couldn't bear to think. I hadn't slept since the accident, unable even to shut my eyes without seeing Isabella's body lying limp on the wooden deck.

I glanced at Francesca, who was standing on the other side of the grave, propped up by Aadeel. She was dressed in an elegant mourning dress that must have dated from the 1950s, but her granddaughter's death had withered her overnight. Standing beside her was Hermes Hemiedes, his hand absently stroking the old woman's frail arm. He returned my gaze, a blank stare devoid of emotion. I looked away.

The sound of wood scraping against gravel jolted me out of my reverie. The casket touched the bottom of the grave and the ropes were pulled out. A bird swooped over the cypress trees and down towards the open grave, the movement of its wings catching my eye. It was a sparrowhawk and my mind instantly leapt to Isabella's tattoo, her Ba. Was this her spirit freed from her body? The extraordinary thought distracted me from my grief. I was interrupted by a gentle nudge to my elbow and turned to see Aadeel there, holding out a spade. The male relatives were expected to cast the first shovels of soil into the grave. I took the spade and stared down at the polished surface of the coffin; the banks of reddish sandy soil around it changed in strata as the grave deepened. A geophysicist committing his wife to the earth; I didn't want to do it. I didn't want to give her up.

The crying of the mourners mingled with the ambience of the world beyond the high walls of the cemetery: the squeal of tram wheels, the clip-clop of horses' hooves, the midday call to prayer from a nearby mosque, the imam's voice threading through the air like a thin purple ribbon. Could Isabella hear any of this from inside her coffin, I couldn't help wondering, trying to distract myself from the excruciatingly tight band of grief now squeezing my heart and lungs. The moment swelled and burst into the next while I stood there, paralysed, dreading the rain of soil against wood, the rattle that signified finality.

The Brambilla family headstone was a large altar dominated by a statue of the Madonna. Set into the marble, in circular frames like lockets, were sepia photographs of the dead — her father, Paola; Isabella's great-grandfather and his wife; her great-uncle who had been killed in the Second World

War; a spinster aunt. I looked for Giovanni Brambilla's photograph, but he appeared to be missing. Was it possible he wasn't actually buried in Alexandria? Below the miniature portraits were empty frames, yawning sinisterly. The idea that a photograph of Isabella would appear there, in a solemn pose that betrayed her exuberance, horrified me.

The warmth of hands wrapping themselves over mine brought me back. Aadeel had stepped up behind me, and together we shovelled the first spadeful into the grave.

\* \* \*

Several ancient black Mercedes stood outside the cemetery gates, waiting to drive the mourners to the wake. Wanting a moment of solitude, I broke away from Francesca and her entourage and walked towards a row of cypress trees. A man emerged from behind a statue and approached me so swiftly I was barely aware of him until he was in front of me.

'Monsieur Oliver Warnock?'

Startled, I looked up. He was short and looked to be in his fifties, with heavy-lidded eyes that blinked like a tortoise's. He looked vaguely bureaucratic in his ill-fitting suit and embroidered fez and, disorientated, for one absurd moment I wondered if I knew him from the Egyptian Oil Ministry in Cairo. He glanced around nervously then pulled me behind a high gravestone.

'You don't know me but I know you,' he said. 'And I have met your wife. Unfortunately, after her demise.'

I assumed he was one of the cheap psychics that operated like parasites amongst the elderly European community. He noticed the repulsion in my expression.

'Many apologies, let me explain. My name is Demetriou al-Masri. I am a coroner at the city morgue. My condolences

Monsieur Warnock. Forgive this interruption but there is something I must tell you.'

'Were you working that night?' I asked him.

'Yes, of course, but this is a strange thing, Monsieur Warnock. Is it okay if I speak frankly?'

'I suspect I wouldn't be able to stop you.'

'Alas, in my profession there are many things that cannot be said delicately.'

A mourner passed us and tipped his hat. Al-Masri lowered his voice.

'Monsieur Warnock, it is my great misfortune and, I believe, my duty to have to tell you that by the time your wife's body arrived at the morgue it was missing several of its internal organs.'

His expression was grim yet nervous, as if he were committing some terrible crime by giving me the information. My mind reeled as I tried to grasp the simple facts.

'You mean there was an autopsy?'

'I mean that several of the organs had been removed before the body came under my jurisdiction.'

Nauseated, I leaned against the gravestone. The idea that Isabella had been violated in such a manner was abhorrent.

'Impossible,' I murmured, clutching onto the idea that the man may be trying to extort money from me somehow.

'It is terrible to be the bearer of such bad news,' he said. 'But I must tell you, the liver, the stomach, the intestines and the heart were gone. I have seen this only once before, twenty years ago. Interestingly, the victim was an Egyptologist, female and about the same age as your wife.'

'Isabella had no heart?'

Again, he looked around nervously. 'Please, it must appear as if I am simply offering my condolences. Even the statues have ears in Egypt.'

'Why didn't you report it?'

'Because, my friend, my relationship with the authorities is tenuous enough without further aggravation, you understand?'

I nodded; I understood exactly.

He moved closer. 'Do you know anything about the art of mummification?' he whispered.

'A little.'

'Then you will know that these organs had great significance to the Ancient Egyptian priests. They would place them in a series of canopic jars, each with a stopper that symbolised the god that would protect the deceased's journey into the underworld. What I don't understand is why the heart was taken as well. Traditionally it is left in the body as it is essential for the ancient ritual of the weighing of the heart. Without a heart, your wife would stand no chance of entering the afterworld. She would be, as you Christians say, condemned to purgatory.'

'But why would someone commit such a disgusting crime? My wife was a Catholic.'

'And I am a Sunni Muslim with a Greek Orthodox grandfather. In this city, religion is not a simple issue. I hope your wife's spirit will find peace.' He bowed, said, 'Good evening, sir,' and slipped away through the gravestones.

I lingered in the shade of the murmuring branches, an overwhelming sense of powerlessness pinning me to the gravelled path. How could any intelligent person believe in mummification? And why had they chosen Isabella's body for such desecration?

# 6

Our car weaved slowly through the narrow streets towards the Brambilla family villa. I glanced at Francesca, her profile solidified in grief. I had to ask: 'What happened to Isabella's body after the ambulance collected her at the jetty?'

'Naturally she was taken to the city morgue, and then to the funeral directors in the morning.'

'You're positive there was no autopsy?'

'Please, we have just laid my poor granddaughter in the ground. Do we have to talk about such matters now?'

'Francesca, you were in control of the arrangements while I was being held by the police. I just need to know if there was an autopsy,' I persisted, determined to get a straight answer.

'Of course not,' she snapped back. 'Is this something to do with that idiot official who approached you at the cemetery?'

She peered at me, her frail frame dwarfed by the huge crimson leather seat, and again I was struck by how she had aged since the drowning.

'You know him?' I asked.

'Alexandria is a village. A village of chattering monkeys making mischief. Be careful, Oliver, otherwise you will find yourself fighting for your own truth along with the rest of us.'

\* \* \*

A marquee had been erected over the villa's courtyard and beneath it stood a long table covered in a variety of both Arabic and Italian pastries. Subdued waiters in tails served coffee and everyone spoke in muted whispers. I knew Francesca couldn't really afford the wake, but when I'd offered her money she had been insulted. Façade was all that many of the European diaspora had left, but it was essential to them to maintain that illusion of wealth.

For the first time, I took note of who had attended my wife's funeral. There were the usual elegantly dressed Italian pensioners who formed Francesca's social circle; also the British consul, Henries, who had recently liberated me from the Alexandrian police, and his wife. On our first encounter, Henries' reaction to my northern English accent had been supercilious, and when he realised the high status of the Alexandrian family I had married into, he had done nothing to conceal his amazement — neither of which endeared him to me.

I spotted a representative from Alexandrian Oil Company, Mr Fartime. Catching my eye, he nodded in sympathy. Despite his political clashes with Isabella, I liked the man. Standing near him was a middle-aged European woman in an ill-fitting grey tweed suit, her flushed face betraying how unsuitable such an outfit was in Alexandria's heat. Amelia Lynhurst. I saw her glance towards me, and then become distracted by the sight of Hermes Hemiedes, still at Francesca's elbow. To my surprise, her expression changed to one of apprehension and she quickly turned away.

A tall, handsome man in his early thirties approached me, his veiled wife beside him. Ashraf Awad, son of Aadeel, Francesca's housekeeper; he had grown up with Isabella and their friendship had lasted into adulthood. I didn't like to think I found Ashraf threatening, but I suspected his relationship with Isabella had more than once slipped into something more intimate. An ardent socialist and supporter of Nasser, Ashraf had completed his engineering degree at Moscow University, which had appealed to Isabella's left-wing leanings. 'Meet the new Egypt' was the way she always introduced him; she saw his education and political fervour as a manifestation of the better side of Egyptian nationalism. Ashraf had visited us once in London en route from Moscow to Cairo. He had slept on our couch and dominated our dinner parties for a couple of weeks, captivating the women and outraging the men with his fervent discourses on socialism and the Middle East. I sensed that he'd never fully approved of me, but Isabella loved him. In many ways he was the brother she'd never had. More importantly, through him she had seen a way she could fit into this new post-colonial society. Noting the full abeyya his wife was wearing and Ashraf's traditional clothes and newly sprouted beard, I wondered why and when he had become a fully practising Muslim.

To my surprise, Ashraf began to weep as he reached to grasp my hand.

'Oliver, my friend, it is a tragedy, a real tragedy. I have lost a sister, you a wife. But Isabella, she had courage. More than perhaps we will ever know.' He embraced me; embarrassed I patted him awkwardly on the back.

I had always secretly envied the openness with which Middle Eastern men expressed their emotions. I couldn't remember my father ever embracing me or Gareth. A hand on the shoulder was the best we could expect, and as a child I had craved the ponderous intimacy of that deceptively casual gesture. In Egypt, men kissed, held hands; fathers openly caressed their sons. I watched Ashraf's tears with secret envy. My grief hadn't broken yet and I wished I could weep like that now.

Francesca, determined to follow protocol, interrupted Ashraf's condolences and guided me to a podium at one end of the marquee. It held three ornate chairs.

'You, as the husband, sit in the centre. I am on your right, while the mother,' Francesca spat the word with ill-hidden disgust, 'sits on your left. People will pay their respects and we shall conduct ourselves with proper decorum. Then my duties as a grandmother will be over.'

Cecilia, Isabella's mother, collapsed into her chair. She moaned quietly, her painted mouth opening and shutting like a beached fish. There was a self-conscious theatricality to her grieving that appalled me. And I noticed Francesca glaring disapprovingly at her.

Despite Isabella and I being married five years, I had never met her mother. Isabella had described her as having a pathological fear of intimacy. 'It makes her claustrophobic to spend time with her own daughter,' she'd told me one night after an argument on the phone with Cecilia. 'She doesn't like to be reminded that she gave birth. This is a woman who is running from her past and she is terrified that one day it might trip her up in the shape of a resentful daughter.'

I could still hear Isabella's scornful tone ringing in my ears. She had reason to be resentful: she was under the impression that her mother had abandoned her to her grandparents. Seeing Francesca's reaction towards Cecilia now, I suspected the situation might have been a little more complex than that.

The Valium was beginning to wear off. I desperately needed something to defend myself from encroaching grief and the tedium of greeting a parade of strangers, but there wasn't a drop of alcohol to be seen.

A man gestured to me from the other side of the marquee. It was Cecilia's husband, Carlos. He was at least ten years her senior and wore the uniform of the wealthy European: panama hat, linen suit, loafers and gold cufflinks that caught the sunlight. Excusing myself, I got up from my chair and walked over to him. Taking my arm, he guided me behind a marquee, out of sight.

'Here, my friend, some grappa from the village I grew up in.' He pushed a silver hip flask into my hand.

I unscrewed the top and took a long, grateful swig. The alcohol burned my throat and seared through to the top of my head, but it obliterated the moment, which was what I wanted.

'I am sincerely sorry we meet in such circumstances. These Brambilla women — before you know it they have swallowed your balls. Cecilia loved her daughter, you have to understand that.'

'She had an odd way of showing it,' I replied. I tried to remember what line of manufacturing Carlos was in, but failed in the fog of tranquillisers and grappa.

'You must remember, Cecilia was born during the Great Depression. She grew up with nothing, just her beauty. Her parents were always working so she, herself, had no mother to speak of. She was only sixteen when they married her off.'

'I'd have thought that very reason would have made her try harder.'

'She wanted to, but it was not allowed. It is far more complicated than you know, my friend. After the early death of her first husband, the grandparents wanted to keep the child. That Giovanni, he was a crazy man, obsessed with the mystical. He could even hypnotise people, like snakes. If you ask me, all the Brambillas are crazy. As for Francesca, she is still angry with Isabella's father for dying so young. In the emotions, she is still a child.'

I thanked him for the grappa and returned to my seat. Francesca gave me a disapproving glare, but she was preoccupied with the Italian guests and couldn't reprimand me further.

I was dismayed to see that my first English-speaking visitor was Amelia Lynhurst. I had first met her at a cocktail party at the British Consulate. When she heard I was a geophysicist working in the oil industry, she had launched into a passionate monologue about how oil exploration was destroying the natural world — or Gaia, as she insisted on calling it, to my great irritation. She had also attempted to cross-examine me about Isabella's research, and I'd found myself taking an uncharacteristically intense dislike to her. She seemed hungry for new information, perhaps for a thesis that would re-establish her ruined reputation. Whatever her intention, I didn't trust her.

'I'm surprised to see you here, Miss Lynhurst.' I failed to keep ambivalence out of my voice.

'Perhaps you didn't expect me,' she replied, 'but please understand, I had a great fondness for your wife, particularly during our time together at Oxford.' She leaned forward and lowered her voice, 'In relation to other, more pressing matters, I hope you understand the implications of harbouring an undeclared antiquity, particularly one of such spiritual value. This country is in the throes of a delicate resurrection and these are perilous times. Such an antiquity has powers you, a man of prosaic interests, could never understand. Others, however, do. If the wrong people were to get hold of such a device, it could prove very dangerous.'

Startled by her directness I felt myself become defensive. Had Isabella been correct in her suspicion that Amelia Lynhurst had known how close she was to finding the astrarium? I decided it would be wise to feign naïvety.

'Oh, we always kept our work very separate,' I replied casually.

Amelia looked sceptical. 'Oliver, if you need my help in any way, you must visit at any time. I'm not sure whether Isabella had a true idea of the value of the object she was researching ...'

Her voice faltered and she glanced over my shoulder. I was surprised to see what I thought was a glimmer of fear in her eyes. I turned to see Hermes Hemiedes coming towards me, followed by the priest who had conducted the funeral.

'I really must leave now.' Amelia pressed her hand into mine then walked away.

Hermes stepped onto the podium, an ironic smile playing over his thin lips. 'Such women are dangerous because they never appear so,' he remarked as we both watched Amelia leave the tent.

'Oliver, Isabella's death is a profound loss.'

He embraced me and I was enveloped by a wave of musk and the scent of the cologne he was wearing — a sharp green tone undercut with a darker shade. In my heightened emotional state, it smelled like the aroma of physical decay. I pulled back, stiffly self-conscious.

'Thank you. I know Isabella respected you greatly, which was rare for her.'

He laughed — a hyena's bark. My eyes fastened on a curious pendant around his neck: a silver depiction of Thoth, the baboon moon god whom the Ancient Egyptians believed gave hieroglyphs to mankind on behalf of Ra.

'The very bright can be very arrogant,' Hermes said. 'I helped make her who she was: uncompromising.'

'So I understand.'

He moved closer, again enveloping me in that nauseating aroma. 'If Isabella did indeed find the astrarium, you should know that the device is very valuable to a lot of people, all of them far less scrupulous than myself.'

He pulled a card from his breast pocket and slipped it into my hand. 'If you respect the ambitions of your dear wife, you will visit me sooner rather than later. Dusk is the best time.'

I glanced at the address, recognising it as the old Arab quarter to the west of the city. When I looked up again, the Egyptologist was making his way through the mourners, his slightly uncoordinated stride parting the crowd.

Now tired of the event, I decided to leave too. I stood, but was prevented from stepping down from the podium by Francesca's hand on my wrist.

'Oliver, you cannot leave now.'

'I can and I will,' I told her. 'It's time I began my own mourning.'

I had never been so defiant with the old woman and she didn't try to dissuade me.

\* \* \*

I was amazed to find that it was near nightfall. A hantour, a small horse-drawn cart, was waiting outside the Brambilla villa. The driver, a rake-thin middle-aged man in traditional clothes, was leaning up against the villa wall and smoking. He threw away his cigarette and stood upright when he saw me.

'Please, get in,' he said quietly but with authority.

Wanting to walk, I waved him off.

'No, for you it is free. Please, Monsieur Warnock, I insist.'

I hesitated, wondering whether he was the secret police, but there was a dignity to his stance and something in his open pleading face that made me trust him. I got in and asked him to take me back to the villa at Roushdy.

We drove through the narrow lanes of the city. The air was fragrant after the recent rain and the soft clip-clopping of hooves lulled me into a gentle trance. The sense of motion momentarily postponed the terrible loneliness I knew I would experience once back in the villa and confronted with remnants of my life with Isabella.

The cart slowed alongside a low archway that seemed to lead into a darkened courtyard. A man wearing a headscarf that covered most of his face suddenly hauled himself into the cart. He was carrying a bag over his shoulder. I reared back, fearing I was about to be mugged. To my immense relief, Faakhir's face emerged from under the dark blue cloth.

'Say nothing,' he whispered. 'The astrarium is in the bag by your feet. I promised Isabella I would deliver it safely to you. Oliver, it is important that you guard the astrarium with your life. I don't know whether it is powerful or not, but there are others who believe they can use it to destroy everything we have worked for in this region — political stability, peace, an economic future …'

With a clatter of wheels we pulled up outside the villa.

Framed in an upstairs window was the lonely silhouette of Ibrihim, switching the lights on ready for my return.

'You must take the astrarium to your friend Barry Douglas. You can trust him. He will be able to open the container and carbon-date the astrarium. This you must do — for Isabella. You know I loved her too.'

I grabbed his arm. 'Why are you risking your life, Faakhir. Who do you work for?'

Smiling enigmatically he shook off my hand. 'Stay safe, my friend.'

He leaped out of the cart to disappear into the shadows.

# 7

I had arranged to meet Barry Douglas at the Spitfire, a small bar just off the Sharia Saad Zaghloul — one of the main avenues in Rue de l'Ancienne Bourse. Established in the 1930s, it had been popular with the Allied troops posted in Alexandria during the Second World War. The proprietor — an Anglophile — had proudly installed a small plaster bust of Winston Churchill draped by a Union Jack in the window. Inside, it was perpetual twilight. This was one of Barry's favourite haunts.

Barry Douglas had quickly become one of my friends as well as Isabella's; I was attracted to his maverick sensibility and classic Australian intolerance for bullshit. We shared a strong disdain for pretence and class-related snobbery. I didn't share his love of all things mystical and spiritual, however; this was a characteristic he had in common with Isabella.

I hesitated at the bar's doorway. When I'd arranged this meeting with Barry, I hadn't had the courage to tell him about Isabella's death; each time I had to tell someone the news it was like living through the drowning all over again and I dreaded that sensation of being swept back into the moment. Besides, I told myself, he was bound to have heard — news tended to sweep through Alexandria like wildfire. Steeling myself, I stepped inside. On the walls hung a gallery of old photographs, dusty black-and-white shots of smiling young men in khaki, arms around each other, hamming it up for the camera — Brits, Canadians, Australians, New Zealanders, the occasional Scotsman in a tam-o'-shanter. Some of them looked like children in ill-fitting uniforms: narrow adolescent shoulders lost in jackets; huge rabbit eyes staring out across time, tiny beads of fear buried in the centre of their pupils and defying the wide smile beneath. It couldn't have been easy defending a territory that many locals regarded as stolen anyhow; dealing with an ambivalent Arabic community not to mention the Italian–Alexandrians, some of whom had already left to fight with Mussolini or the Germans — people like Isabella's father.

Glancing around, I couldn't see Barry, so I sat at the bar and ordered myself a Bloody Mary. Looking at the photos, I couldn't help wondering how many of those young soldiers were now lying in the El Alamein war cemetery. There were seven thousand tombstones there, stretching out in frightening monotony — the most poignant of them marked seven unknown soldiers, five unknown soldiers and so on. Comrades blown apart then thrown together in unimaginably macabre embraces.

'Christ, you're a bloody sorry sight.' Barry Douglas's unmistakably Australian voice boomed across the bar. He pulled up a stool beside me and attempted to perch his massive body on the seat. 'Fucking stools are made for midgets. Aziz!' He yelled at the proprietor who was busy wiping glasses. 'When are you going to get some decent fucking chairs?'

Aziz shrugged, humouring the Australian, who, I knew, was a dedicated regular.

Barry turned back to me. 'At least the beer's cold. How are yer, mate?' He wrapped his huge arm around me and pulled me into a bear hug.

I turned my face away, terrified my reserve might break down. And it might have if I hadn't been momentarily overwhelmed by the mixture of Brut aftershave, stale sweat and hashish emanating from Barry's ancient leather jacket. He released me to wipe a tear away.

'That was some tragic funeral. Hate them myself. When I go to join the great Buddha in the sky, I want my physical remains cooked up in some delicious cordon bleu stew so my molecules are recycled in a meaningful way.'

That was the trouble with Barry: you never knew if he was being serious or not.

'So you were there?' I asked.

'Wouldn't have missed it for the world. I was right at the back, getting stoned. Didn't want to upset the natives.' He blew his nose into a large embroidered handkerchief. 'At least the Catholics put on a good show, unlike the Proddies. You can't have a decent burial without some decent bloody ritual. But Isabella? It wasn't her time.' He thumped the bar to emphasise his point. 'It wasn't her fucking time!'

A furtive couple in the corner looked up from their tête-à-tête, a lone Cypriot sailor turned to stare, and a stray cat bolted from under one of the tables. The tape clicked over and a Kinks track filled the sudden silence — the incongruous youthful yearnings of another world.

Without prompting, Aziz slammed down a glass of beer in front of the Australian.

Barry Douglas was one of those rare individuals whose flamboyance and maverick attitudes worked like an electric shock — his childlike sense of the absurd was both liberating and infectious. Forty-five, he stood at six foot three, weighed twenty stone, and had a tangled mane of red hair and matching beard that made him look like some Celtic god. His skin, permanently sunburnt, bore the wrinkled crusty surface of the Caucasian in Africa. When drunk, he looked and behaved like an outraged bull, but when sober he was capable of charming even the most unapproachable women. The local Arabs loved him, and he had lived in Alexandria for so long they regarded him as a lucky talisman. His clashes with the municipal police were legendary, but even they tolerated his regular escapades with affection. An avid diver and surfer, Barry claimed to have grown up more in the ocean than out. He described his occupation as 'marine expert', though expert on what exactly was never clear. I'd always thought treasure-hunter a more appropriate description, but the longer I knew Barry the more he revealed himself to have extraordinary talents in the most surprising areas.

He left Australia in 1956, and ended up on the west coast of California in the early 60s, where he'd become involved in some of the early LSD experiments conducted by Aldous Huxley at Berkeley. This had led to a complete revision of all of Barry's ambitions. He abandoned academia for adventure and managed to land a job as a diver with Jacques Cousteau, which began his infatuation with shipwrecks. Barry was totally dissolute when he wasn't on a quest, but once he started the hunt he became dangerously focused — a real shark. According to Isabella, the Australian was one of the best restorers of gold, silver or bronze ancient artefacts around, his other skill being his phenomenal ability to carbon-date wood accurately.

After his stint with Cousteau, Barry had continued to work his way around the world and finally settled in Alex. A self-declared sexual compulsive, he was as capable of monogamy as a buck hare and regarded marriage as an abhorrent and outdated institution. This hadn't prevented him marrying three times himself: once to a Hindu, once to a Thai Buddhist and once to a Muslim, all disastrously.

'I loved Isabella, you know.' He took a few long swallows of beer and stared at me. 'I know you're English, but for Christ's sake, Oliver, show some emotion. You're freaking me out.'

I glanced down at my wedding band. 'Can't, not yet. But I suppose in a few days I'll break down into a blubbering mess.'

Barry's eyes drilled into me, his grey-blue irises swimming in a sea of broken capillaries. 'You do realise,' he said, drawing a circle in the air that encompassed the bar, the customers, Aziz in the corner reaching for a cigarette, 'that all of this is an illusion, this quantum foam of particles, matter, bodies, neurons. She's still with you, in you—'

A wave of anger swept through me. I didn't want his sympathy. 'Cut the bullshit, Barry. I'm an atheist, remember? I haven't got some nice little spiritual fairytale to fall back on.'

'I'm not talking bullshit. You can't really think that all we are is mortal flesh and blood? The Ancient Egyptians had it right. There's a whole world beyond this perceived reality we're experiencing right now. I know — I've been a witness to the cosmos.'

'Too many illegal substances, if you ask me.'

Defiant, Barry held up his lager. 'Hey, maybe you're right! Maybe old Barry's grey matter is just a little too fried. But I've met guys with thrice my IQ, physicists, who'd agree with me. Still doesn't change the fact that it wasn't Isabella's time.'

He drained the glass. Following his cue, I finished my own drink and ordered another round.

'You know I was with her when she drowned. I tried to save her ...'

'Mate, there was no way anyone knew that tremor was going to hit. No way. Anyhow, what the hell was she doing diving in the bay? That's strictly no-go. Let me guess, you guys are both MI5 and you were combing the sea bed for military secrets.'

Aziz leaned over. 'Don't joke, my friend. In Alexandria, even the snakes have ears.'

'Yeah? And the mice have cocks.' Barry, miming paranoid, looked under the table then over the counter.

Ignoring the Australian's bravado, I lowered my voice. 'They've already interrogated me about the dive — for twenty-four hours straight. In the end, the oil company phoned the British consul who bailed me out.'

'Bloody bastards, no respect for the grieving.' His tone changed, serious now. 'But Isabella was onto something, wasn't she?'

I looked over to Aziz, who was busying himself with some glasses out of earshot — a deliberate retreat, I suspected. I turned back to Barry.

'She did find something. An object she was convinced was historically important.'

'And?'

'I need you to carbon-date whatever wood you can find. I think the artefact inside is bronze. At least, that's what Isabella thought. I can hardly bear looking at it, Barry, it's just history to me. None of it means a thing — not set against her life.'

\* \* \*

Barry must have driven the company car back to the villa — I was certainly too drunk to do so. The lights were all off except for a small lantern burning on the first floor. Ibrihim had stayed up I noted appreciatively as I staggered to the front door. In those first few days I'd overheard him weeping behind the door of his small room. He had retreated into a formal reticence since Isabella's drowning, as if death, after entering the house, was an important guest who had to be treated with special reverence. The housekeeper had covered all the mirrors, and given away a small kitten Isabella had adopted, claiming it would be bad luck to keep the animal.

As I fumbled drunkenly with the keys, Ibrihim opened the front door. A practising Muslim, he strongly disapproved of drinking. He frowned as I stumbled into the hallway, Barry catching me before I fell.

'Monsieur Warnock is stricken with grief,' the Australian explained solemnly, before belching.

Ibrihim winced in disgust at the stench of alcohol coming from my clothes. 'Indeed,' he replied regaining his composure. 'I have heard that strong coffee is beneficial for such grief. Shall I make some?'

'Excellent idea,' I answered, hoping I wasn't slurring my words. 'My friend and I will take it in the drawing room.'

Barry followed me into the large room and whistled as I switched on the lights.

'Geez, the oil company's looking after you all right. Get used to this shit and it'll be the beginning of your moral demise, not to mention your socialist credentials.'

'What socialist credentials?' I slurred.

'Mate, Isabella dobbed you in.'

'I was a student — I only joined the illustrious Socialist Party of the once Great Britian so I could get laid. All I wanted was to get out of my parents' two-up, two-down and avoid going down the mine. And I succeeded — so shoot me.' I concluded, a little more defensively than I'd intended.

'Oh, c'mon, you're a runner — like me.'

Barry grabbed a First World War British helmet that sat ceremoniously on a sideboard, placed it on his head at a rakish angle and started goose-stepping across the parquet floor.

'You think that if you stop, all your past — your shitty childhood, fucked-up love affairs, compromised ethics and your working-class background — will catch up with you in some catastrophic collision. Bang, bang, you're dead.'

'Something like that.' I sat on the floor, suddenly overwhelmed by the events of the day. 'Barry, I'm too bloody drunk and miserable to philosophise.'

Mercurial as ever, the Australian's mood changed instantly. He replaced the helmet and helped me to my feet.

'Right then, mate, lead me to the golden calf.'

\* \* \*

The steel tube sat in the middle of the bedroom floor, still oozing mud and sea water. Crouching down, Barry tapped against the side.

'Still in there, is it?'

'According to the metal detector. It's some kind of nautical instrument — at least that's what Isabella believed. She also mentioned some kind of wooden casing.'

'Nautical instrument? What era are we talking?'

I hesitated. I guess if I hadn't been drunk, I mightn't have been so candid, but Barry's face seemed so open, his flaming red hair upstanding like the quills of an outraged porcupine.

'Ptolemaic. Cleopatra's time.'

Barry's eyes narrowed. 'Impossible. Nautical instruments don't date back that far.'

'I thought you were the one always going on about how we limit ourselves through our conventional perceptions and expectations.'

'The quote is the expectations of our perceptions, you pissed bastard. Mate, you're holding out on me — what exactly did Isabella think she'd found?'

'Some kind of astrarium with supposedly magical properties.'

Barry's eyebrows shot up at the word 'magical'.

'According to Isabella,' I added quickly.

'Excellent, that clears up a lot of bloody things. Oliver, I know you're a cynic but let's look at the Ancient Egyptians' comprehension of magic. It was inseparably entwined with religious worship and intellectual pursuit. For example … the god Thoth — god of the written word — was also a god of magic. Thoth's task was to classify the creations of the superior deities — Osiris, Horus, Ptah, Amon and Ra. This gave him tremendous power. Any self-respecting magician — like myself for example — would have a well-stocked library; magicians were expected to read every holy word, comma and tome of Thoth's, the idea being that the knowledge would make them as powerful as the god himself. I'm telling you, the concepts were far more bloody sophisticated than the history books make out, and maybe, just maybe, the buggers were right.'

'What's this baloney got to do with the astrarium or astrolabe or whatever the hell it is?' I asked.

He dipped a finger into the mud inside the steel tube and tasted it, oblivious to my disgust. 'Mate, if this is an instrument once used by a magician, you have to adopt their mentality and treat it accordingly, with respect and fear. This artefact, as you insist on calling it, could still be formidable in the right hands. In the hands of someone who knows how to use it. Remember, it was constructed hundreds of centuries before the Enlightenment, before the separation of church and state, religion and science, before the compartmentalising of the psyche. Not that I expect a repressed bastard like yourself to understand,' he concluded affectionately.

I pointed at the steel tube. It stood there, upright, like some obelisk of ill portent.

'Magical or not, or whether it still has power, just remember Isabella drowned for that bloody piece of irrelevant history,' I said, a little more bitterly than I'd intended.

Barry reached into the top of the tube and, with the edge of his fingernail, carefully scraped away some of the mud revealing the edge of what appeared to be a wooden casing.

'This looks way too well preserved for Ptolemaic. You sure Isabella didn't have her dates mixed up?'

'You know Isabella — she was obsessive and thorough in her research. But — you'll love this — it was a mystic called Ahmos Khafre in Goa who finally convinced her it existed.'

'*The* Ahmos Khafre?'

'I imagine so.'

'That bloke's legendary. He was one of the greatest mystics of this century.'

'Yeah, along with Houdini, Crowley and Mickey Mouse. Legitimate or not, Khafre had a total hold over Isabella. So there it is — myth made real,' I finished dramatically, sitting on the floor myself.

Barry peered back into the tube. 'I'll have to take it to my apartment to desalinate it, then carbon-date the wooden casing. Jesus, Oliver, if Isabella was right, do you know how significant this could be?'

To my dismay, Barry's face was lit up with a maniacal excitement I'd seen so many times in my wife.

'Take it, but please get some results quickly,' I said. 'I have to get back to Abu Rudeis in the next week.'

\* \* \*

I watched from my balcony as he walked off down the alleyway, the shaggy outline of his mane visible between the branches of the magnolia tree. Night was Barry's natural domain, along with the subterranean underwater world. He was fearless. Actually, I suspected it wasn't so much fearlessness as active risk-taking — an irresistible compulsion to seek out any situation that would challenge his faculties. It was because of this I had known he would take the job.

He turned the corner and vanished. Exhausted, I leant against the wall, the night air playing across my face. My shirt, damp with sweat, stuck to my back and I realised how much I had begun to fear sleeping, how I'd started to fear that with each passing day my memory of Isabella would fade and eventually she would leave me completely — a terrible, finite abandonment.

I dragged myself back into the bedroom. The bed was large and low; an embroidered quilt with mirrors sewn into it lay over the top — one of Isabella's Indian acquisitions. I dreaded sleeping in that bed alone and the thought of finding it empty in the morning was overwhelming. The reality of Isabella's absence had started to grow like an invisible presence that threatened to eclipse my own desire to keep living. And I knew if I didn't sleep now I probably risked having a psychological breakdown.

Stripping off my shirt and trousers, I walked into the bathroom. As I reached into the bathroom cabinet I knocked over a tin of talcum power and it spilled over the window ledge. Too drunk to deal with it, I decided to clean it up in the morning.

I brushed my teeth and, in an attempt to sober up, plunged my face into a basin of cold water. As I stood there, the water pressing into my nostrils and against my lips, I couldn't help thinking of Isabella's drowned face and how she must have felt. Had she panicked, had she fought to stay with me? I needed to know. I needed to get inside her consciousness — I needed her back. For a moment, I was tempted to breathe in and join her.

I waited until my lungs were bursting, then, spluttering, lifted my face, now streaming with water.

I pulled away the scarf Ibrihim had used to cover the bathroom mirror and barely recognised the face that stared back, covered with stubble. Exhaustion and grief had hollowed my cheeks. Surprisingly, I welcomed my unrecognisable appearance: it delineated the person I had been before Isabella's death and the person I was now. I decided I would stop shaving from now on to emphasise the delineation. I was determined; this new alien Oliver would face sleeping in the empty bed; would block out the hours of lovemaking that had taken place there, the faint scent of her that still lingered on the linen, the taste of her skin imprinted on my senses.

I re-entered the bedroom and threw myself onto the quilt. In seconds I was asleep.

\* \* \*

The sound of a door clicking open woke me. I forced my eyes open and craned my neck to check the digital alarm clock. It read 3.45 am, but as I watched, the digits didn't appear to flip over. The bloody thing's broken again, I thought, then reached over to switch it off when a noise from the bathroom made me swing around. The door was closed but light shone out from beneath it. I froze. I couldn't remember leaving the lamp on.

Then I heard it again — a rustling sound, like someone moving about. A puddle of water began to seep out from under the bathroom door. I wasn't frightened or even surprised; in my muddled near-dream state it all made perfect sense. I got up.

Inside the bathroom, the Art Deco lamp had been switched on, illuminating the pink marble tiles. The bathroom sink was empty, gleamingly clean; a normalcy that was comforting. The sound of water swishing against the bathtub broke the silence. I stopped in my tracks. Suddenly I was aware of another presence in the room; fear crept up the back of my scalp, stretching back the skin. My immediate thought was that it had to be Isabella, yet I knew that wasn't possible.

I turned around slowly. A hand hung over the edge of the bathtub — a woman's hand, long fingers blanched by water and death. My heart pounded against my throat as I forced myself to walk over to the bath. Each step brought me closer to a terror I knew I had to face.

Twisted, the curve of one buttock pressed up against the porcelain, her skin as white as a beached cuttlefish, Isabella's corpse floated in the bathtub. Her eyes were closed; her lips a faint violet. I was close to screaming. The room felt like a vacuum, as if all sound and air had been sucked out of it. I couldn't tear my eyes away. A great bloodless gash ran down the centre of her body and her wet hair floated, suspended like tendrils. Her other hand lay palm up in the water, the fingers plaintive in their curled pleading. As I watched transfixed, her eyelids flickered then opened.

I screamed and woke again in my bed. Terrified, I looked across at the bathroom door. The room was dark and silent.

# 8

The scent of kosherie, a local rice, lentil and pasta dish, floating up from the kitchen woke me. Ravenous, I sat up, only to sink back onto the pillows flattened by a pounding hangover. I waited a couple of moments then bellowed for Ibrihim, who confirmed that it was indeed past midday.

Gingerly, I made my way to the bathroom. A series of bird-claw prints were clearly marked in the talcum powder I'd spilt on the window ledge the night before. The window was ajar, yet I felt sure I'd shut it. What was a bird doing in the bathroom, I puzzled. Could it have flown in through the open shutters of the bedroom while I was sleeping?

The Ba tattoo on Isabella's ankle came into my mind. Then I remembered the events of the night before. Isabella's presence had been so vivid. Had it been real? My terror had been real enough. My mother's warnings of souls caught in purgatory for sins left unconfessed came flooding back to me. As a child I'd hated the fear these tales engendered in me; they had seeded my determination to live unfettered by superstition. But Isabella had lived a 'good' life.

Crazy lapsed-Catholic nightmares, I told myself, as I stood naked in the middle of the bathroom. This isn't rational, it's just coincidence — the dream, the fact that a bird flew in during the night. This is grief stringing together a narrative.

Turning the shower on, I stepped into the cold water, letting it pummel my face and shoulders in an effort to exorcise the night before. But Isabella's gaze of entreaty and bewilderment had seared into my memory.

I stepped out, wrapped a towel around my waist and went to the library.

The small square room was panelled in dark oak with brass trimmings. The walls were lined with bookcases, many of them filled with Isabella's books. The volume I was looking for was on a top shelf, between works by Robert Graves and Giovanni Belzoni: *The Meaning of Ba*.

Isabella had explained to me that the Ba hieroglyph was one of the five elements the Ancient Egyptians believed made up the soul. The Ba represented an individual's personality, the other elements were Ka, defined as the spirit that entered the body at birth — or life force, the other three important elements were Ren — name, Sheut — shadow and Ib — the heart. At the moment of death, Ka and Ba were united. A third significant hieroglyph was Akh, which depicted the successful union of the Ka and Ba that enabled the deceased to progress to the afterlife. If this union failed to take place, the soul was condemned to everlasting death — a fate the Ancient Egyptians dreaded.

I opened the book at a photo of a wooden effigy of King Tutankhamen on his funerary bed. He was flanked by two wooden birds: one with a human face, his Ba; the other showing the face of the sun god, Horus, signifying that Tutankhamen's Ba was that of a pharaoh, a living god. I turned to the next page and began reading:

*The hieroglyph used to write 'Ba' was a jabiru stork, while in funerary art it was represented as any bird with a human head and sometimes with human arms. The manifestation of Ba varied according to the period of Egyptian history and the school — sometimes it was a butterfly, sometimes a human-headed sparrowhawk or a heron. Whatever its image, the Ba was always considered to be attached to the body and freed only in death, after which it could fly anywhere, even into sunlight.*

*Trees were often planted near graves to provide shade for the soul-birds before they soared up towards the stars, taking with them all that had made the deceased human. The Ancient Egyptians facilitated such departures by building a false door or window into a wall of the tomb.*

The head of Isabella's Ba tattoo had her own profile. She'd told me she'd had it tattooed on her ankle to ensure her path to the afterlife. I'd never been able to work out whether she was joking or not, but there was something unnerving about the tattoo — its vulnerable profile with the distinctive nose and large eye; its bird legs and large claws seemingly poised for flight.

Was it possible that I'd experienced some kind of visitation of Isabella's Ba? I entertained the notion for an instant, then dismissed it as ridiculous.

Banging, loud and persistent, on the front door below startled me, followed by Ibrihim's footfall as he ran to answer it. I leaped up, thinking it may be the police, come to search the villa on some flimsy excuse. Instead, I heard Barry's voice roar up the stairs.

'Mate! Get yer clobber on! I'm taking you out!'

* * *

The Union restaurant was one of the last bastions of colonial Egypt. A favourite of Alexandrian society before nationalisation, it still retained some of its earlier glamour. The head waiters were dressed in black suits (now frayed at the cuffs and collars) and bow ties, while the lower waiters wore white skull caps and brown jellabas. The ornate pink and brown wallpaper had started to peel and the velvet curtains were blotched, but the piano was still polished and the pianist wore real diamond earrings. At the height of the Union's glory white caviar was flown in from Iran and French foie gras and Scottish salmon were readily available. Now the kitchen was dependent on the black market. On a good day, it was possible to order Australian lamb chops, mint sauce and couscous and be swept up by a nostalgia you knew wasn't your own while a head waiter points out where Montgomery used to sit and which was Churchill's favourite table.

Barry was a close friend of the maitre d'hotel, Photios Photaros, who was the nucleus of all society gossip and knew not only all the old power players of the European diaspora but their children and grandchildren. He was the story-keeper. Photios, having heard of Isabella's drowning, had placed us at his prize table, in an alcove near the pianist who was playing a mournful rendition of *La Mer*. The maitre d'hotel had also supplied Barry with his customary bottle of Black Label whisky.

We were there to meet an American journalist, keen to get Barry's view on the local reaction to Sadat's peace initiatives. Convinced that no grieving man should be left alone for long, Barry had insisted I accompany him. The astrarium was desalinating back in his apartment.

'Do you believe in ghosts?' I asked him. I was on my third whisky.

'Mate, I believe in everything except mountain trolls in red caps and bells. Although having said that, I have seen a few trolls in red caps and bells — I just didn't believe in them. I've never seen a ghost though — not drunk, stoned or on the stairway to heaven. Why?'

I finished my drink. The whisky's trickling warmth hit the back of my skull and then coursed down to my stomach — I needed anaesthetising even momentarily, it made me forget.

'Nothing. But do you think there may be a psychological reason why someone might think they're being haunted?'

He looked at me. 'I dunno ... guilt, grievance, a sense of unfinished business? But if this is to do with Isabella, forget it. It's more likely her sudden absence has left a shadow; a presence you still expect. I used to get a lot of that back in San Francisco when I was tripping. Also, you have to take into account that time is not linear.'

My heart sank; it had been foolish to expect any empirically based explanation from the Australian. 'So tell me about this journalist.'

'She's the Middle Eastern correspondent for *Time* magazine. Some bright spark told her I was the bloke for the local gossip.'

'Probably terribly earnest and naïve as all hell.'

'Who cares as long as she's buying?'

Just then a visible ripple ran through the male diners in the restaurant — the kind of reaction that indicates the arrival of an attractive woman. Barry and I looked up. A glamorous small blonde woman in a black cocktail dress stood at the door scanning the tables. In an instant Photios was at her side. He pointed our table out to her and she began weaving her way towards us. We both watched, a little amazed.

'Stone the crows, she's a looker. Tuck the bib in, Oliver, we have company.' Sweeping his great mane away from his face, Barry sat up straight in his chair.

As the journalist drew nearer, I realised with a jolt that I knew her. She arrived at our table and reached out to shake hands with Barry; it appeared she hadn't recognised me yet.

'Barry Douglas?' her deep rich voice sending a ripple of memory through me. She still hadn't looked in my direction.

'It might be.' Barry joked, looking like a cat that had just swallowed the cream.

'Rachel Stern, *Time* magazine.' They shook hands, Barry turned to me. 'And this is Oliver Warnock, the best geophysicist in the oil biz. He's a bloody great mess at the moment so I hope it's all right if he joins us?'

Finally she turned toward me. It must have been fifteen years since the last time I'd seen her. She met my gaze with barely a flicker of surprise.

'But we know each other. How are you, Oliver?'

Rachel's expression indicated nothing but a smooth diplomacy. She was older, a wrinkling at the corner of those dark blue eyes whose slant betrayed a faint Mongolian gene somewhere in her Russian heritage, but the rest was as I remembered: the strong nose and chin, the disproportionately full mouth, the play of humour around her lips, the same shock of fuzzy blonde hair that stood out triangularly from her head. However, a sharp intelligence and confidence had replaced the air of curiosity that had defined the young woman I had known fifteen years before.

'Rachel *Stern*?' I asked.

'Stern's my married name, was my married name.' She sat at the table and called the waiter over. 'Can I get you boys another bottle?'

After a quick glance at my dazed expression, Barry said to the waiter, 'Johnny Walker Black Label and a plate of olives, Gamal.' He turned back to Rachel. 'I trust it's at the courtesy of *Time* magazine?'

Rachel smiled. 'You bet.'

I tried not to stare; I still couldn't quite believe it was her. Perhaps it was the fact that I was already quite drunk, perhaps it was the surreal nature of coincidence, but it felt as though another strange twist of fate had just punctuated my life.

I'd first met Rachel Rosen, as she was then, at a cocktail party in London in the early 60s. The host, a mutual friend, was a caustic but erudite socialist I knew through the Imperial College branch of the Socialist Party of Great Britain. I was in the second year of my degree and Rachel, several years older, was completing her Masters degree in International Relations at the London School of Economics. We began our brief affair after an argument about Stalin and it finished when she left abruptly for New York because of family issues — at least that had been her excuse. I'd never been able to fathom whether I'd been too intense for her or the cultural differences had been too extreme, but I was eternally grateful for one thing: Rachel had been the first person to really believe in me, both as a professional and as someone able to transcend his background. And that, to a twenty-three year old with a huge working-class chip on his shoulder, had been invaluable.

Rachel placed the fresh whisky bottle in front of me. 'How nice to see you, Oliver. I heard on the grapevine that you'd ended up working in the Middle East, but I didn't expect to find you in Alex.'

'I'm working at the Abu Rudeis oilfield. I'd be there now except ...'

My voice faltered; I couldn't actually say the words.

'Oliver lost his wife recently, a bloody tragedy,' Barry said bluntly.

'Oh, I'm so sorry.'

The concern in her voice was genuine. I turned away, frightened I might actually cry. The room swayed slightly. Despite knowing I was drunk, I couldn't repress the urge to tell Rachel about the drowning, as if telling someone from my past might make Isabella's death more real. Before I could help myself I'd launched into an explanation.

'Isabella is, was, a marine archaeologist, top of her field. She was conducting a series of dives in the harbour. She was obsessed with this astrarium, a ridiculous piece of tin. I couldn't stop her from making this dive ...' I downed my fourth whisky. 'I was with her when she ... when she drowned.'

Barry coughed and the spell was broken. Rachel reached out and held my hand for a moment.

'I can't even begin to imagine how terrible it must have been for you,' she said, 'and so far from home.'

'Home? I travel so much I don't even know where that is any more.'

I couldn't keep the bitterness out of my voice. I poured myself another whisky.

Barry put a hand on my shoulder. 'Mate, don't you think you should take it easy?'

'Not tonight, tonight I intend to forget who I am.'

'Fair enough, but I reckon you should sit on that whisky for a while.'

He turned back to Rachel. 'So Henries, that silly English bugger, told me you're reporting on the Egyptian reaction to Carter's peace-brokering?'

'And you're the guy, right?'

'Right. Tell you what, come over on Thursday night when the old fellas play their backgammon and I'll introduce you to the local elders. Big respect for guru Barry.'

'I'll do just that.'

They clinked their glasses together in a toast. I watched, vaguely aware that the alcohol had started to make me feel belligerent.

'You can't be naïve enough to believe Carter will actually achieve anything?' I leaned toward the journalist.

'I really think the players are committed this time,' she replied cautiously. 'That's half the battle.'

'You and I both know Sadat and Begin need their people behind them. The Israelis don't like Carter.'

'And they didn't like Kissinger. Listen, Carter's talked to Sadat, Hussein and Rabin. Next week he'll be with the Syrian president in Geneva. Camp David will produce results. Sadat wants peace. He's an Egyptian nationalist; he's not into pan-Arabism. He's a practical individual not a sentimentalist. There are economic reasons why Egypt would seek peace with Israel.'

'Sure, we all know how practical. The Yom Kippur War — remember that little peace initiative? Sadat went to King Faisal to convince him to flex the only muscle he knew the region had over Israel and the West.'

'Right, well maybe now he wants to recoup the benefits. Maybe he's an oil man now, like you,' she teased.

'Hey, I just find the stuff. I see it as my vocation.'

'And what a huge waste of talent. You might know the region but you're wrong about Sadat. Besides, he lost the Yom Kippur War — even more reason to seek peace.'

I lurched on with the argument, feeling as if I was watching myself from the outside. 'Egypt only just lost; that war was far closer than you know. People remember. It was only four years ago; a lot of young men were slaughtered — on both sides.'

'And they're tired of the killing.' She finished her whisky. 'Why oil, Oliver? I'd have thought with your background you'd have pursued something a little more egalitarian, maybe even ecological?'

'Market forces intervened. Happens to the best of us. Right, Barry?'

'No, mate. Yours truly has held onto his socialist credentials, not to mention the credo of Buddha.'

'Bullshit. But here's to American optimism anyway.' I lifted my glass. 'Long may it reign.'

The others ignored the toast, and I could see from Rachel's eyes she'd already passed judgement and found me wanting, but I was beyond caring.

'You are angry,' she said.

'I'm a realist. I've been working in the region for over ten years. It's not enough to get a few politicians to agree — you have to change a whole nation's prejudices and fears. It's a complicated mess that's not going to be solved by a fast-talking peanut farmer.' I failed to keep the sarcasm out of my voice.

'Old stories can have new endings. I'm sticking with my optimism. It's been great catching up, and again, I'm really sorry about your wife. No doubt we'll bump into each other somewhere soon.'

She turned to Barry and handed him a card. 'This is my hotel, I'll see you Thursday.'

Then, to my surprise, she leaned over and kissed my cheek. 'Bye, Oliver.' Her perfume transformed me back into the combustible youth I'd once been, desperate to impress.

I watched her leave, her confident bearing so different from the over-eager young woman I'd once known.

'You've had enough mate, I'm taking you home.' Barry plucked the half-full glass from my hand.

'We have a past,' I said.

'I can see that. For a stitched-up Pommie, you've got taste.'

'I'll assume that's a compliment. Don't worry about walking me — I'll get a taxi.'

'Listen, before you go ...' He pulled me closer and dropped his voice. 'Last night, I came across an old friend, a local. Now it just so happens this bloke used to be the son of the gardener who worked for the Brambillas back in the '50s, when Isabella's grandfather ran the joint.'

'So?'

'So we got talking about the drowning and he tells me he's heard that it was Giovanni who killed Isabella.'

'That's ridiculous. Giovanni's been dead for years.'

'You don't understand — he told me the grandfather put a curse on the granddaughter. Marked her for an early death. Apparently he was considered a great sorcerer by the locals.'

'Giovanni Brambilla?'

'Mate, I'm only telling you what the bloke said. But put it this way, he was shaking with fear when he told me.'

'It's just superstitious nonsense — Isabella's grandfather adored her. It was an accident, Barry, I was there. A stupid, avoidable accident.'

'Nevertheless, I'd be asking the grandmother a few questions. There was something odd about Isabella's childhood, even for around here.'

I speculated about how well he'd actually known Isabella. Better than I'd realised, I guessed.

'How long is it going to take to carbon-date the astrarium?' I asked.

'A week, if you're lucky.'

'I'm due back at Abu Rudeis tomorrow.'

'And if I need to contact you?'

'We have a satellite phone out on the field, for emergencies. Ibrihim has the number.'

Barry pulled me into another of his bear hugs. 'Don't look so worried, mate. You can rely on me.'

# 9

Bill Anderson was waiting for me at the tiny airstrip in Port Said, with a car and driver.

'I thought I'd stay an extra night and catch up with you,' he said. 'My crew left for Texas this morning.' He was a big muscular man just beginning to run to fat, his broad Texan physique incongruous next to the slender Arab driver waiting to drive us back to the camp. He extended his hand, a massive paw, the calloused palm abrasive against my own. 'My sympathies, Oliver. I couldn't believe the news when I heard. It's a rough life, that's for sure, rough and unjust.'

The intensity of his concern embarrassed me and again I found myself wrestling with my emotions. I nodded and we both climbed into the back of the car in silence.

On the way to the camp we drove past the capped oilwell. Floodlit, the well was surrounded by a circle of burnt and charcoal ground; debris from the explosives used to cause the fire to implode and extinguish itself.

'Took a week to figure out the configuration,' Bill said. 'It was probably sheer bad luck but I wouldn't rule out sabotage.

Capping it was a bitch, took way too long — fortunately we didn't lose anyone. This one was a mother, that's for sure.'

'Where are you off to next?'

'Libya, there's a problem at Sarir. That should be exciting,' he added ironically.

I turned back to the open window. Being back in Abu Rudeis was disorientating, my mind kept playing tricks on me, as if I'd slipped back in time to before the drowning. I kept expecting Isabella to ring on the satellite phone; for her to still be in Alexandria, at the villa, waiting. It was a seductive illusion.

The moon had painted the desert in black and white, with just a faint hint of azure streaked across the horizon. The vast scale of the landscape placed human life into perspective. But my grieving had flattened my emotions and the usual sense of cleansing I associated with the desert was absent. The uncomfortable suspicion that I might have unwittingly endangered Barry by leaving the astrarium with him tugged at the back of my mind.

Anderson interrupted my reverie. 'I looked at some of your core samples and the seismic. I hope you don't mind?'

Actually, I did mind. I was fiercely private about my data, and the vague sensation that I'd missed something in my research had been irritating me ever since the Cessna had taken off from Alexandria.

'Not at all, as long as you don't change career and suddenly become the competition,' I joked, trying to cover my annoyance.

'No chance. I like gambling but I'm not that much of a risk taker.'

I noticed the driver glance at his rear-vision mirror as he reacted to Anderson's sharp tone. I lowered my voice. 'Is that what you think I am — a gambler?'

'We're all gamblers in one way or another, but, Oliver, you have to admit this one's a fairly long shot.'

'Did Johannes Du Voor ring you?'

The chief executive officer of GeoConsultancy was a difficult man. He had no conventional training as a geologist or geophysicist but had fallen into the oil business via shipping after his time as a supplies officer in the South African navy during the Second World War. A perfectionist, Johannes Du Voor had an ambivalent relationship with the notion of risk. As a small consultancy that depended on fewer than a dozen large corporations as clients, GeoConsultancy couldn't afford mistakes. Initially, he'd accepted that some of my methods were a little unorthodox, but lately he'd been pushing me to back up that final ten per cent of sheer instinct with data. I had tried fudging it, but sometimes my hunches were so inexplicable even I couldn't account for them. Understandably, the bigger the commission, the more nervous Johannes became.

'We bumped into each other at the executive lounge at Austin,' Anderson said. 'Boy, that man can talk. I don't think he realised we know each other as well as we do. He's changed. The guy didn't look well; he was kinda morbid.'

'He has an eating disorder, in that he eats too much — as if he needs to consume the space around him, literally. What else did the old bastard say?'

'He asked me if you're angling to set up your own consultancy, walk off with his clients.'

I laughed. The idea that I could be that underhanded seemed absurd — at the time. 'The guy's paranoid,' I answered. 'He just doesn't understand the way I work.'

The trouble with Johannes Du Voor was that he imagined the rest of humanity was as ambitious as he was, particularly the few he reluctantly recognised as more talented than himself. He'd recruited me directly out of Imperial College and for two years had insisted I work as his assistant in the field. On our first job together I realised he'd made a mistake; that he was out by nearly a kilometre. It was an important job — the first well in a new structure in Angola — and millions were at stake. I had pored over the seismic data, tested the core samples myself and walked the field sniffing the air. At the risk of being fired, I'd offered him my alternative interpretation. Johannes had listened and had trusted the leap my instinct was pointing to despite his own calculations. To his credit, he corrected the proposed drilling angle, but only after telling me that if I was wrong he would not only fire me but he would also go out of his way to ruin my ongoing career. We struck oil but our relationship altered profoundly after that; he respected this inherent talent of mine, but every new exploration was like free-falling all over again for him.

The car pulled up beside the new drilling rig — untouched since I'd left two weeks earlier. The drill bit hung above the deck, its steel gleaming in the floodlights, poised like some vast mole ready to begin burrowing. Nearby, a deep water well had been drilled to tap bore water to cool the rig in operation. Generators and various other pieces of equipment stood in the long shadow cast by the drill, like a silent audience awaiting a performance. It was bizarre to think that this massive contraption had remained unchanged, as if frozen in time, while my own life had gone through such devastating upheaval.

I made a quick appraisal of the equipment and the operators waiting at their controls, then raised my thumb and jerked it downwards. The giant diesel motors burst into life and the drill started to rotate as the stem was lowered through the deck. Nearby, engines turning the turntable pumped away the rubble and mud.

Anderson, standing next to me, slapped me on the shoulder. 'Rotary drilling, don't you love it!' he shouted over the noise. 'Ultimate penetration!'

Ignoring him, I watched the process for a few minutes. This initial stage was always nerve-racking: one had to pray the drill bit was the correct selection for the rock. So far it was holding.

'I hear rumour there's an oasis about fifty miles from here,' Anderson said. 'The guys told me there's a 1920s Arab-style hotel and it's great swimming.'

'I should stay here.'

'C'mon, there's nothing going on your assistant can't handle. Man, you're suffering a loss. You need some time to gather yourself. I know how that feels.'

I glanced back at the rig. Anderson was right. It would take two days before the drill had gone deep enough that it could change direction and enter the pay zone. Maybe a desert drive would burn away some of my sadness.

\* \* \*

The road was little more than a track. I drove the company jeep like a madman. Somehow the prospect of dying out here attracted me; an instant way of escaping the grief that now shadowed me.

Inland, the Sinai was endless scrub broken by the occasional sand dune. My eyes played tricks, turning the clock back to repopulate the dunes with primordial trees, an inland sea, swooping gulls against a kinder sky. Once, areas of Egypt had been moister, the weather more tropical. There had been swampland, hippopotami in the Nile, lions and crocodiles, but the desert had always been the kingdom of the snake, jackal and scorpion, the domain of harsh death. Much of the Ancient

Egyptian icons reflected this. Anubis, the jackal-headed god of embalming and cemeteries, was an embodiment of the stalking jackal at the edge of the desert inching his greedy way towards the ravaged corpse; Ammut, the terrifying crocodile-headed goddess to whom the hearts of sinners were thrown during the weighing of the heart ritual, was a manifestation of the real predators in the murky waters of the Nile. As my imagination sketched the fecund past against the arid horizon, I was reminded of Isabella's recurring nightmare and then of the desecration of her body before it reached the morgue.

'Anderson, have you ever heard of an illegal organ trade here in Egypt?'

He looked perplexed by the question. 'Not here. Asia maybe, but not in Egypt — why? You missing something?' he joked, then realised I was serious.

'No,' I lied. 'Just thought I might have stumbled onto something.'

'Wow, that's kinda heavy.'

'Forget I even mentioned it.'

We fell back into an uneasy silence.

\* \* \*

Two hours later we arrived at a fork in the road. There was nothing on the horizon in either direction.

Anderson studied the map in frustration. 'Jesus, I thought you said you'd been there before.'

'I have, but I had a local driver,' I answered, smiling.

He swore and tried to trace on the map the way we'd come.

I jumped out of the jeep. Immediately the heat hit me like a furnace; punching me in the lungs and almost sending me reeling. I stood still, shallowing my breath, then wrapped the scarf I was wearing over my head and across my burning cheeks. I loved this elemental pain, this pushing up against the tediousness of physicality, the proximity of death and the sharpness of life it brought with it.

Just then I heard the distinct plod of camels' feet followed by a shout in Arabic. A group of five Bedouin men emerged from behind a small dune, leisurely making their way down to the desert track, their headdresses and robes catching the breeze. They stopped their camels and stared at the jeep.

Uncertain of my reception, I waved. One of them waved back, then the chief whipped his mount on the flanks and galloped towards me, the animal moving with surprisingly elegant strides.

From inside the jeep Anderson whistled. 'Hope your Arabic's good,' he muttered as he climbed out.

'It depends on how thick his dialect is.'

Close up, the hennaed beard of the Bedouin was startling. Now I could see the end of an AK-47 rifle poking out from under his saddle. He stared at Anderson. I followed his gaze; the Bedouin had noticed the old army ID tag the oilman still wore from his service days in Vietnam.

'May peace be with you,' I said hurriedly in Arabic, hoping to distract the Bedouin.

Ignoring me, he pointed aggressively at Anderson. 'Soldier?'

'Say nothing,' I murmured to Anderson, praying the normally loquacious American would stay silent.

By now the others had ridden up. They formed a sullen bunch, staring over the chequered scarves covering the lower half of their faces, wary, waiting for a cue from their leader as to how to react.

'Not any more,' I answered in Arabic, pointing to Anderson's grey hair. 'Old.'

Unconvinced, his suspicious gaze travelled across Anderson's T-shirt, flared jeans and ancient sneakers.

'Old body, young mind,' the Bedouin said deadpan.

Behind him, the other four tribesmen burst into laughter. Anderson, sensing an indignity, swung around to me.

'What's he say?'

'He says you look very strong for a man of your age.'

Anderson narrowed his eyes in disbelief. 'Jesus, Oliver, just ask him where the oasis is.'

'The oasis is half an hour's drive from here. You take the left track,' the Bedouin replied in perfect English. 'Be careful, the desert can be dangerous.'

He swung his camel around and they were gone.

\* \* \*

The gravelly tones of JJ Cale floated out from Anderson's radio, mingling with the rustling of the date palms above us. We were lounging beside a small lake surrounded by a green fringe of reeds and palms. Its surface mirrored the turquoise sky yawning above it. Set back a short distance was the low-lying hotel, its white-yellow desert mud bricks making it barely discernible. Its Moorish architecture, with narrow slits for windows and arches leading to an enclosed walled garden that was cool and shady even at midday, made it a refuge from the incessant heat.

I lay on a beach towel taken from the hotel, left behind from some long-departed tourist, its grey flannel embroidered with 'P&O, Suez Cruises'. Next to my head sat the satellite phone borrowed from the oil company. My contract stated I was to be contactable at all times in case of possible crisis in the field — so where I went the phone went too. Above me, a thick serrated palm trunk leaned over the lake, its reflected counterpart swaying slightly with the movement of the water. It was a perfect isochronism, a parallel world in reverse where anything was possible. I sat up, intrigued by the notion.

Anderson, in voluminous crimson bathing trunks, a copious amount of sun-tan lotion smeared over his reddening face and chest, lay in full sun, resembling a beached starfish. A thick, crudely rolled joint hung between his fingers. He sat up, took a long drag of the marijuana and, holding his breath, handed it to me. After exhaling he fell back onto his towel.

'Boy, how good it is to stop the brain.'

I inhaled gingerly; I had never liked to lose control and marijuana wasn't a favourite of mine, although Isabella had smoked it regularly, claiming that it stimulated her imagination. Personally I thought it stimulated nothing but paranoia, but, for fear of sounding unfashionable and old, I'd never asked her to stop indulging. My preference was alcohol, and I'd never tried any of the stronger hallucinogens around at the time — LSD, mescalin, cocaine. But now I was willing to try anything to stop my mind from slipping into introspection. The smoke hit the back of my throat and seared my eyes. Seconds later a sense of psychological dislocation seeped through my body.

'This is strong, where did you get it?'

'Afghanistan, it's opiated. They always prioritise my equipment so I'm never searched at airports.'

'Sounds useful — I'll keep that in mind.'

'Sure thing, buddy, but I draw the line at firearms and radioactive waste. A man has to have some morals.'

I stared across the lake, the colours blurring into smudges of brilliant blue, emerald green, white-yellow. An ibis flew low over the water's surface, its wings a languid progression of semi-circles rising and falling in a spiral of feathers.

'Do you know why I do what I do?' Anderson's voice was distant and slightly slurred, and my own increasingly inarticulate mind struggled to register the fact that he sounded very stoned.

'For the money, I suppose — maybe the danger.'

'Wrong on both counts, you know I was in 'Nam?'

'Sure.'

'Well, back around '68 — 17th September 1968 to be precise, my platoon was ambushed by the Vietcong and I found myself surrounded by three friends with their guts spilling out. I was the only one left standing. I can't tell you why — wasn't reflexes, wasn't clever thinking, it just happened that way. I missed my death day. That's what I truly believe: I missed my death day and now here I fucking am — amen.' He took another drag of the joint then stubbed it out on a rock. 'But I know, in my heart of hearts, I was truly meant to die that day.'

I lay there thinking about Isabella, her fear of Ahmos Khafre's prediction of her death day. Was that the day she had drowned? It seemed inconceivable. I waited for Anderson to continue. I'd never considered him a religious man or even particularly philosophical; in fact, I'd always assumed him to be the opposite: a realist willing to work for anyone for the right price, regardless of his politics.

'Couldn't it have been simply luck — the angle of fire?' I asked finally.

Anderson rolled over and stared at me, the whites of his eyes reddened. 'Christ, another cynic.'

'I'm a firm non-believer if that's what you mean. Organised religion is the scourge of the world. Look what it's done in this region.'

'That's economics, colonial history and territory and you know it. Anyhow, I'm not talking about religion. I'm talking about the natural span of a man's life and what kind of meaning we bring to our time here on this damn planet!'

Anderson's voice was loud, he was too stoned to realise how loud. I glanced around: the place was deserted except for a peasant woman on the opposite bank doing the laundry. She squatted at the water's edge, her long slim wrists emerging from her robes, her reddened hands a fury of soap suds as she scrubbed the clothes with a pebble on a rock. She looked across then went back to her washing.

I turned back to Anderson, wondering whether to humour the huge bear of an ex-soldier or be honest.

'You know, one of the difficulties I had with Isabella was her belief in all this voodoo. It used to amaze me that an educated, intelligent woman could believe in astrology and ghosts, that some kind of invisible force directed her in her archaeology. I'm a staunch Newtonian. Everything is what you see: gravity is gravity, the laws of physics are immutable and all mysteries are explicable. We're complex animals run by our hormones and ultimately not very important in the grand scheme of things. No more, no less.'

There was a short pause during which I realised we were engaged in the meandering philosophising that smoking marijuana always led to. But I was on a roll, I couldn't stop myself; it was as if I was talking out the events of the past two weeks, trying to incorporate them in a framework that made some logical sense. But why was I so angry? Was I angry with Isabella for dying in her search for something that she believed was a spiritual object — magical even if Barry was to be believed?

'We live and then we die,' I continued. 'People live on in memory; that's the only kind of immortality available, unless you believe in wrapping desiccated corpses in linen and building huge triangular tombs over them. I don't. I'm worse than an atheist; I believe in expendable biology. Maybe that's why I'm terrified of forgetting her because that would mean she'd really left me. You know, that moment she stops appearing in my dreams and I find I can't remember her face.'

There was another long silence. Intoxicated I gazed up into the vast blue. Suddenly I realised that the circling dot above me was a hawk patiently stalking its hunting ground.

Bill lifted his sunglasses and peered at me, genuine emotion crinkling his eyes. 'She'll never leave you — you know that, don't you, Oliver?'

'I guess not.'

Another silence fell upon us, as dense as wood.

Bill collapsed back onto his towel. 'Tom, one of the guys who died with me in Vietnam, a real close friend, had this private joke with me. When we were under fire he'd call me Jerry. Tom and Jerry, see? Humour was his way of dealing with terror; no one else in that platoon, hell, on the whole planet, knew this little joke we had going between us. Anyhow, a couple of weeks after his funeral in Austin, the army put on a commemoration dinner for the platoon — most of whom perished with Tom. So there I am, dressed up like a Thanksgiving turkey, thinking how much Tom would have hated all this hypocrisy and pomp, and I'm looking for my place name on the table. And there it was: Jerry Anderson — not Bill, Jerry — in black ink with a small cartoon of a cat and mouse. It was a sign, you know — Tom joking with me, reminding me that he was still out there, watching.'

'I'd love to believe that random events may have a special significance,' I said, 'but I can't. Maybe it's my scientific training, who knows, but if I had an experience like that I'd just see it as someone's ill-conceived joke.'

'That's bullshit, Oliver. I've seen how you work — not all of it's based on cold logic, not in this game.'

Uncomfortable with the knowledge that he was right, I changed the subject. 'You still haven't told me why you became a firefighter on oilwells.'

Anderson trailed a hand into the water. The drips falling from his fingers appeared huge; deliciously welling miniature worlds of cool, cool water.

'Maybe I just like tempting the gods. You see, every time we set those explosives I'm waiting to die. Just can't shake off the sensation that I'm living on borrowed time.'

'Survivor's guilt?'

'Like I said, I missed my death day, brother. It's as simple as that.'

We lay there flattened by the sun, both very conscious of the unspoken statement hanging awkwardly between us. Finally Anderson spoke.

'Listen, I didn't mean to suggest that Isabella's accident was—'

'Yeah, I know,' I cut in. Then I stood up and waded into the shallow lake.

At the edge the water was warm. I slipped off the bank and moved into the deeper part where it became colder. After taking a deep breath I dived down, four strokes through the greenish water, sand below, the dark stripes of reeds shooting up towards the light, caressing paintbrushes against my body. The cold jet of the current travelling over my burning skin was soothing; my fingers making splayed frog-hands in the aquamarine light filtering from above.

I swam further down and along the bottom. A small group of large fish hovered above me, metal-blue in the subterranean sun then darted away, glinting like thrown silver coins. In that moment I felt something pass by me, something large. Nothing was visible. Ripples ran along my skin, making my body hair stand on end. Treading water, I rotated as fast as I could, just in time to catch the sight of feet and naked legs disappearing into a forest of weeds.

A second later, Isabella loomed out of the lattice of long floating leaves, her loose hair weaving around her face, her breasts luminous. Terrified, I froze, drifting slowly down, as she smiled sadly at me, her face a translucent moon filtering through the green. Then, indicating I should follow, she turned and swam away with that characteristic kick of hers. This is no ghost, I told myself, fighting blind panic.

I followed, only to lose her in the shadowy labyrinth. I searched, fighting the dangerous tangle, stirring up clouds of mud, but found nothing. Lungs bursting, I made for the surface.

Gasping, I broke the water, limbs flailing. Disorientated, I struggled for breath for what felt like minutes then managed to clamber onto the bank where I lay curled on the ground.

I became aware of a strange dull whirring sound — my satellite phone was ringing. I sat up. Anderson was on his feet, frantically waving.

'Are you okay?' he shouted.

Shaking, I got to my knees, trying to compose myself, but Isabella's face still hovered in front of my eyes. I leaned against the sandy bank.

'Fine. I just shouldn't smoke and swim!' I yelled back.

The satellite phone continued to ring.

'Answer it!' I shouted, and then I was back in the water, swimming towards him.

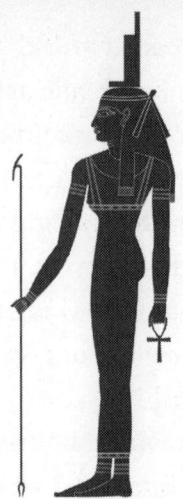

# 10

Barry's excited voice sounded distant, as if he were yelling through a glass wall. 'Oliver, this thing, it's amazing, mate. It's definitely an astrarium, but I've never seen anything even remotely this mechanically sophisticated.'

'What do you mean, it's an ancient artefact?'

'That's what's blowing my mind. It isn't bronze but some other alloy, which might explain why it's so well preserved. It seems to have some unusual magnetic properties — there's a cog-like device at the centre with what appear to be two magnets — looks as if it's meant to spin. Totally freaky. But get this, mate, the first time I carbon-dated the wooden box I thought I was hallucinating, but I've checked it five times now and I'm getting the same result over and over!'

'What result?'

'Isabella was wrong; this astrarium isn't Ptolemaic, it's way older — Pharaonic. I found a cartouche on it — the cartouche of Nakhthoreb, otherwise known as Nectanebo II. That makes it Thirtieth Dynasty — bloody unbelievable!'

My throat was dry and my heart felt as if it was thumping

against the wall of my stomach. If the astrarium was Thirtieth Dynasty it was well over two thousand years old.

'Thirtieth Dynasty, that's not possible. You've made a mistake.' I fought to keep my voice calm.

'Mate, I don't make mistakes.'

'Okay, I'm going to get back as quickly as I can. Meanwhile, I want you to keep this quiet.'

'Oliver, this is the discovery of the century.'

'Just promise me you'll lie low. I don't want either of us ending up in jail for stealing an antiquity. I'll be back in a couple of days. And, Barry, for Christ's sake watch your back.'

The line cut out before he had a chance to answer. I glanced over my shoulder. I was relieved to see that Anderson was fast asleep on his towel and the peasant woman washing her clothes had disappeared.

\* \* \*

I flew to Alexandria four days later. I took a cab from the airport straight to Barry's apartment on the Corniche. The apartment block was one of those neoclassical buildings constructed at the turn of the twentieth century and had a crumbling magnificence. He had lived there for years, and had an arrangement with his Syrian Christian landlady, Madame Tibishrani. Now a voluptuous widow in her early sixties, she lived on the first floor with her handicapped daughter. She maintained Barry's place during his long and often inexplicable absences and operated as an unofficial post box, dutifully collecting his mail. She adored the Australian and was fiercely protective of him, as well as tolerant of the numerous young travellers (almost always female) who'd turned up to stay over the years.

The apartment was on the third floor, with a large balcony that wrapped around the corner of the building. The cab dropped me off.

The sun had begun to set — a blood-red eye staring over the sea already streaked with the darkening clouds of night — and the call to prayer echoed: a lone melodic wailing that never failed to stir something elemental in my soul. The stately white Abu El Abbas mosque with its two domes and slender tower reaching like an outstretched arm to God dominated the square.

Small distinct groups of worshippers had already begun to walk to the mosque. The smell of the sea blew in — a crisp breeze tainted with the scent of distant shores — the familiarity of it saddened me. I glanced back at Barry's apartment block. I immediately noticed that something was wrong. The birdcages that usually hung there were missing and the shutters on the doors were closed. I'd never seen it like that before.

The doorman let me into the building without a word then resumed his position in a plastic black chair by the stairwell. I raced up the stairs. Barry's apartment door was shut; the magic eye carved into it to ward off evil stared back at me as if to mock my growing sense of dread. I lifted the brass knocker and banged. There was no reply.

There was a creak on the stairs behind me; Madame Tibishrani's platinum beehive appeared on the landing below. The rest of her followed, incongruously dressed in an elegant black evening dress. She gasped, startled to see me.

'Monsieur Oliver, you have given me a scare. It has been so terrible, you cannot imagine.'

She hurried up the stairs and joined me outside Barry's door. Even in this dim light I could see that her eyes were swollen from weeping.

'I'm trying to locate Barry. Isn't he in?'

Sighing, Madame Tibishrani stroked my hand. 'My poor Monsieur Oliver, have you not heard? Barry is no longer with us.'

'What do you mean?'

'He had an accident. The police say it was suicide, but I don't believe it, Monsieur Oliver. Barry would never have killed himself. Never.'

Shocked, I leant against the wall, my mind spinning with possible scenarios.

'Do you have the keys?' I stood, pulling myself together.

'Naturally.'

'Let me in, please …'

'But the police …'

'Madame Tibishrani, please. I need to see for myself.'

She glanced down and up the stairs — that furtive look of fear so common in Egypt — then turned back to me.

'*D'accord*,' she whispered, 'but you cannot tell a soul it was I who let you in. The police have been here so many times I think Barry must have been in trouble with the authorities.'

She pulled a bunch of keys from her pocket and, after wrapping the latch with a handkerchief to muffle the sound, opened the door.

The smell was awful — musty, with an overlay of old incense, stale cigarette smoke and cat piss. It was dark, almost pitch black: the heavy velvet curtains were drawn across the windows. Broken glass splintered under my shoes as I made my way across the lounge room, my feet bumping against books scattered across the floor.

'When they searched the place they made such a mess, but I have orders not to disturb it,' Madame Tibishrani murmured from the safety of the doorway. 'No respect for property, no respect for the dead.'

I drew the curtains then opened the balcony doors to let in the sea breeze. Illuminated, the apartment showed itself to be in a state of total chaos. Books had been pulled from the bookcases lining the walls and flung to the floor, as if the intruders had been looking for secret compartments behind the shelves. Several of Barry's prized beanbags had been ripped open with a knife and the stuffing scattered — it looked like a tidal wave of foam had swept through the apartment. A leather armchair, its cushions neatly slit, stood in the centre of the room. I collapsed into it, the cotton stuffing pushing up around me.

'What happened?' I asked.

Madame Tibishrani stepped gingerly into the apartment. Barry's cat, Thomas O'Leary, a thin black and white creature, appeared and wrapped itself around her ankles miaowing. She picked the animal up and stroked it absentmindedly.

'It happened two days ago. I was wondering why I hadn't heard from him — normally he visits every Thursday night and I make him pigeon ...' She blushed; it was an Egyptian belief that roast pigeon was a powerful aphrodisiac. 'But last Thursday there was not his usual knock on the door, so I went up ...' Her face crumpled as she tried not to weep. 'His front door was unlocked, but this wasn't so unusual — you know how Barry believed in keeping his door open for every no-hoper to drop by. Anyhow, I went in and that's when I found my poor friend.'

She pointed at the chair I was sitting in. 'He was in that chair, with a needle in his arm and a leather string ... what do you call it?'

'A tourniquet?'

'*Oui*, like a tourniquet, wrapped further up. He was dead; I think maybe for a day already. But I don't understand ... Barry was not a heroin addict, of this I am sure.'

She was right. Despite his indulgence in many recreational drugs, Barry had always been vehemently anti-heroin. Besides, Alexandria wasn't the easiest place to purchase such a drug. A set-up, it's got to be, I thought as I looked around the ravaged room. Someone had killed Barry and then searched the place. I had the impression they'd left frustrated; frustrated enough to be wantonly destructive.

'I pray for him,' Madame Tibishrani said. 'You know, if it is suicide his soul will not be able to enter heaven. I spoke to the priest about it but he is adamant ...'

As Madame Tibishrani continued worrying about Barry's condemned soul, I found myself wrestling with my own conscience. Had Barry died because I'd given him the astrarium to carbon-date? Was I directly or indirectly responsible for his death? It was a distressing notion. Madame Tibishrani's raised voice broke into my thoughts

'They tried to tell me Barry was cooking up drugs in his home laboratory. Such ignorance! The police, the secret police and the municipality officials have been harassing me constantly since the accident. An Englishwoman even came and questioned me — what gave her the right! I look at her and I think she cannot ever have been Barry's lover; in fact, I doubt whether she has ever had a lover—'

'Can you remember her name?' I cut in.

'Amelia Lynhurst she called herself; some kind of academic, or so she claimed. When I tried to stop her from entering the apartment, she pushed me aside and looked anyway. Crazy, *non*?'

I walked carefully around the room trying to ascertain what could be missing. A huge glass tank stood against one wall — an aquarium filled with tropical fish of which Barry had been immensely proud. It appeared to be the only undamaged object in the room. I found myself wondering what the fish would tell me if only they could speak. I turned back to the landlady.

'Did Amelia Lynhurst leave with anything?'

'Not a thing! So many questions though, Monsieur Oliver. She even asked about you and your poor wife.'

'Outrageous. Madame Tibishrani, do you think you could give me a few moments alone? I would like to say goodbye to Barry in private.'

Again, tears filled her eyes, making me feel guilty for deceiving her. But I couldn't search the room with her there.

'Normally I would say no, but out of respect for you and your poor dear wife who were so close to him ... Besides, I need to feed poor Thomas. Just call me when you have finished.' And she left, the miaowing cat in her arms.

Barry must have known his killer otherwise he would have raised some kind of alarm. There were too many people in this city of over 1.5 million for no one to have heard him call out; and Barry had been on good terms with the other tenants in the building. There was no question in my mind that he had been murdered. What I needed to know now was whether he'd had time to hide the astrarium; and if so, where?

I sat back down in the leather chair and tried to place myself in Barry's mind, follow his line of vision. I closed my eyes then opened them; my gaze immediately fell on the fish tank. I tried to remember how it had looked on my previous visits. Something in its appearance had changed but I couldn't pinpoint the difference.

I decided to check the other rooms. In the bedroom, the futon Barry slept on had been slashed, and the three wooden crates he'd kept his clothes in had been overturned — trousers, sarongs, underwear and wetsuits spilled out in a tangled mess. A small shrine to Buddha had been vandalised. Beside it lay a statuette of Thoth, the god of magic and words — Barry's adopted totem.

I walked into the en suite bathroom where Barry had constructed his home laboratory. Metres of blown glass tubing — vacuum lines — were clamped to metal frames suspended from the ceiling, the tubes threading around and over each other like some bizarre sculpture. The basin had been turned into a workbench, on which stood a small bar fridge, a hammer, a file — still spotted with flakes of dark wood — and a mortar and pestle.

I opened the fridge cautiously, slightly nervous about what I might find. Sitting on the grimy plastic shelves were several corked glass flasks filled with liquid nitrogen — one of the necessary components of carbon-dating. A couple of them trailed curling wisps of vapour from leaky stoppers. Alongside them was an unopened can of Foster's beer. For a moment I was tempted to open it and drink to Barry's health — a ghoulish sentiment I knew he would have appreciated.

Further along the bench, a Pyrex beaker was suspended over a Bunsen burner. I lifted the beaker and sniffed — inside were tiny charred fragments of charcoal. Apart from the flakes of wood on the file and a tiny amount of dark dust — ground wood, I assumed — in the mortar, there was no sign of the astrarium or its wooden case.

After making sure the front door lock clicked behind me, I walked down to Madame Tibishrani's apartment. She answered my knock with rosary beads clutched between her fingers.

'Well, did you make your peace?' she asked me.

'Not entirely. Has there been a funeral yet?'

'*Mon Dieu*, I wish, but no, the poor man is still in the city morgue. They are waiting for the Australian consul apparently — there is a small problem locating Barry's nearest living relative. Although there has been no problem with living ex-wives. Apparently, all three have been informed of his death, and all are claiming that they are still married to him. Barry was such a romantic.' I hastily left before she began weeping again.

\* \* \*

The nearest working phone line I knew of was at the Alexandrian Oil Company office. I went straight there. After practising my Australian accent, I rang the central police station and told them I was a relative of Barry's ringing from Australia and that I was after further details of the circumstances of his death. The officer investigating the case told me politely but firmly that as drugs had been found in Barry's body, they had dismissed the case as accidental suicide, a drug overdose. When I asked about the ransacking of the apartment, he laughed and told me that drug addicts were known for their wild parties.

As I put the telephone down, I had the distinct impression someone had provided the financial incentive for the investigation to be closed down prematurely.

# 11

The morgue was located to the west of the city, in the old Turkish quarter. Built by Mohammed Ali in the nineteenth century, the building appeared to have undergone little renovation. At the reception desk I asked to speak to Demetriou al-Masri, the coroner who had approached me at Isabella's funeral. The sour-faced man behind the desk told me with ill-concealed relish that Wednesday was Mr al-Masri's day off and that I should come back tomorrow. Patiently I explained I was here to see the body of a dear friend. The thirty Egyptian dollars offered under the table seemed to soften his attitude. He called over a youth lounging against a wall and instructed him to take me to 'the European'.

The room was freezing. The sound of a generator battling to maintain the sub-zero temperature filled the room adding to the sensation that I was now standing in a strange antechamber that had some unspeakable ritualistic function. A chemical smell of embalming fluid pricked at my nostrils and sent vague fingers of fear fluttering across the back of my scalp. This was where the new guests were kept, the youth informed me, grinning: the drowned, victims of road accidents, or beggars found curled up in doorways. Each corpse had its own plinth of marble, and one could guess the age and shape of them from the silhouettes of the bodies all covered by grimy white sheets; I couldn't help wondering if Isabella's body had lain on one of them. It was a nauseating thought.

The mortuary attendant pulled the sheet off Barry's corpse. The mane of tangled hair made him look like some majestic statue of Neptune in repose, the white-grey pallor turning his flesh to alabaster. The eyes were open and filmed with a whitish-blue, his chin was unshaved, his cheeks sucked back to the skull in death. In his chest was a huge T-shaped wound — a crude incision that ran from his belly button up to the centre of the collarbone, as if they'd peeled back the chest cavity — roughly stitched with black thread. I assumed they had carried out an autopsy to confirm the cause of death.

The attendant, noticing my emotional reaction, nodded respectfully and left to have a cigarette in the corridor.

The refrigerated air sank into my bones. I shivered, then glanced down at Barry's feet; they were bony, the veins a topography of congealed life stopped mid-pulse. I looked back at his huge barrel chest and the skin below it that hung grey and slack. I kneeled, retching.

Mastering my revulsion, I stood and examined his body for signs that may illuminate the real cause of death. I lifted his beard: under the tangled mass of red hair was a thin purple thread. I'd seen this before in Nigeria on the body of a field worker left propped up on a fence around a well — murdered as a warning to the oil company I was contracted to at the time. Barry had been garrotted. I glanced at his arm and the puncture mark left by a needle — the stigmata of the addict. Whoever had killed him had injected him with heroin after his death to make it look like an overdose. My guess was, they had tortured him to find out where he'd hidden the astrarium. Maybe they hadn't meant to kill him, but he'd died anyway.

I was furious. 'You were never a junkie and you did not commit suicide,' my angry voice bounced off the shiny white tiles.

Tenderly, I tucked his arm up against his body. As I did so I noticed a greenish-blue colour staining his fingernails and fingertips. I knew that colour — I'd seen it underwater, during dives.

\* \* \*

It took an hour to get back to Barry's apartment through the traffic along the Sharia Saad Zaghloul. As the cab sat there, sandwiched between an open truck full of exhausted-looking soldiers and an hantour, I felt someone's gaze burning through the window. I turned and met the eyes of a man sitting at a table outside a café. Shocked, I recognised the scarred face of Omar, the supposed official who had accompanied us on the dive for the astrarium. The sight of him transported me back to Isabella's drowning and, momentarily, I was paralysed by emotion. I stared at him, unable to look away.

The truck in front of us accelerated and my driver was quick to follow suit. We swung into a side lane and away from Omar. Relieved, I promised the driver triple the fare if he went as fast as he could. We reached the Corniche fifteen minutes later.

I raced back up to Madame Tibishrani's floor and persuaded her to lend me the keys for one last time. Moments later I was inside Barry's apartment.

I pressed my face up against the fish tank, the cool glass humming under my skin. On the bottom stood a kitsch statue of Jesus, his feet buried in gravel and his painted eyes turned beatifically towards heaven. He was framed by a stream of silvery bubbles that bounced up behind him through a pump concealed in a plastic treasure chest. Next to this little ensemble was a Richard Nixon doll entwined with a plastic mermaid who appeared to be fellating him — a classic example of Barry's deeply irreverent humour. Then I noticed the metal edge of something half-buried at the back of the slope of gravel. An angel fish, fins rippling like the wings of a hummingbird, swam down and began nibbling at some algae growing on the edge of the object. I immediately recognised the colour of the algae from Barry's fingertips. I peered closer. Between the waving waterweed and the bubbles of the air pumps, part of a smallish box was visible, about the size of an eighteenth-century clock. Despite a thin layer of algae, I could see the serrated edges of two disks.

Transfixed, I switched on a reading lamp and hauled it over to the tank, pointing the light directly at the object. Instantly, thin lines of glittering bronze were illuminated — a tiny inscription written across one of the disks.

'Barry, you clever bastard,' I announced, then, after making sure all the blinds were pulled down, I plunged my hands into the tank.

* * *

Back at the villa, I took the astrarium up to my bedroom — it seemed the safest place. Out of its container it was far smaller and more innocuous-looking than I'd imagined — it certainly didn't look like the powerful weapon Isabella and Faakhir had described.

As Barry had said, the metal resembled an alloy — bronzish in colour but slightly grainy and sparkly, almost as if it had been mixed with diamonds or something flinty. It reminded me of one of the rare earth metals. Running my finger across the surface, I focused on the silvery, slightly coarse texture. I had seen a metal like this before — samarium, which had strong magnetic properties, particularly when combined with cobalt. As such metals were hard to mine for — even today — I couldn't imagine how the Ancient Egyptians would have had the technology, never mind the expertise, to refine such ores. Despite this I knew they had been fascinated by metallurgy. Isabella had told me the Ancient Egyptians believed that the natural chemical changes in such metals so magical that through them a lowborn fellah's destiny could be transformed into that of the most powerful pharaoh — a kind of ancient alchemy. I'd found this idea intriguing, particularly when I discovered that they had cultivated a use for magnetic iron ore from meteorites and tektite glass in their ritual instruments and considered such iron ores to be sacred. Could the astrarium be made from a similar metal?

I examined it more closely. The mechanism appeared to be a series of cogs built around three main disks, whose faces were read through a peephole in the top of the box. There was a main pivotal rod that provided the central axis for the cogs and disks, which finished in what looked like a keyhole at the front. Presumably, one inserted a key or some similar device to start up the mechanism. There was an inscription on each of the three disks: one in hieroglyphs, one in Greek and the third was in a script I could not place.

I suddenly remembered Gareth's drawing of the astrarium and ran to Isabella's desk to search for it. I found it and placed it next to the device. It was uncanny how closely they resembled one another, except the actual device was larger and more complex than they had envisaged. I looked at the cipher written at the bottom of the drawing then peered again at the inscriptions on the astrarium. With a shock, I realised the first two symbols of the hieroglyphic inscription matched Gareth's lettering. Excitement rushed through me as I finally began to believe this was the actual astrarium Isabella had been searching for.

Two small balls — one gold, the other darkened silver — jutted out from behind one of the disks: the Sun and the Moon I guessed. There were five other smaller copper balls — probably the five planets visible to the ancient eye: Mercury, Venus, Mars, Jupiter and Saturn. It reminded me of a miniature planetarium. It was almost inconceivable to think it may be more than two thousand years old. I peered into the central chamber, where, with the aid of a torch, I could just see the two magnets Barry had mentioned. Each sat on its own axis. What would it take to set them into motion, I pondered.

I returned to Isabella's desk. The ghost of her presence hung in the air; I remembered her sitting there in the lamplight that last night, pensive as she studied the illustration of the astrarium, her long fingers trailing the edge of the paper. Then that small gesture I'd forgotten until now — the slipping of something under the ink blotter. I broke open the desk lock. Atop a pile of papers sat an envelope, my name written on it in Isabella's distinctively neat hand. Staring down, grief clutched at my chest. I sat back in the chair until it had passed.

I propped the envelope up against the lamp stand, stalling the moment of opening it, then I glanced at the papers it had been lying on. On top of the pile was a yellowed document with the title: *Nectanebo's Priestess and the Pharaoh's Ba*. The author was Amelia Lynhurst. This must be the thesis Isabella had told me about, the one that had finally discredited the Egyptologist.

I looked back at the sealed envelope with my name on the front. Why hadn't Isabella trusted me more? Why had she lied to me about the significance of the astrarium; the danger involved in finding it? She'd trusted Faakhir with the truth but not me. Had I been so unapproachable?

I sighed and opened the envelope. Under my fingertips the expensive notepaper felt like silk, like her skin. A trace of her distinctive scent — a mixture of musk and jasmine — was faintly discernible. Closing my eyes, it was easy to imagine her heavy hair brushing across the paper, leaving its own olfactory signature.

*28th April 1977*
*Alexandria*

*Oliver, forgive me, I've never been completely honest with you. All those years ago, Ahmos Khafre did not only tell me my death date; he also told me I may be able to save my own life if I discovered the astrarium in time. As I write I hear your voice chastising me for such superstitious beliefs, but the world I grew up in had no borders between magic and myth, the living gods and the dead. Through them I have been a witness, and through you I thought I would escape them. I will always love you.*

*Isabella*

'Don't you dare try to give meaning to a pointless death, Isabella!' I shouted, swept up by sudden rage. 'No one could have predicted that earth tremor. No one! Not even me!'

I punched the cushion on the chair, anger and frustration pounding through me, and the fabric ripped, sending feathers flying up into the air. They floated back down to the floor like lazy snow, covering the envelope at my feet.

The call to afternoon prayer sounded: haunting and melodious. Time was passing. I walked over to the balcony window. Below I could see a gardener pruning a magnolia tree. The simple intent of his gestures seemed so real against the extraordinary events that had begun to shape my choices. I had to know more: the information would free me from my guilt, my doubts. I needed to bury my emotions in my work; I needed to make this world solid. I shouted down to Ibrihim, instructing him to bring me some lunch, then picked up Amelia Lynhurst's thesis.

The illustration below the title caught my eye first. The central figure, a high priestess, sat on a throne and was dressed in a long-sleeved ceremonial robe with red and blue ribbons and a tall pillbox-shaped headdress with flowers sprouting out of it. In one hand she held a sistrum — a rattle-like musical instrument associated with the goddess Hathor — and a garland of morning glory, the hallucinogenic bindweed, lay across her lap. A sparrow was perched at her feet next to a small pot. She was surrounded by handmaidens playing tambourines, who wore dark rose mantles over white gowns, similar pillbox headdresses adorned with a single blue lotus flower, and gold bands high around their necks. The caption told me the image had been found in a tomb in Hierakonpolis on the Nile and was one of the very few depictions of an Isis festival rite. This particular scene had been dated to the reign of Ramses XI in 1000 BC, but the ritual had been carried out through the ages and it was known that Banafrit, Mistress of Good Fate, sister of Nectanebo II, had executed similar rituals.

On the inside page was a portrait of Banafrit herself. The patrician nose, long almond eyes and full mouth were profoundly human in their flawed asymmetry. I would have recognised this face on the street. In fact, it seemed familiar to me. I knew I'd seen it before, but where? I read the text below the illustration.

*This depiction, discovered on the wall of a Hathor temple, is thought to be the only remaining representation of the High Priestess Banafrit (meaning 'of the beautiful soul') who lived during the reign of Nectanebo II in the Thirtieth Dynasty (360–343 BC). Her other titles included Divine Adoratrix and God's Wife, and her power exceeded that of the High Priest and was only slightly less than that of the Pharaoh. As the supreme High Priestess, Banafrit would have worn the royal uraeus cobra on her brow; and would have appointed her own successor to ensure that her magic remained within the Isis sect. There is little written about this powerful but enigmatic figure, although it is reported that several sphinx statues commissioned by the Pharaoh were reported to have carried her facial features.*

I paused, realising where I'd seen the face in the illustration. It was the face of the sphinx that had pinned Isabella to the sea floor. Fascinated, I returned to the article.

*This was one of the greatest honours that could be bestowed upon a mortal, and such privileges were usually reserved for royalty, leading to the hypothesis that Banafrit might have been Nectanebo's youngest sister.*

*The hieroglyphs found below this mural describe how Banafrit had a vision that Nectanebo the II's Ba had been trapped in his tomb and thus being unable to fly in and out had perished condemning the Pharaoh to eternal exclusion from the afterlife. It is possible that Banafrit, clearly a consummate strategist to have achieved such a powerful position, had heard rumour of an assassination plot and was using the vision as a metaphor to warn the Pharaoh. The hieroglyphs mention the construction of a skybox, commissioned by Banafrit, that drew on the skills of all the great astronomers of the realm and would ensure the Pharaoh's destiny. Here the inscriptions become too heavily vandalised to make complete sense but later a passage talks of a following or cult that sprung up around the charismatic Priestess. It is common for such inscriptions to be later 'edited' by enemies of the subject of such narratives. Regardless I believe I have uncovered evidence that proves this cult continued to exist well into Ptolemaic times and that Cleopatra herself might have identified with Banafrit.*

*Interestingly enough Nectanebo himself was immortalised through an account from a translation of an ancient manuscript entitled 'The Dream of Nectanebo' in which Nectanebo recounts a dream in which he overhears the sky war god Onuris complaining to Isis that although he always protected the Pharaoh, the construction of his temple has never been completed. This worried the Pharaoh so much that when he woke he summoned the priests who told him everything was finished in the temple except the hieroglyphs. Nectanebo summoned the best hieroglyph-cutter around, one Petesis. Unfortunately, Petesis was distracted from his task by a beautiful woman whose name meant 'noble Hathor'. Hathor was the goddess of love and drunkenness, but also personified destruction. At this point the account ends abruptly, so we'll never know exactly how angry Onuris was with the Pharaoh. I like to believe his fury might have had something to do with the Nectanebo's demise and eventual disappearance. And then there's the strange way the scribe suddenly stopped writing — as if he himself might have been killed, a murder that would have prevented him from completing his task and revealing the whole story ...*

A photograph of a sarcophagus followed, described as Nectanebo II's empty coffin, now housed in the British Museum.

I examined the photograph, wondering why this paper had been so contentious within the archaeological community. It seemed fairly innocuous to me; certainly insufficient grounds to ruin Amelia Lynhurst's academic career. The reference to the skybox intrigued me. Had Isabella made a connection between that and her astrarium?

I noticed the change in the light outside; evening had fallen without me realising. I glanced towards the astrarium, still illuminated by the desk lamp. It threw a shadow now — the unmistakable silhouette of a robed woman, tall and statuesque. Then, terrifyingly slowly, the shadow turned to profile: the full lips and arched nose clearly defined.

Outside, Tinnin, the guard dog, started barking. When I swung back to the astrarium, the shadow had vanished. Had I imagined it?

# 12

The next morning I was due at the Brambilla family's lawyer's office for the reading of Isabella's will. Deciding it would be safer not to let the astrarium out of my sight, I packed it into a rucksack and slung it over my back.

Popnilogolos and Sons was located in the banking district, two buildings down from the Alexandrian Oil Company headquarters. Dreading another encounter with Francesca Brambilla, I pushed open the heavy brass door. Mr Popnilogolos's secretary showed me into his office.

'Am I early?'

I glanced around, the heavy oak desk was surrounded by piles of documents stacked against the walls. In the centre sat two chairs ominously empty, like props waiting for actors to breathe life into them. I stepped over the files towards one.

'Don't worry, Madame Brambilla is merely late. She regards this as her perennial right.' Mr Popnilogolos, an elegant man in his mid fifties, his hair oiled back, immaculate in a black suit and blue tie despite the sweat prickling at his forehead offered me a cigarette which I declined. He pulled out a box file from the top of a heavily stacked cabinet.

'The Brambillas ... well, I'm afraid, your wife's estate was not worth very much. I hear the mother was at the funeral?'

I nodded. Encouraged he continued.

'An exquisite-looking woman, we all wanted her but Paolo was the only one who was not too intimidated to propose. He was frightened of nothing, except his father Giovanni — eccentric but dangerous, you know.' He swung around, clutching the box file to his chest. 'Here we have it ... Signora Isabella's will.' He sat down behind the desk and sighed ponderously. 'Such a tragedy, appalling. The strange thing is, your wife came to see me only a week before her death. At the time I thought it bizarre: usually clients think about making their wills when they are somewhat older, not in their twenties and bursting with health. Of course, I was happy to oblige, and her foresight was fortuitous. You do realise Giovanni Brambilla left his house to his granddaughter upon his death. Which technically, at least, made Isabella her grandmother's landlady. And now possibly yourself, fascinating.' He smiled; leaving me with the distinct impression the lawyer was indulging in a little Schadenfreude. Before I had a chance to question this surprising information we heard his secretary welcoming another visitor.

'Speak of the devil,' the lawyer said with a wink, and stood to open the door.

\* \* \*

Francesca Brambilla settled into a chair, where she sat stiffly upright, clutching her crocodile-skin handbag as if it were a barricade in a storm.

'Are you comfortable, Madame?' the lawyer enquired.

'As comfortable as possible given the unnatural circumstances. It really should be my will you are reading, not my granddaughter's,' she snapped back.

I tried to catch her eye but she barely acknowledged my presence.

'Indeed, life is tragically unpredictable — as we Alexandrians know too well,' Popnilogolos responded smoothly. He turned to me. 'Monsieur Warnock?'

'You may proceed.'

He cleared his throat and began reading: 'I, Isabella Francesca Maria Brambilla, bequeath all of my estate to my husband, Oliver Patrick Warnock, including my books, research and collection of artefacts. To my grandmother I leave the jewellery I inherited at the time of my father's death. Dated 22 April 1977.'

The two of us waited; I sensed we were both expecting something more conclusive, some kind of absolution even.

'Is that it?' I finally asked.

The lawyer nodded.

Francesca's hand shook as she grasped the ivory head of her cane. 'This will was written seven days before her death?'

Mr Popnilogolos smiled weakly. 'Perhaps Madame Warnock had a premonition?'

The old woman swung around to me. 'Has this got anything to do with you?'

'I promise you, Francesca, I had no idea she'd made this will. Nor that Giovanni left the house to her.'

A difficult silence settled over the room like dust. Francesca's deep voice stirred it up as she finally spoke.

'My husband and I had a disagreement towards the end of his life. There were aspects of his behaviour that I did not approve of. Rewriting his will was Giovanni's way of punishing me. I don't think he ever imagined that Isabella would die before me.' She turned back to me. 'Does this mean you wish me to move out of the villa? You are the new owner apparently.'

'So it appears.'

Watching her discomfort, it occurred to me that there was a way of taking advantage of the situation.

'Mr Popnilogolos, would you give us a few minutes of privacy?' I asked.

'Certainly.' After a short bow, he stepped outside.

'I'm happy to allow you to stay on in the villa on one condition,' I told Francesca.

'Which is?'

'You tell me the truth about what happened to Isabella's body. Why was she buried without her heart?'

The elderly woman's cane fell with a clatter to the parquet floor. 'She had no heart?'

'No heart, no internal organs.'

She seemed shocked but not completely surprised. As I watched, another expression swept across her fine wrinkled features — one of realisation.

I picked up the dropped cane. 'You know something, don't you, Francesca?'

'I know nothing,' she replied tersely. 'I am as horrified as you.'

Clutching the arms of the chair, she rose to her feet. 'If you wish to evict me, I would appreciate at least twenty-four hours' notice.'

And without another word, she opened the door, pushed past the lawyer waiting outside and left.

\* \* \*

I walked down towards Mohammed Ali Square, where the Bourse, Alexandria's cotton and stock exchange, once stood. It had existed for centuries in one form or another. E M Forster had written about it, even ancient Arabic writers such as Ibn Jubayr. A symbol of old colonial Egypt, the Bourse had been burnt down in the hunger riots earlier in the year. You used to be able to hear the cries of the bartering merchants every morning. Now the site had been reduced to a vacant lot that functioned as a temporary car park. Somehow it seemed emblematic of modern Egypt.

As I made my way through the narrow streets I kept thinking about Isabella's missing organs: had it really been an ambulance waiting for her body on the jetty or something more sinister? I was conscious of the weight of the astrarium on my shoulder, I reflected on the experts I knew and who I could really trust to help me work out what to do with the device. Faakhir's grim expression as he warned me of those who would use it to destroy the region's political stability came back into my mind. So far, both Hermes Hemiedes and Amelia Lynhurst had offered their help, but could I trust them? Amelia's reaction to Hermes at the funeral was bizarre; was she frightened or threatened by him somehow? There were political divides and conflicts within the archaeological world that were beyond my understanding. I'd witnessed firsthand Isabella's frustrations over such struggles as she herself had fallen victim to them again and again. The astrarium was an enigma the ramifications of which I couldn't even begin to comprehend. All I knew was that Barry had been murdered because of it, and that more lives may be at risk, including my own.

My mind returned to Amelia Lynhurst's thesis and the reference to the sphinx statues with Banafrit's features. I tell you, at this point it felt as if Isabella herself was some kind of sphinx challenging me to solve a riddle the answer to which, I suspected, lay beyond the conventions of my thinking.

I stopped in front of the intersection of Salaymar Yussri Street and El Nabi Daniel. Opposite stood the broken pillars of the Roman amphitheatre. Kom el-Dik was the only official archaeological dig in Alexandria. Standing there, I remembered how Hermes had taken Isabella and me there for lunch with the Polish archaeologists one day. She had clearly trusted the man and the memory propelled me towards a decision. Crossing the road, I made my way to the tram stop that I knew would take me west into the old Arabic quarter.

\* \* \*

The tram was nearly empty. An old man, his jellaba stained with the day's work, slept with his head lolling back; a lone schoolgirl sat next to him, painfully self-aware in the way of all adolescents; a group of intense young men huddled in a corner talking rapidly, their hands a flurry of illustration — university students, I concluded. Opposite me was a middle-aged woman, well dressed in western clothes. She smiled, one eyebrow cocked suggestively. Ignoring her, I stared out at the passing streets, the astrarium safe in my rucksack on the seat next to me.

The tram stopped at the lights and a car pulled up beside it. I looked down into it and saw Omar in the back seat. He smiled at me, then leaned forward and tapped the shoulder of the man in the front passenger seat. The stranger swung around to stare at me. I couldn't drag my gaze away.

He had a distinctive angular face, and the only expression he carried was one of absolute menace, a kind of terrifyingly intense hatred.

The lights changed and the tram took off. An elderly woman who had just climbed aboard fell to the floor, pomegranates scattering from her shopping bag. Several of the students rushed to help her up, blocking my view of the car. Taking advantage of the distraction, I leaped down from the other side of the tram and ran down a side alley.

# 13

By the time I reached Hermes Hemiedes' apartment block it was early afternoon. The smell of frying fish filled the tenebrous foyer and from somewhere in the building came the sound of a wailing baby. As I entered, a mangy dog curled in the corner lifted its solemn head and gazed at me blankly. Then, as if it had completed its duties as guard dog, it flopped back to the ground.

I glanced at the list of residents — the name Hemiedes was written in gold lettering next to *'penthouse apartment'*. A handwritten sign in Arabic announced the lift was out of order. I began hauling myself up the stairs.

\* \* \*

The view from the roof was spectacular. In front of me, Pompey's Pillar arched up into the sky, flanked by two sphinxes. Made of red granite, it had been erected in AD 300 to commemorate the Roman emperor Diocletian, who saved the city from famine. It was a magnificent sight, with the city stretching back to the

Mediterranean. I turned back to the roof garden. The top floor of the penthouse was a small apartment constructed on a roof terrace that housed a cane sofa and chairs with a plethora of cushions, all covered by a canopy of vines growing out of huge clay vases. Brass wind chimes hung like strange fruit between the branches, their atonal chimes accompanied by the strains of David Bowie's 'Ziggy Stardust'. It was a bizarre combination.

The boy who had let me in — whom I presumed to be Hermes' companion rather than his servant — placed a pot of mint tea and a glass on the low table in front of me and began to pour. Dressed in a sari, with gold hooped earrings, kohl smeared over each eyelid and a purplish lipstick on his lips, he looked about thirteen years old and was incredibly effeminate in his movements. The classic catamite, I thought; a tradition that stretched back for centuries. He'd told me in halting English with a strong American accent, no doubt picked up from watching black-market movies, that Hermes was taking his customary morning walk and would be due back around three and that I should wait for him. The speech had been accompanied by a series of fluttering flirtatious gestures.

His eyes wandered to the rucksack I'd placed beside me on the couch and, protectively, I put a hand on it. He grinned, an absurdly innocent smile, then to my amazement took off the sequined scarf draped around his thin narrow shoulders and began to dance to the music — an outlandish pirouetting that seemed to be an exaggerated version of contemporary dancing he must have seen once or twice. He sang along in a high falsetto that dipped occasionally when his voice broke; it was strangely beautiful and poignant to hear this child-man's voice interweaving with Bowie's lyrics.

He moved towards me, gyrating his hips in a clumsy seduction attempt. I wasn't sure whether I should laugh, cry or run.

'Usta!' Hermes' voice bellowed out from the open French doors, followed by a sharp clapping of hands. The boy immediately stopped his dance and went sulkily to the record-player to take the LP off.

Hermes stepped onto the terrace. I stood up to greet him. He was dressed in an embroidered kaftan and a pair of pearl earrings shone between the strands of his lank dyed hair; a matching necklace hung around his wrinkled neck. He resembled some kind of latter-day alchemist who'd bought his accessories at an up-market duty-free shop. Clicking his fingers he ordered the boy to leave us.

'I apologise,' he said. 'The silly child wants to be a rock star and live in New York. Still, perhaps he is not entirely without talent. Please, sit, finish your tea.'

I placed the rucksack on the table before him. 'I've brought you something,' I said, 'something I need your expert advice on.'

Hermes opened the rucksack and pulled out the astrarium very gently. Almost as if he were making love to the object, he peeled off the tissue I'd wrapped it in. Finally it stood revealed on the glass-topped table. Hermes muttered what sounded like a prayer and sat back.

'My poor Isabella, so close to her discovery ...' He looked at me. 'Has anyone else seen it?'

'Only one other person and he's dead. I suspect he was murdered.'

'People have accidents so easily these days. I like to regard such unfortunate events as historical phenomenon. After all it is a very *accidental* era we're living in.' Hermes replied cryptically, 'I am honoured that you have brought the instrument here.'

'I was hoping you might be able to translate the inscriptions on the disks.'

'I will certainly try.' The Egyptologist pulled a pair of glasses from his waistcoat pocket and peered through them. 'There are three languages as far as I can see — Greek, Babylonian and hieroglyphs. It will take time — I have to make a rubber impression of the etched letters. Leave the instrument here and I will have the translation finished by tomorrow evening.'

I hesitated, not wanting to leave the instrument overnight, acutely aware its very presence might endanger Hermes' life.

'I can give you four hours. I'll wait here while you work.'

'Please, you must trust me.'

'Four hours, Hermes. It will have to suffice.'

He stared at me, then laughed and reached out to shake my hand. 'A cautious man is a wise man.'

'A cautious man is a living man and I made a promise.'

'I fear the astrarium will demand further sacrifices. Do you think you were followed?'

'I lost him.'

'Good. There are spies everywhere in Alexandria; everyone wants to ingratiate himself with someone. Such shocking promiscuity. Come, you will wait in my reception room.'

I followed him back into the apartment. One wall of the small reception room was covered in photographs, most of which looked as if they dated from the 1930s and '40s. I peered closer — they all appeared to be of lavish social occasions: polo matches, beauty contests on Stanley Beach, yachting races, opera nights. There were even images of a masked ball, characters in ornate evening dress — tribal from the neck up — frozen in time as if caught in some clandestine illegal rite. With a shock I recognised some of the famous faces standing next to a younger, slimmer Hermes Hemiedes who smiled arrogantly out of the photographs as if he were already conscious of the awed gaze of the viewer: Lawrence Durrell,

Daphne Du Maurier, King Farouk, Lord Montgomery, Maria Callas, the Egyptologist had even been photographed with Winston Churchill.

He sighed wistfully. 'The glory days, when Alexandria was a real metropolis. Nowadays there is such a grinding earnestness, sometimes I wonder whether I am witnessing the death of imagination itself.'

'Don't worry, imagination hasn't died, it's just been replaced by paranoia.'

Hermes laughed and I found myself warming to him despite my reservations.

'So I'm curious,' I said, 'what was Giovanni Brambilla like? You were close, weren't you?'

'At one time, the best of friends. Oh, Giovanni was a wonderful fellow, a visionary in his own right. We shared some proclivities — a weakness for ancient beliefs, you could say. However, he had strong opinions; he wasn't frightened of alienating people. He adored Isabella, she was his little princess. She was such a serious little girl. We visited some sites together; Behbeit el-Hagar was one. A minor site, but an important one in relation to the last days of the empire.'

'The empire?'

'The great reign of the Pharaohs.' The nostalgic tone of his voice made it sound as if he'd lived through it himself.

I turned away from the photographs. 'I apologise for the urgency, but I have to return to Abu Rudeis as soon as possible ...'

'Oliver, the astrarium is a precious antiquity but many would also see it as a working tool, you do understand that? It may even be regarded as a weapon in the wrong hands.'

'Whose hands exactly — government, political groups, private individuals?'

'I have an idea, but I'd like to keep my theories to myself for the time being. Just remember, whatever your other priorities may be, to treat the astrarium as anything less than extremely powerful would be very foolish.'

'Then I should make it clear: I am only investigating the astrarium for Isabella's sake. Personally I don't believe in astrology or ancient mysticism.'

'Even so, you must appreciate that there is much about the material world that we do not understand. And there are certain individuals who have gifts … gifts of interpretation—'

'And naturally you'd describe yourself as one of them?' It was impossible to keep the irony out of my voice.

'Rest assured I am not alone in that assumption. Please, take a seat. Usta will bring you more mint tea, but now I really should get started.'

He left the room and I sank back into the embroidered silk cushions. Four hours later, I was woken by Usta.

\* \* \*

Hermes was working in a study at the back of the apartment. The astrarium stood on a table: sheets of tracing paper covered with pencilled inscriptions lay beside latex casts of the machine's disks — the faint imprints of the hieroglyphs visible in the raised rubber.

Hermes placed the first page of the transcribed hieroglyphs before me. 'First, let me say that I regard this instrument as the predecessor of the Antikythera mechanism, as Isabella had anticipated.'

I nodded, curious to know whether he would also confirm Barry's findings.

After a glance at me, he continued. 'But Isabella was wrong: it is not of Cleopatra's era, but from that of the Egyptian

Pharaohs — the Thirtieth Dynasty to be precise, the reign of Nectanebo II.'

'Jesus, Barry was right.' I spoke aloud without realising it.

I scanned the lines of hieroglyphs. The inscriptions on the bronze wheels were tiny, barely millimetres tall. In the larger format, I recognised a couple of them — the sign for Sun that doubled for Ra; the god of embalming, Anubis, symbolised by the jackal's head. I reached out and touched the serrated edge of one of the cogs. So the device was Pharaonic, but was that reason enough to kill for it? Or to die finding it?

Hermes' voice interrupted my reverie. 'What do you know about the Thirtieth Dynasty, Oliver?'

'I know it was roughly 400 BC, and the last dynasty of the Egyptian Pharaohs — during the reign of Nectanebo II, as you said.'

'Indeed. By the time Nectanebo II came to power, Egypt was little more than a banana republic, only kept safe from again being annexed to Persia by the employment of Spartan mercenaries. Nectanebo II faced two major challenges at the beginning of his reign. The first was to hold onto power; the second, to balance the ever-threatening Persians with their sophisticated weaponry and the dangerous greed of the Spartan mercenaries employed as Egypt's protectors. More than anything the young king had to unite Egypt, to reinstate the nation's self-esteem. In some respects there are parallels with Egypt today ...' Hermes' voice drifted off for a moment and then he recovered his train of thought. 'Nectanebo rebuilt Egypt's confidence in three ways. One was by reminding his people of Egypt's former glory days when it ruled the world and the Persians and Greeks were primitive upstarts in comparison. The second way was by reinforcing his influence with priests, peasants and the intelligentsia alike by emphasising his alliance with the gods. This led into the third way: building as many temples as he could during his reign. The astrarium was designed for one of those temples — the star attraction if you like.'

'And the inscriptions confirm this?'

'Well, the astrarium itself consists of three primary disks behind which a far more complex mechanism sits. The largest outer disk is made of an alloy I don't recognise; it appears to be etched with a scaled-down version of the Dendera zodiac — based on Egyptian astrology. The next disk describes the movements of Venus and Mars — Hathor and Horus to the Egyptian astronomers. The final disk follows the trajectories of Jupiter, whom the Egyptians identified with Amun-Zeus, and Saturn, the dreaded deity Seth.' He paused to sip some tea. 'As to the inscriptions themselves, the majority are written in Egyptian hieroglyphs. Some are simply instructions on how to operate the mechanism. Some describe the history of the machine and chronicle its feats. There is a small amount of Ancient Greek, but I suspect this might have been added later — during the time of Ptolemy. There are a few lines of Aramaic, suggesting Hebrew scholars were also involved in its construction; and the remainder suggests a token acknowledgement of Babylonian astronomy, which the Egyptians also respected.

'There is also mention of a key, called a Was, which is a reference to the staff of dominion carried by all sky deities.' He pointed to the small keyhole-like cavity I'd noticed before at the centre of the disks. 'It appears to have been hand-operated.'

'But the key is missing.'

'Indeed. I suspect that in ancient times there would have been an official keeper of the Was. Possibly he drowned in the shipwreck and the Was key was lost; or perhaps he survived and the key is who knows where? Reunite the key with the astrarium and you have a very dangerous device. Just look at this ...' He held a sheet of the traced Greek inscription under the light and began reading. '*This illumination of the skies and of Fate* — I use the word "Fate" here loosely as it is the nearest translation I can think of, but really it is a combination of passion and destiny. Somehow it suggests greater free will than the contemporary notion of Fate. *This illumination of the skies and of Fate is the inherited property of Her Majesty and earthly manifestation of Hathor, Aphrodite and Isis, Cleopatra VII ...*'

As Hermes looked at me, I noticed his hands were trembling with excitement.

'It does appear that Cleopatra was quite possibly the last owner of the astrarium,' he said. 'But there is something that disturbs me ...'

'What's that?'

'It's this.' He pushed an almost blank sheet of paper towards me. I recognised the cipher I'd seen in Gareth's drawing. 'Do you know what it is?' he asked.

'I've seen it before. Isabella already knew of it when she was searching for the astrarium. She told me it was a cipher.'

'But did she tell you what it meant?'

'She never got the chance.' An instinct told me not to tell him that my brother may have the answer to the riddle.

'I found it standing alone below the main body of text,' Hermes said, watching me carefully. 'For the life of me, I cannot decipher it. But its isolated position indicates its importance.'

Despite the long hair combed back over the domed forehead, the rouge smeared roughly on each hollowed cheekbone, there was something entrancing about Hermes. I could see why Isabella had been so captivated by him: it was impossible not to find his passion and his depth of expertise compelling. He was one of those individuals who sweeps others up in his enthusiasm. His animated explanations made me struggle with my usual detachment.

'The translation of the hieroglyphs is as follows: *Whoever sets his birth date upon these dials will change/transform the path of his Ka. I will give to the slave the life of the Pharaoh; I will make Anubis bark the date of his demise.* This astrarium is also a predictive tool. In fact, I believe its predictions might have been the reason why Nectanebo fled Egypt. Some say he went to Ethiopia, or the Macedonian mainland. There are even those who believe that Aristotle was really Nectanebo II, and that he tutored his nemesis, the young Alexander, in the sciences of mathematics and astronomy.'

From somewhere in the apartment came the sound of cutlery being rattled, a tap turned on then off. It was hard to stay in the present, to avoid being thrown back into the history that seemed to emanate from the artefact itself.

'Isabella's sole intention was to prove that the ancient world knew the Earth rotated around the Sun long before Copernicus,' I retorted, trying to anchor my thinking to a familiar reality.

'My friend, you and I both know that isn't entirely true. I fear you are letting your own prejudices dictate your perceptions.'

'And I fear, as in quantum physics where the observed particle is influenced by the observer, this astrarium's purpose changes according to the expectations of whoever is examining it. It seems to have become a metaphor.'

'In any case, what we think is irrelevant,' the Egyptologist replied. 'I don't believe you have the slightest idea of the astrarium's importance or the danger it brings. The Ancient Egyptians believed that the most important principle of life was to maintain a balance between Maat, universal order, and Isfet, universal chaos. The astrarium was constructed as a means of restoring balance, a way of controlling chaos and evil, personified by Seth, and harmony and light, personified by Isis and Ra. The Pharaoh it was made for — Nectanebo II — was a worshipper of Ammon, also known as Amun-Re. Amun symbolised concealment and mystery, while Re represented visibility and transparency. The name Amun-Re united this duality in the one god — a duality of light and dark. The astrarium could be used in the same dual capacity: to predict positive events — the correct positions of the planets for successful navigation — there is even a suggestion that it can lead you to treasure — auspicious dates for magical rituals and the like; and negative events, such as the loss of a battle, or even one's death date. The deciding factor was the true — or, in modern parlance, unconscious — motivation of the user.'

I shook my head. 'You're trying to tell me the astrarium itself makes a judgement about the true motivation of the user?'

'Oliver, the machine has a soul, a kind of independent will. This is what the Ancient Egyptians believed, and it is what I believe.'

'That's ridiculous.'

'It would be dangerous to ignore me. Most of us live the unexamined life — we live in Isfet, in chaos. Seth rules this century, my friend. There are those who seek influence at such times. Amelia Lynhurst, for example, is a woman with dangerous aspirations.'

'Really, why do you think that?'

'She was very proprietorial of Isabella when she was at Oxford — the relationship was more than that of mentor and student. Isabella was impressionable, putty in the older woman's hands. For Amelia to seduce her was unethical; to abandon her was worse.'

I wasn't entirely surprised to hear Isabella had had an affair with a woman — her understanding of sexuality had been far more fluid and open-minded than mine. Isabella had been ten years younger than me and her experiences were very different from my own. My generation had been shaped by the drabness of the economic deprivation that followed the Second World War. Isabella had been luckier, benefiting from the economic boom and cultural openness of the 1960s. But Amelia Lynhurst? Somehow I couldn't quite believe it.

'That was the real reason for them falling out?' I asked.

'Believe me, Amelia does not have either your or Isabella's interests at heart when it comes to the astrarium,' Hermes told me. 'If you go to her, not only will she betray you to the authorities; she will claim discovery of the instrument and use it to promote her own ambitions.'

His warning echoed the concerns Isabella had expressed, and it was this that influenced my final decision to trust him.

'What do you know about Banafrit, Nectanebo's priestess?' I asked.

'How do you know about Banafrit?'

'I found Amelia Lynhurst's treatise on her in my wife's possessions. She claimed Banafrit commissioned the construction of the astrarium.'

'So you know more than you have suggested, Oliver.'

'That doesn't make me a believer.'

'Whether you believe or not, Amelia Lynhurst is convinced that she is the living reincarnation of Isis. More importantly, I suspect she might have convinced others.'

'That's absurd.'

'As I said before, this is still a working mechanism. It can manipulate the destiny of the individual who dares operate it.'

I realised he'd steered the conversation away from Amelia Lynhurst and the possibility she may be involved with a sect; that was interesting, I thought, an observation worth remembering.

'A working mechanism missing its key,' I pointed out, looking back at the astrarium.

'Again, I urge you to leave the mechanism here. I will try to find the key for you.'

I pondered my options. In another place, at another time of my life, I would have rejected such an obvious manipulation outright. But sitting in that richly decorated room, the lamplight catching the bronze dials of the astrarium, Hermes' rapt face poised in anticipation, I was almost convinced. Egypt had that effect — it was impossible to escape the history and mystical lineage of the land, no matter how sceptical one might be. Besides, I reminded myself, some of my physicist friends would say that the laws of physics were just a model too and there was still so much we didn't know. But there was something else at stake here; Isabella's commitment to the astrarium she had died pursuing. 'No, I'll hold onto it for the time being. I want to continue my own research.'

His face closed over and, to my surprise, for a second I thought I detected a glimmer of fury. 'As you wish,' he finally muttered.

I carefully wrapped the astrarium up again and placed it into my rucksack. 'I just have one last question. What's the significance of a manifestation of a person's Ba?'

'If the deceased's Ba is seen after burial, it usually means that person's task on earth is unfinished and their soul cannot complete its journey to the underworld.'

As I left the building, I had the distinct impression of invisible wings brushing by my cheek.

# 14

I wound my way back to the city centre, my mind a whirling mass as familiar axioms battled a plethora of new hypotheses. With each step, the astrarium in the rucksack on my back bounced against me. I kept thinking about Hermes' warning about the power of the device; then remembered Barry's explanation of the Ancient Egyptians' belief in magic, their intertwining of religious worship, intellectual pursuit, sorcery and science.

Walking helped me organise my thoughts; it was a habit borne of my childhood wanderings across the Cumbrian Fells. As the rhythm of the streets pounded up through my legs a destination began to take shape in my mind. A couple of old men were playing Shesh Besh outside a shoe stall. I glanced down at the backgammon pieces, calculating the moves to win, and then made my own decision. I would go to the cemetery to talk to Isabella, to take her the astrarium.

It was illogical, but this time, unlike on the oilfield where I'd legitimised my decisions with science, I was relying solely on my intuition.

\* \* \*

I walked on up Bab el-Mulouk back toward Rue Sherif and past the Antiques Market toward Cairo Station Square. My path was broken by two long queues of people; women in one, men in another, all clutching their ration cards, snaking out of a gamaya — the ubiquitous co-op grocery store where the locals collected their rationed food: meat, rice, oil and flour. Such queues would form with each new shipment of rare imports — New Zealand lamb, butter and tea. Once commonplace such items had become scarce in the economic tumult caused by Sadat opening Egypt up to the free market earlier that year.

Here toward the centre of the city, the buildings became more westernised, and the old cosmopolitan Alexandria, elegant and ostentatious, began to appear: the neoclassical old Lloyds Bank building, the Banco di Roma and the Bank of Athens — all originally landmarks of colonialism now under the banner of the National Bank of Egypt. I passed Bank Misr with its balconies and arches, more Ottoman than classical, then walked past the Anglican church of St Mark, and the old offices located in ornate neoclassical city blocks. Along Fouad Street, the grand villas started appearing: Villa Salvago, Villa Sursock, Villa Rolo — phantoms from a past world.

As I weaved between the pedestrians I became aware of the sound of a motorcycle behind me. I knew from the distinctive engine note that it had been trailing me for some time. A cab hooted next to me, the gesturing driver touting for business. I leaped in and instructed him to take me to Chatby Cemetery.

As he drove away I glanced out the rear window. For a moment I thought I saw the menacing face of the man who had been in the car with Omar earlier that day. Then a minibus crammed full of commuters got in the way and by the time it had passed, the motorcycle was gone.

* * *

*Isabella Francesca Maria Brambilla — b: 31/1/1949 d: 29/4/1977.*

I stared at the engraved letters and numbers, their crisp edges confirming their newness. Isabella's face, wryly smiling, gazed up from the black-and-white photograph set into the large marble headstone next to the oval portraits of her father and uncles. Once again, I noticed the absence of Giovanni's photograph. It seemed inconceivable that he would not be buried with his family. The photo of Isabella looked as if it had been taken at her first communion; I barely recognised her. It represented a period of her life I'd never had access to and I found myself momentarily flooded by a strange jealousy.

It horrified me to think of Isabella lying in that grave incomplete, as if I had failed her in death as I had in life. Despite my own lack of spirituality, I couldn't shake the disturbing thought that Isabella would not be able to rest until her heart was returned to her, that her Ba might be trapped in this life forever.

Carefully I laid the astrarium, still inside my rucksack, onto the marble slab covering her grave. I waited — for what I wasn't sure; perhaps a sign that she was finally united with the object she had spent years searching for. There was nothing, just the creaking of a tree branch and a faint breeze — time breathing out.

I concentrated on an old wreath of lilies propped up against the headstone, the petals now brown and curling. One bloom had broken loose and fallen onto the grass. I crouched to pick it up, and noticed a small hole at the far end of the marble slab. I kneeled down and looked closer: it was a chiselled hole about four inches in depth, three inches across. Someone had even bothered to give it the appearance of a miniature door with an etched outline. I knew it hadn't existed when we buried her, yet somehow the image seemed hauntingly familiar.

'Oliver?'

The voice was feminine, lilting and Italian in accent. I looked up: Cecilia, Isabella's mother, stood at the head of the grave, her expensive Chanel suit looking ridiculously out of place. In one hand she held a small bunch of chrysanthemums; the other was trying to stop the breeze ruining her coiffured hair.

'I'm so sorry,' she said. 'I have disturbed you in a private moment.'

Realising she'd assumed I was in the middle of a prayer, I swiftly stood, dusted my knees and, worried that she might notice the chiselled hole in the tomb, stepped quickly back onto the pathway.

She reached out and took my hand between her gloved fingers. 'You poor man. We never think of the young and the talented dying. Such deaths are an obscenity, a joke against God, don't you think?'

Unlike her daughter, Cecilia was tall and had a Tuscan blonde beauty honed by the polish of Rome. Slender and green-eyed, she seemed entirely aware of the power of her own attractiveness. She was only eight years older than me, which made her a very youthful forty-six. To my great chagrin, a spasm of involuntary desire shot through me like electricity. To make matters worse, I had the impression Cecilia sensed my dilemma. I pulled my hand away.

Smiling faintly, she crouched down to place the bouquet next to the lilies. My words spilled out nervously as I tried to distract myself from the sight of her skirt riding up her thighs.

'I couldn't stop her from making that dive. God knows I tried, but she was insistent. Still, I can't help thinking that if I had ...'

'Oliver, it was an accident, a consequence of a chain of events that led to a moment you had no control over. Who is to say whether that moment might or might not have happened?'

She glanced apprehensively around the cemetery then stepped closer. 'I know Isabella would have told you terrible things about me.' Cecilia's voice was little more than a whisper. She paused, as if waiting for me to protest. I did not.

'You have to understand,' she continued, 'I was bullied into letting Isabella go. I made a grave mistake. Giovanni was an immoral man, desperate to influence events beyond his control; he even began to involve Isabella in his activities — activities that were not appropriate for a child. Maybe I have been a bad mother. But I was only twenty-five when I was widowed, and Giovanni Brambilla was a very frightening man. He is powerful even now, beyond the grave.'

'What kind of activities?' I asked.

'Once, when Isabella was about nine, Francesca wrote telling me she was worried about the way Giovanni had started to involve Isabella in the strange "performances" he put on. I immediately bought a plane ticket, but when I tried to get back into the country they refused me a visa. I believe Giovanni used his influence to bar me. After that, whenever I confronted Francesca about it, she denied she'd written to me at all.'

'Isabella had nightmares,' I told her. 'The same one again and again. A gathering of people performing a ritual — one of the Ancient Egyptian rituals she'd studied …'

Cecilia's face fell in horror. 'Mio povero figlia!' she murmured, near tears.

Behind us, a twig snapped and we both turned. I glimpsed a movement between the trees, the flash of a figure now hidden.

Cecilia's expression changed instantly to one of fear. 'You should know that people here will go to any lengths to reinvent their history, even their recent history,' she whispered.

We started walking back to the entrance. The cemetery appeared empty but I had the strong sense of being observed. Above us, the cawing of ravens filled the blank sky. I grasped Cecilia's hand briefly. For the second time that afternoon she smiled.

'You know, Isabella did finally contact me, about a month before her death. No letter, just a box of photographs from our early days, from when her father was alive. I cried when I opened it. It is strange, no? Not to hear from your daughter for so long, then out of the blue she sends you old photographs a month before she dies? Oliver, I'm afraid I don't believe in coincidence.'

\* \* \*

As I waved her Mercedes off, I remembered where I'd seen the miniature door before — it was like the portal engraved into the wall of an Ancient Egyptian tomb; the symbolic door that allowed the deceased's Ba to fly in and out.

Who would have carved such a thing into Isabella's gravestone?

\* \* \*

Later that night, taking advantage of Ibrihim's visit to his mother in Ar-Rashid, I buried the astrarium in a waterproof box beneath one of the magnolia trees — a temporary hiding place should anyone break into the villa as they had Barry Douglas's apartment. I planted a small pomegranate bush with shallow roots over the top, so the earth didn't look disturbed. It was only after I went back inside that I remembered how Persephone had been tricked by Hades into eating seven pomegranate seeds, condemning her to stay with him in the underworld for seven months of each year. It was a disturbing association.

It was past midnight, I sat on the edge of the bed clutching the Valium the company's doctor had prescribed for me, wondering if I could, again, face that wave of treacly darkness, the loss of sensory control that now allowed me to sleep.

I decided against taking the pill and climbed into bed. Then, feeling as bewildered as a child, I stared at the ceiling and the shifting shadows of the tree branches thrown by the street lamp outside. Finally, my eyes closed and I drifted off.

I dreamed I was in sunshine. Bright light, a beach perhaps, the sense of a soft grainy surface beneath my sun-warmed skin, then the soft weight of another body curling around me. I recognised the shape and scent instantly. I didn't dare open my eyes in case I frightened her away, but the urge to see her overwhelmed me.

I opened my eyes and, found to my relief, I'd stayed dreaming. Isabella stared back at me, her eyes filled with that dark violet I had lost myself in so many times. Smiling, she lowered herself down onto me. The touch of her skin almost threw me into consciousness. It felt indisputably real — the warmth, the velvet moisture, the intimacy of her scent.

In wonder, I reached up, threading my fingers through that thick veil of hair, the familiarity of touch quickening. Her lips caught my lower lip, the promise of other caresses silently mirrored in the lovemaking of our mouths; a kiss that sprung open all the memories of our earlier embraces. The first weeks of our courtship, when we would make love all night then stumble around the markets of Calcutta drunk with exhaustion; when just the smell of her hair would make me hard, her voice whispering out all our future plans, spinning patterns against those tropical nights. This and every other moment ran through my mind like a kaleidoscope, but by now her mouth had started to travel down my chest, her long cool fingers as real as the taste of her; her lips, a tight band of heat throwing tremors down my thighs.

Then I remembered her death; the memory reverberating through me like one of the subterranean explosions I'd choreographed.

# 15

It was well after midday when I woke. The sun was a crimson prickling against my eyeballs, forcing the lids open. I lay there in that delicious non-state like an amoeba, happy for a time, until a burning sensation across my shoulders threw me into full consciousness. I sat up and reached behind me to touch my smarting skin. My fingers were sticky with blood.

I got up and walked over to the mirror: four deep scratches ran across my shoulders. I touched them — it felt as if I'd caught my back on a row of pins or nails. Then I remembered the dream, the lovemaking with Isabella. I studied the marks again, but they seemed too closely spaced for fingernails.

I flung back the covers on the bed; the bottom sheet was spotted with blood. Several long black hairs lay on the pillow and halfway down the mattress, a tiny brown feather. I lifted it and blew it across the bed. Could it have come from one of the pillows?

The miniature doorway chiselled into Isabella's gravestone came to my mind. I went to the library and looked up Nectanebo II in one of Isabella's reference books. All the information I'd gleaned from Hermes and Amelia Lynhurst's thesis was there, along with a photograph of the Pharaoh's empty sarcophagus and a sidebar with information about it and where it was now housed, in the British Museum. I noticed the sidebar was credited to Hugh Wollington of the British Museum. Presumably the man was an Egyptologist; perhaps he'd be able to give me more information about the astrarium — information I'd sensed Hermes was withholding. He may also be able to confirm whether there was any correlation between the hieroglyphs inscribed on the astrarium and those on Nectanebo's sarcophagus.

More importantly, a trip to England would allow me to see my father and my brother. At the thought, a wave of desire to be with family and in familiar surroundings engulfed me.

I was interrupted by a knocking at the front door, and with some trepidation I looked through the peephole: a youth of about sixteen waited on the other side. I recognised him from the offices of the Alexandrian Oil Company.

'From Mr Fartime,' he told me, handing me a note as I opened the door.

\* \* \*

The garish modern décor of the Alexandrian Oil Company's headquarters on Sherif Street reflected Mr Fartime's personal dilemma. He regarded himself as a twentieth-century entrepreneur trapped in a nineteenth-century paradigm that barely creaked along. He'd done his utmost to defuse the classical proportions of the office with oddly inappropriate modern furniture, but hadn't been able to apply the same modernisation to the organisation of the company and was constantly bombarding me with long anecdotes about the antiquated bureaucracy he was forced to work within.

As I entered his office, Mr Fartime struggled out of the white leather chair he'd been sitting in, a copy of *Time* magazine still in his hand. I noticed the cover featured a smiling Noam Chomsky. Before I had a chance to wonder what Mr Fartime made of the American activist, he'd tossed the magazine onto his desk and was reaching out to shake my hand.

'Thank you for coming so quickly, Oliver. Again, my condolences on your terrible loss ...'

'Thank you,' I replied, reflecting that the last time Mr Fartime had seen Isabella was at a dinner party during which they'd argued over the ecological merits of the Aswan dam. Fortunately the dispute had been interrupted when the hostess — a well-to-do Syrian-Egyptian socialite with many connections to the European community — had lost the microphone concealed in her low-cut evening dress. She was leaning across the table to make a point when the device fell out and landed in the soup tureen. The American ambassador had fished the microphone out and remarked, 'If you must spy, Madame Abdallah, allow us the honour of supplying you with the latest technology. Our Soviet friends tend to be a little clunky in the design department.' At which the whole table had burst into laughter.

I sat down opposite Mr Fartime, wondering if he too was recalling the occasion.

He indicated my beard. 'My friend, have you joined my more religious brothers?' he joked — a reference to the bearded Muslims who had started to appear more often in the westernised city.

I smiled. 'No, no new-found faith. I've just been too busy to shave.'

'I understand. I trust the additional security at the villa is to your liking?' he went on. 'I was concerned by the unduly rough treatment you received at the hands of our esteemed police force after your wife's demise. The Alexandrian Oil Company may be a government institution but we like to look after our consultants, especially our "Diviner". I promise that from now on we will be better hosts.'

Mr Fartime's English was a quaint mixture of Victorian phrasing and Arabic proverbs. Despite Isabella's reservations about his politics, I had always liked the man. Nevertheless, I watched his face carefully now. Were his comments a way of assessing my response to the police interrogation? Perhaps even an attempt to find out whether Isabella had discovered anything during that final dive?

'The extra guard does make the place feel more secure,' I replied, 'so thank you. But I'm sure this isn't the reason you called me in so urgently. Is everything all right at the field?'

'More than all right. The drilling rates are holding up nicely. You are indeed the Diviner. No, this is a personal matter.'

I shifted in my seat, a little nervous now, racking my mind for any transgression I might have committed.

'There is no need to look so anxious, my friend. I have received some news of your younger sibling, Gareth.'

I sat up. The last phone conversation I'd had with my brother came back to me: the broken words, his sudden weeping at the end. Ever since my mother's death, my brother had become more isolated despite the entourage that hung around him. Then there was his addiction — the aggrandising that came with amphetamine use, the manic phone calls. And, in the throes of these depressions, Gareth had always turned to Isabella for emotional guidance.

'He hasn't—'

'He is alive, fear not,' Mr Fartime cut in. 'His female friend rang the office this morning looking for you. Your brother has taken a turn for the worse, as they would say in England. His friend seems to think you should return to England as soon as possible to provide some guidance. She was most insistent — a rather strong-willed young woman.'

Mr Fartime's smile was entirely without irony and I sensed his concern was genuine. Gareth had mentioned a girlfriend on the phone, Zoë, but I'd never met her. At least she sounded responsible, I thought. I'd been concerned that Isabella's death would cause Gareth to relapse and the promise I'd made to her to look after him now reverberated in my mind.

As if reading my thoughts, Mr Fartime leaned across the desk. 'I had a brother too, once. He was ten years younger. I lost him in the '73 war. There are many things I would have done differently if I had been given the chance, and knowing my brother better would have been one.' He paused, a little embarrassed at venturing into such intimate terrain. 'Go to him, Oliver. The company is happy to give you four weeks. The field can spare you and, given your own personal circumstances, it is the least we can do.'

There was another awkward pause as he stared down at his shoes. 'I knew your wife's father, you know. My father worked as his manager at the cotton mill — before 1956, naturally.'

'Naturally,' I repeated, surprised again by how entangled Alexandrian society was.

'We trust that you will return at the end of those four weeks, Oliver. There is more work to be done at Abu Rudeis, and after that minor earthquake ...'

He coughed politely, embarrassed that he had to refer to the tremor that had killed Isabella. The memory of the sphinx tumbling down to the sea floor flooded my mind.

'The fault line reached as far as the oilfield?' I asked, surprised. 'Why wasn't I told?'

'The well was undamaged, and you had enough on your mind at that time.' Mr Fartime coughed again.

'I'll be back by the end of the month, I promise. The reservoir is my project too, don't forget.'

'I will keep the villa vacant for you,' he said with a nod. Pushing back his chair, he hauled his large frame upright and shook my hand again. 'Tell me, what was your wife really looking for during that dive?'

The question took me by surprise. Was Fartime spying; and if so who for?

I thought quickly. 'A rare fish,' I said. 'You must remember what an ecologist she was?'

Mr Fartime chuckled. 'Alas, I'm afraid I do.'

\* \* \*

I spent the next day organising my trip back to London. Throwing myself into packing was a way of distracting myself from my growing anxiety about leaving Isabella's grave behind; I couldn't help feeling I was abandoning her.

That evening, I sat on the bed, Isabella's letter in my hand. Her distinctive handwriting pulled images of her like threads from my memory — Isabella cheering with my brother during a Carlisle United match; Isabella giving a paper at the Royal Archaeological Society in London; Isabella dancing wildly in the flat to the Rolling Stones.

I looked back at the page; one paragraph jumped out from the rest.

*Oliver, forgive me, I've never been completely honest with you. All those years ago, Ahmos Khafre did not only tell me my death date; he also told me I may be able to save my own life if I discovered the astrarium in time.*

The fact that Isabella had really believed the mystic made me realise how profoundly our cultural and philosophical outlooks differed. If I'd had the courage to confront those differences when she was alive, instead of hoping that she'd grow out of such beliefs, could I have saved her? A sickening sense of guilt swept through me: I should have stopped her from diving that day; we should never have came back to Egypt.

I walked over to the balcony and glanced down at the garden. The pomegranate bush I'd planted above the astrarium had buds that were beginning to unfurl. It was as if I could feel the presence of the astrarium through the thick canvas I'd wrapped it in, through the wooden box, through the foot of soil above it. And as I kept staring, I had the distinct impression it was staring back.

How was I going to get it to England? If I took it in my luggage, there was the chance I'd be arrested at the airport for attempting to smuggle an antiquity out of the country. I couldn't afford another interrogation. Perhaps I could just take the pages with the transcribed hieroglyphics Hermes had given me — would they be enough information for Hugh Wollington? But the more I thought about it, the less I wanted to leave the astrarium. I was bound to it now, committed. And if whoever wanted it was prepared to kill Barry, I knew it was only a matter of time before they got past the security here. I had to take it with me.

Then I remembered Bill Anderson's boast days earlier.

\* \* \*

I met Bill at the Alexandria Sporting Club. Once a prestigious country club where only the privileged few could be members, it boasted its own racetrack, croquet and lawn bowls grass lawns and an eighteen-hole golf course. The large reception room with its Tudor-style wooden beams and hunting trophies reminded me of an English country house. The two of us sat sipping mint juleps on a terrace looking over the immaculately mown lawns and topiary, the gentle thud of tennis balls echoing in the distance. In one corner of the room sat a dignified older gentleman wearing a red pasha hat and a red carnation in his blazer. He was holding court to a group of women who must have been well into their seventies, dressed in faded but elegant day dresses and hats. We watched as he kissed the hand of one of the women, who laughed coquettishly.

'Who's that? Methuselah?' Anderson asked, grinning.

'That, my friend, is Fargally Pasha, once known as the King of Cotton and past friend to kings, film stars and dictators,' I answered. 'Now condemned to his memories.'

'We all end up like that sooner or later,' Bill quipped and raised his glass to the old man.

Smiling, Fargally Pasha toasted us back.

The American turned to me. 'So what's this mysterious favour I can do for you?'

I leaned forward. 'In the Sinai you said you could get anything through customs under the guise of emergency equipment?'

'Wasn't I under the influence of an illegal substance at the time?'

'Come on, Bill, I'm serious. There's something I need to get back to London; something Isabella cared about very deeply.'

He stared at me then thoughtfully stirred his cocktail with the sprig of mint that decorated it. 'How big is it?'

'It's stored in a box about eighteen inches by twelve. If it were opened, no one would recognise it except a very experienced archaeologist.'

'Jesus, Oliver, you're not getting into that game.'

'If you think I intend to flog the damn thing to the highest bidder, you're wrong. It'll end up back in Egypt sooner or later. I'm just carrying out Isabella's last wishes — trust me, it's not what I want to be doing.'

Anderson's eyebrows shot up in disbelief. 'The best I can do is fly it direct to Aberdeen on the company's private plane, then have it couriered down to London. If it's marked with the company's insignia, no one's going to open it.'

'That's good enough. How quickly?'

'I can organise for you to put it on the plane yourself, and it should get to London a couple of days after you. My equipment flies on before me.'

I lifted my cocktail glass in a toast. 'Anderson, I owe you.'

'And I intend to collect.' He clinked his glass against mine.

# 16

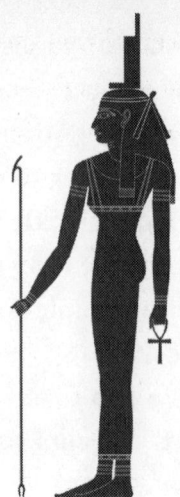

On the afternoon of my departure I visited the Brambillas' villa. When I arrived, Francesca was sitting in a reclining chair, eyes shut, in the walled courtyard in a small circle of sunlight beside the pond. Several carp, hopeful for food, weaved over each other in a blur of pale gold, gathering under her shadow where it fell across the water.

The garden was still beautiful despite its neglect. Frangipanni branches cut a maze across the sky and vines trailed across some of the paths. Someone — probably the teenage son of the lodger — had spray-painted a rough facsimile of football goalposts on the stone back wall and scrawled *Viva Al Olympi!*

I sat down in an empty chair beside her, wondering whether to wake her or not.

'So you have come to evict me?' she said abruptly, her eyes still closed, her voice resounding through the courtyard like the cry of a tragedienne.

I stayed silent, and after a moment she opened her eyes and gazed at the weaving mess of fish.

'I just want some answers, Francesca.'

'Answers, what kind of answers?'

'Why was Isabella's body violated?'

'If my granddaughter's body was violated I know nothing about it.'

I tried to read her face but it was as closed as her knotted hands.

'I would love to believe you, but I don't,' I replied carefully.

She sighed, still staring down at the fish. 'Do you have any idea how terrible it is to be born on the wrong side of history?' Only now did she look at me, her gaze bitter. 'Of course you don't; you're English.'

'I was born on the wrong side of class.'

'That's different. You can buy yourself out of that situation, as you yourself, Oliver, have done,' she replied harshly, then reached into a pocket and pulled out a cigarillo.

Reaching into my own pocket, I offered her the gold Gucci lighter a Saudi client had once given me. Francesca lowered her face towards the flame and the tip of the cigarillo burst into a glowing ember. She exhaled; a great curl of white smoke hung on the still air.

'No,' she continued, 'to be born on the wrong side of history is to be trapped in great sweeping circumstances over which one has absolutely no control. This was our country. Mohammed Ali personally invited my grandfather, a civil engineer, to Egypt, placed him into his cabinet. And my grandfather built roads, waterways, great architectural feats. But even if my family's hearts were Egyptian, their souls were Italian. This was what I was taught, and it was not a contradiction.'

She was becoming hysterical. Aadeel emerged from the villa — I guessed he had been listening — and hurried over to the elderly woman.

'Madame, the lodgers,' he murmured, pressing a blue pill into her hand.

'A curse on them,' she muttered, but took the pill with a sip of water from a glass Aadeel held out. Then she waited, ostentatiously disregarding the servant until he slipped back into the house.

'My son was also an idealist,' she said, more calmly. 'We all thought that Mussolini, like Julius Caesar, would unite Alexandria with the Mediterranean world. We were not alone in this delusion: the Greeks thought the same, only their great dream was the old Ptolemaic order — Athens and Alexandria. Dreams like that have their own fuel — economic polarity, the ambition of a new order where everyone knows their natural place.'

Francesca's philosophising riled the humanist in me. 'There is no such thing as people having a natural place,' I interjected.

But the old matriarch was determined to finish her tirade. 'Those soldiers marched into that desert knowing they were going to die, and many did. The rest were herded together and interned, like animals. That was the first time this family was on the wrong side of history. The second time was Nasser and the revolution. Even then my son stood firm. "Times will change, Mama, you'll see. Our time will come, we just have to wait," he told me — the fool. The third time was the Suez Crisis; again, it was the English who let us down. Do you know what they call that incident here in Egypt? The triad of cowardice — the French, the British and the Israelis. We Italians, along with every other European, lost everything overnight. The Jews were the first to leave, or disappear mysteriously in the night. Others followed. But not this family. Paolo was determined. "So now I am the manager of my own company, but I will own it again, you will see, Mama." The wrong side of history, Oliver — it killed him, thirty-seven years old. And we, his parents, had to watch him die of humiliation!'

Again, I could see Aadeel hovering in the gathering twilight. Indifferent to his anxiety, Francesca continued. 'Paolo's death turned Giovanni into a desperate fool. And desperate men reach out for all kinds of false hopes. He thought he could use the old ways, the ancient ways, to change things back. I had no choice — I had to pretend I didn't know what was happening. In the end, it was all Giovanni had left.'

'Is this to do with the "performances" you wrote to Cecilia about?'

'You have been talking to Cecilia?'

'She mentioned a few things …'

'She is a liar! Giovanni loved Isabella. We were parents to her, not grandparents!' She fell back into her chair, exhausted by her fury. 'I have said enough. Throw me out of my own house, but I refuse to betray my husband.'

'What about your granddaughter? Doesn't she deserve respect?' I grabbed her hand; the wrinkled liver-spotted skin was as thin as rice paper. 'Francesca, they stole her heart.'

She snatched her hand away, her face closing over like stone. 'You should have protected Isabella. Isn't that what husbands are for?' she said with quiet spite.

In the branches above us, a dove began to coo, an ironically peaceful sound considering the tension between us. Enraged, I battled the impulse to hit out at the old woman.

'I told you, I know nothing.' She tried to stand, her elbows shaking wildly as she grasped the sides of the chair. 'Aadeel, begin packing our things! We are to be evicted!'

Her shouting startled the dove who flew noisily out of the tree, dislodging leaves that showered down over the old woman's shoulders. She did not brush them off.

Aadeel glanced at me.

I stood. 'It's all right. No one is going to be evicted. I just came to say goodbye. I'm going away for a few weeks.'

Francesca sank back into her chair. I waited, unable to pull myself away without a final goodbye.

'Of course you're going. The English always do,' she muttered into the descending dusk.

\* \* \*

I sat back against the leather upholstery of the oil company's ancient Bentley; the rich smell of the interior mixed with the driver's cigarette smoke. I'd placed the astrarium into the cargo hold of Anderson's jet earlier that day and the thought of it flying on ahead of me was consoling; as if something of Isabella would be waiting for me upon my arrival in London. Cocooned in the car, the painful events of the last month seemed to stream behind us like the wake of a ship.

I wound down the window and the music of the city — honking vehicles, the cries of the street vendors, the bells on the horses' harnesses — rushed in. Old Ramadan decorations stretched gaudily between two buildings, tired tinsel and paper ribbons waving palely. Twilight. Already the streets were bustling with night shoppers; street pedlars selling figs, dates, peanuts, fresh fish caught that day — their wares carefully spread out on sheets of canvas; young women with extravagant hairstyles and western clothes hurrying home from offices and shops; the old men holding court at the café tables.

The memory of Isabella's child-like pride at showing me her city, her hand holding mine in this very seat, sputtered on and off like a faulty fluorescent light.

'The airport?' the driver shouted over the traffic noise. 'We go to airport, right!'

'*Shukran*, thank you.'

I turned back to the window, trying to suppress an unexpected wave of anxiety. Leaving is not losing her, and memory is a kind of afterlife, I told myself, but I found no consolation in the observation.

The car headed out towards the airport, past the sewage works and the satellite towns beginning to spring up around the outskirts of Alexandria, and into the cool desert. The oil refinery's flaming towers roared up against the darkening horizon like great primordial torches and finally my panic began to flatten out. With the blind sky yawning above the speeding car, I thought how Isabella would have loved this night.

# 17

## London, June 1977

The hazy English sunlight was a shock after the glare of Egypt. The drive from Heathrow took me through the factorylands, into the outer London suburbs, then onto Chiswick with its large Victorian houses and gardens, into denser Shepherds Bush, past the terraced boarding houses of Notting Hill and finally into West Hampstead. The suburban landscape dragging me back into the smells, sights and sounds of England.

I stepped out of the taxi. There was the faint sound of reggae music, birdsong, and that particular humidity that always laced the early summer air — a languid sensuality that invariably surprised even the Londoners. I glanced at the Victorian terrace; our flat was located on the top floor. The curtains were pulled across. Staring up it was as if I saw Isabella parting them and peering down, her anxious face searching the street for me in that way she always did when she was expecting me back from a trip. But the curtains stayed closed and my legs almost buckled underneath me from grief.

'You all right, mate?' The taxi driver leaned out of his open window.

I nodded, and turned to lift out my suitcase. The cab drove off, and as I carried my luggage up the pavement I noticed the twins from next door watching from their front garden, one nonchalantly picking his nose while the other scratched a scabby knee. Children of a recent divorce, their working mother was rarely home and Isabella had often brought them up to our apartment for tea and the Turkish delight Francesca sent from Egypt.

'Mister Warnock!' called Stanley, the older brother, now hanging from the garden gate, his prematurely aged face peaky and worried. I turned reluctantly: this was the moment I'd been dreading.

'Where's Issy?' he demanded, his voice trembling with anxiety. 'You've not gone and got divorced, 'ave yer?'

'Stanley, I've just got in from a long flight and—'

'She's left yer, 'asn't she?' Alfred joined his brother on the gate, the two of them glaring at me in defiant accusation, blond hair shaved tight against their narrow skulls, precocious in their distrust of all things adult.

I hesitated. They had both adored Isabella. She'd even taught them a few words of Italian, which they'd repeated solemnly in atrocious north London accents, captivated by her expressive gestures — *buongiorno, buonasera, arrivederci*. Momentarily overwhelmed, I sat down on my suitcase, too distressed to reply. There was the creak of the gate as it was swung open. A minute later I felt small cool fingers slip between my own.

'Mister Warnock, it's bad, innit?' Stanley stood in front of me, his eyes wide with a sense of tragedy that belied his age.

I stared up at him. 'I lost her,' I whispered.

'Lost her? How can you lose a whole person?' Alfred, incredulous, still hovered behind the gate. But one glance at Stanley's trembling face and I knew the older twin had understood.

'C'mon, Alfred.' With his eyes screwed tight to stop the tears, Stanley led his brother back to their front garden.

\* \* \*

Our flat was in West Hampstead, a suburb filled with the dispossessed middle class: the divorced, the bachelors, the perpetual spinsters alone in their studio apartments huddled around the electric kettle. But it was my favourite part of London; I liked the semi-urban location. The apartment was tiny — I'd purchased it at the beginning of my first job, using the position as leverage to secure a mortgage. It had been a momentous occasion: I was the first member of my family to ever own property, and at twenty-four I felt I was already soaring above a cycle of poverty that went back generations.

It was a one-bedroom apartment, really a glorified attic conversion. The kitchen was the size of a large cupboard with a view of next-door's concreted courtyard. The lounge room, which doubled as the dining room, was split-level; a small set of wooden steps led up to a sleeping area with just enough space for a double bed. The ceiling was so low I could hardly stand. The best thing about the place was the small roof terrace that lay beyond the double windows of the sleeping area. It was located between two tall Victorian red-brick chimneys; a sanctuary hidden from the windows of the surrounding buildings that offered an unencumbered view of northwest London. When the weather was good, I'd carry out the large telescope I kept folded against the bedroom wall and set it up on its spindly tripod. Beyond the orange city sky, the stars were my metaphysical ladder, a way to escape the claustrophobia of both London and the apartment.

I pulled my suitcase along the entrance hall and onto the staircase. The paintwork was battered and splintered, the carpet stained and worn by a thousand tenants before us, and the strong smell of curry wafted down from the apartment of the young Indian Sikh couple who lived on the first floor. I paused on the landing.

'Oliver?' My neighbour peered through his partially opened front door, the door chain still on.

'Hello, Raj,' I said.

Sighing with relief, Raj unlatched the chain and stepped out. He was wearing a sweaty vest, white turban and the trousers of his bus driver's uniform. His eyes were tired and anxious.

'Just come off the nightshift?' I asked, surprised by the happiness I felt at the familiar sight of him.

'That is right.' He reached out, his voice cracking with emotion. 'Oliver, your brother told us about your terrible loss. My wife and I are most grieved, you know we both loved Isabella very much.'

'Thank you.'

I could see his sari-clad wife hovering shyly behind him. Shaking his hand, I tried to hold down the balloon of emotion now banging against my ribcage. Embarrassed, Raj tactfully turned back to the apartment.

'Aisha, he is back.'

His wife, her slim figure radiating a glass-like fragility, offered me a biscuit tin. 'Please, you must be tired and hungry, and your fridge will be empty. I have some samosas for you. Please?'

Thanking them both profusely, I slipped the tin under my arm.

After the door closed behind them, I stood staring up at the next landing, my own front door, achingly familiar with its blue paint and brass doorknob, beckoning through the banisters. Clutching the biscuit tin as a drowning man might hold onto a buoy, I made my way up the stairs.

The flat was a darkened cavern that stank of stale cigarette smoke and frying bacon. With all the curtains drawn, it held the gloom of somebody else's life, a past I now barely recognised. Even in this dim light I could see several dirty plates on the floor, a dressing gown thrown across the television. A lava lamp glowed in the corner, its nebulous mass congealing in slow motion like an errant fungus.

Isabella had insisted Gareth should have a set of keys so he could use the flat as an occasional retreat from the frenetic world he existed in. It was obvious he'd stayed over and failed to clean up after himself. I picked up the plates and carried them into the kitchen. Well, at least he's eating, I reassured myself. The task of dealing with my brother's latest bout of addiction loomed; a depressing prospect.

I turned the dripping tap off and went back into the lounge room. It was a time capsule, the objects within might, themselves, have been submerged — the dust and microscopic human debris from a lifetime before, a lifetime suspended in the still air.

I climbed the wooden steps to the sleeping area. Isabella's dressing gown hung on a hook on the wall. Burying my face in the silk, I breathed in deeply. The smell of our sex still lingered in the folds, the love twistings of leg and skin.

Kneeling on the floor, I buried my head in this tent of memory, wondering if I could go on. I was free-falling in her absence. If I'm entirely honest with myself, I think I might have been waiting for some kind of external sign to give me a reason to continue, for Isabella to talk to me from beyond that invisible wall that divided the dead from the living.

There was nothing but silence. Then slowly the sound of a distant ice-cream van playing a tinkling 'Greensleeves', and the roar of a plane passing overhead came into focus. And suddenly

I wanted to wipe all of it away — the clinging labyrinth of Egypt, the astrarium, the incessant misery of loss.

Grabbing the steel wastepaper bin, I pulled open the chest of drawers and began to pull out Isabella's clothes: sweaters, blouses, skirts, lingerie — all ghost clothes now, a ghost I was determined to exorcise. I stuffed as much as I could into the bin then carried it onto the roof terrace. After emptying a bottle of lighter fluid over the clothes, I held a match to the pile.

Sliding down, I sat with my back to the wall. As each item crinkled then burst into flames, I remembered the occasions she'd worn it: an Indian cotton dress flying around her tanned legs as she danced at a rock concert; a business suit she wore for her lectures; a nightdress she would put on, without consciously realising it, when she wanted to make love.

Emotionally exhausted, I curled up and closed my eyes.

\* \* \*

The sound of footsteps woke me. Silhouetted against the afternoon sky was a young woman, her wild hair framing her face like a mane.

'Oliver?' she said.

Disorientated, I stumbled to my feet. I must have slept for hours.

'I'm Zoë. Gareth's girlfriend. Sorry,' she indicated the open window she must have climbed through to reach the roof, 'I was audacious. I let myself in. Gareth had the keys. He doesn't know you're back or anything …'

'You're forgiven. So you're the person who rang my office in Alex?'

She stepped into the shade and I could finally see her clearly. She wore Dr Martens boots, purple fishnets and a blue

Lurex ball gown that flared from the waist, her hennaed hair fell to her shoulders, and her face had a pre-Raphaelite beauty that formed a jarring contrast with her dress. Despite the heavy purple eye shadow, she looked ridiculously young.

Candidly, she looked me up and down; to my annoyance I found it a disarming sensation.

'You look like him, only older,' she said.

I moved the subject onto safer ground. 'Is Gareth all right?'

'Depends on what you classify as all right. He's playing tonight so I thought you could come and see for yourself. Personally I've never seen him so self-destructive.'

'In what way?'

She looked me fully in the eye then decided to be honest. 'Speed. I mean, we all indulge. It's just that with Gareth it's got so bad he's frightened to sleep. Like really frightened, as if it might kill him to close his eyes. Most of the time he's rational, but then he'll start talking about people coming to steal his soul.'

'That isn't rational.'

'Isn't it?' she replied with a nonchalant irony.

Reaching into the still-smouldering bin, she pulled out one of Isabella's half-burnt bras, all underwiring and lace, and held it up. 'I don't think everything is rational.'

She waited for an explanation; I didn't give her one. She dropped the smouldering bra back into the embers. 'I think we have a bit in common.' She flung the remark out as if it were a paradox.

'Apart from my brother?'

'An interest in stone, rock ...'

I glanced at her quizzically.

'Didn't Gareth tell you?' she continued.

'Afraid not, we've never talked much, my fault as much as his,' I replied, now wondering how much he'd told her about me.

'I'm a sculptor, I work in marble.' Her earnestness was endearing. 'You're a geologist, aren't you?'

'A geophysicist, that's far less romantic.' I smiled. 'How old are you?'

'Does my age preclude the possibility of being taken seriously?'

'As an artist or a woman?'

'I'm asking you.'

'I think,' I leaned forward to emphasise the point, 'I'm old enough to be your father.'

'But you're not. And, if you have to know, my father died last year in a road accident and I suspect he was several years older than you.'

Suddenly her façade of hardened indifference slipped away. I fought the impulse to hug her.

'I'm sorry.'

She flinched. 'So you see, we have something else in common.' She glanced out at the rooftops before turning back toward me. 'I met your wife once, at the squat. She told Gareth to break it off with me — she thought I was too intense, and probably too young.'

I laughed. 'That sounds like Isabella — she was always giving him advice about his love life.'

'It's okay, she was right. I am too intense ...' Her voice trailed off and she indicated the smouldering bin. 'It's hard to find the words ...'

'That's because there aren't any.'

She nodded and, squatting down against the wall, lit a cigarette.

'Marble's made from seashells crushed together over millions of years, isn't it? That's why it has that translucency — the light of all those ancient oceans.'

'Exactly,' I answered, smiling. 'And oil is made from organic matter crushed together over millions of years, and that black-gold tint is the treacly light of money shining through.'

'But isn't working just for money ultimately corrupting?' she persisted.

'I'll let you into a secret. It's not the money but the hunt that gets me excited. Finding something I can sense is there.'

She nodded. 'I feel that when I look at a piece of marble. I see the shape hidden in the rock, then release it by carving.'

'Bingo, that makes three things we have in common,' I joked.

Zoë's face wavered then settled into seriousness. 'So what do you think happens to us when we die, when we're crushed together over millions of years?'

I stared out over the languid summer evening; the laughter of children playing below floated up with the faint scent of mown grass. 'We become one with the universe, nature recycling itself. It's that simple,' I answered finally.

'Nothing's simple.' She threw her cigarette away. 'I'm eighteen, in case you're wondering.' She stood up. 'She's still here, you know.'

For a moment I thought I'd misheard. 'Sorry?'

'Your wife, she hasn't left yet. She's still here, all twisted up in your shadow.'

'Look, I hardly know you—'

'Oops, I'm being audacious again, sorry. It's a gift I have and sometimes I speak out of turn. You'll have to put up with it. Come to the gig tonight — please. Gareth really respects you. He'll be thrilled if you are there. I wouldn't have rung if I didn't think the situation was serious.'

She smiled; a poignant half-smile that broke the ferocity of her make-up. There was an unnerving maturity about her despite her youth, and her beauty was hard to ignore.

'He doesn't know you're back or that I rang you,' she continued. 'Proud family, your lot — Gareth would rather die than ask for help. I'm sorry about your wife. She must have been amazing. Gareth took the news really badly.'

'They were close.'

'The band's playing at The Venue. They're on in an hour so we should get moving.'

I hesitated. I hadn't calculated the possibility of actually seeing my brother sing. In fact, I'd never seen Gareth's band play — that had been Isabella's domain, and I'd semi-consciously avoided the gigs, a part of me terrified that he might not be as talented as I hoped. I needed to believe in his future in the way my parents had never believed in mine, which meant I needed him to be good, really good.

I glanced out over the rooftops, the urban regularity jarring after the skyline of Alexandria. The sun had begun to slip behind the horizon.

'Come on, come with me,' Zoë said. 'It's got to be better than hanging around here. But there's no way you're wearing that daft suit.'

# 18

The Vue was an old ballroom someone had decided to re-create as a rock music venue. Apart from some fluorescent ceiling hangings and a stage backdrop with a massive black A on a red background ringed by a circle, the original décor looked relatively intact. Ornate plaster reliefs decorated the balconies, a huge crystal chandelier hung from the ceiling, imaginatively strung with pink electric lights, while a strobe painted the walls in blindingly blue-white staccato.

The bar was located on an upper balcony, encircled by large booths with a neon sign of Betty Boop having sex with Mickey Mouse pulsing over the counter. I pushed my way through the crowd cradling a vodka and four pints of Guinness. By the time we'd arrived, the band were backstage preparing to go on and the bouncers wouldn't let us see them. So Zoë had guided me to the bar, pointed to where Gareth's housemates were waiting, and instructed me to buy the drinks. I reached the table, self-conscious in the battered leather jacket Gareth had left at the flat and which Zoë had forced me to wear.

I felt I'd entered some kind of Hieronymus Bosch netherworld populated by young women and men dressed in the most fantastical outfits and hairstyles. They lounged against the walls and on the chairs; a couple even appeared to be having sex on the table of one of the booths, oblivious to the incurious bystanders. Another couple sported bright-pink mohawks over a foot high; the man, a good deal shorter than his girlfriend, reminded me of a bizarre peacock. His eyes were carefully outlined with black kohl and eye shadow, while the shaved halves of his scalp either side of the stiff pink spikes glistened like a pale pancake. A torn T-shirt held together by oversized safety pins sat under a black leather jacket covered in zips and studs, and his skin-tight trousers were made of rubber. His girlfriend wore a leather bra — the kind of thing one might purchase from a sex shop — and a tartan miniskirt, under which the suspenders holding up her fishnet stockings were clearly visible. The two of them had a tribal grace, and the youth particularly, with his long naked skull and aquiline features, reminded me of a pale version of some of the Nubian tribes I'd seen in central Africa. I'd never thought the English could be capable of such decorative and imaginative dressing, and for one bizarre moment I speculated whether such fashion wasn't a brilliant fusion of colonial Britain and the urban dispossessed.

Gareth's housemates were seated in one of the booths, Zoë beside them. I placed the beers down on the table then sat opposite. They looked as out of place as I did, I couldn't help noting with some relish. They were a curiously eclectic group who looked like they had nothing in common except the squat they lived in — in Harlesden, a semi-industrial, unprepossessing suburb on the outskirts of northwest London. The narrow Victorian terrace was one of a whole cul-de-sac marked for demolition until Gareth and his friends had taken illegal occupancy eighteen months before. Despite my disapproval, I couldn't help admiring the energy they had poured into repairing the place — clearing the ancient sewage drain that led under the street, emptying the back garden of litter, replacing the shattered windows.

'Excellent, my friend, the beverages have arrived intact despite the unruly herd,' Dennis announced.

At forty, he was an active member of the International Marxist Group and a borderline schizophrenic; a passionately literary character who, when he wasn't reading Nietzsche, worked as a bookie. Next to him was Philippe, a short corpulent Frenchman with long hair who had come to London to escape military service, or so Gareth had told Isabella. My brother had apparently recruited the draft dodger at an anarchist meeting.

The third housemate was a diminutive thirty-year-old Irishman called Francis, with straight red hair that ran down in flat streaks to his waist and a matching goatee. Never seen without his embroidered beanie, he resembled a studious garden gnome.

'Thanks, Oliver, you're a gentleman and it won't be forgotten,' he murmured in his soft southern Irish brogue as he reached for his drink.

A tall, stunning pneumatic blonde in bondage trousers and a net vest sauntered past; her pendulous breasts were clearly visible, as were her large pierced nipples. All three men paused, glasses in midair.

'Would you look at that? An angel in hell and I know exactly the man to deliver her from such terrible damnation,' Francis said admiringly.

'Be my guest — these punky girls look like their pussies have teeth. Me, I would have concern for my manhood,' Philippe responded before sipping cautiously at his Guinness.

Dennis turned to Francis. 'You don't get it, do you? The desecration of the body is an anti-beauty statement, and yet the desecration itself becomes a fetish, then a subculture with its own individual ways of delineating beauty — so all this protest becomes self-defeating. It's a loop. All of history is just loop after loop.'

'Jesus, Dennis, I bet you're fun in bed in a modernist kind of way.' Francis swung around to me. 'What about you, Oliver? Does that bird lift your wick or what?'

'Francis! The man's just become a widower, he's not interested in getting laid,' Dennis retorted. 'Sorry, Oliver, my associates are emotionally insensitive at the best of times. Francis didn't mean to be offensive.'

'No offence taken,' I replied, concluding that the only way I was going to survive the night was to get drunk.

'Leave the poor bastard alone,' Zoë ordered. 'Can't you see he's in culture shock as well as acoustic.' She turned back to me. 'But don't worry, the girls here won't bite — unless you ask very, very nicely.' She grinned wickedly.

Luckily, any further humiliation was staved off by the lights dimming. The MC came on stage and immediately the audience broke into a chorus of wolf-whistles. 'The Alienated Pilots!' he screamed through the microphone.

Dennis rose to his feet, his face cadaverous under the fluorescent lights. 'Well, comrades, it's time the troops turned up for the parade,' he announced solemnly and began making his way to the front of the stage.

We all followed, except Francis who took the opportunity to finish off our beers.

From the back of the darkened stage came a low drum roll and then a cymbal clash. A ripple of expectation ran through the crowd as a follow spot flicked on, illuminating my brother in a pool of blue-white light. Gareth looked like a beautiful sixteenth-century Spanish carving. His bared torso was a washboard of cascading pale ribs with a bleeding heart crayoned onto his chest; his leather trousers slung low on his hips ringed by a studded belt. His head was tilted back, his eyes shut. A crown of plastic barbed wire was pushed low over his forehead, pearls of fake blood rolled down over his cheekbones, he held the microphone clasped in one hand like a sceptre. He lifted his muscular arms up as if in crucifixion. The religious references appalled me — clearly he hadn't escaped our mother's influence. He looked thin but not emaciated; I hoped, against all evidence, that Zoë's concern had been unwarranted.

The audience fell into awed silence. I couldn't help thinking how proud Isabella would have been of Gareth at that moment. I almost felt her standing beside me in the dark, radiating excitement. Instinct made me turn, half-expecting to see her face, but instead I found myself glancing at Zoë, who was staring at a space just above me. I looked over my shoulder, wondering what she'd seen, but there was nothing. As if in answer, she suddenly reached out and fluttered her fingers above me, as if shooing something away.

Then, her face avid with anticipation, she leaned across and whispered into my ear. 'The trouble with your brother is that he has no continuity — he reinvents himself from moment to moment. But that's exactly what will make him famous.'

She looked like some magical sage, her kohl-rimmed eyes shimmering silver under the lights. Suddenly Gareth's voice rang out over the crowd.

'This is for Isabella — may you shine on forever,' he announced, and a great sweep of emotion rushed through me.

The next minute, he burst into low gravelly song, his body throwing itself into pose after pose: a svelte Pierrot with the stance of a bullfighter. The effect was undeniably sensual and I couldn't help wondering what had happened to the small child I used to take walking on the downs. 'The Fens have shadows,' he'd once told me, 'but when night comes the shadows fly away and leave the Fens alone, all cold and shivery.' I'd never forgotten the passion of his six-year-old conviction, and now there it was, up on the stage.

*My love wears green*
*Like the dragonfly she shines*
*Slices my heart into shimmering pieces*
*My love wears green ...*

The chorus was a pounding cacophony of guitar chords that ignited the audience. At the front, a row of skinheads leaped up and down, their shaved skulls glistening with sweat. In a violent frenzy they pushed aside the surrounding spectators as the lights changed to a deep blood-red strobe fragmenting Gareth's movements like time-lapse photography.

*She takes the mighty*
*And strikes them blind*
*She sleeps with all my friends*
*Yet swears she's mine*
*My love wears green ...*

It was as if my brother had been transformed into someone I'd had no idea existed under that indolent façade. There was an old-world Celtic quality to his lyrics despite the punching brutality of the chorus. The next three songs had the same lurching romanticism as the first — seductive ballads splintered by violent refrains. At the edge of the stage near Gareth's feet, a small group of girls had gathered, their faces illuminated as the spotlight swung into the crowd like a beam from an aberrant lighthouse. Each girl appeared to be undergoing a private dialogue with the sinewy figure, as if he were singing for her alone. They reminded me of worshippers at an altar, transfixed, transported. It was hypnotic to witness and, envious, I found myself imagining what it must be like to hold such power.

Just then a boy who looked about fifteen, a Union Jack safety-pinned to his vest, pushed past, spilling his beer down the front of my trousers. I reeled around but he carried on indifferently, stumbling into the swaying audience. The three vodkas I'd consumed collided with my exhaustion in a sudden dizziness. I made my way through the crowd and leaned against the wall, looking on as my brother sang his way through a kaleidoscope of emotion.

\* \* \*

Gareth's dressing room was far less glamorous than I had imagined. Painted white, it had a chipped mirror glued to one wall, a battered Formica table covered in a couple of sticks of stage make-up, empty beer cans, and ashtrays spilling over with cigarette butts. In one corner stood a steel clothes rack on wheels with various performing outfits hanging off it.

Wearing sunglasses, Gareth leaned against the edge of the table surrounded by a small crowd of groupies, fans and band members, a beer can in one hand and Zoë nestled adoringly under his other arm. Under the fluorescent light I could see that sweat had run rivulets through his make-up. He appeared jittery, still high from his performance, but I also recognised the influence of amphetamines in his manic gestures.

He caught sight of me. 'Oliver! Oliver! I can't believe you're here! I almost didn't recognise you with that beard.' He addressed his entourage. 'Everyone, meet my brother — fresh from the land of the Pharaohs!'

The small crowd stared at me, then, seemingly disappointed at my ordinariness, turned back to their drinking and chattering.

Pushing his way through them, Gareth took off his sunglasses and pulled me into a hug. The shock of the embrace made me freeze.

'Did you like the dedication?' he asked. He smelled of cigarettes and Old Spice aftershave.

'It was really moving.'

'I'm so sorry about Isabella.'

Hating myself for the inherent awkwardness of the men in my family, I pulled away. 'It's been terrible.' My voice broke despite my reserve.

'You're home now. It's good to see you.'

I changed the subject. I couldn't bear to talk about Isabella, not now, not with Gareth. 'You were brilliant out there. I couldn't believe you were my brother.'

'Did you all hear that? Oliver here thought we were bloody brilliant!' he shouted to the room. 'And he's a bloody Tory!'

His entourage grinned inanely and nodded in dumb approval.

'I'm not a bloody Tory,' I muttered, embarrassed.

'Yeah, but you're a capitalist, same bloody thing.' He suddenly swung back to the others. 'Fuck off! The lot of you!'

They paused, murmuring amongst themselves, wondering if he meant it.

'Now!' he yelled, spittle flying.

The room emptied in minutes.

Gareth turned back to me, grinning. 'Oh, the sheer power of celebrity. They're sheep, the whole bloody lot of them.' He extracted a crushed cigarette packet from the back pocket of his tight leather trousers and lit up a crooked cigarette, inhaling deeply. 'Fuck, it feels so wrong — without Isabella you're nothing. She was your inspirational self, your evolved feminine side, she made those exploitative mud scramblings of yours poetic.'

Gareth's speech tended to oscillate wildly between an ornate Oscar Wilde-style patter and contemporary slang, as if his personality was some grand work in progress whose foundation hadn't quite settled yet.

'The word is "geophysicist" and it's not mud, it's oil.' I looked into his eyes, trying to gauge the size of his pupils. 'You're speeding, aren't you? Do you know we're all worried sick about you?' My voice reverted to the northern accent of my childhood as I spoke — the tongue of my family.

He pushed me away and put his sunglasses back on. 'Give me a break. You've been gone for months, and Da's been on my back every bloody week.'

'When did you start using again? I thought we talked about that—'

'Isabella talked about that. You were never bloody interested until now. Did you bring her back?' he demanded abruptly.

'What?'

'I thought maybe you'd bring the ashes back or something.'

I stared at him — the amphetamines were making him manic. 'Isabella had a Catholic funeral, it was what her family wanted.'

'I just thought we could have our own service — you know, scatter her ashes on the heath or something. I could have sung. Isabella liked my singing.'

'Christ, you're unbelievable.'

I turned to walk away, but Gareth reached out and put his hand on my shoulder.

'Listen, I'm sorry, all right? It must be hell for you. I know I wouldn't have survived it. You two were symbiotic: silence and song.'

For a second a window opened onto the man he might become; rarely had I heard Gareth sound so sincere. I decided to take a risk.

'Gareth, you made a drawing for Isabella, a drawing of the astrarium ...'

His whole demeanour changed; it was as if he sobered up instantly. He went to the door and, after checking no one was loitering in the passage outside, closed it. 'Come back with me tonight, Oliver, back to the squat. We need to talk.'

\* \* \*

My brother's bedroom, on the top floor of the terrace, had black walls and a dark blue ceiling onto which he'd stuck fluorescent decals of planets and stars — a fictional galaxy that in no way resembled the Milky Way or any other known astral body. He lay on a mattress on the floor, while Zoë and several others of his entourage — Philippe, the drummer, a couple of drunk bouncers — lounged around the room. I sat awkwardly beside my brother, my back hard against the cold wall, the discovery that he was virtually never alone a growing source of irritation.

Gareth had just turned off the light to display his celestial artwork and the others were staring reverently at its greenish glow.

'I'm telling you, on this hash it's better than the Sistine Chapel,' Philippe murmured, curled up on a beanbag.

'You should see what it's like on acid.' The drummer rolled over onto his back, high as a kite.

'Yeah,' Zoë affirmed in a reed-thin voice.

'Gareth,' I hissed, 'I thought you wanted to talk to me alone.'

'We are alone.'

'No, we're fucking not.'

'I meant existentially.'

'That's it, I'm out of here.'

I struggled to my feet but Gareth grabbed my arm.

'I'm sorry. Listen, don't go, we'll talk in a minute, I promise.' He pulled me towards him, his breath stank of Guinness. 'How did she die really? Did she find the astrarium? Is that how it happened?'

I paused, my mind reeling in the dark, I hadn't realised he'd known Isabella had been diving for the astrarium in Alexandria.

'She drowned searching for it,' I whispered.

I wasn't going to tell him we'd found it. It wasn't that I didn't trust him; simply that I wanted to protect him.

'Come with me.' Gareth pulled me to my feet.

We stumbled our way to the door, tripping across outstretched legs, splayed arms and a chorus of expletives. The tiny room he took me to was lined with cardboard egg cartons and illuminated with a single naked electric bulb. A battered desk with a sound mixing board on it ran along one wall, while opposite stood a small bookcase holding titles such as Rimbaud's *A Season in Hell*, John Fowles' *The Magus*, *Ways of Seeing* by John Berger — all the usual reading for a 22-year-old art student.

'This is my workshop,' he said, 'it doubles as a recording studio and drawing space. Only a privileged few are allowed in. There are fans out there who would give their virginity just to get through that door.'

'You're safe then. I lost my virginity years ago,' I joked.

'Thank fucking Christ for that.' Gareth reached for the copy of *A Season in Hell*. 'This is what I think you're after.' Between the pages was a photocopy of the drawing of the astrarium he'd made for Isabella. 'She showed you this?'

'Yes, the night before she ...' I faltered, unable to say the words.

Gareth put his hand on my shoulder, a brief reassurance.

'I just need to know whether she explained the symbols at the bottom?' he asked.

'She told me she was going to tell me when she had the actual astrarium in her hands, but I know you'd worked on the cipher together.'

Gareth grinned. 'I was always good at puzzles, remember?'

He ran his finger over the letters almost as if they were Braille, then picked up the paper and folded it carefully so the symbols lined up against each other. 'I'd been staring at it for hours. There was something about the symmetry or lack of it that kept annoying me.'

He held up the paper. The way he'd folded it made it apparent that the symbols were actually halves of whole symbols or hieroglyphs; and once each symbol sat against its opposite, eight letters became four. He pointed to the four new hieroglyphs.

'They're basic Egyptian hieroglyphs you can look up in any library: Where/Place, Sun/Ra, Never/Endless, Sets/Finishes. The translation is "Where the sun never sets" or, as Isabella put it, literally: "When the sun floats forever". At first we thought it must mean when time stands still, you know — a moment frozen in time. We spent hours before you guys left for Alex trying to understand the context — what such a phrase might be doing on an astrolabe, a time calculator. Then weeks later, it came to me. I was on a bender — I'd been up for days. Anyway, in the middle of the night I had this epiphany — it was just a couple of weeks before Isabella drowned. I booked a call through to her immediately and asked her, "What if 'Where the sun floats forever' means the end of time or, in human terms, immortality, the end of death?" There was a long silence and then she said quietly, "My God, Gareth, you've solved it. Ten years of searching and you've given me the key." I'll never forget her voice.'

'Isabella was always a little dramatic.'

'Look, it's an ancient riddle, some kind of metaphor for eternal afterlife, right? But now we'll never know, will we?'

I avoided his gaze, anxious that he'd guess the astrarium had been found, even that I had it in my possession. He looked back at the photocopy.

'There's something else — I only worked it out in the last few days. I think the way the cipher's constructed is symbolic in itself. Two halves that mean nothing until they're put together. I reckon that the astrarium, if Isabella had ever found it, would have been incomplete. It needs something else — its other half — to be activated. Two halves making a whole — it's almost like a love story. There you are, that's Gareth the drug-fucked Romantic's version.'

I looked back at the hieroglyphs, trying to cover my amazement. Gareth had intuitively understood the need for the Was, the key to the device.

Reaching out, I put my hand on his shoulder. 'You're to tell no one about the hieroglyphs or their meaning, understand? This is important — important for me, important for Isabella. You're to destroy the drawing and forget about the whole thing. Promise?'

He nodded solemnly.

'And I want you to come and stay with me,' I continued, determined to persuade him while he was vulnerable. 'I'm only here for a couple of weeks, but it'll give you a chance to get clean. And, frankly, I could do with the company.'

But Gareth was already backing away. 'I can't do that — I have art school, gigs, it's impossible ...'

'Please?'

'No, Oliver.' His voice had dipped into sullen aggression and I knew there was no point in arguing.

'Then at least ring me every day to let me know you're okay?'

'That I can do.'

He pulled his lighter out of his trouser pocket and lit the corner of the photocopy, watching the paper curl and turn to ash.

'Goodbye, oh sister mine,' he whispered.

# 19

That night, too drunk and jet-lagged to make my way home, I slept in Gareth's bed. He'd gone to stay at Zoë's place. I collapsed onto the sheets beneath an old quilt I recognised from my childhood. With my head buried in a pillow that smelled of patchouli oil and stale sweat, I fell instantly asleep.

Isabella sat on the concrete pavement, black hair spilling over olive skin, dressed in the embroidered dress she'd married me in. Looking up at me, she smiled then threw two small grey stones onto the concrete as if she were playing jacks. As they hit the concrete, the stones began to spin; balanced on their ends, they turned faster and faster, like two magnets spinning around each other.

I awoke not knowing where I was, the angled walls of the darkened bedroom completely alien to me. I stared up at the ceiling covered with glowing fluorescent stars and planets. As I watched they dissolved into a greenish fiery loop, travelling faster and faster until they lifted away from the ceiling and swooped towards me in the shape of a body in flight.

I woke again, this time for real, drenched in sweat, dehydrated, the beginnings of a hangover pounding my temples.

* * *

When I got back to my building, it was early morning and a box marked 'Private Air Delivery' was sitting inside the front door. I instantly recognised the insignia of Bill Anderson's company, Runaway Wells, and my own scrawled handwriting. As if propelled by my nightmare the astrarium had arrived.

Set on the Formica kitchen table, the mechanism looked as if it were from another world entirely. I sat down at the table, part of me hoping the jumble of cogs might have assembled themselves into working order during the journey, but it continued to sit there motionless.

The outer bronze dial etched with the Babylonian symbols for the five major planets glinted dully under the light. The middle dial, made of a silver-like metal, was etched with more recognisable Greek zodiac symbols — the twins, the archer, Taurus the bull — along with the crocodile and the ibis. The smallest dial, made of a gold alloy, was etched with Egyptian hieroglyphs and seemed to contain the centre of the mystery.

I peered through the small opening at the base of the main shaft around which the cogs turned. Hidden in the middle of the mechanism were two magnets facing each other — small grey disks that looked like stones; a little like the pebbles in my nightmare. They appeared to be waiting — to be set spinning?

If I found the key to activate the mechanism, would that put Isabella's spirit to rest? Was it possible, in some abstract, esoteric way she, herself had ended up living out the prediction of the cipher, hovering in a halfway world — a dimension where the Sun never sets — a trapped soul?

Through the thin wall, the abrupt ringing of my neighbour's alarm clock made me jump. I was being ridiculous, I told myself; the nightmare meant nothing. Still, the vividness of it haunted me.

I reached for the telephone and called the operator to get the number of the British Museum.

\* \* \*

The sarcophagus stood in an alcove in the large hall. Hieroglyphs encircled it, describing the life of Nectanebo II — his military conquests, his wives, his palaces and wealth. They also narrated the journey he would take in the afterlife, even though the sarcophagus had never actually fulfilled its function.

I was acutely aware of the astrarium in the rucksack on my back as I walked slowly around the granite coffin studying the hieroglyphs. I stopped at a small doorway etched into the side — the gateway for the Pharaoh's Ba. What had happened to Nectanebo II? Had he died in some obscure corner of Africa? Or had he ended up as an official in some foreign court, living under a secret identity?

The desire to reach out and run my fingers across the hieroglyphs was overwhelming; as if by touching the gateway I would be able to tell where the Pharaoh's restless Ba still hovered — Greece? Iran? Egypt? If I lifted out the astrarium and held it up against the tomb, would there be some kind of synchronicity between the two?

I scanned the display hall — the security guard had turned his back. Quickly I reached out and stroked the carved surface, the narrative whispering out from under my fingertips.

'Wonderful, isn't it?'

Snatching my hand back, I swung around. A stocky man in his late forties, a large band of eczema covering his forehead, stood before me. Despite his naked pate, he sported sideburns that ran thick and black down each cheek. He was dressed in maroon corduroy trousers and an orange shirt, giving the impression that he was compensating for his unprepossessing physical appearance.

'Don't look so worried,' he said, 'people touch it all the time, they can't help themselves. It's compulsive — subconsciously we're all searching for a gateway into the afterworld.'

He gave a bark of a laugh riddled with irony, then held out his hand. I shook it tentatively.

'Hugh Wollington. You must be Oliver Warnock.'

'I am. Thanks for making the time to meet me.'

'My pleasure. Besides, it's flattering to be sought out. I don't get that many enquiries — my area of Egyptology is rather specialised.'

I turned back to the tomb. 'So tell me, is it true no one knows where Nectanebo II is buried?'

'He fled Egypt, abandoning his post so to speak—'

'After retreating to Memphis ...'

'You do know your stuff.' He began pointing out the various inscriptions. 'Here the scribes have written how the Pharaoh was known as the Great Magician. Nectanebo II was famous for building a record number of temples and reminding the populace of his own divinity — basically using mysticism and religion as tools for political propaganda. Irrational to our way of thinking, especially in the context of modern politics—'

'Oh, I don't know. Apparently the King of Saudi Arabia frequently consults astrologers about political decisions.'

'He does indeed. Do you know the king?'

'Not personally, but I worked on some of his oilfields.'

'Fantastic country. I was posted out there in the '50s when I was still in the army — it's a landscape that burns away all affectation. But you'd know all about that in your industry.'

'I don't know — plenty of affectation in oil.'

We both laughed again, and I warmed to his enthusiasm. It seemed to be anchored in a pragmatism that was appealing after Hermes Hemiedes' fantastical interpretation of Egyptian theology; and the fact that he was ex-army was reassuring — it grounded him somehow.

'The challenge is to put yourself into the cultural mentality of the Ancient Egyptians,' he went on, 'virtually impossible for a Judeo-Christian Anglo-Saxon living in a modern democracy. But if you can imagine a total belief in the power of sorcery, and a regular dialogue with a whole plethora of deities one had to appease and second-guess in order to survive, then you begin to get the picture.' He pointed to a particular hieroglyph. 'This tells us that at one point Nectanebo decreed he was the living embodiment of Horus — an astute political decision, as this was a way of using the myth of Horus's defeat of Seth as an allegory for his own power over the Persians. As a marketing strategy it worked brilliantly until—'

'Until they invaded for the second time.'

'Exactly. Nothing like a second invasion to destroy one's reputation for invincibility.' We both laughed again.

'I've been fascinated by Nectanebo II since I was a student,' he said. 'It was the combination of military strategist, wizard, spiritual visionary and the puzzle of his disappearance. I was an impressionable youth, always looking for heroes, probably because I was so patently unheroic myself — anything to get out of Hendon, you see. Suburbia is a great motivator. I suppose that's why I joined the army, but you can blame Luxor for making me into an Egyptologist — seems like centuries ago now.'

His evident intelligence endeared him to me even further. I wondered if I could trust him.

As if he read my hesitation, he lowered his voice. 'I heard

about your wife, Mr Warnock. Archaeology is a small community. My deepest condolences — Isabella's death is a great loss. I met her at a conference once. She was a lovely woman, passionate about her subject. So many of us are fossilised old sticks — I mean, assembling shards of ancient pottery can be rather introspective ...'

His sincerity touched me. I glanced at the sarcophagus. The desire to take out the astrarium and place it next to the hieroglyphs was almost unbearable. I turned back to Hugh Wollington, teetering on the edge of confession. I needed his expertise desperately, and he seemed to have respected Isabella. In that second, I made a leap of faith.

'If I told you I have with me an artefact that might be Pharaonic, would you examine it for me?' My words spilled out recklessly.

He looked startled. 'You do realise possession of such an object could be illegal?'

'I realise I'm taking a huge risk trusting you. My wife found the artefact just before she drowned.'

Hugh Wollington glanced at the rucksack. 'Please, come this way.'

He led me into a huge hall toward the colossal granite head of Amenhotep III. The beatific expression of the young Pharaoh was somewhat ruined by the fact that he was missing most of his chin and the royal false beard that was an indication of his deity-like status. Had the false beard been hacked off by early Christians in an attack on the old pagan icons? Or had the rough handling of irreverent English sailors destroyed it during transportation on some nineteenth-century sailing ship? Either way the young Pharaoh now suffered the indignity of gazing into infinity missing half his face. Taking me by the elbow Hugh Wollington guided me around the statue.

There was a discreet door set into the wall behind it.

As we stepped through, the lofty ambience of the museum was transformed into the musty neglect of the civil service. Here was the private face of the institution, a labyrinth in which historians made fetishes of their particular domain — Greek, Roman, Celtic — absorbed in their individual worlds, like fishermen throwing out their nets and painstakingly hauling in each forgotten clue. Several small offices led off the passage, some cell-like rooms were visible through glass windows — their occupants bent over lamplit desks busy categorising and assembling new exhibits, restoring the old, casting moulds from the broken — an ant's colony of activity.

We arrived at a door painted hospital green and embellished with a small brass plaque bearing the legend *H W Wollington*.

'The W stands for Winston in case you're wondering. My mother was a huge fan,' Wollington remarked cheerfully as he pulled out a key attached to a chain from a waistcoat pocket. 'Welcome to the inner sanctum — beyond the yellow brick road.' He ushered me in.

The strong odour of preserving fluids assaulted my nose immediately. I recognised the smell from the laboratories Isabella had taken me to: acids to eat away layers of calcification — desalination chemicals. I unpacked the astrarium then placed it on the desk where it sat glinting under the lamplight. Wollington inhaled sharply — almost in wonder, then sighed.

'Fascinating.' Holding up a magnifying glass, he bent over the device. 'The first thing I notice is a cartouche — the royal insignia. The distinctive ostrich feather motif suggests the astrarium belonged to Nectanebo II, a mechanical ephemeris to navigate destiny might be a better way of defining the device. Of course, adding a cartouche is common practice in the attempt to authenticate fake antiquities. In truth, the notion that a sophisticated object such as an astrarium existed in Pharaonic times is highly unlikely. Egyptian astrology was considered a sacred science to be kept out of the hands of the uninitiated, which means that most of what we know of it today is only surmised — educated guesses based on the belief systems of contemporary cultures. Unfortunately, we have no other points of reference.'

'So I'm discovering when it comes to my own ability to suspend disbelief,' I joked.

'Easier for some than others; it really depends on your own spirituality. But you must remember, Nectanebo II absolutely believed in his own mystical powers, as did his followers. In fact, in his own time and in the generations to come, he was considered one of the greatest sorcerers and astrologers ever to have existed. Of course, his mysterious disappearance only added fuel to the myth. Some say he still lives to this day.'

I was shocked to see not a trace of irony on his face.

He smiled and went on: 'If the myth of immortality is to be believed. It is extraordinary what lengths humanity will go to in the search for eternal life. There was a huge export industry in mummies between the twelfth and seventeenth centuries — Europeans believed that drinking a concoction that contained powdered mummy would make them live longer. It proved such a profitable export, the Egyptians resorted to sending over far more recent desiccated corpses.' He smiled ghoulishly. 'Even now, American tourists spend large amounts of money bribing tomb guards to allow them to sleep overnight in the pyramids in the belief that somehow this might extend their lives. The astrarium, a machine that could control one's destiny, may also have been assumed to confer immortality — such an idea would certainly have seemed reasonable in Ancient Egypt.'

I sensed a change in his attitude towards me — a definite coolness underpinned by something else: a concealed arrogance.

'I have heard of the existence of the astrarium before,' he went on. 'It has become something of a holy grail amongst certain archaeologists, not only your wife.'

He walked over to a filing cabinet and pulled out a facsimile document. 'This letter, dated 1777, was sent from Alexandria by Sonnini de Manoncour to Napoleon. It details how although he failed to find Nectanebo's instrument of prediction, he had the good fortune to find a section of an inscribed stone tableau which he was convinced was of great religious and magical value. As you can see, the letter was bequeathed to the British Museum by the Coptic Egyptologist and mystic Ahmos Khafre.'

I realised this was a copy of the very letter Isabella had seen all those years ago in Goa. Fascinated, I tried to read the ornate archaic French script.

'So Ahmos Khafre was reputable?' I asked.

'As an Egyptologist, his reputation was impeccable. As for his other beliefs, I'm not one to pass judgement. But the letter has been proved authentic.'

'How did the museum get hold of it?'

'Khafre bequeathed all of his possessions and writings to us — some were more useful than others. Interestingly, he told the museum exactly when to expect them. He predicted the date of his death, you see — to the hour. Amazing.'

He pulled on white cotton gloves and lifted the astrarium to examine the underside. 'Of course, it's always amusing to see how these fakes work.'

'Fake?'

'Yes, I'm sorry to tell you this is probably a folly — possibly seventeenth century. Most likely constructed for an alchemist as part of his collection of tricks to convince prospective clients. Any object that could be associated with Nectanebo II, the great Egyptian magician Pharaoh, would be marvellous for setting the scene.'

I stared at him. I knew he was lying; the question was why.

'I tell you, I was there when my wife excavated it from the sea floor,' it was hard to disguise my anger at his superciliousness.

'I'm sorry to disappoint you. I didn't say it wasn't an expensive folly. Besides, as I said before, it is ridiculous to think that something of the Pharaonic period, and as complex as this, would be in such pristine condition.'

His tone of voice had become distinctly patronising, further convincing me the artefact was genuine. So he wanted the astrarium as well. But why the clumsy attempt at deception? Even if he managed to persuade me of its worthlessness, surely he couldn't believe I'd leave it with him?

'As a geophysicist, I can tell you such preservation is rare but not unheard of,' I said. 'Sometimes the mud on the ocean floor is so dense, oxygen can't permeate it. It also appears that the mechanism might have originally been preserved in oil, which would have created a watertight seal.'

I'd raised my voice, and through the glass partition I could see other museum officials looking up from their desks.

'Mr Warnock, you are clutching at straws,' Wollington said. 'Naturally I understand you are upset given the circumstances of its discovery.'

His earlier wry humour appeared extremely disingenuous now.

'Well, if it's a worthless fake, I'll just take it home,' I said.

'Actually, as I warned you earlier, there are protocols to be observed, even for fakes.'

His whole tone had changed and I caught a glimpse of the soldier beneath the academic — a quiet but palpable violence. I was momentarily intimidated. Then, just as quickly, he reverted to a neutral friendliness.

'Look, it won't take long. If you don't mind waiting here … ?'

Reluctantly, I sat down. Perhaps I was being paranoid. I watched through the glass partition as he entered the adjoining office and approached an officious-looking colleague. They exchanged a few words then looked at the partition. Their gazes didn't connect with mine and I guessed it must be one-way glass. They appeared to be arguing. The older man reached for the phone but Wollington grabbed his wrist, preventing him from picking up the receiver.

Wollington's shirt sleeve rode up, revealing a tattoo. Although it was hard to be sure from that distance, I thought I recognised the distinctive shape of a Ba, a similiar tattoo to Isabella's. The unexpected congruence of images hit me with a jolt.

The sound of a door slamming nearby galvanised me into action. I put the astrarium back into my rucksack and left the office as fast as I could without attracting attention.

\* \* \*

The museum's entrance hall was milling with tourists. I sauntered towards the exit door with the rucksack over my shoulder. As I passed the reception desk, a phone rang. The young girl answering it didn't even bother to look up. I must have been ten feet from the revolving glass doors when she called over the security guard. Without looking back, I exited then immediately hailed a taxi.

As the cab swung around the corner, I caught sight of the security guard racing out of the building. I ducked down in my seat.

# 20

It was hard to sleep that night — half of me was afraid I might have another visitation from Isabella, while the other half anticipated a raid from the British authorities or whoever Hugh and his cohorts were. At about five in the morning I abandoned the bed and tried to distract myself with some research. While I was reaching up to a top shelf for a box file, a book dislodged from a lower shelf and fell onto the carpet. It was a collection of English poetry. As I picked it up, an inscription on the inside cover caught my eye: *For Isabella — all my love, Enrico Silvio, Oxford 1970.*

Slipped between the pages was an old black-and-white photograph. A group of people stood poised in front of an archaeological dig, a strange formality to the composition, as if they were members of a travelling group or club. In the front row, crouching down and smiling into the camera, was a very young Isabella. Her hand rested on the knee of the woman seated behind her — Amelia Lynhurst. To my surprise she had once been quite attractive. Seated next to her was Giovanni Brambilla, Isabella's grandfather — I recognised him from the family photographs. He wore a safari suit and an embroidered fez, and looked authoritarian even in his eighties, his deep-set eyes and heavy eyebrows scowling at the camera. Standing behind him was an effeminate-looking man with long hair; he stood in profile — a younger Hermes Hemiedes. On his other side stood a vaguely familiar figure, a man in his late thirties with a mane of unruly black hair and a piercing gaze. He wore a British army uniform and to my amazement I recognised the facial features despite the unfamiliar framing of hair — Hugh Wollington, the Egyptologist at the British Museum. So he had known Isabella, but not from some conference.

On the back of the photograph were inscribed the words:

*Behbeit el-Hagar, 1965.*
*The ceremony of innocence is drowned;*
*The best lack all conviction, while the worst*
*Are full of passionate intensity.*

The lines of poetry resonated. I glanced at the book the photograph had been hidden in — was there any connection? I searched through it and found the three lines in Yeats's poem 'The Second Coming':

*Turning and turning in the widening gyre*
*The falcon cannot hear the falconer;*
*Things fall apart; the centre cannot hold;*
*Mere anarchy is loosed upon the world,*
*The blood-dimmed tide is loosed, and everywhere*
*The ceremony of innocence is drowned;*
*The best lack all conviction, while the worst*
*Are full of passionate intensity.*
*Surely some revelation is at hand;*
*Surely the Second Coming is at hand.*

> *The Second Coming! Hardly are those words out*
> *When a vast image out of Spiritus Mundi*
> *Troubles my sight: somewhere in the sands of the desert*
> *A shape with lion body and the head of a man,*
> *A gaze blank and pitiless as the sun,*
> *Is moving its slow thighs, while all about it*
> *Reel shadows of the indignant desert birds.*
> *The darkness drops again; but now I know*
> *That twenty centuries of stony sleep*
> *Were vexed to nightmare by a rocking cradle,*
> *And what rough beast, its hour come round at last,*
> *Slouches towards Bethlehem to be born?*

What had the group been excavating? I remembered Hermes telling me how Behbeit el-Hagar was an important site in relation to the last days of the Pharaohs. Was it linked to the astrarium in some way? And why had Hugh Wollington lied to me?

I touched the inscription on the inside cover, the slight indentation unfurling a whole scenario in my imagination. An affair, lovemaking, that lay embedded in my wife's past, secret, unshared; the shadowy figure of a man she'd never told me about. Each new disclosure about Isabella's past separated us further. How well had I really known her? Was the woman I'd loved an artifice? A composite of all that I'd wanted her to be rather than what she actually was? The idea was too distressing to dwell on. I needed to believe in us, in the authenticity of the marriage — there was little else left.

I glanced back at the name, racking my memory. Enrico Silvio ... I'd never heard it before. I knew the Yeats poem was about the end of Christianity, but the imagery reverberated nevertheless — the circling falcon that had lost its master, the sphinx galvanised into a slow awakening by the possibility of the end of the known world, the crowing of the desert birds flying wildly around the blinking eyes of the colossus; it was an allegory that felt uncomfortably relevant to my own disintegrating world.

I looked around the room. Hanging on a hook on the back of the door was a collection of old handbags Isabella was always promising to throw out. There was a beaded shoulder bag I remembered her wearing when we were courting — I knew she'd had it since her student days. The inside smelled musty and the torn silk lining was stained with perfume, lipstick and crumbs of what I suspected might have been hashish. I turned the bag inside out. I was in luck. Slipped between the lining and the bag itself was an address book. I opened it; the handwriting — a simpler, more looped version of the script I'd known — made my heart lurch in sudden sorrow. I sat down and tentatively turned to the letter 'S'. It was just a hunch, an instinct I wasn't sure I wanted to play out. But there it was: 'ES' followed by an Oxford phone number.

I knew it was a long shot, the number must have been over five years old, but it was worth a gamble. I glanced at my watch — it was already nine in the morning and light now filled the living room. I reached for the phone and dialled the number. It rang for ages. I was just about to give up when a woman answered; older, foreign. In a curt voice she told me that Enrico was currently in hospital but was due home later that day.

I gave her my name and number and asked her to tell him I was the widower of Isabella Brambilla. Widower. The word felt like a tragedy that had befallen someone else. The woman's voice tightened at the mention of Isabella's name, but perhaps I was imagining it.

I put down the receiver, suddenly wanting to escape the history of my marriage, the claustrophobic flat, London itself and my growing sense of being watched.

The ringing of the phone startled me.

'Hello?'

'Hi, Oliver. Gareth here ... just checking in like I promised.'

My brother's voice sounded slightly slurred and I wondered whether he'd slept at all since the gig.

'How are you?' I asked. 'Have you been home yet?'

'Well I am now. Did you get back to West Hampstead okay?'

'Kind of, but are you taking care of yourself?'

'Didn't I say I would?'

His voice was sullen, hostile; I had to bring him back.

'I'm going home later, to see Da. Any messages?'

'Yeah, tell him I'm not dying. Then the old bastard might get off my back.'

There was a click, then the dial tone. He'd put the phone down but the genetic thread between us was still there, vibrating like a lightly plucked guitar string.

\* \* \*

Later that morning, the astrarium packed in my rucksack, I caught a train to my father's village. The station was exactly as I remembered it — the painted sign hanging over the platform, the wooden tubs of roses at each end. The only new additions were a Cadbury's chocolate vending machine placed discreetly next to the ticket office and a brand-new telephone booth installed next to the toilets. Mr Wilcott, the stationmaster, who I remembered as a youthful man in his forties, was now in his sixties. He stood at one end of the platform, a tall, hunched over individual with a limp from a wound he'd received in the Second World War — a story he used to regale us schoolboys with. After whistling to signal the train's departure, he limped down the platform towards me.

'Oliver, is that you?'

'The one and same, Mr Wilcott.'

'I'm sorry about your wife, lad. I only met her the once but she were a lovely lass.'

The familiarity of his voice hauled me back into safer times, to the never-changing landscape of my childhood. As I listened to his thick northern accent and the small talk about nothing and everything, I suddenly realised how much I missed the unquestioning acceptance, the anchoring, of village life.

'Did Da tell you?' I asked.

'Oh aye, he were very upset, you know. He'll be glad to see you. With us long?'

'Just the night, I'm afraid.'

'Shame. Your da's been ever so lonely since your mother passed. Stay longer, surely it'll do you good to see a few old faces?'

'I'd like to but I can't afford the time.'

'In that case, I'll see you off tomorrow — the 10.45 is it?'

'Aye.'

I walked down the stairs and onto the street, the rucksack hoisted over my shoulder. I'd planned to walk to my father's house through the village — the same route I'd taken every day to and from school decades before. But now I didn't feel like meeting anyone else; I decided to cut through the small field that led onto the row of terraces where my father lived.

The meadow was filled with buttercups and daisies whose tiny stems bent with each gust of wind coming off the Fens. There was the faint smell of cow manure and the tang of wet peat. This had been one of the places where I'd done my dreaming as a child, staring up at the sky and imagining each cloud was a magic carpet on which I could escape — to exotic places, to new faces and landscapes. I stood, breathing in deeply, strongly tempted to lie down in the grass in the hope that time would reel back and I'd stand up as a ten year old. Cleanly. Innocently. Instead, I hoisted the astrarium back over my shoulder and kept walking.

\* \* \*

My father stood waiting at the door of the small terrace house, his frame, once angular and impressive in its height, buckled with gravity, like an ancient tree. It was a shock seeing him so aged, and I realised it must have been several years since I'd visited.

The house was part of an estate built for miners in the 1920s — a harsh grid of narrow streets and small, terraced, architecturally monotonous red-brick houses. The railway line ran behind the terrace my father was in, and alongside it stood a neat patchwork of allotment gardens. The one that belonged to my father was filled with marrows, tomatoes, strawberries and the occasional rose bush. This small oblong of territory was his pride and joy. It was where he'd disappear to for hours after church on Sundays. It was also a place we, his sons, were excluded from. Even now it was impossible to look at the allotment without feeling resentful.

The house had two bedrooms upstairs, a front room with a fireplace and a kitchen at the back. There was an outside toilet at the end of the concrete yard; no bathroom, no place to wash except for the kitchen sink. We'd bathed in front of the fire in an old tin bath every Sunday night. Da first, then my mother, then myself, and finally Gareth. I would watch my father from the other side of the fireplace, his long skinny back mottled with the blue-black of coal dust, the mystery of his cock and balls a swinging shadow as he gingerly folded himself into the short tub. This rebirth of his, this transformation from black-faced Cyclops with the miner's lamp on his forehead to mere mortal both fascinated and appalled me. I too wanted to go down into the earth, but I didn't want it to poison me.

In the early 1960s, at the end of my first year as a successful consultant, I'd offered to pay for an extension to house a bathroom. My father had been furious. 'I'll not take charity from me own son,' he'd told my mother. It had been a year until he'd agreed to talk to me again. But that was my father — as proud and truculent as the landscape he'd grown up in.

'I thought you'd come in one of your fancy cars,' he barked awkwardly from the door. I noticed he was clutching a walking stick, his huge bluish knuckles knotted over the wood. He was also wearing a woman's cardigan, the top pearl button fastened tight, the pale pink wool stretched over his vest. I didn't dare ask where it was from.

'I took the train,' I said, 'the car's still garaged, I haven't had a chance since I got back to collect it.'

He stared at me, his deep-set eyes searching my face. His skin was hollowed under the cheekbones, the wrinkles a topography of disappointment and anger. Today, though, the eyes were kind.

'I've had tea on the table for over an hour,' he said. 'But I can put the kettle on again.'

'That'll be nice.'

Without touching, we both entered the house.

Later that night, we sat in the tiny front room watching an episode of *The Benny Hill Show* — one of my father's few indulgences — on the small black-and-white television I'd bought my parents five Christmases before, mainly to entertain my then invalided mother. The silence between us was deafening. I'd often suspected this had been one of the many reasons I'd married Isabella — her voice had always run like a stream over my own impenetrable silences. In four hours, my father still hadn't mentioned her death. We'd talked about Gareth's health, the weather, the latest disputes the miners' union was having with management, Harold Wilson, Enoch Powell, the failing train services and the state of my father's meticulously maintained allotment. We circled around the drowning like crows over a recently ploughed field.

*The Benny Hill Show* finished with the rotund comedian chasing a buxom, pig-tailed blonde across the screen and my father, who still believed that using the television wore it out, got up to switch it off. On the way back to his armchair, he opened the sideboard drawer where he'd always kept a tin of sherbet lemons. Pulling it out with a rattle, he offered me one.

'So how's Gareth really?' he said.

'Surviving.'

'Well, that's a comfort. How's that musical group of his?'

'I saw them play. They were good, Da. You wouldn't have recognised him. I asked him to stay with me — he refused, but he promised to ring in every day. I think he'll pull through; it's a stage he's going through.'

There was a silence in which I supposed my father was trying to imagine the scene. Then, abruptly, he said, 'I've never said this, but I appreciate you looking out for him. He were always his mother's son, coming so late in the marriage, like. I know that now. Words don't come easily between us, not like me and you …'

I smiled, saddened that my father's perception of our communication could be so different from my own.

'But he's close to you,' he went on. 'You'll take care of him, you know, when …'

'Aye, you'll have no worries there, Da.'

We both sucked noisily on our sherbet lemons. The fire spat a sudden ember.

'In case you're wondering, the cardigan was your mother's,' he said. 'Silly really, but wearing it comforts me. I suppose it still smells of her.'

'You don't have to explain.'

'But I do.'

He leaned across and poked at the few burning coals in the fireplace, as if he were too embarrassed to look at me.

'What's happened is unnatural, son. Isabella were a young girl, she weren't meant to die like that. Promise me you'll not end up rattling about like your old da, not knowing whether it's Sunday or Thursday. Worse still, not caring. It's no way for a man to live.'

He sat back in his armchair, as if exhausted by the effort of uttering so many words at once. To my great shame I was speechless. I couldn't remember him ever speaking so intimately to me.

'She was very fond of you, you know that, don't you, Da?'

'Aye.' He sighed, a long and hollow sound that seemed to contain all the injustices of the world and, worse, his beaten-down resignation to them. He coughed, as if to change the subject, and sat forward. 'You know, I decided to finish that project your mother started just before she died. You remember how she'd begun to research her family tree — the Irish side, the McDermotts?'

'Oh aye.' Hypnotised by the flickering flames of the fire, I was almost asleep, more relaxed than I had been in weeks.

'I'd always thought her father's family were a bunch of misplaced Irish peasants who'd ended up on the wrong side of the sea, but would you believe I discovered a famous ancestor — your great-great-grandfather, Connor McDermott. He was a diviner, quite renowned in some parts. Seems he had a gift for finding bore water. I even found something about a trip he took to southern Italy in 1790 — apparently he was successful in breaking a drought there. Maybe that's where you get it from, son.'

I sat up, interested. 'He actually had the ability to sense where to dig?'

'Oh aye. I even wrote to the Dublin library and got posted a whole file of clippings on it, lad. One newspaper said he talked about being able to hear where the earth sang. But the silly bugger got it wrong once and that was the end of that. Be careful, lad — one mistake is all it takes. But then, who knows, he could have been a trickster all along. A chancer on the make.'

'Could be,' I said.

Sitting there with the fire warming my knees I suddenly remembered a conversation I'd had with Isabella a few years before, after she'd seen me at work on an oilfield in Italy, in the southern Apennines. Her face lit with passion, she'd called me a diviner, told me I had a gift and that I was wasting it. Her conviction had disturbed me. Was it a reaction to my mother's blind, passive faith that had frustrated me so much as a child, or had I been unconsciously frightened of something else? In any case, Isabella must have felt it as yet another occasion when I'd trivialised her beliefs. Little surprise she'd chosen to confide in Gareth and not myself. Why had I always avoided the issue of her mysticism — was it because I sensed something about my own inherent abilities? Now there was the suggestion my divining skill had been inherited, carried in the bloodline and re-emerging like a seam of rock suddenly pushed back to the surface.

My father had lapsed into another long silence and I could feel the old sense of suffocation and ennui rising up in me; the same restlessness that had propelled me out of the village as a teenager. I didn't belong then, and I knew I didn't belong now. Secretly thankful I was leaving in the morning, I wished the old man goodnight.

I was sleeping in the second bedroom, Gareth's room once I'd left home. It seemed to be still waiting for a thirteen-year-old boy, with its ancient *Beano* comics, the dusty model aeroplanes hanging from the lamp, a Boy Scouts' flag pinned over the mantelpiece. Mixed in with these were remnants of adolescence — a poster of the band Queen, an old copy of *Rolling Stone* magazine with Marc Bolan glaring out from the cover on the side table. Sitting on the desk, still in the rucksack, was the astrarium — my talisman of Egypt.

Pulling back the sheets, I squeezed into the single bed.

## 21

The next morning, I tried to ring my brother at the squat. I woke Dennis who informed me that he'd only seen Gareth for a couple of hours in the past two days. This wasn't comforting.

The train back to London was strangely empty, and as we drew into Victoria Station the platform was hung with Union Jacks and signs announcing the Queen's Silver Jubilee. I'd forgotten that it was the seventh of June. By the time I got back to my flat London was in full celebration. The road was blocked off and the cul-de-sac itself had been transformed.

In the centre of the street, under a canopy, stood a long table covered in cakes, sandwiches, jellies and other manifestations of English home cooking. Small stalls selling a plethora of souvenirs flanked the display. There were china mugs printed with pictures of the royal family, a teacup and saucer with the Queen's face smiling up from the bottom, Silver Jubilee spoons, butter knives, postage stamps and souvenir programs.

A reggae band playing Bob Marley's 'No Woman No Cry' stood at one end of the street, while at the other end an amateur string quartet played Elgar. Banners strung overhead proclaimed the twenty-five years of the Queen's reign, and Union Jack flags hung out of various windows, fluttering like garish laundry. Neighbours, friends and families milled excitedly around the tables.

Several food stalls were set up along the kerb, one selling West Indian cuisine — fried plantains, curried goat and rice; another with Indian curries and samosas. Another stall advertised English pork sausages, pickled eggs and jellied eels. The air was filled with a dissonance of smells — curry, hot chips, incense and the occasional whiff of burning toffee.

Two Rastafarians with waist-length dreadlocks chatted to a middle-aged couple dressed as a cockney pearly king and queen, their button-covered jackets shimmering in the sunshine. There was a buxom brunette dressed as Britannia sitting on a throne, sceptre in hand, as several drunken husbands posed to have their photograph taken with her. One old man had dressed his rather plump white British bulldog in a tailored Union Jack jacket.

Families danced together on the tarmac: waltzing to the violins or bopping to the reggae band. Children darted among the intoxicated adults, chasing each other and screeching with excitement. There was something gloriously pagan and uplifting about the whole event and, momentarily, I forgot the ordeals of the past two months. After grabbing a sandwich, I half-danced and half-pushed my way towards my front door, almost unrecognisable under the streamers and balloons adorning it.

I felt a tug on my jacket. Stanley stared up at me solemnly, then, putting two fingers into his mouth, gave an ear-splitting whistle. Alfred headed towards us from the other side of the road, pulling a thin older man, Mediterranean in appearance, by the hand.

Stanley's eyes narrowed accusingly. 'It's an Italian gentleman. He's looking for yer. Probably 'cause he knows you murdered Issy.' His fist tightened around the sleeve of my jacket.

I crouched down so I was at eye level with the eight year old. 'Stanley, Isabella died in a very sad accident—' I started, but was interrupted by a tap on my shoulder.

'Mr Warnock?'

The stranger stood in front of me, awkwardly holding out his hand for me to shake — to the amazement of the watching twins who were obviously expecting some kind of citizen's arrest. The man's face was heavy in the jowls and his mouth had a sensual fullness. He looked like an ageing voluptuary. I guessed he was in his late fifties, but his skin tone was an unhealthy grey and, on closer inspection, his face was etched with a web of fine lines, as if he'd recently suffered some great tragedy.

'My name is Professor Enrico Silvio,' he said in an Italian accent. 'I was your wife's tutor at Lady Margaret's Hall, Oxford.'

\* \* \*

I closed the window and the sound of the steel drums and bass guitar outside diminished. Professor Silvio stood scanning the living room as if trying to glean the history of my marriage from the surrounding furniture and photographs. Sensing my gaze, he swung back to me.

'It was kind of you to invite me into your apartment, Mr Warnock.'

'I know an intelligent face when I see one and in any case, it was I who called you initially,' I replied.

'And here I am. Tell me, what else do you see in my face, Mr Warnock?' His broad features gleamed with a resigned amusement.

'Honesty. Besides, if you were going to rob or attack me you would have done it by now.'

'Attack you? Why should I attack you? Are you a man with many enemies?'

'I seem to have acquired a few lately,' I said wryly. 'I'm sorry if I've offended you. I work in the oil business. Isabella's world is sometimes quite alien to me, alien and bewildering.'

'I can imagine.' He sighed and fragility shone out again through the stretched, pale skin. 'I am dying, Mr Warnock, that is what you have seen in my face. Honesty is a characteristic I have developed only later in life. I have been waiting for your call for years. I've always wondered what type of man Isabella might have married.' He moved to a side table and picked up a framed photograph of Isabella. 'I thought maybe an artist, or some kind of left-wing revolutionary, but never a businessman. She was looking for a zealot, I was convinced of it.' He put the photograph back on the table.

'It sounds as if you knew her well,' I said.

My statement seemed to agitate him. He began to move around the room restlessly.

'Mr Warnock, one of the benefits of confronting one's mortality is a sudden appreciation of the brevity of life. I have no time left for subtlety or nuance. As a dying man I must speak directly.'

'You and Isabella had an affair?'

A twitch ran like quicksilver over one cheek. He paused, remembrance clouding his eyes.

'Yes, we were lovers, but to call it an affair would be to trivialise our relationship.' He dropped his head in his hands, then swept his fingers through his hair: the habitual gesture of a once-handsome man. 'You must understand that I am not proud of how I was at that time of my life. I was ambitious, but I had traded too long on the originality of the thesis that had made me famous. Isabella was remarkably lateral in her thinking, even at that age. Her cultural perspective gave her a unique angle on archaeology. For her it was a living subject; it was in her blood. She came to me with the story of this remarkable device she was going to base her doctorate on. She trusted me, but I betrayed her. Yet you have to believe I loved her.'

He paused, as if wanting my permission to continue. I waved my hand — a small conciliatory gesture implying an emotion I didn't feel.

'I told Isabella that her thesis sounded too improbable, and that if she continued with this subject she risked not being taken seriously. I genuinely wanted to protect her, but I wasn't entirely honest. I had come across some evidence of the astrarium myself, many years before. While researching in the Louvre, I discovered a small stone naos — a box-like shrine — that dated from the late Thirtieth Dynasty and had been found at Hierakonpolis. It was covered in hieroglyphs that no one had yet translated. It appeared to be a prayer to Isis asking for her blessing for a skybox made for the great Pharaoh Nectanebo II. I believed the device Isabella was researching might have been the skybox referred to.'

'Quite possibly,' I said. 'Isabella herself had several pieces of research referring to the astrarium as a skybox — though I don't understand why she maintained it was Ptolemaic.'

'She might have told you that, but, trust me, Isabella had a strong sense of how old the astrarium might actually be. It was around this time that she started having nightmares.'

'You know about the dream?'

'I do, and I can't tell you how much I grew to hate her grandfather, a man I never even met. There is some dark history there.'

I sank into a chair, defeated by the knowledge that, again, Isabella had been unable to confide in me, her husband.

Professor Silvio sighed. 'I made Isabella my research assistant, and then I seduced her. At first it was a calculated move, but then, to my great horror, I fell in love. I promise you that part of the story was not calculated—'

'You appropriated her work and published it yourself?' I interrupted.

I didn't want to hear about the affair. His confession felt like a transgression into a past Isabella had kept secret; a decision I felt I should respect regardless of my own emotions.

But he was not to be swayed. 'I even thought of leaving my wife for her,' he went on.

Now resigned, I helped myself to a whisky, then listened as he spoke about an angrier, younger Isabella; an Isabella I had glimpsed on occasion but certainly not known.

'She embodied everything I had once aspired to — she was gifted, disciplined, she didn't care about the professional protocols, the stratagems of academia that had castrated me. Being with her broke all the rules that had crippled me over the years, all of them.'

'You stole her work?' I repeated, wanting him to at least acknowledge his treachery.

'She was a young woman and a foreigner. I didn't think the academy would take her seriously. At least, that was my excuse to myself. I didn't appropriate all of it — just the hypothesis that Nectanebo might have created a prediction myth to justify his flight from the Persians. She never forgave me.'

'So is that why you're here — for absolution? The confession of a dying man?'

'No. I need to see it with my own eyes, I need to know it exists.'

'See what?'

'Please don't be disingenuous, Mr Warnock. Two days ago I received a phone call from the British Museum. After a somewhat heated exchange I told Mr Wollington I couldn't help him with his enquiries. A day later my office was broken into but nothing was taken. I believe you have the astrarium; and, if that is the case, you are correct that you have acquired some dangerous and powerful enemies. I can help you.'

'How?'

'You know the astrarium is missing its other half, the object that will make it spring into life. Perhaps if I show you this I will convince you of my sincerity.'

He reached into his jacket pocket and pulled out an object about four inches in length, packaged in tissue. He unwrapped it to reveal a fork-like object with a finely cast stem of bronze. It had an animal carved at one end and two key-like prongs at the other. I took it from him and examined the animal: it was a falcon with a tiny human face — the minute head of a Pharaoh.

'Is this the key, the Was?'

'It is. The falcon symbolises the Ba of Nectanebo II, his soul-bird. You see, the astrarium wasn't only designed to protect the Pharaoh's living destiny; it would protect his spirit in the afterworld.'

Would it have protected Isabella's Ba too, I pondered. Then felt surprise that I'd even considered such a far-fetched notion.

'How did you find it?' I asked the professor.

'I stole it from a colleague — an English archaeologist who taught for a semester at my college. She was someone Isabella greatly admired.'

'Amelia Lynhurst?'

'It is not something I am proud of.'

'And how did Amelia come by the key?'

'On a dig some years before. She'd never made the find public.'

'Was the dig at Behbeit el-Hagar?' I asked, remembering the younger Amelia in the group photograph I'd found in Isabella's poetry book.

'So at last the mosaic is beginning to make sense, Mr Warnock.'

'But why there?'

'Behbeit el-Hagar is the birthplace of Nectanebo II — another piece of the mosaic.'

'Did Isabella know you had the key?'

He looked at me, his face drained of colour. 'It is the most appalling thing I have ever done. It was after she'd left me — I thought I could use it to bribe her to come back, but she had already met you.' He paused. 'It is guilt that brings me here. Without the key, the astrarium is nothing. I should have given it to her.'

He sank into a chair and buried his face in his hands, his scalp glimmering palely through his thinning hair. He looked completely defeated and it was hard not to pity him. I reached for the rucksack.

\* \* \*

'Wonderful, it is so sublime in its design.' Professor Silvio ran his hands lightly across the top of the mechanism. 'I never thought I would live to see it.' He leaned closer. 'You see these three disks?'

I nodded, anticipation clawing at my throat. The astrarium had begun to disturb me, and now, with the key about to activate the mechanism, its power over me felt even stronger.

The professor's trembling fingers caressed the edges of the cogs. 'These dials served to calculate the orbits of not just the

Moon and Sun but also the five planets known in those times — Mars, Mercury, Venus, Jupiter and Saturn. Those calculations were used to decide the most auspicious dates for religious festivals as well as for divining purposes. This is where the astrarium becomes an instrument of war. Quite possibly the astronomical calculations were made by Eudoxus of Cnidos, a Greek who worked with the priests of Heliopolis. He wrote a treatise on the subject, of which I published a translation.'

He peered down the shaft that formed the pivot for the cogs. 'And here is the keyhole.'

The Was slipped effortlessly into the slot. We both stood there, suspended in awe. Then, almost as if directed by the astrarium itself, I moved my hand towards the key.

The professor's gaunt fingers locked around my wrist. 'No! Don't turn it until you have heard what I have to say.'

I stepped back from the table. Night had descended and the music outside was punctuated by the distant explosion of fireworks as the Jubilee celebrations reached their climax. There was a smell of fecundity in the air — the aroma of summer that had always made me so restless as a younger man, the sense that something exciting was happening elsewhere and I was compelled to go out and find it, whatever the risk.

I glanced back at the professor. The shadows under his eyes had deepened and his skin looked even greyer, as if he had aged in the last few hours.

'I have stomach cancer,' he said, 'an advanced case. I have about two, three months, they don't know exactly. Funny, the Ancients thought the stomach was the seat of all emotion. Perhaps they were right; perhaps I am dying because I have denied my emotions for so long.'

'Give me the facts, Professor' I said coldly. 'Something the geophysicist in me can understand.'

'The facts? You have that wonderfully English capacity to make everything sound so dry.'

He pointed to the three hands, each one longer than the preceding one, that rotated across the three dials, like the hands of a clock. 'These mark three time periods — the Ancient Egyptian equivalent of day, month, year. If my translation is right, the hands are currently set at what I believe to be the date of the Battle of Actium.'

'So the astrarium did belong to Cleopatra?'

'Exactly. If you turn the key, two smaller hands will appear — one made of gold, the birth-year hand; the other made of black silver, the death-year hand.'

'The death-year hand?' I repeated, shocked by such a concept.

'If you enter your birth date into the machine, it will calculate your death date. I believe that is what Isabella had planned to do, except, of course, she wanted to try to change her death date. But there is more to this instrument. It can bend time and events to serve your desires — actual and unacknowledged — fame, fortune, even self-destruction. That makes it very powerful but also very dangerous. Because — let's be honest — how many of us know what we really want? One could describe it as a Faustian device, bringing a judgement of its own.' He smiled.

I was fascinated despite my scepticism. I just couldn't believe a navigational device, thousands of years old, could have saved my wife's life, never mind alter the outcomes of events. It had to be a metaphor — an object of wish fulfilment that thousands had imbued with their belief over centuries.

'I'm not a religious man, Professor Silvio. I believe in the Big Bang, evolution and free markets. This device is an enigma, that's obvious. For a start, parts of it are made of an alloy I've never seen before. Then there's the two magnets at its core — they're unusually powerful. Rotating magnetic fields have interesting properties, but affecting destinies? Come on. Besides, if all you've said about this machine is true, then you'd be the first to turn the key — after all, it'd stop your disease in its tracks.'

The academic smiled sadly. 'Indeed it would, but I am not afraid of dying. I am a devout Catholic: God has chosen this path for me and I must follow it. Besides, I suspect there is a twist in its promise, a sting in the scorpion's tail.'

'How do you mean?'

'Why do you think the key was separated from the machine before the Battle of Actium? I believe Cleopatra was entirely aware of the astrarium's magical powers. With one turn of the key, she could have influenced the outcome of the battle to her advantage — but she chose not to. The pivotal question is why?'

I stared at the astrarium sitting there on the table, the soft lamplight picking out the various hues of the metal. Again, I was struck by the sense that the machine appeared to be observing me as I examined it.

'The key should remain in the device but it must never be turned. You understand, Oliver?'

I nodded, not entirely convinced.

'And promise me you will hide it somewhere safe — not here in this apartment. Do not underestimate Hugh Wollington. He has powerful alliances and he is ambitious. He will do anything to achieve his goals.'

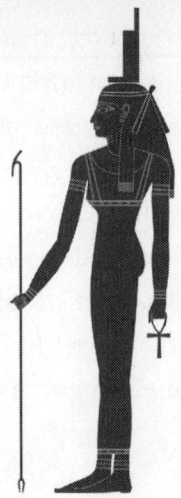

# 22

I picked up my car, garaged near the flat and drove over to Lambeth. Behind Waterloo Station was a Turkish bathhouse and gymnasium I'd frequented since my student days. Situated in a small seventeenth-century building sandwiched between two office blocks, the baths had originally been established to service gentlemen of leisure. I suspected they were now used for more clandestine encounters too, but chose to ignore the undercurrent of homosexual flirtation that occasionally drifted through the clouds of steam.

The gymnasium had the most basic of equipment — two bench presses, free weights and a couple of exercise bicycles. An autographed photograph of the English boxer Henry Cooper hung on one wall. There was also a steam room, a dry sauna and a large tiled area with plunge pools. I usually worked out then spent some time in the steam room before immersing myself in the cold plunge pool. It was a brutal regime but one I had become addicted to — it was one of the few ways I could clear my mind of the obsessive analysis that was an integral part of my personality and my job.

Now I was there with an entirely different motive. I hurried up the narrow stairs, the astrarium in a small bag tucked under my arm. There were several men in various stages of undress in the locker room. A huge West Indian gentleman, his black skin gleaming with droplets of water, was towelling his great shiny back, the rolls of flesh rippling down to his waist. Two young cab drivers, just off the nightshift, were exchanging anecdotes about dodgy customers in thick East End accents, while a sullen-looking adolescent in a pair of grubby Y-fronts sat in the corner reading a martial arts magazine with Bruce Lee glaring out from the cover. They barely looked at me as I unlocked the battered steel locker and placed the astrarium deep inside. After throwing several layers of gym clothes on top of it, I fastened the lock, stripped and then headed to the steam room.

I settled myself on a bench and stared at the pinewood panelling, thinking over the past few days. Professor Silvio's confession, which made me think I had never really known Isabella, emerged from everything else, floating around the sauna like a curling phantom of steam. The moisture condensed and ran down my forehead and a vague recollection took shape in the steam. It was about seven months ago, just before we were due to leave for Egypt. Isabella had received a letter earlier that day and I'd found her sitting at her desk staring at the scrawled Arabic. She'd looked tense. Worried that it was bad news, I'd asked if it was from her childhood friend Ashraf, who wrote regularly. But she told me it was an invitation to a conference from a society of archaeologists she used to belong to and it had surprised her — she hadn't been involved with the society for years. Trying to lighten the atmosphere, I'd flippantly asked if it was some kind of coven. To my surprise, Isabella had lost her temper. Now I wondered whether it had anything to do with the photograph taken at

Behbeit el-Hagar. A couple of months after she'd received the invitation she'd gone to a conference in Luxor. Was that the same conference Hugh Wollington had mentioned?

Exhausted, I fell into a deep sleep. I was woken by the sullen adolescent, his acne-marked face leaning over me.

'Thought we'd lost yer, guv,' he said gravely as he shook me awake. 'You should be careful. People die in the most peculiar places nowadays.'

\* \* \*

As I swung the car into my street, I saw Dennis sitting on the doorstep of my building. He was dressed in an old pinstriped suit beneath which the cuffs of pyjamas were visible. Wondering how he'd got hold of my address, I steeled myself for bad news before pulling up in front of the house.

'Something's happened—' I started, but his grim expression cut me off mid-sentence. All my anxieties about my brother's self-destructiveness shot through me.

'We've been trying to ring you for hours. We didn't know where to look for you. It's Gareth.'

'Has he overdosed?'

'It was an accident …'

'No.' The possibility of his death made me reel. Dennis grabbed me by the arm. 'Oliver, Gareth's still alive. He's in a coma, at the Royal Free. Zoë's with him …'

Before he'd even finished his sentence I was back in the car.

\* \* \*

My first impulse at seeing Gareth lying there so unnaturally still was to tear the tubes from his body, lift him out of the bed and run with him out of the hospital, to whisk him back to my father's house, and tuck him under the hand-stitched quilt. To magically return him to the boy I used to read to; mapping out his future with dreams filled with adventure. But I couldn't. Gareth had done this to himself, had pushed the life out of his own body until there was almost nothing left but a papery shell.

As I watched, tremors ran under his eyelids, as if he were scanning the horizon of an interior world inaccessible to anyone else. I pulled my gaze away from the clear plastic tube that ran from his wrist up into a drip, terror of further loss rising up in me like bile.

'I knew he'd done too much, and then he wanted a bath — I should have stopped him.' Zoë rocked herself in a chair beside the bed. She looked at me, her face drawn thin around her eyes. 'We had to break the door down.'

I took Gareth's hand. It was cold. I barely noticed the doctor entering the room. He glanced with disapproval at Zoë's unbrushed hair, miniskirt and fishnet stockings, then turned to me.

'You're the brother?' he asked brusquely.

I nodded.

'He's been in a coma for over ten hours, I'm afraid. It's too early to tell what the outcome will be.' He waved the chart in his hand. 'The blood tests indicated high amounts of both amphetamine and cocaine. The combined effect plus the heat of the bath most likely caused the seizure. Frankly it's a miracle he didn't drown.'

On the other side of the bed a heart monitor blipped regularly. The guilt of not forcing him to come and stay with me, of not watching him all the time, washed over me. I knew I wouldn't survive the death of somebody else I loved, not now. I wished then that I believed in God, in any kind of afterlife. Dread threatened to overwhelm me. To combat it, I focused on Gareth's appearance; on how ridiculously young he looked without all the fashionable paraphernalia and eye make-up — like the boy I'd known. Someone, a nurse probably, had combed down his hair into an even parting. Gareth would have hated that.

'Will he live?' I asked. 'Is his brain damaged?'

The doctor hesitated. 'It's too early to say. But I must tell you that his brain was without oxygen for quite a few minutes, we don't know how many, and the longer he remains in a coma the worse the prognosis. We must hope he regains consciousness soon.'

I stood up, towering over him. 'For God's sake — is there nothing you can do?'

The doctor stepped back nervously. 'Mr Warnock, you should prepare yourself for the possibility that Gareth may already be virtually brain dead. We just don't know yet.'

Incredulous, I looked at my brother's prostrate figure. 'Brain dead?'

'The next twelve hours are crucial.'

\* \* \*

Having escaped the oppressive atmosphere of the ward I stood dazed at the entrance of the hospital, watching the rest of the world bustle along in sickening normalcy. The daughters helping their elderly mothers through the glass doors, the pregnant women clutching overnight bags, the ambulances pulling up at the side entrance. Zoë stood next to me. Sighing she lit up a cigarette.

'Hampstead Heath is nearby — we could take a walk,' she ventured. 'Doesn't have to be for long, but it might help?'

I nodded blankly.

\* \* \*

It was late afternoon by now. Pollen smudged the light as dandelion puffs floated through the air like tiny parachutists intent on flight. We walked from South End Green up towards the Hampstead ponds. Above us, a corridor of chestnut trees waved majestically. The heady scent of lilac conjured memories from my youth: of Gareth as a boy playing cricket on the green, of us fishing illegally in the village pond, of taking him out for his first drink down at the local pub. And I was filled with irrational anger — at my brother for his utter disregard for his own life, for the people who loved him; and at the rest of the world that kept on functioning, seemingly indifferent.

Zoë and I walked in silence; words seemed superfluous. She stopped, her settling foot breaking a twig. There was a fine film of sweat on her upper lip and the sunlight illuminated her skin as if she was lit from within; I imagined all the blood corpuscles, her unmarked youth, racing under its surface in an abundance of hope and health. And, despite my fear and anger, I found that I suddenly wanted her.

As if she knew, she reached up to kiss me. I responded, then, filled with chagrin, broke away from her.

She smiled at my mortification. 'It's okay, you know.'

'No, it's not, you're my brother's girlfriend.'

'We haven't got that kind of relationship. Gareth would understand.'

'I don't.'

We'd reached a clearing, a hidden sunlit circle set away from the path, and I threw myself down on the grass. I couldn't help feeling I had betrayed Isabella by desiring someone else. But then I realised I was angry with her too; angry that she'd withheld so much of herself from me — her past, the real nature of her work. I stared up, Zoë beside me. The tree branches above us formed a swaying tent of dark green and lime, of blue and the burning globe of the sun.

'Want a cigarette?' Zoë asked.

'No, thanks, I've given up.'

'Thought you might have.' She lit up, exhaling against the sky. 'Tell me, what's that bird that follows you around?'

Shocked, I sat up. 'What bird?'

'C'mon, you know what I'm talking about — it's like a small hawk. I saw it that night at the gig, just about here …' She waved her hand around my shoulder. 'Don't look so surprised. I see things — didn't Gareth tell you?'

'There is no bird.'

'There is, but if you don't want to admit it, that's fine. Is it something to do with Isabella?'

Amazed, I stared at her; I couldn't afford to tell her the truth, not now with Gareth possibly dying. 'There is no bird.'

'If that's what you want to believe.' She blew smoke into the silvery air. 'Gareth will live, won't he?'

Her question pulled me sharply back into the moment. 'I don't know.' I closed my eyes again, the sun a dancing red dervish against my eyelids.

'I wish there was a way of turning back time,' Zoë said. 'I used to fantasise about that, you know, when my father died. There's the minute before and the minute after. If only it was possible to undo events — or at least manipulate the outcome. But we can't. We just stumble on, thinking we're in control, until we're confronted with our own death.'

Her words seemed to drift like the pollen in the air. But as she talked on an idea began to manifest in my mind; crazy irrational but persistent. What if Enrico Silvio's theory about the astrarium were true? If I turned the key, would I influence my brother's destiny? An absurd thought, but, as hard as the rationalist in me argued, I couldn't repress the idea that at least it would be like rolling the dice.

'What if you could manipulate destiny?' I found myself saying out loud.

Zoë turned. 'What do you mean?'

'What if a person's death date is the result of a combination of circumstances — a belief that you're fated to die on that day, which leads to a subconscious vulnerability as you abandon the precautions you usually take instinctively? And what if there's a way of changing that date?'

'I suppose it might be possible,' she answered cautiously.

The urge to get to the astrarium was overwhelming. I leaped up and reached into my pocket for two five-pound notes.

'Here,' I said, handing them to Zoë, 'this is the cab fare back to the squat. Get some sleep. I'll go back to Gareth,' I lied.

She stared at me, her green eyes questioning.

\* \* \*

By the time I reached the Turkish baths it was almost six o'clock. The locker room was full of day workers finishing their evening workouts — amateur body builders, city businessmen looking for a way to unwind. I went straight to my locker and collected the astrarium.

Back at the flat, I hurriedly unpacked it and set it on the kitchen table, the key beside it. I felt as if it was coaxing me, calling me in some insidious way. I took the key between my trembling fingers and studied the mechanism.

In the oilfields I had witnessed the potential of belief; it amazed me how many oilmen were susceptible to superstition. I'd even known geophysicists who performed their own special rites before the final test to separate the oil from the porous rock cuttings — the test that would decide whether they'd hit black gold or not. Men with IQs well over 150 would cross themselves, kiss a good-luck charm, rub a lucky talisman, before leaning over the UV box to watch whether the dripping perchloroethylene would change the colour of the sandstone chips from milky white to shimmering blue. The more spectacular the hue, the better the quality of oil detected — many described it as the colour of heaven.

Despite Professor Silvio's tutelage, I barely recognised the hieroglyphs on the astrarium, and the Babylonian numbers were completely incomprehensible. I searched the shelves for a reference book I'd seen Isabella use in her translation work. It contained a graph correlating the Ancient Egyptian calendar with the Christian calendar, with a projection forward that Isabella had boasted was accurate to the day.

I calculated the day, month and year of Gareth's birth according to the ancient calendar then turned the lamp onto the astrarium's dials. The tiny etched symbols danced under the bright light. Holding my breath, I turned the outer dial so the marker was aligned with my brother's zodiac sign: the two twisting fish, Pisces. Then I turned the other dials to the corresponding year, month and day of his birth. To my mortification, I found myself muttering the Lord's Prayer and I confess my hand was trembling as I lifted the Was.

I inserted it into the machine and turned it.

I waited. At first I thought nothing had happened. Then, just as I was about to give up, a faint ticking sounded somewhere within the ancient jumble of cogs. It was extraordinary, but as I listened the ticking became stronger and stronger. An image of Nectanebo II flashed into my mind: dressed in his ceremonial robes, the Pharaonic headdress tilting forward as he too listened apprehensively for the clicking of the mechanism. Filled with disbelief at my own actions, I froze. What was I doing?

Bronze teeth clicked over one another as the cogs moved. As Professor Silvio had predicted, the death-date pointer slid into view: it was blackened silver and tipped with a miniature sculpture of a dog-like creature with a forked tail and long hooked snout, like the elongated nose of an anteater.

Ninety-five seemed a good age for Gareth to live to. I slowly turned the key and the death-date pointer ticked past the tiny dashes that marked the decades. Professor Silvio had estimated 340 BC as the most likely year for the construction of the astrarium, so the actual year I selected was 2042 AD.

And then I sat back and waited … for what? The telephone to ring? For my brother, resurrected, to walk through the door?

But at least I had acted. It was a consoling thought.

On the street below, a group of revellers from the nearby pub strolled past. Their conversation was reassuringly pedestrian: one man complained about his sister-in-law, another boasted about his football team's prowess — normal life, twentieth-century realities. Yet here I was, gambling with arcane sorcery, a desperate man resorting to desperate measures.

A slight whirring sound, almost imperceptible, interrupted my thoughts. I bent my head to listen, then peered inside. The two magnets were now spinning, revolving around each other at a speed that amazed me. The heartbeat of the machine appeared to have been activated.

I remembered the spinning stones Isabella had shown me in the dream. She had wanted to set the machine in motion to postpone her own death. It should have been Isabella who turned the key all those weeks ago, and perhaps our own lives would have spun on untouched, seamless, innocent.

'If not Isabella, then Gareth, please,' I prayed. I couldn't remember the last time I'd made such an entreaty.

# 23

It was after hours, but the night nurse had taken pity on me and allowed me into the ward on the proviso I didn't wander into any other area of the hospital. I sat by the bed watching the shadowy angles of Gareth's face under the dim night-light. Unconscious, the softness of boyhood eclipsed the sharpness of age. I'd been sitting beside his thin, motionless body for over an hour. The astrarium, packed in its rucksack, was on the floor beside me.

Gareth's breathing reverberated through the room like some distant sea breaking on an invisible coast. My mind wandered back over the past few weeks and fastened on Isabella that last night, her face bent over her research, her expression one of apprehension. Finally, I was beginning to understand that it had been her desperate search for a way to cheat death. I reached down and laid my hand on the rucksack, the shape of the astrarium pressed up between my fingers. Would it work or was I completely deluding myself?

I thought of the promise I'd made to my father. If Gareth died, I would have failed him and my brother, in the same way

I'd failed Isabella. Was I inherently incapable of protecting the people I loved?

No longer able to bear the sound of that regular breathing — a lie when he seemed so far away from life — I retreated to the waiting room and sat in the dim light barely aware of the television flickering on the opposite wall.

A voice from the TV mentioned Egypt and I looked up. The program was *Panorama* — a discussion on the Middle East, the Yom Kippur War of '73 and its impact on Egyptian–Israeli relations. The panel comprised two academics, a front-line war correspondent, the Egyptian ambassador to Britain and the compere, Robin Day, who reminded me of all the armchair socialists I'd known as a student, annoying in their middle-class prophesying. Then, much to my amazement, he introduced Rachel Stern. Again, I had the impression that my life was folding in on itself, youth and adulthood smashing up against each other as if time had become irrelevant.

Robin Day gave a laudatory summary of Rachel's expertise in Middle Eastern politics then asked her: 'Sadat is making noises that suggest some appeasement towards America. Do you think there might be a peace agreement with Israel itself?'

'I believe he'll make some very unexpected moves in the next couple of months towards that goal,' Rachel said. She radiated a brittle intelligence. 'You have to remember that Sadat wants to push Egypt into the world marketplace. He wants trade and stability. There have been hunger riots in the past twelve months, and there are internal pressures arising from the shift from Nasser's socialism to Sadat's economic policies — this hasn't been an easy transition. Another dimension to consider is that President Carter wants to make his mark on the Middle East and Sadat has his ear. Of course there are potentially disruptive factors in the scenario — Colonel Gaddafi in Libya; the President of Iraq, Saddam

Hussein; President Assad of Syria; and various wild cards including Prince Majeed of the Saudi royal family who is particularly outspoken in his hatred of both America and Israel.'

'Indeed, and we're lucky enough to have some rare footage of the prince ...'

The screen cut to shaky black-and-white footage of a group of men in battle fatigues on a barren hillside. At their centre was King Faisal of Saudi Arabia, distinctive in his traditional dress, with a young bearded man by his side, Prince Majeed. A man, obviously a henchman of the Prince's, stood on one side. Tall and swarthy, he looked familiar. I pulled my chair nearer. It then came back to me: this was the man I'd seen in the car talking to Omar. His menacing persona radiated out of the screen across time and space — it was hard not to feel threatened. I stared at the television, wondering about the connection. Had this man hired Omar to be on the boat that day? And why would Prince Majeed be interested in the astrarium?

A hand was suddenly placed over the camera lens and the screen went black. Robin Day appeared again, but I didn't hear his comment on the footage as the night nurse rushed into the room.

'Your brother's regained consciousness, Mr Warnock.'

\* \* \*

Gareth was still lying flat in his bed but now his face was turned to one side, staring out the hospital window to the black sky beyond. I was terrified that he might have woken impaired, his mind broken.

'Gareth? It's Oliver.'

'So I'm back on the planet?'

His voice was little more than a whisper. A great wave of emotion rattled through my body and, losing all inhibition, I finally cried — for Isabella, for Barry, for the lost innocence of my marriage.

Gareth, aghast at seeing me so undone, clutched my hand.

\* \* \*

Incredulous at the speed of my brother's recovery, the doctors reassured me that Gareth's brain patterns appeared normal. At five-thirty in the morning, in the narrow pea-green hospital corridor that smelled of disinfectant, I slipped coins into a payphone and rang the squat. Zoë answered. I told her the news and left her weeping with relief.

As I put the receiver down I had the prickling sensation that I was being watched. I glanced down the passage — there was no one except a hospital cleaner pushing a mop across the tiled floor.

Before I went home, I drove to Primrose Hill and climbed to the top. The sunrise that morning was the most inspiring I'd ever witnessed: a huge crimson sphere ascending over London; the streaking clouds catching coral, blue, mauve. Up there, I had a sense of absolute power, as if I could dictate who woke and who slept on in the city. It was intoxicating, as if I lived above and beyond the lives spread out before me. Was this how Nectanebo felt? That he had control over people's lives and deaths — a living god?

I arrived at the flat exhilarated but exhausted. I collapsed onto the couch. On the table next to me, the answering machine blinked. After pressing the button Johannes Du Voor's voice boomed into the room, demanding that I meet him at the Ritz at ten — a nasty reminder that I was still on the payroll. I hadn't known the South African was in London, but that was typical of Du Voor — he was always showing up at the most inopportune moments. I checked my watch: I had an hour to get there.

\* \* \*

Built in 1910, the Ritz was one of those last bastions of old-fashioned service in London. During my first years in the job, as a working-class northerner, I'd always felt distinctly uncomfortable in the large and luxurious arched reception hall with its huge crystal chandeliers and marble pedestals, as if the hotel staff could sense an impostor. But, after studying my clients, I soon learned to adopt the nuances of class, how to, at least, feign a relaxed indifference, accepting it as natural to be served and waited upon. The CEO of GeoConsultancy, my employer — Johannes Du Voor — was under the impression that such venues still made me uneasy, which was exactly why he always insisted on meeting me at the Ritz every time he visited London. It gave me the psychological edge to maintain his illusion. What he didn't know was that over the years I'd stayed at the hotel for the occasional retreat — with and without Isabella.

Johannes shifted uncomfortably, his vast bulk squeezed into the Louis XVI chair, dwarfing the table with its linen cloth, silver tea set and delicate china. He lifted his cup to his lips then put it down in disgust.

'Jesus, weak as bloody piss. You'd think that here out of all bloody places they'd get the tea right. That's the trouble with the English — arrogant and complacent. You should be careful — I sometimes feel the same about your bloody hunches.'

'What does it matter if I get the results?'

A waiter holding a tray of scones had hesitated at the sound of Johannes' booming voice. I beckoned him over.

'Have a scone,' I told my boss. 'You know eating calms you down.'

'Fuck you, Oliver. If you weren't a recent widower, and the best geophysicist I know, I'd have fired you yesterday. My condolences by the way.'

His huge paw of a hand swept two scones off the tray and onto his plate.

'Thank you, and thanks also for the wreath.'

'Proteas. Bloody difficult to find in Egypt. I wept, you know, when I heard about Isabella. She was a great girl, strong, fierce, bloody gorgeous — too good for you.'

I watched him pile a huge spoonful of clotted cream onto the scones followed by a large blob of strawberry jam. There was a rumour at GeoConsultancy that Johannes had become so fat he no longer fitted into a first-class seat and was now looking to buy a private jet with custom-built furniture.

'Why are we here?' I asked him. 'I thought I'd made it clear I was taking a few weeks off.'

'Does it look like we're working?'

A rivulet of jam travelled down his chin. Undeterred, he continued to demolish the scones.

'For example, this last job — I looked at the geology, the maps, the seismic but could see nothing at that depth. And yet you insisted on drilling.'

'You're wrong, there was something. The data was clear to me.'

'Maybe to you, but to nobody else. You're becoming a real wildcatter, Oliver, reading signs the rest of us just don't bloody see. Even the Dutch are beginning to think you're a mystic. You've begun to rely too much on your gut and not enough on the science.'

'I disagree.'

I knew I didn't sound convincing. Johannes continued his tirade, oblivious to my self-doubt.

'I'll give you another example — that job in Nigeria you were calculating. You sent through the depth and size of the reservoir before the survey was even completed. Explain that!'

'That was just a mix-up in the post. You received my calculations before you received the survey results. You're just confused.'

'Oliver, you telexed your calculations.'

I fell silent. He was right: I had sent in my approximations of the depth and size of the reservoir before the survey had been completed. It wasn't hubris on my part; it was I who'd got the dates confused.

'Look, I'm not complaining,' he went on. 'How can I? You're the best there is. And right now I'm looking down the barrel of a gun and in need of a few miracles myself ...' He pressed a hand to his chest.

I'd heard rumours Johannes was ill but this was the first time he'd actually mentioned it.

'Heart?' I guessed.

'The good news is that, despite what the ex-wives say, I do actually have one. The bad news is that it's more than a little tricky. So I need a fuck-up on my watch like I need a hole in my head. Oliver, when you get it wrong, I'm the one responsible; and the way you're going, you'll get it spectacularly wrong one day — it's inevitable.'

'Is it?'

I didn't want to explain myself. And, as I reflected on all the explorations I'd initiated, I knew I didn't have the language to describe that moment when speculation transmuted into certainty — a gut sense that began as a small knot in my stomach, then flowed through my fingers and feet as I literally felt the hidden folds and ripples of the earth beneath me.

Johannes peered at me, searching my face. It was as if he was looking for some glimmer of understanding — of illumination, something to hope for. I'd never seen him so vulnerable before — it was unnerving, all his confidence had collapsed into a bewildered perplexity.

'How do you do it, Oliver? C'mon, rattle the bars of this old sceptic's cage. Because I'm staring into the void, my friend, and I need something to believe in. Throw the old sinner a bone.'

It was one of those confronting moments when someone I had held at a distance had stepped across the boundary with a genuine need for help — Johannes wanted me to turn him into a believer. But I couldn't answer him. There simply wasn't enough trust between us; or at least that's what I told myself at the time. The truth was, I didn't want to expose myself to what I thought could be ridicule.

'So you want me to be more orthodox in my methodology?' I asked.

A fleeting expression of crushed expectation ran across his features before he slipped back into his characteristic aggressiveness.

'Do I?' He buttered another scone. 'I suppose I do, yes. I suppose we're all asking for explanations and the nice neat rational ones are the easiest to sell. And, after all, that's what I am, Oliver, isn't it? A salesman who's running out of time. And now you're taking a bloody month off. But in case you're thinking of doing something stupid, remember I have you under contract for at least another year.'

Bill Anderson's warning came back to me: that Johannes was paranoid I might break away and start my own company. Wasn't it obvious I just needed some time out? A police car screeched past, heading down Piccadilly — another IRA bomb scare I couldn't help thinking.

'Oliver?' The South African's nasal tones drew me back to the point.

'Johannes, I'm not going anywhere, I promise.'

'Good, but we need you back in Egypt within two weeks — that's the best I can do. Maybe I should get you a decent shrink who specialises in bereavement — you look like shit. Two weeks. No show after that and you're fired.'

'I'm coping,' I said. 'Isabella left some loose ends and they're a little preoccupying.' A classic English understatement that hung in the air a little longer than I'd anticipated.

'Yeah? Well, I just hope it isn't the kind of loose end that's going to upset the Egyptian government. You know how much time, effort and diplomacy it took to set up that relationship, not to mention the money. Destroy that and I'll happily destroy you.'

Shifting uncomfortably, I tried to guess whether Bill Anderson had told Johannes about me smuggling an artefact into Britain. Keeping my expression neutral, I answered as innocently as I could, 'Now why would I do anything like that?'

I stood and picked up my rucksack. Johannes stayed seated and I didn't bother shaking hands with him.

'Don't worry, I've got the bill,' he said, and reached for another scone.

'Have a good flight home, Johannes.'

As I walked away, I heard him bellowing at the waiter for some decent tea.

# 24

As I turned into my street, a police car and an ambulance came into view. Raj's wife, Aisha, stood by the gate talking to a policewoman who was scribbling diligently in a notepad. I could see Raj sitting in the back of the ambulance while an attendant wrapped a bandage around his arm.

Aisha, looking tearful and pale, ran up to me as I got out of my car. 'Oliver, a shocking thing has happened. Thieves and no-gooders have desecrated your property! My Raj, he was a hero!'

'I was not a hero,' Raj yelled from the ambulance. 'I just behaved as a good citizen should. But, Oliver, what they have done! It is terrible!'

'What's happened?'

Before Raj could answer, a detective stepped up behind me. 'Mr Warnock?'

\* \* \*

The front door was ajar, several books and a camera case jammed between it and the doorframe. Even from here, I could see the extent of the devastation. I faltered at the door, a sense of violation flooding through me.

'We believe the break-in occurred around one in the afternoon, sir. It was a professional job, no fingerprints, and they've taken some care to search the premises in an efficient but ruthless manner.'

The detective, in his late thirties, was coolly professional but I found the conciliatory tone of his voice instantly irritating. We stepped over a smashed photograph — Isabella in her wedding dress stared out of the cracked glass.

'Sorry about that, sir.' He picked up the photo. 'Your wife is recently deceased, isn't she?'

'She drowned in a diving accident, six weeks ago in Egypt.'

'That must be difficult. And now this, and you've only been back in the country ... what, a few days, sir?'

'Just over a week.' I could hear myself sounding defensive.

We progressed into the lounge. The curtains had been ripped from the windows, several pillows lay disembowelled, and the cover of the couch had been slashed making the white stuffing protrude obscenely. Books had been tumbled from the shelves, an antique clock — the only thing I'd inherited from my grandfather — lay on its side, the wooden back torn from the casing. The invasion of privacy was nauseating. It felt like a kind of rape.

'We believe there was more than one intruder. It was a very thorough job. Your neighbour ...' he glanced down at his notebook, 'Mr Raj Ahuja, tried to prevent the second man escaping over the back fence. He was kicked rather violently in the arm for his trouble. According to Mr Ahuja, the thief was brandishing a small handgun with a silencer attached. Mr Ahuja thinks he recognised the gun from a James Bond film. Interesting that — the fact that it had a silencer. It would suggest that the intruders had more than theft on their minds.'

He looked right at me. 'The odd thing is, sir, if they have actually stolen anything, they've left behind a lot of objects of evident value, such as your telescope, sir, over there — interesting thing to own, a telescope — or your gold cufflinks on the dresser, or the television. It looks like they were after something specific. Any idea what that might have been?'

Instinctively, I shifted my shoulder so the bag holding the astrarium slipped further behind my back and looked the officer squarely in the face.

'None at all. I don't even keep a safety box on the premises.'

'I see. Your neighbour told us you work in the oil business. Could they have been after something of corporate significance, information of some kind?'

'Anything like that, survey reports, maps and so on, are kept at my employer's offices. Like I said, there's nothing of much value here other than sentimental.'

'I know this is a distressing possibility, sir, but is there any reason someone might want to harm you?' he asked lowering his voice as if it were an impolite question.

Several candidates came to mind — a couple of old clients, an ex-girlfriend and, of course, Hugh Wollington. I fought the impulse to touch the bag over my shoulder to reassure myself the astrarium was safe.

'No reason at all,' I said, keeping my gaze steady and direct — a technique I'd acquired in my business negotiations.

'Then it's a real mystery,' he said, studying my expression.

'Indeed.'

His eyes travelled back to the photograph. 'An attractive woman, your wife. You must miss her very much.'

\* \* \*

The police team left an hour later. I sat on an upturned wooden crate in the centre of the living room and stared at the scratched walls, the ripped posters, the torn curtains and cushions, and tried to imagine the fury of the intruders when they realised the astrarium wasn't there; how angry they must have been to wantonly destroy the objects around them and risk being caught. Somehow the violation seemed apt, as if they'd deliberately smashed this section of my life firmly into the past tense.

A knock came at the front door. I kicked aside a torn book and a pillow to open it. The twins looked up at me.

'We've got some information for yer,' Stanley declared in a whisper as Alfred scanned the empty hall behind them, as if looking for spies.

'Private information,' Alfred added, before slipping under my arm and into the flat.

* * *

They sat on the edge of the slashed couch swinging their legs. Alfred, eyes wide, couldn't stop staring at the broken furniture now propped up against the wall. 'Mum said Isabella was taken by angels,' he said gravely.

'Underwater,' his brother added, failing to hide the suspicion in his voice, "cept they don't 'ave angels underwater.'

'Mermaids then,' Alfred contributed hopefully.

Stanley snorted, 'Alfred believes everything. I know better.'

'We loved Issy, she was an angel 'erself.'

'Shut up, Alfred.' Stanley swung back to me, shoulders bristling. 'This information, it'll cost yer,' he announced

'What's the information about?' I asked, wondering why I was taking a couple of eight year olds so seriously.

Stanley's eyes grew to the size of saucepans and his voice lowered to a croak. 'We saw them, didn't we, Alf?'

'Yeah, but we're not tellin' you 'til we get our price.' Alfred kicked his feet against the couch, triumphantly assertive.

'What's your price?' I asked.

'We want a piece of her,' Alfred pointed to the cracked wedding photograph, 'so we can remember.'

'Done,' I said. 'Now tell me what you saw.'

'There was two of 'em,' Stanley said, 'big geezers with big ugly heads. We saw 'em come over the wall and past our bedroom window, isn't that right, Alf?'

'And we saw the getaway car outside,' Alfred elaborated then nudged his brother excitedly.

'And that man who was driving, he was the ugliest of them all.'

'Yeah, he had these funny bits down the side of his head, like caterpillars they were.'

'Ugly black caterpillars hanging upside down,' Stanley concluded helpfully.

\* \* \*

The twins left, Alfred clutching a photograph of Isabella. Alone again, I slid down the wall and sat on the floor. I guessed I'd been lucky Hugh Wollington and his cohorts hadn't broken into the flat before. I imagined they might have had me followed the whole time. Wollington had mentioned that he'd spent time in Saudi. Was it possible he had some connection with Prince Majeed and that man I'd seen with Omar? I felt as if I was descending into paranoia, the sense of being hunted all consuming.

I glanced around. The room was a maelstrom of debris. I couldn't possibly spend the night here. Pulling the rucksack over I lifted out the astrarium — at least I'd kept that safe. I left it on the floor while I gathered some clothes to pack into the rucksack underneath it.

As I sorted through the chaos, I heard a small thud. I looked around. To my amazement, a metal cigarette lighter on the floor had fastened itself to the astrarium. I pulled it off, placed it back on the floor some distance from the mechanism, and watched it slide across the carpet to stick to its side again. It was clear the astrarium had become magnetised.

What could have activated the change, me turning the key after thousands of years? I applied a scientist's logic to the problem. What about those curious alloys — was there a way of analysing their components without damaging the device? I racked my brains; the myriad of information mirroring the tumult around me — it was bewildering, disorientating and overwhelming. I no longer knew what I believed in. Had Gareth's recovery been simple coincidence?

Suddenly I lost my temper. 'Damn you! If you have any kind of power, show me! Do your worst, you bloody heap of ancient tin!'

Trembling with frustration, I set the dials to my own birth date, grasped the key and turned it. Again the magnets began to whirl, the cogs clicking over each individual bronze tooth across the centuries. Part of me was terrified the death pointer would spring up; another part of me defiantly dared the machine to challenge me.

The death pointer didn't appear.

'Just as I thought — a glorified wind-up toy!'

As if in response, a short burst of clicking sounded from the mechanism. Fighting the impulse to kick it, I began searching for the telephone. I finally found it under the couch next to a pile of broken wooden chess pieces. To my surprise it still worked. I rang the Ritz and reserved a room.

\* \* \*

It was evening, the sky a soft blue, the heat of the day prickling up from under the tarmac. Rush hour had passed and the roads were quiet, but there were people everywhere, enjoying the summer evening. Again, I had the sensation I was being followed. I glanced in the rear-vision mirror — there was no one behind me. Nevertheless feeling as if I needed to escape I accelerated.

As I roared past Green Park, something smashed into the windscreen. Swerving, I ran the car up onto the kerb and came to a halt. Shaking, I sat with my hands still on the steering wheel. The window had fragmented, transforming the skyline into a thousand pieces of a jigsaw puzzle. Blood rolled down the glass in lazy drips.

I wrapped my fist in a handkerchief and punched a hole through the shattered glass. The sound of evening birdsong flooded into the car. Climbing out, I began searching for whatever had hit the windscreen. A few yards down the road I found a sparrowhawk, wings spread, head lolling on a broken neck.

Shocked, I kneeled and looked for the collar around its ankle. The only way a sparrowhawk could be patrolling the London skies was if it belonged to some eccentric falconer practising his craft from the safety of a nearby park. As a child, I'd sometimes found the corpses of such birds on the Cumbria Fens. But there was no collar. The creature's black claw lay limp in my hand.

Around me, the sky shifted imperceptibly, like a glass prism that had just been manoeuvred, and I wondered whether I wasn't still dreaming.

## 25

The rooms in good hotels have a soundless vacuum-like quality that I found myself craving now: the sealed-off luxury of an anonymous refuge that brought nothing with it — no past associations, no memories — merely the comfort of being one of many to sleep within its four walls secure in the promiscuity of transition. It is the womb men like me seek, the place we know we can safely return to on our travels. I'd checked in under a false name. The staff, most of whom knew me, were discreet enough not even to raise an eyebrow. I walked through the hotel room, marking my territory out in short paces — past the Louis XVI desk and chair, the gold and blue silk curtains, the canopied bed then made my way straight into the bathroom and ran a bath.

The waxy white marble tiles jolted me back to the morgue and Barry Douglas's corpse lying on the slab there. The Australian would have loved the irony of my setting the astrarium to my own birth date. I could hear his voice cajoling me into an admission that perhaps, finally, my cynicism and deep-seated belief in scientific rationalism were breaking down.

'We'll see if the damn thing has any power over my life,' I said out loud, answering his grinning ghost.

After the bath, I called to book a flight back to Egypt. Sitting there in the hermetic silence, it struck me that it was only ten hours earlier that Gareth had still been in his coma. The morning seemed to have receded as if it were months ago and not merely hours.

Wrapped in a bathrobe, I sat down at the small desk that doubled as a dressing table. The curtains were still open; below, the traffic streamed down Piccadilly. The night was alive. The thin moon pressed against the black sky as delicately as a porcelain teacup, unchanging, eternal. I gazed out, thinking about Isabella, Gareth, the people I loved in my life, working out a strategy that might allow me to regain control of events.

It wasn't just Gareth's carelessness that terrified me but his vulnerability. His youth gave him that illusory sense that life stretched out forever, that one never had to be responsible for one's actions. I knew the illusion well: it was how I'd lived for my first twenty years, fallible in my spontaneity, culpable in my impulses. Now I felt as fragile as glass. Gareth had survived, but how would he live now?

And what about Isabella, who had lived so much more intensely than I did, despite all my adventures? Her passion and vivacity had sometimes created a gulf between us. Was it my innate trait of stepping back and observing rather than being fully present in a situation that had enforced this final, fatal separation? I didn't know. Perhaps I'd become caught up in this obsession with the astrarium as a way of trying to undo past wrongs; an unconscious bid to win her back. Did I think that by solving the enigma of the astrarium I could put to rest all those unresolved arguments? Put her to rest?

Pulling the curtains closed, I shut out the city and the moon, now janglingly bright.

\* \* \*

Hours later I was still awake, lying in the bed staring up at the ceiling. I checked the bedside clock — it showed 6 am already. It would be 8 am in Egypt, and I knew Moustafa, my assistant, would have already been at the oilfield site for a couple of hours. I decided to distract myself by checking on the progress of the well. I rang him on his field phone. The line was bad but in the background I could hear the distant thudding of the drill. The sound swept me right back and suddenly I found myself missing the reality of the field — the frenetic activity, the pungent smells, the shouts and sounds; the concrete world I knew.

'Moustafa, it's Oliver. How's it going?'

'Oliver! Fantastic, you are the man I have been trying to reach for days. Du Voor told me you had gone underground …'

'It's complicated. How's the drilling going?'

'Wait, I will find some privacy to talk in.'

The shouts of the roughnecks faded as he walked away from the field. A minute later he was back on the phone. 'Oliver, I have exciting news. We have encountered oil-bearing sandstone, and we haven't even reached the main target. But there's more — there seems to have been substantial subsurface movement since the seismic data, and nothing is matching up. You must come back to the Sinai, Oliver. I think we should run another couple of seismic lines.' His words tumbled over each other in his eagerness.

'Moustafa, slow down, this could be bad news, not good news.'

'I don't think it's bad news. We have at least two hundred feet of net oil pay and I believe this new structure could extend a long way to the east, well into the new block. From the helicopter, it seemed to me—'

'Hang on, land formations don't appear overnight.' I yawned; my jaw ached and there was the throbbing balloon of a headache over one eye.

'Of course, but there was the earthquake a few weeks ago.'

I sat up. 'Around the twenty-ninth of April?'

'That's right, how do you know about it?'

'Fartime told me about it — it was the same tremor that killed my wife. I just hadn't realised the fault line extended that far. Have the original well and field held?'

'There's no leakage — it appears unaffected. But it's this new reservoir rock that is so promising — a trap has appeared, it's like the substructure itself has altered. Even from the air it looks different — you can see signs of the shear. It must have been a thin fault line that ran down from Alex.'

Moustafa usually erred on the side of caution. I'd never heard him so animated.

'Okay, I'll bring my flight forward,' I said. 'I'll be in Port Said by Thursday.'

'Thank you, Oliver. You won't regret it, I know it. *Inshallah*.'

As I put the phone down, I noticed the outline of the astrarium gleaming in the electric glow of the alarm clock.

My suitcase sat in the corner of the hotel room; it contained a couple of pairs of jeans, a suit and an old denim jacket. I would pick up anything else I needed in Cairo. Fifteen minutes later I had a seat on the evening flight to Egypt. The running man, but running to what?

\* \* \*

Gareth's vocals, dancing above the pounding bass, competed with the droning commentary of a football match playing on the television hanging above the bed. The song finished in a lingering note that swept through the hospital room like light.

My brother, looking flushed and comparatively healthy, clicked the tape machine off.

'There was a rep at The Vue gig, he's asked us to come in — Stiff Records, could lead to something, you know.' He collapsed back on his pillows.

'That's great, Gareth. The band deserves a break.'

'I get out of here tomorrow — they're just finishing the last tests on my kidney and liver functions. It's all looking pretty good considering I was dead all of two days ago.'

'Not exactly dead, comatose.'

'Head banging in Heaven. And thanks for the upgrade to a private room. I feel like a right toff.'

'It's the least I could do.'

On the television, the stadium broke into a roar as Carlisle United scored. We both swung around to watch. I knew that stadium from my childhood: the wooden railings, the old billboard running along the pitch, the hard men of the north up on their feet roaring.

'Da will be happy,' I murmured.

'Happy? He'll be hanging the bloody flag out.'

There was another beat between us; the quiet, undefined pleasure of being with family. Then Gareth spoke.

'Thanks for not telling him …'

With my face still turned to the television, I reached across and took his hand. We sat there watching the football, our hands clasped.

'I wasn't trying to kill myself.' Gareth pulled his hand away, a man again.

'I know that.'

'It won't happen again, I promise.'

'I know that as well.' I met his gaze. 'But this is a chance to really clean up,' I ventured.

To my dismay he sank back into a sullen defensiveness.

'Fuck it, I made a mistake, that's all. I haven't got a problem. I'm going to be a bloody great success, you'll see.'

'Just promise you won't do anything stupid again?'

He stayed silent.

I stood and picked up my overnight bag, the astrarium packed safely inside.

Gareth looked up. 'Don't be away too long this time, will you?'

'I don't plan to be. And remember, if you phone the office they can get hold of me easily enough.'

I leaned towards him, determined to embrace him however awkward the gesture. As I did, I noticed a sketchbook sitting on the side table, folded open to a pencil sketch of a woman's face. She looked familiar. I lifted it up to examine it: Banafrit. I recognised her from the photographs in Amelia Lynhurst's thesis and, more disturbingly, from the shadow the astrarium had cast that evening in Egypt. The deep-set eyes, the heavy eyebrows and full mouth were unmistakable.

'Who's this?' I asked.

'I don't know. She was in my head when I came out of the coma. Zoë insisted I draw her. It was as if she'd visited me. A face like that could turn a man to crime. I was right about the astrarium, wasn't I, Oliver?'

I shut the door and sat down again.

'Listen, if anyone should turn up asking questions, you know nothing, and you've never worked with Isabella, understand?'

'Are you in trouble?'

'Someone broke into the flat — smashed up the whole place.'

'She found it, didn't she, Oliver?'

I barely nodded.

'Christ, do you know how amazing that is!'

'Please, Gareth, this is serious. There are people out there who want it, dangerous people. I want you to forget we even had this conversation.'

'I've already forgotten, but what are you doing going back to Egypt? Surely it's only going to be more dangerous there?'

'I have business to carry out, and I made a promise to Isabella.'

I began to make my way to the door.

'One last thing,' he said. I swung around.

'Don't do something stupid like getting yourself killed, promise?'

'Promise.'

\* \* \*

There was an hour left of the British Airways flight and already the Mediterranean was visible below, the shadow of the plane rippling across the blue waves. I glanced back at my copy of *The New York Times*: the news of Elvis Presley's death covered the front page. I remembered my father miming to 'Hound Dog' as it played on the radio — one of the rare occasions I saw my mother laugh.

So many events this year had made me feel as if an era was coming to an end. Perhaps it was just that the naïve optimism of my generation was now history, to be replaced by scepticism and a growing awareness of a moral void. People younger than myself — Isabella's peers — were angry and understandably disenchanted. Elvis's demise from over-eating, over-indulging and generally imploding into his own myth seemed to me like yet another terminal disillusionment.

Staring down towards Cairo as we flew across the Nile Delta, I realised I too had started to change. I didn't like to dwell on the real reasons I had set the astrarium to my birth date; it wasn't just the Newtonian in me challenging the mechanism, it was also a perverse desire to discover whether Isabella could have possibly saved herself. At least by returning to Egypt there was a chance I might put her to rest. I couldn't bear the idea, however superstitious it seemed to a non-believer like myself, that she may be trapped in a kind of purgatory.

I glanced up at the overhead locker. The astrarium was safely stored inside. At the departure gate I'd told the airline that I was carrying geological apparatus. Initially suspicious, they had waved me on when I showed them my first-class ticket.

The engines shifted to an accelerated roar as the plane began its descent. Without warning, it dropped then stabilised. Stumbling, the hostess steadied herself against the back of my seat. I glanced out the window — Cairo was below, a mirage of high-rise buildings and sandstone. There wasn't a cloud in the sky.

'Turbulence?' I asked the hostess.

After checking the other passengers weren't listening, she leaned towards me. 'Confidentially, there seems to be some disturbance with the instruments. Something's gone wrong with the autopilot; it began at take-off and hasn't corrected itself. So we're landing the old-fashioned way. But don't worry, the captain is an excellent pilot, ex-air force, the best.'

I glanced at the overhead locker again, speculating whether the magnetic qualities of the astrarium were affecting the plane's navigational instruments.

The jet wobbled again, the fasten-seatbelt sign flicked on and I leaned towards the window. The three pyramids were visible as we passed over Giza. Standing in silent communion, they were a monumental testimony to man's attempt to conquer the finality of death. Ten minutes later, the plane made a smooth final approach and, with a shudder, the wheels hit the runway.

# 26

Once I was out of the arrivals gate, I headed to the set of lockers British Airways reserved for their first-class passengers. The first-class lounge was policed and one of the only places I knew of in Egypt that you couldn't bribe your way into. After making sure the cloakroom was empty, I placed the astrarium in a locker, locked it, and then hid the key between the upper sole of my shoe and the leather beneath — a place I concealed my money when travelling in Africa.

The next morning, after an early breakfast, I hired an old Honda and drove to Port Said. Every few miles or so was the sign: *Foreigners must not leave the road.* I crossed a bridge and waved at the guard sitting on an upturned wooden crate, his rifle slung casually across his lap. All bridges were guarded in those days because of potential military conflict, and it was forbidden to photograph them. On the other side, I began to see debris from the Egyptian–Israeli conflicts: burnt-out gunposts; old army tanks, upended; the wreck of a military helicopter half-buried in the sand, the blue Star of David still visible on its side. These tragic remnants of an age-old hostility lay tossed aside like toys that had once belonged to a giant child. I continued along the desert road, a single dirt track, swerving around potholes and the occasional goat. The car engine rattled like a cheap moped and I prayed that it wouldn't break down: troubled by the possibility of ghosts, the faint shimmer of a soldier smiling shyly by the roadside, hitching a ride back to a world that no longer existed.

I turned the radio on — immediately Elvis's deep voice filled the car; 'In the Ghetto' sounded out, a broadcast from an American military base in Iraq. I drove on, the desert sky rolling over me. Lulled by mile after mile of track, I felt my recent experiences in London evaporate into the wavering glass-like horizon that constantly hovered just in front of the car. As I travelled, a dust storm blowing up behind the tyres, a keener sense of myself — stripped back, liberated from memory — settled into the driver's seat. For all its irritations and eccentricities, I now remembered why I loved this country.

* * *

The four-seater Cessna swung to the left, its wing tilting up to the sun as it circled back over the area we'd just covered. I watched the horizon go from horizontal to diagonal and a thrilling feeling of omnipotence flooded through me, as it always did when I was surveying. It was the exhilaration of seeing the whole formation of the landscape spread out below — the glorious impression of being above humanity, above millions of years of history, as if reading the topography of the mountains and riverbeds enabled me to see that transcendental past and also the faraway future. I could see how the world had stretched and shrunk, how the oceans had eaten the coast, how the continents themselves had moved, how volcanoes had etched their fury down sweeping slopes. More importantly, I could see where the earth was hiding her treasures in folds of shale and carbonate reefs.

After my phone call to Moustafa from London, I'd spoken to the Alexandrian Oil Company and then to the Ministry of Oil itself. The adjoining block, where the new pay zone appeared to extend, was earmarked for licensing to friendly foreign oil companies as part of Sadat's new economic policy. But I'd agreed with the ministry that we'd use some of our existing equipment and personnel to take a look at the block — whatever we found could only help their negotiations.

Moustafa and I had met in the tiny Port Said airport and sat in the departure lounge — a glorified alcove furnished with an old vinyl lounge suite and a dusty photograph of Nasser in army uniform hung over an empty counter upon which sat a fan spinning forlornly — and we had analysed the landsat image of the area that the Alexandrian Oil Company had on record. Taken from the NASA satellite in 1972, it covered most of the area east of the Suez Canal. The section we were interested in showed little geological potential — it appeared on the images as a light-coloured flat area not much higher than sea level. This meant that the ridge we were now searching for from the plane really was new, possibly related to the earthquake. We didn't have the data yet to understand it; we needed to get down there to explore it.

'There it is!' Moustafa, two surveillance maps open on his lap, pointed out the window.

I looked down. The jutting derricks of the Abu Rudeis oilfields looked as if they were made of Meccano, the discoloured sand around each one spread out like an ink stain. But the part of the landscape Moustafa was indicating was a white scar of a ridge that ran for about twenty kilometres directly below. I tapped the pilot's shoulder. The horizon tipped again as he flew the plane down for a closer look.

'See here,' Moustafa traced the formation on the map for me.

I noticed the map was labelled in Hebrew and, surprised, looked at him questioningly. He grinned.

'Israeli — I got them on the black market, dated 1973. Probably military, but they are the best charts.'

The area with the ridge was marked as flat on the surveillance map, as it had been on our own satellite images. There was no sign of any external feature, of the edge of a basin or of buried carbonate platforms, the kind of geological conditions that promised a hidden reservoir of oil or gas. I looked out of the window again. Now that we were lower, the ridge was clearly visible — one side a smooth slope, the other side with an incline of about ten feet, giving a hint of the substructure beneath.

'It looks like God has suddenly stamped his foot and the carpet has a wrinkle,' Moustafa said.

'Nicely put but not exactly scientific.'

He laughed.

I checked the map again; it was the second time we'd flown over the formation and I knew the reference points were accurate. Here it was on the page, flat as a pancake, but out of the window the mound was undeniable.

'Has there been instability here before?' I asked, still puzzled.

Moustafa pushed the second map towards me; this time the labelling was in Russian. 'This map dates from the late 1950s but you can see it is just the same as the 1973 map. There is nothing in this valley except goats and rubble. Now it looks as if the pay zone we just encountered in the adjacent oilfield,' his finger ran across the map toward Abu Rudeis, 'might extend all the way to here.' He grasped my wrist in sudden excitement. 'Oliver, if this were so, this could be a huge discovery!'

My own oil sense had been ignited the moment we sighted the ridge — it looked like a textbook illustration of where to drill. And there was something about the slight discolouration in the rocks on the far slope that had made my heart rattle with adrenalin. But I'd hidden my enthusiasm. I trusted Moustafa, but before I'd commit to anything I needed to know exactly what we were dealing with, and who else Moustafa had discussed this with. And, of course, I wanted the data, but most of all I wanted to walk the ridge.

'Let's go down,' I said.

\* \* \*

The plane landed on a flat area of scrub just before the slope rose to the crest of the ridge. The terrain was bleak and barren, twisted bushes clustered around the occasional boulder. Moustafa and the pilot unloaded the gravity meter — an instrument that measured changes in the gravity field and would indicate whether there was a change in the structure of the crust, the possibility of source rock and, above it, reservoir rock. There was also a machine called a sniffer that detected minute traces of hydrocarbons. If any of these tests indicated a possible oilfield, then we would turn to seismology, using explosives to create shock waves that would reflect off the substructure and allow us to create two-dimensional, even three-dimensional, images of the oil-bearing strata beneath.

I walked to the top of the crest and stood there looking over the terrain. I took a deep breath and inhaled the faint scent of salt, and something else under it that I was beginning to believe may contain that elusive trace of oil. Thinking it could be coming off the established oilfields to the west, I turned in that direction, then realised the wind was blowing from Upper Egypt, entirely the other direction.

I peered down the other, sharper side of the slope. An old Bedouin shepherd sat in the shade of the crest, watching a bunch of scrawny goats graze on the scattered clumps of desert grass. I shouted a greeting before going down to join him.

'*Salaam alaikum*,' I said.

'*Alaikum salaam*,' he replied, then patted the flat boulder where he was sitting to indicate I should join him. I bowed in greeting then sat beside him. He offered me a piece of chewing tobacco, which I accepted then discreetly slipped into my pocket.

'How long have you worked this particular piece of land, my friend?'

'Many years, many years.' He waved vaguely towards the east. 'But now I am confused. I was here four full moons ago and none of this was here.'

'None of what?'

'This.' He patted the boulder we were sitting on, then pointed to the ridge behind us. 'It has grown in the night like mushrooms.'

'Mushrooms in the desert?'

He laughed, which became a hacking cough finished with a stream of tobacco-stained spittle that bled into the sand.

'There are many things I cannot explain — stars that are older than light, a woman's change of heart, President Sadat's dreams — yet I believe them because I see them with my own eyes. It may be sorcery but it is there, it is God's will, and so I believe it.' He smiled again, pulled out an evil-eye pendant that hung around his neck and pressed it to his forehead.

A dark lump lying on the ground caught my attention. I picked it up and sniffed it. It smelled pungent and rich; a lump of tarry oil, surface seepage probably brought up by the earthquake and already decaying in the air and sun. A pounding sense of excitement rose up in my throat. Concealing my emotion, I slipped the lump into my pocket.

I stood and tracked a strata of darker sand that finished at a small crevasse, a dead bush sprouting from it. I kneeled and examined the base of the bush; all around it were bird-claw prints baked into what looked like mud. Birds of prey weren't that unusual in the desert, but mud? It had been years since it had rained in this region.

'Oliver!'

Moustafa's voice startled me; he appeared on the crest waving a piece of paper in his hand. 'The geophysics look very good! We're close, I know it!'

As I scrambled up the slope towards him, the Bedouin caught my arm.

'This is God's work. It is not to be ravaged without consequence, consequences that will affect us all. Don't forget, you are a mere man, my friend, Allah is mightier.'

\* \* \*

Back at the oilfield, I walked around the drilling rig that I'd helped set up months earlier. It had been moved one kilometre to the southwest and was drilling into the same reservoir we had penetrated with the original well, which now rested at over fifteen thousand barrels per day. Mud and oil roared up through the derrick and it seemed clear that the new well would be as productive as the discovery well.

Nearby, the shale shakers — great sieves — were steaming as the hot underground mud rippled out of the drill pipe like the entrails of some subterranean beast. The shale shakers sifted and shook the mud out from the cuttings, after which it showered down into the mud pits, filling the air with the raw smell of oil and pungent earth. I waved at the mud logger who stood over the pit full of drill cuttings then I pulled Moustafa away from the roar of the generator.

'This new potential field, it's on land leased by IPEC?'

'Naturally.'

'And you haven't spoken to Johannes about it?'

'I work for you, Oliver, not Du Voor, you know that.'

I nodded, then, appalled by my sudden avarice, looked away to the horizon. A truck drove along it, hauling sections of well casing to be used in completing the current well. The sight reassured me. This was industry, commerce, the great cogs of progress. This was a terrain I knew and trusted.

I turned back to Moustafa. 'Let's run some seismic lines, see what they say before telling anyone. I think that might be wiser.'

'I agree, my friend.'

Moustafa held out his hand, and we shook — a sealed pact.

But as I walked away, Enrico Silvio's warning about the astrarium offering a kind of Faustian contract seemed to echo under the thudding oil well. I couldn't ignore the coincidence of this new reservoir appearing immediately after I'd put my own birth date into the astrarium. No matter how much I tried to rationalise I couldn't rid myself of the notion that perhaps the earthquake had somehow been a result of the discovery of the astrarium, the releasing of some kind of inexplicable force that reached across time and space. What had I really done by setting the dial to my own birth date?

# 27

It was late afternoon by the time the silhouette of the camp appeared on the horizon. Already the temperature had started to drop as the desert cooled. As we neared the huts, the outline of a police car parked outside my hut came into view.

'Oliver, are you in some kind of trouble?' Moustafa asked.

'Perhaps.'

The driver pulled up and we sat in the jeep for a minute.

'Let me deal with the police,' Moustafa murmured in English. 'You know I have connections.'

I glanced at the driver, then reached down into my shoe and pulled out the locker key. I slipped it into Moustafa's hand.

'Guard this with your life. If they take me, go to the BA first-class lounge at Cairo. The locker is listed under the company name. There's a rucksack inside.'

He nodded. 'I won't open it. What I don't know won't harm me, *inshallah*. As always, you can trust me.'

\* \* \*

The camp quarters were simple — there was a single wrought-iron bed with a striped lumpy mattress, an electric kettle, a bar fridge, a ceiling fan and an old tea chest that functioned as both storage and a table. I'd never spent more than a week in such accommodation, but most of the crew weren't so lucky; some spent weeks stationed out on the site. The hut they'd assigned me still contained the possessions of the previous occupant, an Italian-Catholic well borer. I hadn't bothered throwing them out. A tattered print of the Virgin Mary ascending to heaven on a cloud hung on the wall over the bed. A bookcase made from a plank balancing on two rusty nails held an eclectic collection of worn paperbacks: *Futureshock*, *Roots*, *Fear of Flying* by Erica Jong, *Love Story* (in Italian), *Watership Down* and, I suddenly noticed to my distress, *My Name is Asher Lev* by Chaim Potok, a Jewish writer. The Egyptian military police wouldn't like that.

As Moustafa and I entered the hut, two officers were ripping out the lining of the tea chest. My meagre items of clothing were strewn on the floor beside them. Another officer — obviously their superior — lounged on the bed watching them. Seeing me, he lazily got to his feet with as much disrespect as he could muster.

'You Mr Warnock, British citizen, yes?'

I stepped forward, blocking the view of the Potok novel. I was afraid they would assume I was Jewish, possibly even Mossad.

'Is there some problem?' I asked.

'Maybe.' The officer shouted at his men in Arabic, ordering them to turn the mattress over, then swung back to me. 'Maybe you spy?'

The old blue-striped mattress fell to the floor in a cloud of dust, revealing two *Playboy* magazines, dated 1968, lying on the rusting base. The officer held them up accusingly. 'Yours?' he demanded.

'Of course not!' I snapped back in the most authoritative tone I could muster.

The officer burst out laughing, his two comrades joining him. Moustafa and I remained stony-faced. Displeased, the officer cracked his baton against the iron bed frame.

'Is funny, no? Very funny.'

Moustafa joined in the laughter. I followed, my heart pounding as the officer flicked through the magazine pages. He stopped at a centrefold displaying a blonde grinning inanely above a pair of enormous pink-tipped breasts. Wearing a leather cowboy hat, she sat astride a saddle perched on a hay bale. He held the page up. The centrefold smiled out at me her blazingly white teeth mockingly perfect next to his stained and irregular grin.

'She your sister, no?'

The atmosphere thickened as the other men, instantly registering the extent of the insult, turned to me.

'Careful,' Moustafa said quietly in English. I remained silent. To defend myself may infuriate the officer further, yet not defending myself undermined my position. I knew he'd been instructed to arrest me, otherwise he wouldn't be taking such liberties.

'Or maybe you like boys?' he went on. 'I'm sorry for you if you do, my friend.'

This time no one dared laugh. I felt my hands curling into fists, the miner's son readying himself for a brawl. But to resort to violence would be suicidal.

Sensing the danger, Moustafa stepped between us. 'Officer, Mr Warnock is Egypt's friend. He is employed by our government. There has been a mistake.'

'No mistake. He is to be escorted back to Alexandria and interrogated.'

'On what grounds?'

'That is between Mr Warnock and my commanding officer, Colonel Hassan.'

Moustafa broke into a warm smile. 'Colonel Khalid Hassan? From Mansoura?'

Flustered, the officer glanced from Moustafa to me. 'The same. Why?' he asked suspiciously.

'Then there is no problem. Khalid Hassan is a good friend of mine. We were at El-Orwa el-Woska together as children. He will be very unhappy when he hears you have arrested a friend of mine.'

'We are not arresting him, we simply want to ask him a few questions.' The officer shoved me towards the tea chest and the scattered clothes around it. 'Collect your things, we go now.'

\* \* \*

I looked up at the single barred window; the bluish light of dawn had just begun to thread its way through the night sky. I tried to measure the time since they had bundled me into the jail — at least twelve hours. During the short walk from the police jeep to the cell, I'd recognised the building from my previous interrogation: the police headquarters on Al Fateh Street in Alexandria. Behind its austere façade was a warren of small rooms that ran around an inner courtyard. The atmosphere was dank: the acrid smell of urine and carbolic soap, undercut by something else — the smell of fear.

They'd been questioning me for hours. The fluorescent light above blazed down; I felt as if it was burning actual stripes across my brain. If I concentrated, I imagined I could smell my soft grey matter frying like old bacon. I was beyond exhaustion and my thoughts reeled like a drunken boxer. So far the officer had focused only on the circumstances of

Isabella's death, reiterating over and over that the dive had been illegal and had taken place in a restricted military zone.

'I told you before,' I said wearily, 'on the day she died — I had no idea the dive was illegal until we were actually on the boat. My wife hadn't been entirely clear on the matter.'

'She was lying to you, sir.'

The officer, a disarmingly polite man in his late forties, kept apologising to me; a ploy I'd fallen for until the questioning stretched into hours and I wasn't allowed to rest or go to the toilet — deliberate tactics to humiliate me and break me down.

'Okay, perhaps she lied to me — what does it matter? She drowned before we found anything.'

My head sank to my chest. All I wanted was to sleep; my eyes felt as if they had sunk into pits and my trouser legs were streaked with urine. Bizarre snippets of phrases kept popping into my head, along with lines from old pop songs — The Beatles' 'She Loves You'; The Monkees' 'I'm A Believer'. Exhaustion and dehydration were sending me into a delirium peppered with moments of surprising clarity. Did they know about the existence of the astrarium? Had anyone else been detained? Hermes Hemiedes? Moustafa? Maybe even Francesca Brambilla, although I couldn't imagine the matriarch tolerating such treatment.

'Your wife worked with Faakhir Alsayla, a diver?'

I lifted my head and tried to focus on the officer's gaze. His eyes swam around in circles, a swarm of deceptively compassionate brown irises. If only I could grab one and squeeze, I thought irrationally.

'I don't know that name,' I lied.

'So perhaps you know a Hermes Hemiedes?' he persisted.

When I refused to reply, the interrogator nodded and one of the policemen flanking me hauled me to my feet. I caught sight of a man at the glass window of the door, staring in. His face was eerily familiar and I tried to remember where I'd seen it before: the *Panorama* show on television in London, Prince Majeed's henchman, Omar's companion. A new fear clawed at my throat.

Another policeman came in and told the officer that Mosry was waiting outside. The name seemed to sear the air like a hot coal. Wanting to memorise it, I held onto the sound: Mosry. The officer nodded and Mosry entered the room; instantly it was as if the temperature had dropped. I remembered an encounter with a warlord a few years previously in Angola, a man who recruited and butchered child soldiers. For the second time in my life, I knew I was in the presence of evil.

The officer gave the newcomer a nod of nervous deference. Now I wondered whether I was going to survive the interrogation.

The questions began again, with a new aggression. 'Answer me!' the officer barked, then slammed his fists on the desk.

'I have no idea what you're talking about,' I said.

'Perhaps this will help your memory.' He reached into a file and pulled out a black-and-white photograph of Hermes and myself at Isabella's funeral.

'May I telephone the British Embassy?' I asked. 'As a British citizen I have rights …'

I'd forgotten how many times I'd made this request; it had become a collection of words I clung to like a raft, a means of keeping my fading sanity afloat. The actual words had stopped making any sense to me; they had become a medley of sounds strung together at the end of which salvation seemed to beckon.

Ignoring me, the interrogator picked up a stubby pencil and drew on a piece of paper, which he shoved towards me. 'Do you recognise this?' It was a crude rendering of the Ba hieroglyph.

'Of course, from my wife's work. That's Ba, the Ancient Egyptian soul-bird.'

'A primitive symbol from a primitive culture — only the West romanticises such fairytales. It is also the symbol for an organisation — an organisation that is illegal, Mr Warnock. Do you know this organisation?'

By now the room was beginning to spin. 'Can I sit down?' I asked.

The officer looked towards Mosry as if waiting for an order. The other man nodded and the officer lunged at me, as if to hit me. At the last minute he punched the air and I fainted.

\* \* \*

It was her perfume, a spiralling thread of musk and lemon that took me back to the first time I ever met her. If I opened my eyes, she would vanish; it was a magician's trick, a sunspot, the dancing shadows on a lake. I breathed in deeply, wanting to stay basking in her presence no matter how illusory.

The tickling on my face continued, but I fought to stay asleep. I sensed that if I woke completely, pain would flood through my swollen legs and feet. I'd once read of a bereaved neurophysiologist who developed a hypothesis that the dead continued to exist in the way our memory imprinted our experience of them upon our brains. Not an endless loop of disjointed images but a real and ongoing discourse based on decades of observation, of 'knowing' that person. Was this what I was doing now? I didn't care. I held out my hand, blind fingers touching warm flesh.

'Isabella.'

Not a question, just naming the unnameable. She stood over me, her black eyes shining with that wry expression so achingly familiar, wearing the same clothes she'd worn that last evening before the dive.

'Isabella.'

As if in answer, she reached out and touched the prison wall where graffiti was carved into the plaster in desperate scratches. Her fingers outlined the crude drawing of a fish, then a bull, and finally she pointed to a woman's head crowned with writhing snakes.

'The fish, the bull and the Medusa,' I whispered, the images burning themselves into my memory.

Then, as she kissed me, I sank back into unconsciousness.

\* \* \*

I woke with a jolt, my whole body a knot of twisting pain. The gaunt face of the guard came into focus as he rattled the keys above me, indicating I was free to go.

As I sat up, I turned to the cell wall — the graffiti had vanished.

# 28

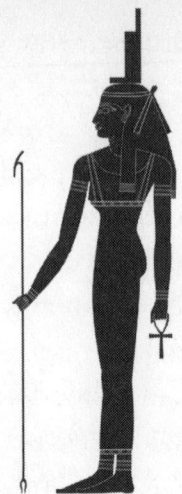

Henries, the British consul, dealt with the infuriated prison official with icy politeness, then marched me out of the building. As soon as we were out of earshot, he told me Moustafa Saheer had informed him of my arrest and it had taken several hours of phone calls and some pressure from the Alexandrian Oil Company to engineer my release, none of it helped by the fact that it was a Friday, the Islamic day of rest.

'You do seem to be leaving an unpleasant trail of half-truths and accidental deaths, Oliver. God knows, losing one's wife is a ghastly experience, but clearing up after you could become somewhat tiresome. I wouldn't want you to become a DBS.'

'A DBS?'

'A Distressed British Subject — the poor dears can float around for decades. A bit like your unfortunate Australian friend Barry Douglas — another headache, but not mine, thank God. I suppose he was a DAS, a Distressed Australian Subject. What a dreadful thought.'

Henries' car was parked along the street, a short distance

from the prison entrance. His driver got out and opened the rear door for him.

'Whatever you're up to, stop it now,' Henries told me forcefully. 'I won't be able to bail you out next time, no matter how many phone calls I have to field from the head of BP, Shell or whomever. Even oilmen like you are expendable when it comes to international affairs. You are on borrowed time, Oliver.' He tapped his watch to emphasise the point.

The limousine drove off. I stood on the street, dazed and dehydrated. A man stepped out from the shadow of a shop doorway and took me by the arm. I shook him off, then realised it was Hermes Hemiedes.

'Come, my dear fellow, let me escort you to the safety of your villa,' he said.

I pulled him back into the doorway. 'How did you know about my arrest?'

'It's a small country. I had news of your arrival back in Cairo. Naturally, out of concern for yourself and the astrarium, I have been tracking your progress.'

'Are you crazy? You shouldn't be anywhere near here. They asked about you, they wanted to know if I knew you. What's going on?'

'The authorities have never approved of the kind of Egyptology I am involved in. You must know by now that they felt the same way about Isabella.'

'Hermes, I was questioned and humiliated for hours!'

A short whistle came from behind me and I swung around. Ibrihim, my housekeeper, was standing on the other side of the street some distance away, nervously watching the armed guards at the sentry box outside the police headquarters. The company car waited next to him. He shot Hermes a glance of utter disdain then gestured frantically that I should join him.

I turned back to Hermes. 'It seems my every move is watched.'

'More than you possibly realise. Would you like to come with me?'

'No. Stay away!'

He gripped my arm. 'Don't forget, whenever you need me, I'm here.'

I shook him loose and, without looking back, crossed the road towards Ibrihim and the car.

\* \* \*

Back at the villa, Ibrihim pressed the rucksack containing the astrarium into my arms.

'Your friend Mr Saheer delivered it. He told me to tell you that sometimes it is better that the heart does not know what the hands are doing. But please, Mr Warnock, I have a wife, and a son at university. I don't want trouble.'

'I promise, Ibrihim, no trouble.'

He looked at me disbelievingly, then shrugged and disappeared into his room.

I carried the rucksack upstairs into the bedroom, then locked the door and pulled down the blinds. After placing the rucksack on the desk, I waited, my nerves rattling, half-expecting a heavy banging on the front door below, convinced the villa would be raided at any moment. There was nothing but silence.

I carefully lifted out the astrarium and stared into its mechanism. To my surprise, the two magnets were still whirling furiously, the dials turning. What avalanche of fate had I activated?

So many people wanted this mysterious instrument. Did they really believe it could influence lives, events, even history?

I looked around the room. The instrument had to be hidden, but where? Despite the extra night guard the Alexandrian Oil Company had put on after Barry's murder, I still felt insecure about keeping the astrarium in the house. I went to the balcony, pulled aside the blind and stared down into the garden. On Ibrihim's side of the house, there was a makeshift yard where Tinnin the Alsatian was kept. Muslims regard dogs as unclean, but Ibrihim had explained to me that he tolerated Tinnin's presence because he was a good guard dog. There was a kennel there, large enough for something to be buried at the back of it.

\* \* \*

Later, I took a walk along the Corniche. Battling the gusts of wind coming off the Mediterranean, I crossed the road and sat on the sea wall. The scent of roasting chestnuts floated from a brazier nearby, reminding me incongruously of Oxford Street at Christmas. Courting couples, some in traditional dress, others in western clothes, strolled past, the wind making sails of their garments. The women were beautiful, vivacious, luxuriant in their flesh; the men thin-faced and earnest. Their intimacy suddenly made the absence of Isabella painfully apparent. I was reminded of a walk I'd taken with her only months before. I looked out over the sea, to the right was the islet upon which once stood that great wonder of the ancient world — the Pharos. Isabella had taken me there, describing the lighthouse in detail, as if she had lived through that era herself. The lighthouse was built during Ptolemaic times to protect the increasing number of trading ships from being wrecked in the harbour. Isabella told me the Pharos would have appeared to defy gravity in its soaring height and, for the religious pilgrims of the era, must have been a spiritually transcending vision with its flaming beacon burning day and night. As she stared out at the site that day, I remembered being struck by how convincing her description sounded, as vivid as if she had seen it herself.

\* \* \*

In the Café Athenios the old men had begun to congregate for the evening, chatting over hookah pipes, small cups of thick black coffee and baklava. I sat at a table outside and ordered a coffee. I needed to put my scattered thoughts into some kind of order.

I remembered what the police had said about the Ba hieroglyph being the symbol of an illegal organisation. The fact that Isabella and Hugh Wollington both had a Ba tattoo suggested there was a stronger connection between them than I'd suspected. Were all those people in that photograph from Behbeit el-Hagar involved? Perhaps Enrico Silvio was a part of it too. But what kind of organisation was it?

The printed image on the front of the menu caught my eye. It resonated somehow, this drawing of a woman with snakes for hair. Then I remembered the head of Medusa that Isabella had pointed to in my dream. There had been a fish and a bull scratched onto the cell wall too. Where would one find those three images together?

'Mr Warnock?'

Startled, I looked up. Aadeel, Francesca's housekeeper, stood at my table looking flustered.

'I went to the villa in Roushdy — your housekeeper told me you would probably be here.' He looked at the cut above my eyebrow and lowered his voice. 'You have been questioned again?'

I nodded. 'It was unpleasant but it could have been far

worse. I suspect I got preferential treatment as a European. Did Ibrihim tell you anything else?' I was worried he might have mentioned the astrarium; I trusted no one now.

'Do not worry, he was discretion itself. No, I had to find you because of Madame Brambilla. I fear the grief is destroying her, she is losing her mind. Please, you must come now.'

\* \* \*

Francesca was sitting in the drawing room, the French doors thrown open to the garden. Despite the warmth of the afternoon she was wearing a blanket around her shoulders. Terrified by my appearance she clutched at my arm.

'So you have finally come to take my house?'

I sat down on the sofa beside her chair. Her grand authority had been replaced by a childlike bewilderment. It was devastating to witness. 'I'm not going to take anything or send you anywhere, Francesca. You're safe here.' Trying to reassure her I stroked her hand.

'It was my fault, Oliver, I killed her. It was that woman. I knew Giovanni was a fool to trust her. Do you hear that, Giovanni?' she cried, addressing the empty space in front of her. 'Do you hear?'

She appeared to be slipping in and out of a mild dementia.

'Which woman?' I asked gently.

'The English woman, the one who helped Isabella go to Oxford. She was always scheming.'

'Amelia Lynhurst?'

'Giovanni chose her to be his high priestess … they had so much power together, then she wasted it, all of it …' she began rocking herself in the chair. 'The body always lets us down so what does it matter? The poor child was already dead.'

I assumed she was talking about Isabella's missing organs. I leaned forward, trying to hold her gaze and pin her to some semblance of lucidity.

'Francesca, who took Isabella's body to the mortuary?'

'The men who work for our church, that is what I arranged. I didn't want the autopsy but the police insisted.'

'And how long did the priests have her?'

Again she appeared to lapse into dementia. 'A Brambilla has never been cremated. We are always buried, like the great kings of Egypt. We are immortalised by our ancestry.' She grasped my hand. 'Isabella was born on a very auspicious day. She was destined for greatness. She was chosen, you know. My husband had her astrological chart calculated; he believed in such matters.'

Reaching into my jacket pocket, I pulled out the photograph of the group shot at the Behbeit el-Hagar dig. 'Do you recognise any of the others in this photo?' I asked.

Francesca pointed to Hugh Wollington. 'This man, he visited here a few times as a student. I didn't like him, but he worshipped Giovanni. A good wife never asks her husband certain questions. Marriage is a mutually agreed conspiracy. Sometimes it is a travesty,' she finished bitterly. 'Come, it is time you met my husband.'

She reached for her cane then hobbled towards an archway. I followed, apprehensive as to how lucid she actually was. We arrived at a small door covered by a curtain. She pulled the curtain across, then lifted a key hanging off a chain around her neck and inserted it into the lock. I pushed the heavy door open for her.

'This was Giovanni's study. Only a privileged few were allowed to enter. Nothing has been altered since his death.'

The large room was filled with antique furniture. A Napoleon campaign desk sat at one end, in front of a bay window. On top of it was an oval portrait of a middle-aged man in his fifties wearing the uniform of the Italian Fascist Party, a falcon perched on his outstretched arm. Next to it was a photograph of the same man with a young King Farouk, looking remarkably slim and handsome; the two were shaking hands. A stuffed falcon peered down from a ceiling corner, its glass eyes glinting. A scaled-down model of what appeared to be the family cotton factory, made from balsawood and matchsticks, stood under a dusty bell jar on a stand to the right of the desk. At the opposite end of the room was a small camp bed made up with sheets and a blanket, set discreetly behind a sofa. It was a poignant sight.

Catching my gaze, Francesca remarked defensively, 'I sleep with the ghosts of my family. They make me safe. But I wanted to show you these ...'

She led me to a wall covered in framed pictures and pointed to a row of group shots, all men. The photographs were dated in neat inked script from 1910 through to 1954. I noticed that the war years, 1939 to 1945, were missing. All appeared to be taken at the same spot, on the shore of Lake Mariout, an area where many wealthy Alexandrians used to hunt duck and other waterfowl. In one of the latter photographs, dated 1954, a small girl stood proudly beside a middle-aged man sporting a moustache and dressed in a hunting jacket and hat. He held a falcon on his outstretched arm and the child's concentration on the bird transported the viewer straight into the moment: I could almost hear the cries of the disturbed heron as they flapped out of the rushes, the rustling wind in the swaying palms, smell the water. I recognised Isabella in the child immediately.

'There she is,' Francesca said, 'five years old and already hunting with her father and grandfather. That is Paolo, my son, with the falcon. The other men had hunting dogs, but

Paolo had birds of prey. Our family have always kept falcons — since the sixteenth century in Abruzzo. My granddaughter loved that bird.'

She pointed to the stuffed bird hanging from the ceiling. 'That is it there; that ridiculous creature lived longer than my son. That is life: full of banal surprises. After his death, Isabella would take the falcon out herself. "Nonna," she used to say, "why don't I have wings?" She should never have left Egypt; she should never have studied abroad. She would be alive now.'

'How do you mean, Francesca?'

'*Basta*! It is all meaningless now. The line is finished.' Angrily she hit the leg of an armchair with her cane.

I walked over to a low bookcase and kneeled to look at the titles: *Ancient Astrology*, *The Ancient Art of Mummification*, *The Egyptian Book of the Dead: Spells and Incantations*, *Nectanebo II — Magician or Politician?*.

The old woman shuffled up behind me. 'Giovanni's tomes, they travelled everywhere with him. At first I humoured him, I even joined in with his little re-enactments, but then it got serious ...' She faltered, as if she had revealed too much.

'Serious how?'

Her face closed over. 'You can't stop the men,' she said bitterly.

I pulled out a book entitled *Popular Stories of Ancient Egypt* by Gaston Maspero — a name I knew from Isabella's bookshelves. The book fell open at a page relating the dream of Nectanebo, the one Amelia Lynhurst had described in her thesis. A pressed flower slipped onto the floor. Despite its desiccated state, an exquisite scent flooded the room. I picked the flower up — it was a dried blue lotus, the blue of the petals still faintly visible. I knew it was a sacred flower and was regularly depicted on the walls of the temples and in scenes with members of the Egyptian court elegantly poised over the blossom. Isabella had told me it was an hallucinogen.

'Was Giovanni researching Nectanebo II?' I asked.

'The Pharaoh was his obsession. Giovanni was fascinated by the notion of racial purity and Nectanebo II was the last truly Egyptian ruler. Those that followed, my husband described as colonial impostors — the Persians, then the Arabs, then the Turks, French and English. I think that was why my husband was so fond of King Farouk; he was truly Egyptian.'

'There's no such thing as racial purity,' I said.

'The 1930s were a different time — people looked for certainty then, it made them feel secure. You must understand, we were all desperate, especially here in Egypt. We Italians wanted to belong. Giovanni knew there was change coming; he wanted to secure his family's future, to ensure we would not lose everything.'

'Just how did he think he was going to achieve that?'

'Enough! I have told you too much already; I will not betray my husband!'

'I'm not asking you to betray your husband, just to save your granddaughter.'

'It is too late for that, Oliver. We have lost her, don't you understand? We have both lost her.'

'But is she at peace, Francesca?'

'At peace? Don't be an idiot. Look around you — I am surrounded by the dead, all screaming for retribution. When I die it will be the same.'

I slipped the book back onto the shelf. 'I need to know the name of the priest who handled Isabella's funeral,' I ventured, unsure whether I'd lost her trust altogether.

To my relief she answered me. 'Father Carlotto, at St Catherine's. The parish has served the family for years.'

Her hand was a collision of delicate bones resting on my arm as I escorted her back to the study door. Once we were in the corridor, she locked the door and turned to me.

'You cannot visit him tonight; tonight your duty is to me. You must accompany me to the opera house. The Bolshoi Ballet is visiting and they are putting on a production of Stravinsky's *Orpheus*.'

Disturbed by her sudden fey tone of voice I thought she might have slipped back into the memory of some past event, but just then Aadeel appeared in the shadows. 'Madame Brambilla would be most indebted if you could accompany her,' he said. 'Truly, it is the event of the year — everyone who matters in Alexandria will be there. And Madame must attend for the sake of the family's reputation.'

I fingered the cut on my forehead thoughtfully. Aside from the authorities, not many people knew I was back in Alexandria. There were advantages to being seen so publicly — it would be a defiant gesture to my pursuers and may force them out into the open. It occurred to me, somewhat disturbingly, that in my attempt to transform myself from the pursued to the pursuer, I was resorting to using myself as bait.

# 29

The Sayed Darwish Theatre, known as the Mohammed Ali in its colonial heyday, was a small but ostentatious neoclassical building adorned with great sweeps of gold paint and peeling plaster. From the mid-nineteenth century until 1952, the European diaspora had kept it vibrant with visiting orchestras, ballets and singers. It had been one of the cultural centres of old Alexandria. But since the revolution, the venue had lost much of its original audience and had become a cultural anachronism in the newly affluent Arab-dominated society.

The orchestra began and I glanced down the row Francesca and I were sitting in: it was an eclectic congregation — various European dignitaries, several Egyptian officials and a smattering of tourists. In the row in front of us sat Henries and his wife. Sensing my gaze, the consul turned and tried unsuccessfully to hide his displeasure at my presence.

I felt awkward squeezed into the tuxedo, starched shirt and cummerbund Francesca had insisted I wear; all once belonging to Giovanni Brambilla. The shirt prickled the back of my neck, the satin necktie knotted expertly by Aadeel pressed tight against my Adam's apple. And it was hard not to be uncomfortably conscious of the cuts and bruises that still marked my face.

On stage, Orpheus, clad in a painted body stocking, sat before Hades and Persephone, the King and Queen of the Underworld, and plucked at a golden lyre. His solo of pirouettes and leaps — a desperate plea to allow him to lead his wife, Eurydice, out of Hades — was starkly emotional, full of grief and longing, and especially poignant to me.

A rustling to my left distracted me — Amelia Lynhurst, making a late entrance, whispered apologies as she pushed past those already seated to the empty space in my row. I was still mistrustful of her given Hermes' comments that she had 'dangerous aspirations' and possibly believed herself a reincarnation of Isis. There was the story of the key to the astrarium too — how Amelia had found it and Enrico Silvio had stolen it from her. Francesca didn't trust Amelia either; she'd claimed her to be a scheming woman. Nevertheless, I knew I had to confront her. During our conversation at Isabella's funeral, Amelia had made it clear that she believed I had the astrarium; more importantly, she'd seemed to know a lot more about it than I did.

A musical crescendo interrupted my musings. Eurydice, clad in a diaphanous veil and echoing Orpheus's dance steps with heartbreaking grace, followed her husband to the entrance of the cave that led out of the Underworld and into the living world beyond. Orpheus's frantic yearning to turn and see his wife was evident in the half-spins he made, almost turning but not quite, the choreography teasing out the suspense, the terrible knowledge that if the poet did surrender to temptation he would condemn his wife to a second death and lose her all over again.

My whole body knotted in empathy, his longing mirroring

my own desire to have Isabella alive again. And then, with a teasingly slow spin, Orpheus turned, arms outstretched, to embrace his wife as she stood on tiptoe, arched like a willow tree, at the portal between death and a second life, and so condemned her.

It's embarrassing to admit but I actually cried out loud when Eurydice collapsed lifeless again under the gaze of her husband. Mortified by my outburst, I watched in silence while Orpheus, destroyed by his own desire, traced out his distress in a series of agonised leaps.

\* \* \*

There was a reception being held in the foyer. I made my way past several Russian ballerinas now mingling with local dignitaries, past a table covered with brochures advertising package holidays to the Soviet Union toward Amelia Lynhurst.

'We should talk …'

I guided her into a small alcove decorated with a marble statue of Mohammed Ali in his customary fez. 'What do you know about the murder of Barry Douglas; or about my arrests for that matter?' I couldn't repress the aggressive tone in my voice. Startled by my directness Amelia glanced around then leant toward me.

'I understand that Mr Douglas killed himself. As for your arrest, I did warn you and you failed to take heed,' she answered in a lowered voice.

'Barry didn't kill himself and you know it. Why should I trust you? Isabella didn't.'

'Isabella was led into the wrong alliances. That was her tragedy, and now it's yours.'

'Alliances like the sect you belong to?' I said sharply.

To my amazement, she laughed. 'Define sect.'

'A group of people who believe blindly in the same philosophy or religion to the exclusion of all others,' I replied without smiling. 'One might even call them zealots. Dangerous people.'

'The future belongs to the zealot, whether we like it or not. But I don't belong to any "sect" as you put it.'

'I want to know who killed Barry.'

'If it wasn't suicide, then I imagine it was the same people who were behind your arrests. All are actions that would require considerable influence with the Egyptian authorities. Think about it.'

I grabbed her wrist. 'Did you know they violated Isabella's body?'

Several bystanders turned at my raised voice, and I could see Henries talking furiously to Francesca Brambilla at the foot of the wide marble staircase. Amelia struggled in my grasp.

'I can help you, Oliver. You should know that like Orpheus, Nectanebo II is a great love story—'

'No more myths, Amelia. I've read your thesis — I know about Banafrit and that, supposedly, it was she who designed the astrarium. What I want to know is why you want it, just like the others?'

'The astrarium chooses its own keeper and it is my duty to protect that person. Like Orpheus, Banafrit was willing to go into the Underworld to save her lover. Just like you might have to, Oliver.'

'I said enough riddles!'

Over Amelia's shoulder I could see Henries making his way across the foyer towards us. I spoke quickly and quietly, my voice beaded with threat. 'Then tell me, why didn't the astrarium prevent Nectanebo's demise?'

'At the beginning of his reign Nectanebo suppressed a possible coup from the Delta. There was growing dissent within Egypt. Powerful priests claimed Nectanebo had insulted Isis herself and that the only way to appease the goddess's wrath and save Egypt was to build her an extraordinary temple, and an extraordinary device to place within the temple, a device that would talk to the stars itself. But there's something else — a story inscribed on a naos that dates from about fifty years after Nectanebo's disappearance.'

'Professor Silvio's naos?'

She looked surprised, then recovered herself. 'How is the professor?'

'Dying.'

'I'm sorry to hear that; he was once an honourable man. The naos Professor Silvio discovered described a skybox that had prophesied the Pharaoh's death and so the priests had to save the skybox from being destroyed by the Pharaoh himself.'

'But why would the astrarium suddenly change its function?'

'Because it developed a soul.'

'I've heard this theory before — it's absurd. Inanimate objects don't have souls,' I retorted, determined not to be drawn into any more mysticism.

'The function of the astrarium was to talk directly to the gods, therefore it became the embodiment of their will. To the Ancient Egyptians, it had a soul. Now, let's just say that one day the astrarium was being transported and it got knocked, and deep within the mechanism a spring was loosened and the second pointer sprang out. An arbitrary accident takes on meaning — the Pharaoh's death is written in the sky! This would be heresy, and as such would mean the death of the astronomers and astrologers, as well as the priestess, who had been involved in the construction of such a device.'

'All of which could have pointed towards a potential coup or possible assassination ...'

'Now you are beginning to understand.'

'So I have nothing to fear.'

'As long as the astrarium remains sleeping. I trust you have not activated it?'

Before I had a chance to reply, Henries joined us. Amelia made an excuse and disappeared into the crowd.

# 30

Back at the villa, a progress report from Moustafa on the new oilfield was waiting for me; the gravity data we had been unofficially collecting looked increasingly encouraging. If I could secure the finances and the licence, I could end up a very wealthy man. I debated whether Johannes Du Voor would support the project, then I remembered his warning about relying too much on intuition and decided to wait until I had more concrete data before telling him about the potential find.

I got up and walked out onto the balcony. I could see the shaggy outline of Tinnin flopped halfway out of his kennel; the rucksack containing the astrarium was still buried behind it. As if sensing my gaze, the Alsatian growled in his sleep.

My mind returned to the ballet I'd seen that evening and a longing for Isabella to be standing beside me swept over me. I was now as entangled in the mystery of the astrarium as she'd been, but where to next? Had she been trying to tell me when she visited me in my dreams? Where did the symbols lead me to? The fish, the bull and the Medusa. A fish — I knew it was a Christian image. And then I remembered Francesca telling me the name of the priest at St Catherine's.

\* \* \*

I paused with my hand on the cool wall of the cathedral, thinking about the first time I'd stood on these same steps, with Isabella. We'd visited the cathedral only months before and I remembered her face avid with passion as she told me about its namesake, Saint Catherine. Like many academics, Isabella was convinced that Catherine was merely a Christian appropriation of Hypatia of Alexandria, a pagan philosopher crucified for making her intellectual beliefs public. I saw again her dramatic gestures as she described all of this to me, then realised with a jolt that my second visit to the cathedral had been for Isabella's own funeral.

I stepped inside and felt instant relief from the late afternoon heat. The high vaulted ceiling was a mosaic of coloured light. I walked towards the main altar, my footsteps echoing in the profound silence. A foreman sweeping the marble floor spoke to me in Italian, offering himself as a guide. When I asked for Father Carlotto, he disappeared through a side door. I took the opportunity to wander around the cathedral, recalling how it had looked during the funeral, how dreamlike the altars had seemed to me with their gilded wood and lurid stained glass.

I stopped before one window that showed the figure of Christ, the crown of thorns cutting into his forehead, his limbs emaciated. He was reaching towards an older man who was offering him a set of keys, and it was this older figure who had caught my attention. I stared at the grey-haired man, his peasant's face infused with benevolence. I knew him from my Catholic childhood — Saint Peter, the gatekeeper. But it was the bird that hovered over his left shoulder that fascinated me. I knew it immediately — a sparrowhawk. Then I remembered Zoë asking me about the bird fluttering around my own left shoulder. Instinctively, my hand went up to touch the place.

'Our Saviour handing the keys to Saint Peter. Beautiful, isn't it?'

I swung around and recognised the short tanned man in his early thirties from Isabella's funeral. If he hadn't been wearing a cassock, I might have mistaken him for an insurance salesman.

'What is the symbolism of the bird?' I asked.

'The sparrowhawk was the emblem of Saint Peter. Of course, the early Christians took from the culture around them and so the Copts assimilated some of the Ancient Egyptian symbols — the sparrowhawk was important to them as well. You have an interest in such things, Mr Warnock?'

'You remember me from the funeral ...'

'With some difficulty. With that beard I almost mistook you for one of my Coptic brothers.' He shook my hand, his palm surprisingly cold. 'How can I help you?'

I glanced around. The cathedral appeared empty but I wasn't prepared to take a risk. 'I wanted to ask you about the body of my wife.'

'*Scusi*?' He looked flustered, as if he thought he might have misheard.

'Francesca tells me she organised for your staff to collect the body from the ambulance before it was delivered to the city mortuary.'

'Francesca?'

'Madame Brambilla, my wife's grandmother. Surely you know her? After all, your church has looked after the family for decades.'

'No, there has been a mistake.'

'No mistake. Madame Brambilla told me herself.'

Father Carlotto guided me to one of the smaller enclaves; a family shrine. 'Monsieur Warnock, the Brambilla family was excommunicated many years ago,' he murmured discreetly.

'Excommunicated?'

'In 1946 I had to look it up in the records when Madame Brambilla begged me to hold your wife's funeral in our cathedral. I had to have a rather difficult conversation with the Bishop, but we concluded that the sins of the father — or in this case, the grandfather — had nothing to do with the granddaughter. May God rest her soul.'

'But what about Paolo Brambilla, he died in '56, wasn't he buried through this church?'

'He is buried, it is true. But not by this church.'

I looked away to disguise my amazement. My gaze fell on a stained-glass depiction of Saint Sebastian stuck with a dozen arrows, his face twisted in a tragic grimace.

'Why were they excommunicated?' I asked.

'That is a private matter between the church and the family.'

I pulled my wallet out. 'But I am part of the family. And you know, on behalf of the family, I was thinking we should make a donation — say, a hundred dollars. I noticed on the way in that you are in the middle of restoring your roof.'

Father Carlotto hesitated, pursing his lips. Finally, with a certain resignation, he threw up his hands. 'Indeed, and such a generous donation would be most welcome. But, Mr Warnock, you cannot bribe me into surrendering the secret records of the church.'

I picked up a prayer book that had been left on a pew and tucked two fifty-dollar bills between the pages. 'Please, Father, for the sake of my wife. I have reason to believe her spirit is not at peace.'

I pressed the prayer book into his hands. He stared at me, as if deciding whether to trust me or not. Finally he took the book.

'Indeed, I am sure she is most certainly not at peace. Her death was a great tragedy, perhaps an unnecessary one. As to the excommunication, apparently the grandfather had some unfortunate associates — eccentric people who indulged in all sorts of strange rituals. Harmless really, I suppose, just fanatical historians who got carried away. This country has many echoes; they can creep into your head and make the imagination run. My predecessor was prepared to ignore them, but some of the congregation got upset, and then when Nasser came,' he lowered his voice, 'there was a witch hunt. No one was safe.'

'And my wife's body?'

'I have no idea. I only ever saw the coffin. I can show you the entry in the record book.'

'That won't be necessary. One other thing, Father, the fish is a Christian symbol, isn't it?'

He smiled, relaxing at last. 'The fish represents the disciples of Jesus, some of whom, as you know, were fishermen. It was used as a secret symbol in the first century AD by early Christians who maintained their faith against the hostility of the Roman Empire. The tradition has continued over the centuries — it has never been easy being Christian in this part of the world. Even now, some of the young Copts here in Alexandria have hidden tattoos to indicate their faith. The symbol also appears in murals in the tombs at Kom el-Shugafa, a place some of my congregation still believe is haunted. Interestingly, the site was linked with Giovanni's activities if I remember the report correctly.'

He hesitated, then went on in a whisper, 'But there is something else you should know … Your wife came to see me before she died.'

I tensed. 'About what?'

'She came to confession. It was the first time in years, she told me. She was frightened, Mr Warnock. I believe she had found herself involved in things beyond her control. Spiritual things. I'm afraid I wasn't able to give her much sound advice — perhaps if I had suggested she left Egypt ... But she was almost hysterical, she wasn't really making much sense. I'm deeply sorry now that I didn't take her fear more seriously.'

'When was this?'

'About two weeks before her death.' He stepped closer. 'Listen, my friend, if you should need sanctuary at any time, we can help you. My Coptic brothers at the Deir Al Anba Bishoy at Wadi El-Natrun will take you in for as long as necessary. They have helped others this way, and despite your loss of faith, you are still a Catholic, no? And with that beard you would be almost invisible.'

I stared at him, wondering how much he actually knew about Isabella's death and the astrarium.

He placed a hand on my shoulder. 'Please, sometimes in life one must simply trust. Remember my offer.' And he left, the prayer book clasped in his hands.

\* \* \*

I stood beside the huge pipe organ that sat beneath a stained-glass window depicting the trials of Saint Cecily. What terror had compelled Isabella to resort to confessing to a priest? I knew she'd occasionally gone to church but I'd never known her to go to confession. What had she been running from?

The sound of a familiar voice speaking in English broke my reverie. It was coming from a side chapel; a woman's voice asking about candles. I walked towards it, and entered an alcove with a marble relief depicting a martyred female saint against the far wall. Photographs of children and small offerings of flowers had been placed at the saint's feet. There was even a rusting, unopened can of Pepsi-Cola. The woman had her back to me, but I still recognised her. She kneeled and placed a small bunch of gardenias with the other offerings.

'Saint Sabine, isn't she the patron saint of children?' I asked.

Startled, Rachel Stern rose to her feet. 'Do I know you?'

'Rachel, it's Oliver.'

She regained her composure. 'Oliver! I didn't recognise you with all that hair on your face. What a surprise.'

'A pleasant one, I hope. I'm sorry, I've disturbed you in prayer.'

'Shh, don't tell my rabbi. The offerings are for my sister — she's been trying to conceive for years. Apparently if you genuflect enough, the saint will come to the rescue, although I hope it isn't an immaculate conception — there are enough martyrs in the family as it is.'

She hauled her bag over her shoulder and began walking out of the chapel. I followed.

The sun blinded us for a moment as we stepped out of the cathedral. A young boy in rags slipped out from the shadow of a doorway, stretching out the stump he had for an arm. I pressed a few coins into his other hand.

Rachel armed herself with a huge pair of sunglasses then assessed my crumpled linen jacket and jeans.

'I heard about your friend Barry,' she said, 'I was so shocked. He didn't seem the type to commit suicide.'

'He wasn't.'

A group of boys in uniform leaving the courtyard of the cathedral school ran past us laughing and I found myself relishing not being alone. I needed company. 'Look, would you like to go for a drink?'

'A drink? Last time we spoke I had the strong impression you didn't even like me.'

'I was drunk and belligerent. I apologise.'

She studied me quizzically. 'No, I don't think you're sorry at all.' She walked away.

I followed her. 'Please, I just need to talk to someone who knows my history, someone I trust …'

She spun around. 'You really are in trouble.'

'Please, Rachel, it's been really lonely …'

She hesitated, searching my face for something, perhaps a trace of the idealistic student she'd known, and then linked her arm through mine.

# 31

The Centro Di Portuguese was a relatively new and exclusive bar in the same expensive suburb as the oil company's villa, Roushdy. The club was a converted villa with an open-air bar in the courtyard and a disco upstairs. The entrance was hard to find and there were a couple of bouncers at the door, well-built ex-security types. The clientele was a curious mix with two things in common — wealth and loneliness.

We sat under a canopy of woven rushes looking out over the courtyard. At another table, a group of Italian naval officers, drunk, were arguing about who was the greatest entertainer: Michael Jackson or Caruso. Nearby, a white Ugandan (rumoured to be an arms dealer) lifted his eyes away from the buxom young blonde he was flirting with and nodded slightly in my direction, the kind of sly acknowledgement one man makes to another when he thinks the other is involved in some clandestine event, like infidelity.

Rachel was on her third whisky; the only effect the alcohol seemed to have upon her was to make her more loquacious. I didn't care. Once we'd arrived I'd found myself unusually taciturn. I suppose I was frightened she'd be sceptical, or worse, if I confided in her. And yet I desperately needed to discuss the events of the last few weeks with someone who might help me reach a more objective perspective. I'd already wasted half the evening arguing politics, but Rachel had indulged me, as if she sensed my sudden reticence. Our intellectual sparring anchored me to the world I knew before Eygpt, before Isabella's death. And, despite her tough veneer, Rachel had an underlying humanitarianism that appealed to me, as well as a strong sense of self-parody, a characteristic that hadn't existed in the younger woman. It was as if she'd become sharper with age. Now there was a muscularity to her thinking that meant I felt slightly at war — a sexy wrestling match that promised to end in orgasm, defeat or death. That night I was ready to embrace all three.

'So what exactly happened to your marriage?' I asked her.

'Oh, it's complicated. Basically, although Aaron claimed he loved unconventional women, I don't think he really wanted to be married to one. And you?'

'We are ... were gloriously happy.' To say Isabella's name felt like an infidelity, and yet I hadn't planned to seduce Rachel — not consciously. 'Tell me, why did you leave all those years ago?' I went on.

'Let's face it, Oliver, we were the most mismatched couple in the world. It wouldn't have lasted.'

'Perhaps not, but it hurt like hell at the time.'

'As it should at twenty-three,' she retorted, smiling.

The dance hit 'Disco Inferno' blasted out from the disco above. I glanced up: the DJ, a young rake-thin Arab in a floral yellow silk shirt, was gazing wistfully at the deserted dance floor.

Rachel sighed. 'Innocent times. I think about them nowadays. Sometimes I feel drenched in a kind of existential cynicism. It makes me feel so old. And you?'

'Me? I'm barely surviving from hour to hour.'

She looked at me. I knew she thought I meant surviving the loss of Isabella. She finished her drink then moved closer. Before she began speaking there was that moment of hesitation, the beat of blind faith one takes before free-falling into intimacy.

'My marriage broke down because we lost a child. A stillbirth. Aaron was able to deal with it better than me. I just buried myself in work. Then one day at breakfast I looked across the table and didn't recognise him any more. So there you have it — the end of the dream.'

I reached across for her hand. 'I'm sorry.'

'But we're both still here.'

I noticed she didn't remove her hand.

'Rachel, if I told you something astonishing, something barely believable, could you keep an open mind?'

'Hey, if there's one thing I've still got it's an open mind …'

\* \* \*

I took her back to the villa and, while she waited in the living room, I slipped out to the kennel and collected the rucksack. Then, with the rucksack slung over my shoulder, we made our way to the Sheraton Hotel where she was staying. I needed her to see the astrarium while I told her my story.

\* \* \*

In the lift going up to her room, I was aware of the growing erotic tension between us — her scent, the warmth of her body brushing against my bare arm. I wondered whether my senses were deceiving me. I knew I wanted her, and it occurred to me that seducing her might be a way of exorcising Isabella. It was a disturbing but tantalising idea.

Catching Rachel's gaze, I realised the attraction was mutual. I pulled her towards me into a clash of tongues and lips. With an almost electric shock, I realised how much my body had missed being touched over the past weeks. I vanished in her skin, the feel of it so completely different from my wife's. Rachel's taste was green, if I could find a colour for such things. Isabella had been a deeper hue. We moved slowly and luxuriously, tentative in our exploration, my hands finding her nipples hard against my palms. The lift shuddering to a halt interrupted us, making us both break into self-conscious laughter.

We stumbled down the empty corridor, still kissing and struggling with each other's clothes. Once inside her room, the realism of the pasty green walls and vinyl-covered cabinets sobered me up, but Rachel pulled me back into an embrace, then walked over to the bed.

'I drive this,' she said with a grin, then pulled her smock top over her head, revealing her small breasts, her slim hips arching out of the low-slung jeans like some exotic musical instrument. 'I'm so deprived of touch I think I've gone half-mad; I can't even remember the last time someone hugged me. I always seem to be running — hotel lobbies, pressrooms, airports. But oh boy, do I want you now.'

I moved towards her then paused. In that moment of hesitation, I realised that I was deceiving myself — I wouldn't be able to escape Isabella in this desperate lovemaking. I wasn't looking for a lover but a confidante. Someone who would convince me I wasn't going mad. Anything else — sexual or emotional — would get complicated, and I knew Rachel was complicated.

On the bedside table was an old black-and-white passport photo of a much younger Rachel: her face shiny with the blind belief of the idealist, her curly hair tortured into one long side plait. I recognised her expression. I touched the glossy paper; the faint memory of a smile in a London doorway seemed to come off like a smudge on my finger. Next to the photograph were a seashell and a dog tag. I picked up the shell and held it to the light. It was a small nautilus shell, pearly and ribbed, a luminous subterranean cathedral fated to shine for eternity.

As if my action were a cue, Rachel lay down on the bed. She looked at me, smiling, her hair spread above her head. Like snakes, like the Medusa.

'That seashell is from the beach where I lost my virginity,' she said. 'The photo's from the ID badge I wore on my first Democrat campaign, and the dog tag belonged to a soldier in Vietnam I interviewed, who was killed the same day. Love, faith and destiny — I carry them everywhere as a reminder of how far I've come and how precarious life is. But I think you know that already, right?'

In lieu of an answer, I put the seashell into my mouth and placed it onto her belly button with my tongue; the salt of her skin caught at my groin in a sudden erotic tumescence. I pulled her jeans and pants below her knees and worked my way down. Rachel gasped, her sex now wet against my face. Groaning, she reached for my fly; my cock was hard in her hand, and then in her mouth. Sitting up, she pulled my hands away from her and concentrated on pleasuring me, her eyes closed in sensual relish. It was as if she was determined to take me, not to be taken.

Trying to control the sudden surge of pleasure, I steadied myself with one hand against the headboard. Then, wanting to give to her, I pulled her up. Pushing her jeans off, I made her stand as I kneeled. 'No,' she moaned and tried to pull me away, but I held her close, the rich musk of her filling me as I sucked and probed and she clawed at my shoulders. Then, finally, we toppled to the floor and she slowly lowered herself onto me, teasing me, both of us teetering on the edge of orgasm. I felt her bite my neck, her tongue in my ear, each breast filling my hands perfectly, each nipple hard against my palms.

It became a primal struggle of limbs as I threw her onto her back and, with her knees up against my chest, took her violently. With a glorious abandonment each of us surrendered to our own pleasure. She came screaming, triggering my own climax, then, to my astonishment, she broke into gales of laughter. Her hysteria was infectious and soon we were both rolling on the carpet. Perhaps we were giddy with the sheer relief of having experienced intimacy, or perhaps we were both secretly terrified — of our history, of the unspoken understanding that under the surface we were both singular creatures.

A framed poster of the Corniche slid off the wall and hit the carpet with a dull thud, missing Rachel's head by inches.

'You see, we're both watched by ghosts,' she declared, then got up, wrapped herself in a bathrobe and walked out onto the balcony. After pulling on my underpants I joined her.

The narrow concrete balcony looked out over the Montazah Gardens. The lights of the palace glimmered on the far side of the park and the tops of the tall palms that ran along the avenues swayed darkly, scratching at the night. Beyond were the fairy lights of the yachts moored at the jetty. It was one of those electric nights with a sense of timelessness, a certain agitation carried on the breeze that seduces fools like me into thinking they're immortal. Only this night I didn't feel immortal. Something was making me uneasy, something else in the air, a creeping, inexplicable dread.

'I haven't had sex for over three years, not since before my divorce.'

Rachel's statement floated out over the ugly iron railings and down into the street below where we both watched it evaporate in the steam of car noise and the vitriol of two men arguing at the corner.

'That's far too long.' I wrapped myself into the warmed wings of her bathrobe, against her hot, thin body. 'But, Rachel, I'm not here to be your lover; I need you to be my friend. Could you be that for me?'

She nodded against my bare chest, her cheek a burning tattoo. Below, the two men continued to argue: real time, real life. I led her back inside and reached for the rucksack.

\* \* \*

We sat on the bed with the astrarium between us. I couldn't bear to look at her now, convinced my disclosure had condemned me entirely. Her hand crept along the tousled bedsheets towards my own.

'It's okay, Oliver, I believe you. You're lucky — if you'd told me these things five years ago I would have dismissed you as simply another westerner seduced by eastern mysticism. But I've seen some weird things myself. When I was in Kampuchea, I watched the Khmer Rouge recruiting witchdoctors to terrify the peasants — a campaign that worked, by the way. Then a couple of years ago I was cursed by a Papuan Highlander when my photographer stupidly took a photo of his wives. But there's something else that makes me believe in the power of this … astrarium or whatever it is. Prince Abdul Majeed. He's religious, fanatical and dangerous, and absolutely the kind of man who'd believe the power of something like this. He hates the West and would do anything to destroy Sadat's peace initiatives. There've been attacks on western interests in the region — a naval base in Turkey, the US embassy in Damascus, others you don't even hear about. It's unofficial, but those who should know know, it's Majeed. He's got a henchman, Mosry, who's his muscle. You can bet that if the astrarium is indeed believed to have influence over events, or is even viewed simply as a talisman of an older, more powerful Arabic civilisation, then Majeed will want it and he'll get Mosry to kill for it.'

The memory of Mosry staring into the interrogation room at police headquarters shot through me.

'You might want to take some safety precautions,' Rachel continued, 'like get yourself some body armour, a gun, maybe even disappear for a while. Majeed is ruthless.'

She turned back to the astrarium, which I'd wrapped up again as she was talking. 'But this ... this is totally amazing: history incarnate. To think the Ancient Egyptians were so sophisticated. I would have liked to have met Isabella, she must have been fascinating.' She stretched then stood. 'But now I really have to shower. See you in ten.' She disappeared into the bathroom.

The early morning sun had begun to filter through the thin curtains. I glanced at the clock radio beside the bed. It showed 6.30 am. I got up and walked out onto the balcony. A strange birdcall sounded over the early morning chorus. For some reason it reminded me of London and the last morning when I'd driven away from the flat. The memory brought with it an increased sense of foreboding. I looked over at the balcony of the apartment next to us — the curtains were open and the room appeared vacant. The sound of a van pulling up drew my gaze down to the front driveway of the hotel. The security guard, looking oddly nervous, stepped out of his sentry box and walked to the van's window. I could see money being exchanged, then, to my amazement, the guard walked away from his post and the hotel. The van pulled up at the main entrance and two men in white uniforms jumped out. Something about the urgency of their movements made me more uneasy.

As if sensing my gaze, one of them looked up towards the balcony, staring right into my face before I had a chance to duck down. By the time I'd stood up again, the men had disappeared.

I went back inside. Rachel stood in the centre of the room towelling her damp, curling hair. She sat on the edge of the bed and smiled seductively. 'Come back to bed — the rest of the world's asleep.'

I hesitated. Outside in the corridor, I could hear the sound of running footsteps. I gestured to Rachel that she should keep quiet, then went to the door and opened it as gently as I could. At the end of the corridor were the two men I'd seen outside, now with guns in their hands. I shut the door softly then grabbed Rachel's arm and pulled her from the bed.

'Out, now!' I hissed, sweeping up the astrarium with my other hand.

Rachel threw on some clothes, grabbed her travel bag and followed me to the balcony. We climbed over the low wall onto the balcony of the room next door. The glass doors were unlocked. We ran into the room.

Through the thin wall we heard pounding on Rachel's door, then the sound of it being kicked in followed by footsteps running into the room. Rachel turned to me in bewilderment. We both glanced at the door of the apartment we were in. In seconds we were at it. After making sure the corridor was empty, we slipped out then bolted. As we turned the corner, we ran into a bellboy carrying a set of towels.

We were already running through the empty lobby when we heard shouting behind us. The desk staff watched us in amazement.

'What the hell, Oliver!' Rachel yelled as she ran beside me.

'Just keep running! They're right behind us!'

We pushed through the main glass doors and bolted into the grounds and beyond onto the sleeping streets. We ran past a row of parked cars then ducked into a side lane. Behind us we could hear the men following.

Desperate, I glanced around. A covered cart stood by a market stall, the thin horse harnessed to it chewing on a wad of hay in the gutter. I pulled up the tarpaulin: the cart was half-empty, a layer of dry cement dust covering the bottom. There was room to hide.

Grabbing Rachel, I hauled her up and we both cowered under the tarpaulin, trying desperately to quieten our panting breath. Minutes later we heard the men entering the lane.

'You sure it was him?' one asked in a gruff voice. He spoke in Arabic with a Saudi accent.

'Absolutely. Mosry had a photo,' the other replied.

Rachel's nails dug into my wrist as she heard the name. We waited, motionless, not even daring to breathe. The men left but we stayed hidden for another five minutes. I could feel the pounding of Rachel's heart through her fingers, and the smell of both our fear cut through the odour of the tarpaulin and the powdered cement. Tentatively, I lifted the tarpaulin — the lane was empty. I leaped out and helped Rachel down to the ground.

'He said the name Mosry, didn't he?'

Her voice was drowned out by a boom, a flash of light and a shudder that seemed to travel in a wave under our feet. Thrown to the ground, we lay there as plaster and debris showered around us. I waited until all of my senses were sucked back into the present.

'What the fuck was that?' Rachel sat up. Apart from a few tiny scratches on her face, she appeared unharmed.

'That was Mosry trying to ruin Sadat's peace initiatives,' I replied.

I turned towards the hotel, visible at the end of the lane. One side appeared to be completely demolished, the plaster walls falling away in a void of rubble and mangled iron girders. Patches of sky showed through shattered windows and doorframes.

'But if they were after the astrarium, they wouldn't have given up. They'd have killed you!'

'Rachel, I wasn't meant to be there. They were after the journalists, the foreign press — people like you.'

'Oh Jesus, no.' She froze in horror.

From the street behind us came the sound of men shouting. Convinced we were still being searched for, I pulled Rachel to her feet and we started running again. Half-dressed and covered in plaster dust, we raced through the dawn streets like ghosts, horrified people scattering from us. I clutched the astrarium to my chest, counting the years of my life as a way to distract myself from the roar of my damaged hearing and the thudding of my heart. I wasn't entirely aware of where I was going, but some instinctive sense of geography must have been activated, the compass of the survivor, as we found ourselves outside the shop of a barber whom I knew well. Abdul had been cutting my hair ever since Isabella and I had arrived in Alexandria. A friendly man in his mid-sixties, he was a socialist and a poet and we'd spent many hours debating the failures and successes of various regimes and exchanging opinions on poets such as Seferis, Rilke and Lorca. I knew he would help us.

Abdul and his assistant were prostrate on the floor in the middle of morning prayer. Surprised, they peered up at us.

'Mr Warnock! You look terrible!' Abdul stood, dusting his knees.

'We need a room, Abdul. Now!'

Abdul took one look at Rachel's terrified face and immediately ushered us to the back of the store, shouting at his assistant to close the shop. In the distance there was the wail of sirens as ambulances and fire engines converged on the Sheraton.

# 32

The room above the barber's shop was equipped with a single iron bed, a small camp stove upon which sat a pot of mint tea, and a low wooden chair. There was a shelf holding several books, including a couple of revolutionary texts and a collection of Constantine Cavafy's poems, and various hairdressing supplies scattered around. There were two small windows; one looking over the street market below, the other opposite, looking over a panorama of rooftops.

Rachel, now dressed in a plain traditional kaftan Abdul had supplied, collapsed onto the bed. 'Are you absolutely sure it was Mosry's men?'

'I saw the white van drive up,' I said. 'That's probably where the explosives were. They must have seen me on the balcony and decided to try to get the astrarium, assuming I had it with me, before detonating the bomb.'

'Oliver, it could have been anyone — the Syrians, the Jordanians. No one wants this accord except Sadat.'

'Rachel, you heard them mention Mosry's name yourself.'

'Francois Paget from *Le Monde*, Eric Tullberg from *Der*

*Spiegel*, George Del Sorro, *The Washington Times* — Christ, they were all there, Oliver.' She looked at me, her face white with shock, bits of plaster still caught in her blonde hair.

I glanced across at my rucksack sitting on the floor. Following my gaze, Rachel said nothing.

'Don't you think it's a little miraculous?' I ventured.

'What, having your hotel room blown up? I'd say it was very bad luck.'

'I mean having survived.'

'If it is Mosry then next time we won't be so lucky.' She stood up. 'I have to get to a phone to file the story.'

'Shouldn't you see a doctor?'

'All I need is a shower and a strong coffee. I'll sleep later, if I can find a spare hotel room. I suppose I should be thankful Mosry's after you and not me.' She smiled grimly.

'Listen, I need a couple of favours ...'

'If it involves confronting two large Saudi gentlemen, count me out,' she joked.

'Can you take a message to my housekeeper and collect some things for me? Then I need you to visit the priest at St Catherine's and ask him whether you could borrow a Coptic monk's cassock. If you tell him it's for me, he'll understand. Please, Rachel? I'll be indebted to you for life.'

'For life, huh? That's tempting.' She picked a large piece of plaster out of my tangled hair. 'I guess there's a story in it eventually. Is this barber trustworthy?'

'Completely, although we disagree on the merits of Rilke and he's itching to shave off my beard. So you'll do it?'

Rachel nodded. She left minutes later, with a letter for Ibrihim and some money I'd borrowed from Abdul.

When she was gone, I unwrapped the astrarium. Amazingly, it was intact, the magnets still whirling. I sat there hypnotised by the spinning mechanism. I thought I saw a light flicker behind me and spun around, half-expecting to see Banafrit's shadow stretched across the wall and ceiling. There was nothing.

* * *

The face reflected back in the sliver of mirror propped up against the wall was almost unrecognisable. My beard, thick and black, covered most of my chin, and with the suntan I'd got out at Abu Rudeis, only my blue eyes gave me away as English. The robe, shirt and black priest's cap Father Carlotto had given Rachel fitted me perfectly. It was disturbing that I, a fervent atheist, could take on the appearance of a cleric so convincingly. It was, however, the perfect disguise.

'Wow! You look totally legit.' Rachel stared at me, amazed. 'Even I wouldn't have recognised you.'

I reached into the bag packed by Ibrihim, pulled out a pair of sunglasses and put them on. 'And now you wouldn't even suspect I was European.'

Rachel had had to negotiate the police barricades that had been set up around the city centre and the Sheraton, but had managed to slip by with some hefty bribes. When she arrived at the villa, Ibrihim had been almost hysterical. The night before, while he was visiting his mother, the villa had been broken into, my bedroom and study searched, and Tinnin the Alsatian poisoned. It seemed Mosry's men were getting closer.

'What else did Ibrihim say about the break-in?' I asked.

'It was hard to get much out of him, he was very nervous. He did tell me he'd fired the night guard. He was convinced the guy had been paid off.'

'Better that than murdered. Was there much damage?'

'They'd smashed up some of the furniture, your clothes and books were all over the bedroom, some of the wall panels had been torn off. Ibrihim told me you should stay invisible for at least another week and keep away from anywhere you're known. Promise me you won't take any unnecessary risks?'

I kissed her. 'Promise.'

It felt like a lifetime since we'd made love early that morning, but now, holding her, despite the bruises and scratches I'd collected during the morning, the memory of that lovemaking echoed under my skin.

'Ever had sex with a priest?' I asked.

\* \* \*

Rachel left an hour later. She'd taken a room at the Cecil Hotel and was hoping to file a story on the bombing before New York woke up. I felt a lot lonelier and, frankly, scared without her.

Ibrihim had followed my instructions perfectly: apart from the sunglasses, he'd packed several changes of clothes, a few of Isabella's reference books, a work diary, money, passport and a knife, which I now slipped into my belt. There was also food: cheese and bread. Outside I could hear a street cleaner singing as he went about his work. I had to hide the astrarium, but where? I looked around the small room. In the corner stood a male mannequin that looked as if it dated from the 1940s, a dingy black toupee was perched on its shiny plaster pate. Halfway down its torso I noticed a hairline join, as if it might unscrew at that point.

Wrapped in cloth, the astrarium fitted perfectly into the hollow torso. 'Stay sleeping,' I found myself saying out loud to the mechanism as I carefully twisted the two halves of the mannequin back together.

I stood in front of the window, eating, still dressed in the priest's cassock. Shoppers and workers eager to return to their families were milling in the street below. Just then, a group of older Arabic women, their shopping piled high in baskets carried up on their shoulders, passed beneath the barber's shop, and weaving her way between them was a slim European woman with black hair down to her waist. My heart jolted in recognition: Isabella. If not her, her double. She glanced blindly up at the window and I stepped back out of sight. When I looked again a moment later, I could see her face clearly. I was convinced it was her, and despite my rational mind telling me it couldn't possibly be her, every molecule in my body screamed out for confirmation. She turned and began pushing through the crowd — with that distinctive way of walking I knew so well. Without thinking about the consequences, I reached for the priest's cap and ran down the back stairs of the shop.

I pushed through the crowd after her, but each time I got close she darted on ahead, leading me away from the centre of the city and out towards the old Arab district. Occasionally I caught her half-profile, the strong nose and chin discernible in the fading light. The crowds dropped away, the streets became narrower and more ancient: low mud-brick buildings and the labyrinths of street markets replaced high-rises, neon and the occasional petrol pump. She ran ahead, her long hair tumbling around her shoulders. I followed as closely as I could as she slipped from shadow to shadow, always frustratingly just out of reach.

The gates of the catacombs of Kom el-Shugafa appeared in front of us. I called out, but the girl stepped through a side door and was gone. Without hesitating I followed.

The air at the bottom of the central shaft that led down to the catacombs was chilly and damp. I knew from previous visits that the catacombs dated from the time of the Roman emperors Domitian and Trajan, when Alexandria was already a Roman colony. The limestone walls dripped with moisture and I was thankful for the electric lights strung up in the corners. I glanced back at the spiral steps I'd climbed down into the shaft, bewildered to find myself suddenly underground. It was almost as if I'd fallen under a spell; how on earth had I allowed myself to be lured into this godforsaken place?

I spun around, staring into the shadows, looking for the girl. It seemed impossible for a human being to have disappeared so quickly. *Was* she human or some crazy projection of my own mind? Perhaps the guilt of my night with Rachel was combining with my shattered nerves to play tricks on me?

I tried to gather my rationality around me like armour, scouring my mind for facts I knew about the catacombs that would help me navigate them. I remembered that the dead had been transported to their tombs via this main shaft, and that it also provided the necessary ventilation for the mourners, who returned on holy days to celebrate their deceased.

Ahead lay a room called the triclinium — a small square hall with stone benches and a stone table permanently in place — built especially for these subterranean picnics with figs, grapes and cheese laid out on the cold stone table top while children and family gathered around, drinking wine and exchanging anecdotes about their dead. Better that than the secret shame we'd made death into in the twentieth century, I couldn't help observing.

My movements were hindered by the long skirt of my cassock, so I stepped out of it and stored it in an alcove; I'd collect it when I left. A noise behind me made me jump and I swung around to confront the girl. Instead, a rat scurried past; now I was thankful for the small hunting knife hidden in my belt.

Where was she? I moved forward, stepping carefully over the broken paving stones at the entrance to the catacombs. The doorway was framed by two pillars, with a bas-relief either side showing the Ptolemaic two-tailed cobra god Agathodaimon, the divine guardian of second-century Alexandria. One tail was coiled around the wand of Hermes, while on his head he wore the shield of Perseus showing the snake-haired head of Medusa. I examined it — here was my first clue. Isabella's double had led me exactly to where the Isabella of my dream had wanted me to be, but why?

Cautiously, I moved further into the chamber, wondering if she was now hiding behind one of the stone funereal statues.

There were two niches either side of the tomb's entrance. In the left stood a statue of a woman, while in the niche opposite was her male counterpart, eerily serene in his stance. Neither statue bore any inscription but they seemed to be husband and wife: a marriage immortalised. Over the entrance was a carving of the sun disk of Horus, flanked by the wings of the royal falcon. There was mixed allegory everywhere, a reflection of a culture in flux, a hybrid aristocracy seeking legitimacy from both the Pharaonic past and a Hellenistic present, and looking forward towards the Roman future while terrified of insulting anyone — a culture in fear. Thinking the girl might be behind one of the reliefs I stepped into the tomb.

Carved into the wall, were two reliefs of Anubis, the jackal-headed god of mummification. In one, the grinning jackal's head sat atop the body of a Roman legionary, his muscular torso clad in a leather kilt, one arm holding up a spear, the other resting on a shield. The realism of the statue seemed somehow more sinister than the stylised Egyptian iconography. It was a poignant illustration of how a dictatorship could assimilate local religious beliefs to reinforce its own power. I could almost hear the soldier-jackal breathing, a low growl that threatened violence.

I shivered; it was as if the dead hovered in the chilly air, waiting for some indication of approval of the splendour of their last place of residence.

In the centre of the burial chamber was the main sarcophagus. It held the body of a woman and was decorated with carvings of floral garlands and Medusa heads. The bas-relief above it showed the Ancient Egyptian burial rite, the embalmed body lying stiffly on the funerary bed. A priest of Anubis stood over the dead woman, and at her head I recognised Osiris, king of the underworld, wearing his Atef crown and holding the traditional crook and flail.

I reached out and touched the worn features of one of the Medusas, undoubtedly carved there to scare off grave robbers. She seemed to embody many of the characteristics of the women I was attracted to: fearlessness, curiosity, a beauty that had been frozen into a fierce intellectualism. But where were the other clues Isabella had pointed out, the bull and the fish?

I heard scurrying and had the sudden frightening sensation I was being watched. But as I peered around the dimly lit chamber, nothing moved, not even the hanging lights or the shadows of the statues.

To my right was a side sarcophagus with a bas-relief above it that featured Apis the sacred bull, a goddess stretching out her wings to protect him. So there was the second symbol. Now I needed the final clue — the fish, the secret sign of the early Christians.

Just then the sound of murmuring voices came from the stairs leading down into the central shaft. I hid in a niche behind a statue as the footsteps grew louder — it sounded like quite a large group. There was a rhythmical beat to their footfalls, almost a ritualised tempo, and I could smell the strong fragrance of burning incense. They were moving towards the burial chamber, towards me.

I held my breath. The footfalls stopped inches away, followed by the sound of stone scraping against stone. Frozen against the damp stone I was terrified, nevertheless, hidden by the statue, I peered out. To my astonishment, I caught sight of a figure carrying a blazing ceremonial torch and dressed in the pleated robe of an Ancient Egyptian priest. But what was most startling was the ibis mask he wore. I knew it represented the god of knowledge, Thoth, its curved beak symbolic of the moon's crescent.

The figure descended into an opening in the stone floor — the scraping noise I'd heard was the cover being pushed aside. As I moved to see more clearly, I knocked a small rock with my foot. The Thoth figure swung around at the noise, the bird's head staring blindly towards me. I ducked back into my hiding place, fascinated yet also deeply disturbed.

# 33

I waited until the light from the torches had disappeared from the tunnel entrance and I could no longer hear the diminishing footsteps then emerged from the niche. I peered down the narrow stone shaft with steps carved into it — I thought it was Roman or perhaps even earlier. Walking softly down ten steps, my hands traced the roughly hewn walls scarred with chisel marks. A little further down, carved into the rock above my head, was an inscription. Calling on my schoolboy Latin, I translated it: *To descend into darkness is to know oneself.*

There was just enough light filtering in from the electric lights for me to see the first of the winding steps. Those who had descended before me must have known exactly where they were going — there were no rails, just the slippery walls, clammy under the palm. I touched the hunting knife in my belt before continuing my descent. I had never felt more vulnerable, not diving, not potholing. The whole tunnel felt as if it were alive, as if its very walls had absorbed centuries of violence, mute witnesses to unmentionable horrors.

About halfway down the light faded away completely and I was plunged into total darkness. It was an unsettling experience; I could see nothing at all, just smell the damp stone and feel it under my groping hands. I moved tentatively forward, feeling out every step. After a couple of minutes I lost all notion of what was external and what was internal. It seemed to me that this profound darkness had become an extension of my body — even my psychology as if I'd crossed the threshold — from physical to metaphysical.

My foot hit the level floor, no more steps. Along the walls I could feel where the limestone fell away to rectangular hollows. My fingers fastened around a long hard object, a stick of some sort, I thought. With a shock, I realised I was holding a bone, probably human. I now knew what the hollows were: loculi — horizontal burial shafts each containing a skeleton. Horrified, I pulled my hands away and relied solely on my feet to guide me.

A breeze coming from deeper inside the catacombs brushed my face. I blinked, my eyes adjusting as they scanned the darkness for light. Nothing, just this seamless black. Following the direction of the faint wind, I felt my way around a corner. Figures became visible at the end of a long passage, moving around each other in slow, ritualised movements, as if choreographed. It was like watching some slow underwater dance.

Sliding along the wall, I moved closer until I was about fifteen feet away. I realised the figures were inside a chamber; a blazing torch was set up in each corner. There were five of them, all dressed like Pharaonic gods. A huge set of scales stood to the left of the chamber, its ebony and gold arms stretching a good ten feet from side to side. Gold chains held the plates of the scales; one tray was empty, while the other held a single white feather. The pivotal pole was topped with a carving of the goddess of truth, Maat, recognisable by the ostrich feather she wore on her head.

In that moment I understood the symbolism of the ritual taking place on a raised stone platform. It was the weighing of the heart, the same ritual Isabella had dreamt about over and over. It was unmistakable. Now I knew why I had been led here. I was transfixed; it was as if I'd been transported into Isabella's nightmare, into her very psyche.

An African man wearing a jackal mask kneeled by the scales, his black, muscular arms shimmering in the torchlight as he held a gold platter on which sat a shrivelled piece of flesh. Anubis. Beyond the scales lay a pool of dark water. Next to it stood the man in the ibis mask; he held a scroll and a quill. Thoth would transcribe the good deeds and the sins of the deceased, whose heart would be weighed against the weight of a feather. The heart! Horrified, I looked again at the shrivelled object on the gold platter, the dark desiccated flesh visible in the flickering light. Was it a human heart? Isabella's?

Could it be possible? If so, what was the role of the young girl who had led me here to witness this bizarre re-enactment?

Next to Thoth, in the place where the deceased would usually stand waiting to be judged before the throne of Osiris, were four Canopic jars carved with the heads of the sons of Horus. I was appalled. I knew Canopic jars were used to contain the mummified organs of the dead. Did these jars contain Isabella's organs? Their bright colours and the hieroglyphs painted vertically on each one looked completely authentic. The whole theatrical display seemed meticulous in its historical accuracy; garish yet sombre with a rigid authority that had kept such a civilisation — with its chaotic underworld — so powerful for centuries. The purpose and effort behind such a fanatically correct presentation was terrifying. And judging by the participants' concentration they appeared to be convinced by the power of their own symbolism; they weren't just re-enacting the weighing of the heart ceremony — they were living it.

Osiris's throne was a gilded chair on a podium, its base carved with serpents and jackals. Behind it stood two figures in profile, Isis and her sister Nephthys, as if they expected the king of the underworld to manifest any minute. Isis wore an elaborate costume that covered her arms and hands, its long skirt reaching to the ground. Her golden breastplate was moulded in the shape of a woman's breasts and her face was a painted mask framed by a long black wig. In contrast, her sister goddess was unmasked and near naked — it was almost as if one goddess was meant to represent artifice, the other nature. Nephthys looked as if she was in her twenties, and I peered closer, wondering if this was the woman who had lured me into the catacombs. But her face did not resemble Isabella's in any way.

I crept forward along the clammy wall. Another figure with a falcon mask, Horus, started a low chant in a language I didn't recognise. His stance and stature were vaguely familiar to me. Horus's role was to lead the deceased to the ritual, but as yet the deceased appeared absent in the tableau. Had they not arrived yet? The other worshippers joined in and the hypnotic monotone echoed off the limestone walls, weaving and blending into one note that bored its way into my head. I tried to remember the exact order of the gods in the murals I had seen that showed the ritual. Osiris sat on his throne to the right, with Isis and her sister behind him. Here he was missing, the throne empty. Horus and Thoth stood next to the scales that weighed the heart. Horus would dictate the sins of the deceased while Thoth would write them down. What did the jackal-headed Anubis do? I thought frantically but I couldn't remember exactly. And there was another god missing — a figure that always appeared at the bottom of the murals, a large crocodile-type creature snapping at the heart on the scales. Ammut, that was it — Ammut the devourer of the dead, a fusion of all the creatures that terrorised the Ancient Egyptians in real life. She had the head of a crocodile, the body of a lion and the haunches of a hippopotamus. Ammut's task was to eat the hearts of those found guilty by the gods, thus destroying any hope of an afterlife for them. Would she appear? Although the monster had a peculiarly comical look, it had always disturbed me; there was something primordially terrifying about the sly ferocity of the reptilian jaw, the jagged teeth waiting to tear apart the sinner.

A great rustling burst up around me. Crouching, I glanced back at the stage. The masked figures appeared indifferent to the cacophony, which grew louder and louder until what appeared at first to be a swarm of black rags of cloth came streaming from the back of the catacombs. They swerved at the last minute to avoid the stationary figures on the raised platform and I was buffeted by a huge wind as thousands of beating wings missed me by inches. Bats; they poured past me and continued towards the tunnel's entrance.

I felt an arm wrap around my neck and I stumbled. Someone pinned my hands behind me and a needle jabbed into my shoulder. I fell back, not understanding what was happening. My captor hauled me into the full light of the torches and pushed me to my knees. The torches began to spit small meteorites of flame and the masked figures on the podium gravitated slowly in my direction. They seemed to grow in height as they moved.

Horus stepped forward and his falcon's head sprouted feathers, its beady black eyes swivelling towards me. I tried to speak but my tongue felt too swollen to move. Belatedly I realised I'd been drugged, but the knowledge didn't stop the violent rush of fear as the bird-god stepped down from the podium, his huge gnarled claws rattling against the stone floor. This can't be real, this isn't real, I told myself, but dread swept through me in a wave of sweat and blind terror.

Horus stretched out his arms as he reached me, revealing a small tattoo on his forearm — the Ba symbol. Struggling to stay focused, I racked my memory for the image — I'd seen it recently ... Hugh Wollington! Was it him behind the mask? There was so little of the human about the figure now kneeling before me. The falcon cocked its head and opened its beak to speak.

'We welcome you, Lord Osiris.'

I blacked out. When I came to, I was strapped into Osiris's throne, my legs and torso bound to its sides, only my arms from the elbow down were free. The god's tall crown was pressed low on my forehead and his crook and flail were tied across my chest. I was wearing a robe of shimmering fabric threaded with gold. All my senses were heightened by whatever they had injected me with; every movement of the creatures before me carried a multitude of after-images — one sweep of an arm was a thousand arms breaking like a wave, one turn of a god's head made many, the appearance of the players undeniably real; the fusion of fur and flesh, scale and skin, seamless and horrifically organic.

Horus and Anubis advanced, Anubis carrying the gold platter with the heart on it, two valves trailing from the rippled purple flesh. Ears twitching, the canine fur and flesh fusing into the muscular neck of a man, Anubis held up the plate. Isabella's heart, it had to be. Struggling, I tried to shout but again I had no voice.

Horus's falcon head began to speak. 'Oh Lord, we are gathered here in the hall of truth and justice to judge the life of Isabella Brambilla, to weigh her heart against that of the feather of truth, the symbol of the goddess Maat who will tolerate neither sin nor lie. If the deceased's heart balances against the feather, she will be granted a place in the Fields of Hetep and Iaru. But if her heart is heavy with the weight of wrongdoing, Ammut will devour it and the deceased's soul will be condemned to an eternity of oblivion. I seek your blessing, Lord Osiris, as embalmer to the gods and kings.'

Isis stepped in front of the throne. I could see now that the goddess was wearing a painted mask over her features, bejewelled with turquoise eyes and crimson enamel lips that shone fantastically in the flaring torchlight. As she spoke I thought I recognised the voice — Amelia Lynhurst's perhaps, only deeper now and resonating with authority.

'My Lord, you must bless Anubis if you wish to save the soul of your consort.'

The heavy black wig covered her torso, concealing the figure beneath the breastplate, but there was something genderless about her shape — the shoulders too wide, the waist too thick. I struggled to remember Amelia's figure, whether it had any similarities. My drugged state meant it required extraordinary concentration to make any coherent sense of the scene and I kept slipping back into hallucination. I tried to speak again, but only managed a groan. Impatient, Isis yanked the flail from where it was tied across my chest and blessed Anubis herself.

Anubis carried the heart over to the scales and ceremoniously placed it onto the opposite tray to that holding the white feather. The scales balanced for an instant then tipped violently to the side the heart was on.

'This heart is heavy in deceit!' Horus shrieked, his voice like a bird's cry. Thoth, holding his feathered quill high, started writing on his papyrus scroll, while either side of me Isis and her sister, Nephthys, began to ululate in that hair-raising manner of Arabic mourners.

A small wave suddenly ran across the surface of the pool behind the scales. I turned at the motion; it resonated in my drugged mind, echoing some frightening image: Ammut, the devourer. In terror, I struggled in my chair as the air became pungent with a fishy stench. The water rippled again and this time I was convinced I saw the flaring eyes of a crocodile in the torchlight.

There was a splash and the gnarled, horny head of a crocodile lifted out of the water, its long yellowed teeth snapping at the heart. A lion's mane hung from its reptilian scales, a travesty of wet and matted fur.

I retched.

A figure stepped from the shadows beyond the flaring torches and walked towards me — normal, human, dressed in a simple cotton dress. This was no double — this was surely Isabella! My fear slammed into the back of my throat, my heart a rattling cannon. I tried to stand, to walk towards her; my arms tore against their bindings and began to bleed.

'Will you save your consort and surrender Nectanebo's skybox?' Isis whispered.

At the mention of the astrarium I was jolted out of the artifice. 'What!? What's that got to do with all this?'

The words tumbled out of me as I tried to close myself against the image of my wife, iridescent in its ordinariness. Now I could see the spreading stain of dark blood across her chest, oozing from the wound where her heart had been removed. Whose terrible imagination had concocted this?

'Give up the astrarium.' Isabella's voice sounded in my head but her lips didn't move. 'If you do not, I will have no afterlife. I will not even live on in your memory. You will be my condemner, my murderer.'

She had articulated my worst fear; that I had failed to save her and that — equally disturbing — I might forget her entirely. But what on earth did this have to do with the astrarium? Even with the drugs coursing through me, I knew there was no appeal, no loophole, to the weighing of the heart. Hoping the pain would jolt me into clearer thinking, I pushed my torn skin against my bonds, but still my mind reeled under the effects of the drug.

'Osiris, speak your judgement. The heart is heavy, the deceased is guilty!' Anubis barked.

Ammut's bulky reptilian body slithered out of the water and she shook herself like a large dog. I could see that the glistening lion's pelt merged at her waist into the shiny black hide of a hippo. The creature shook herself dry like a large dog — somehow the familiarity of the gesture was even more frightening. The heavy crocodile head swinging from side to side as tremors ran down the goddess's torso.

'Save me! Tell them where it is!' Isabella whispered urgently.

This was why people believed in visions, I suddenly understood, as the realism of the hallucination battled my intellectual comprehension that I was caught up in some horrific drug-induced sham.

'No!' I shouted, my anguished cry sounded solid set against the ephemeral nature of the scene before me.

Her crocodile claws scraping against the stone floor, Ammut slithered closer to the heart sitting on the scales.

Isabella clutched at her chest as if in pain. 'Tell them, I beg you!'

'No! None of this is real!' I screamed.

Ammut lunged forward and grabbed the heart between her jaws as if it were a piece of old meat. She turned her head towards Isis, the heart hanging from her mouth, as if waiting for a command.

'Not real, my Lord? What is real? The waking world or the sleeping one; the world beyond the mind or the chaos that lies under order?' Isis's words were like icicles. 'You must fulfil your role or your consort will be denied entry to the afterlife.'

The light flickered wildly as a huge shadow fell across the blazing torches. The goddess, now silent, was staring at the back wall of the cavern. Across the ceiling, extending down to where the black water lapped the bottom of the limestone stretched a massive silhouette: a dog-like creature with four slender legs, a long tail with a forked tip, a long beak-like snout and two raised blunt-ended ears. The players all fell to their knees, foreheads to the ground. No one was looking at me, and they seemed too terrified to look at the giant shadow.

With a supreme effort I yanked at my bonds. To my amazement, they broke. I leaped from the chair, snatched the heart from Ammut's jaws and bolted down the long corridor towards the steps that led back up to the surface. Behind me I heard chaos erupting — shouts and footsteps.

I ran up the stone steps — sheer terror propelled me forward. At the top, a figure carrying a torch pulled me aside into an alcove. To my relief and further astonishment, it was Faakhir.

'This way!' he cried.

We ran towards the light of an open door. Outside, a car was waiting. As I fell into the back seat I managed to murmur the name of the barber's shop before slipping into unconsciousness.

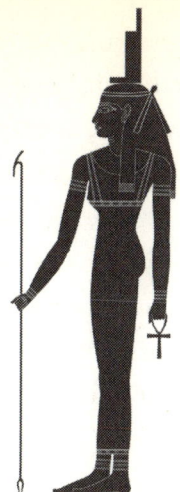

# 34

I woke sweating in the small iron bed. An embroidered blanket had been thrown over me. Shooting pain burst rhythmically over each eye and it was hard to swallow. The naked electric bulb seemed to swing against the smoke-stained ceiling. My mind was numbed into a sensorial jumble that made it difficult to actually make sense of where I was, even who I was. I lay there waiting as my frenetic thoughts slowly collected themselves. I glanced down at my wrists and the red bands burned around them — the marks of restraint. Now flashes of the night before began to flicker across my memory: the catacombs, the ceremony, Faakhir helping me to the door of Abdul's shop, telling me not to look for him, but that he would be watching me.

I looked over to the back window. Beyond lay the rooftops of Alexandria. The sun was high; it was about midday I guessed. Beside the small camp stove sat a bowl of fresh fruit and a bottle of water. Abdul had obviously left some supplies. I reached out and my fingers brushed against a small box next to the low bed on the floor. I sat and picked it up, slipping my hand into the open top. My fingers hit something sticky and organic in texture. I pulled out a purple lump of muscle tissue; the withered dark flesh bulged out between my fingers.

Disgusted, I threw the heart back in the box and leaned over the side of the bed, retching. After the shivering stopped, I lay back and considered the events of the night before. Why the weighing of the heart ceremony? And why had I been designated as Osiris? Who was the woman who lured me there? Had it really been Hugh Wollington playing Horus or had that been a figment of my imagination, a desperate attempt to link events and make sense of them? But who else would go to the trouble of creating such an elaborate and macabre charade in order to obtain the astrarium? And if it was Wollington, how did he know of the connection between the ritual and Isabella's recurring nightmare?

The Coptic robe Father Carlotto had given me lay neatly folded at the bottom of the bed. Somebody must have collected it from where I'd hidden it in the catacombs. Had they been watching me the whole time? And what was Faakhir's role in all of this?

I glanced back at the box containing the heart. I wasn't even sure it was human, then I remembered I knew someone who would be able to tell me.

\* \* \*

Demetriou al-Masri peered through his thick half-moon glasses at the heart on the laboratory dish and prodded it.

His office was a windowless annexe off one of the city morgue's main chambers; I suspected it might once have been a large cupboard. Dressed in my Coptic robe, I'd entered the morgue with remarkable ease. Upon seeing my disguise the coroner had immediately pulled me into his tiny office.

We'd both been staring at the heart for at least five minutes and I was beginning to doubt whether I was going to get a conclusive verdict.

Finally he cleared his throat and sat back. 'It is a human heart, from a smallish body, quite possibly female. I would say around thirty years of age.'

My own heart started rattling the bars of my ribcage. 'My wife's?'

'It might be, it might not. That is not something I can confirm.' He sighed and began packing the heart back into the container I had brought it in. 'May I ask how you came by the organ?'

'It was delivered to the villa, anonymously.'

The coroner studied me, then handed me the container. 'Run, my friend, run as fast and as hard as you can. I do not want to find myself staring down at your body tomorrow.'

He opened the door and the room was immediately flooded by the greenish fluorescent lights of the morgue beyond. I glanced back at the windowless room. Demetriou al-Masri followed my gaze.

'I had a view once, but they demoted me. Curiosity can be very bad for one's career. You should be careful. These are dangerous times, even for a cleric,' he added with an ironic smile.

\* \* \*

I went straight to Chatby Cemetery, clutching Isabella's heart. My air of purpose must have been apparent for people parted to make way as I strode along the crowded streets, indifferent to my fate, intent on only one thing.

It was extraordinary to watch how people reacted to me. Some moved respectfully out of my path; others brushed past roughly, as if being deliberately rude. All of them appeared to take me for a cleric.

The cemetery was empty apart from a few gardeners patiently clipping the trees that ran in avenues between the graves. I walked through the dappled light, unrecognisable as the man who had walked the same path a couple of weeks before.

Someone had laid fresh flowers — white lilies — across the marble slab of Isabella's grave. The scent reminded me of the flowers she used to bring back from the street markets in London, filling the apartment with their fragrance. Whispering apologies to my dead wife, I dug a small hole in the earth at the foot of the grave and buried her heart. Now, at least, all of her was buried together. As I stood up I noticed the small portal was still open on one side, the miniature door for her Ba.

\* \* \*

In the room above Abdul's shop, I pulled the astrarium from its hiding place and upacked it, my hands trembling. My experience in the catacombs had unnerved me and, staring at the small glinting clock-like mechanism, I could now conceive how it might have destroyed kings, ruined nations. This device could make a beggar into a Pharaoh and, in a moment of obstinate egoism, I had challenged it. I peered closer. The pointer was still turned to my birth date but, to my horror, the small silver-black death pointer had sprung up.

I gazed at it, incredulous. How could the pointer have appeared by itself? I had only put in my birth date; I hadn't even touched anything else. Thinking it must be some mechanical fault, I inserted the Was and tried turning the dials again, but the cogs were fixed. I pushed the key to the point where I was frightened it might snap in half. The pointers stayed immobile: fastened on the date of my birth and now, supposedly, of my death. A slow dread filled me. Was I going to die, like Isabella, before my time? I'd survived the blowout at Abu Rudeis, the explosion at the hotel and then the ritual in the catacombs, but I couldn't deny the very real sense that death had begun to shadow me.

I peered at the death pointer and began to draw the outline of the tiny silver figure at its tip onto a blotter — a dog-like beast with an elongated face and forked tail. I held it up. Shuddering I recognised the creature whose shadow had appeared on the wall of the catacomb just before I'd fled. Frantically, I counted the tiny dashes running between the hieroglyphs of the full moon on the dial. The next full moon was in eight days. Did that mean my death date was just over a week away?

Suddenly I had a visceral comprehension of Isabella's blind panic those few days before she drowned. Despite myself, I felt the same desperation. I tried to repress the fear that swept through me. It's all just ridiculous superstition, I told myself; the device was originally constructed as a piece of political propaganda, a way of intimidating and impressing Nectanebo's followers, of confirming his status as a great magus. Amelia Lynhurst had told me how the Pharaoh's enemies had turned the device against him and used it to orchestrate his death date. It was merely a toy that could be manipulated any way the user chose — just dials and a clockwork mechanism. It had no control over anything. But I couldn't prevent my mind returning to the same question over and over: could it have stopped Isabella dying on the death date predicted for her?

The impulse to smash the device swept through me but I kept my fists clenched at my sides. To destroy the device meant I believed it had power over me. I refused to succumb.

'There is no death date,' I told myself aloud. 'No one is going to frighten me into anything.' My voice bounced back off the walls.

Sounds and images flooded my mind: Isis's voice, Horus's shriek, Ammut's bloodied crocodile mouth tossing the heart from side to side. I found I remembered Isis's voice exactly, as if the drug I'd been injected with had heightened my memory. Its vocal inflections had seemed similar to Amelia Lynhurst's yet the voice had been deeper. I didn't think it was Amelia, but if not her, then who? And why were they so desperate to get the astrarium? Were they connected with Prince Majeed in any way? I doubted it; I couldn't see Mosry taking such a subtle and complex approach to getting the instrument for his employer.

The ritual made me think of the stories I'd heard about Giovanni Brambilla, the performances he'd got Isabella involved in as a child, which in turn led me to that photograph taken at Behbeit el-Hagar. I already suspected Hugh Wollington had been behind the Horus mask. What about the other people in that photo — Amelia Lynhurst, Hermes? There was only one person who would know.

\* \* \*

A black Volga sat outside the iron gates of the Brambillas' villa. A tall man in flared jeans and a shirt that was several sizes too small leaned against the box-like Russian car, smoking and staring blatantly at the house. I recognised him from the Sheraton Hotel — one of the men in the white van. Mosry was obviously having the villa watched. Disguised as a Coptic monk, I decided the best plan was to be as audacious as possible. I slipped on my sunglasses and, mustering my courage, walked towards the iron gates.

As I passed I greeted him in Arabic. 'Lovely weather, my friend.'

Slightly embarrassed, he dropped his cigarette butt in the gutter and replied, 'It is, Father.'

I continued to approach the villa, smiling back at him — he hadn't recognised me at all. I entered the iron gates and saw Aadeel nearby, on his knees weeding the enclosed garden. 'Aadeel!' I hissed.

He looked up, his face infused with suspicion when he saw my Coptic outfit.

'It's me, Oliver,' I whispered.

His face softened and he glanced over at the man watching the house. He waited until we were inside before he spoke.

'Allah be praised. We were worried. Where have you been?'

'I'll tell you later. Right now, I need to talk to Francesca.'

'She is resting, she hasn't been well …'

I pushed past the housekeeper and strode along the hall into the back parlour. The old woman was sitting in a large armchair facing the open French doors, an old photo album resting on her lap. She continued to stare out vacantly, despite my entrance.

'Francesca, last night I was drugged and forced to take part in a re-enactment of an Ancient Egyptian ritual,' I said bluntly, angry at being ignored.

She didn't respond.

'Is that what Isabella had to endure as a child? The kind of mad nationalism Giovanni believed in — voodoo and bad theatrics?'

I felt a hand on my shoulder. Startled, I wheeled around. Aadeel stepped between me and his mistress.

'Mr Oliver, Madame cannot answer you. She has had a stroke, she is paralysed. But my son Ashraf is here in Alexandria, and I believe he may be able to help you.'

Shocked, I glanced back at the old lady who was still staring blankly ahead. 'Oh, Francesca, I'm so sorry.'

\* \* \*

The housekeeper lived in an extension built at the back of the villa. It consisted of a bedroom and a kitchen that also doubled as a lounge room. A photograph of Ashraf in his graduation gown hung proudly on the wall, next to a portrait of Nasser. I sat on the edge of a sofa still covered in its plastic wrapping. Outside I could hear Aadeel welcoming his son.

Ashraf entered, dressed in traditional clothes, the bruise on his forehead — the result of cumulative hours spent praying in the mosque — the mark of the devout. He greeted me with a warm handshake. 'May peace be with you.'

'And you,' I replied.

He sat opposite, in a kitchen chair. Aadeel's wife, a silent shadow, handed him a mint tea.

'My father tells me you want to know about Monsieur Brambilla's ... special activities?' he said warily.

'Let's call it what it was — it was a cult, wasn't it?'

He stared at me. I knew that despite his close relationship with Isabella, Ashraf had never entirely trusted me.

'Oliver, you know Giovanni Brambilla was as close to me as my own grandfather,' he said, 'this family is my family. I would never betray them. But I loved Isabella and she loved you, otherwise I would not be sitting here with you.'

I stifled a wave of anger. 'You knew about this as children, didn't you? He was re-enacting these ancient rituals in some desperate attempt to conjure up the gods — for what reason? So he could keep hold of his money?'

'Please, Monsieur Oliver, you are shouting.' Aadeel got up

and pulled the window shutters closed. 'You understand we cannot talk about these things openly.'

Ashraf calmed his father then spoke to me again. 'I was the son of a servant so there were some … privileges that I did not share. In that respect I was lucky. I saw a ritual once — I must have been eleven and Isabella was eight, I think — her mother hadn't left long before. It was the year Nasser humiliated the Europeans, when we defeated the invading armies of the British, Israelis and French. I remember the fear in this household. Giovanni Brambilla knew that if Nasser nationalised the Suez Canal, he would eventually nationalise everything, including the cotton. Giovanni was terrified he would lose the mill, the house, his millions.'

Decades of resentment spilled out in Ashraf's voice. His father put a hand on his arm. 'Please, Ashraf, these things are in the past.'

'And the past has marked us,' Ashraf replied in Arabic before turning back to me. 'We were children, but Isabella was the innocent one, she had been protected. He would hypnotise us, both of us. It was his party trick. I knew better. I knew this crazy sorcery the old man was up to was his desperate attempt to manipulate events. His friends and associates, the old colonials, had lost their influence and Giovanni's bribes to the new guard, some of them socialist sons of the fellahin, hadn't worked. There was one young officer who'd taken over the management of the Alexandrian Cotton Mill, run by another Italian — a Jew. Giovanni knew it was only a matter of time before this officer destroyed the Brambilla fortune. The old man hated him, but he could do nothing but wait. He was terrified. It was in November — just after the British landed in the Sinai.'

'The sixth of November?'

'Exactly. People were frightened, they didn't know which way it was going to turn. The streets were empty — the young

Egyptian men had all run to the train stations to volunteer for the fighting; the Europeans had locked themselves up in their villas. Yet Giovanni and his friends drove out to the catacombs.'

'You followed them?'

'I knew Isabella was with them. In my heart she was my sister.'

Ashraf hid his face in his hands, overwhelmed by grief. His father stroked his head and after a few moments he collected himself and continued.

'I chased the car on my bicycle, driving through the empty streets at some distance, somehow knowing I was doing wrong. When I got there, I followed the sound of voices down the passages. The light of the torches flickered on the walls like the fires of hell, their chanting like that of demons. I have never forgotten it.'

He ran his hand across his face, his fingers trembling. Aadeel glanced at his wife and indicated that she should leave the room. She walked out with a swish of her long skirts. Ashraf took another sip of mint tea.

'There they were, eight, nine of them standing on a stage — all the old gods with their primitive animal heads that I'd seen in the books Giovanni had shown me, books he kept in his study. I remembered the name Horus, because I had wanted to be him. Only it was Isabella there, half-naked and carrying a silver dish with some kind of flesh on it. I almost called out to her, but something stopped me. I knew that what was happening was wrong but I was desperately afraid.

'There was a huge set of scales set up on the stage, and Isabella placed whatever was on the dish onto one of the trays. They all stood there watching silently, like statues in their masks. I recognised Giovanni but the others I didn't know — their faces were hidden. And then …'

His face went blank as the memory passed through him.

'Then what?' I prompted.

'There was a terrible screaming. Evil came into that place and it had a shape.'

I didn't need to ask him anything more. I had seen the same shape myself, both in the catacombs and carved at the end of the death pointer on the astrarium. Thanking him, I stood to leave. Just as I was about to step out the door, Ashraf looked up.

'Oliver, that young Egyptian officer who was in charge of repossessing the cotton mills — he was killed by the British on the seventh of November, the very next day. Maybe it was because of the old sorcery, maybe not. But maybe you should ask the Sudanese.'

'Sudanese?'

'The Egyptologist who was a friend of Giovanni's — he was always in the house in those days.'

# 35

Usta, Hermes' young companion, answered my knock. I pushed past him.

The living room was empty, its brightly coloured cushions scattered across the floor and a hookah pipe still smouldering. From somewhere in the apartment came the sound of Hermes yelling for his companion. I followed his voice.

The bedroom was dominated by a large low bed tented with a mosquito net. Through its lace I could see Hermes lying curled up on his side, his yellowed face in profile against the pillow. His back, naked, looked curiously feminine. I ventured into the room, which was filled with the cloying scent of cologne. Edith Piaf's voice soared out of a record-player, immediately evoking both Paris and, bizarrely, the smell of rain.

'Who's that?' Hermes asked.

I flicked up the mosquito net. 'Oliver Warnock.'

Startled, he covered himself with a silk dressing gown incongruously patterned with images of Paddington Bear. His hair, streaked with white, hung loose down his back and his skin was shiny with some kind of cream.

'You're ill?' I asked.

'Fatigued, my dear friend, nothing more. I had to attend an all-night vigil for one of my associates recently and I am getting too old. Be kind enough to avert your gaze,' he added and made to climb out of the bed.

Perplexed by his coyness, I dutifully turned my head.

'I went down to the Kom el-Shugafa catacombs, following a lead,' I began.

'A little too contemporary a location for my archaeological tastes. Anything after first century BC is really rather derivative of earlier times.'

Hermes, standing now and wrapped in his dressing gown, slipped his feet into leather slippers. His eyes were streaked with kohl and two patches of rouge had been carelessly daubed onto his withered cheeks.

'Contemporary or not,' I said, 'I stumbled upon a re-enactment of the weighing of the heart ceremony, in which I was forced to take part — drugged and humiliated. You weren't there, were you?'

Hermes sighed heavily. 'An interesting proposition.' He looked at me. 'So, which role were you cast as?'

'Osiris.'

'The king of the underworld, as you, a geophysicist, are. I did warn you life was about to become eventful. Come.' He led me back into the lounge, where steaming cups of Turkish coffee now waited on a low table. 'It was the group of individuals who seek the astrarium, no? This was a tactic to frighten you, I assume.'

As Hermes stirred his coffee I found myself staring at his painted fingernails wondering why his vocal rhythms were so familiar. Had he been in the ritual? Perhaps I was mistaken in thinking Hugh Wollington had been Horus. Just then the sleeve of his dressing gown slipped up as he lifted his cup —

there was no tattoo. Besides, it didn't make sense to suspect Hermes. I had already entrusted him with the astrarium and, in fact, my life.

'Give the instrument to me,' he went on. 'You know it is dangerous. It will seduce you, or those seeking it will destroy you.'

'Too late, it's already seduced me. I've started seeing meanings in everything, everywhere, all linked back to that device.'

He laughed, a dry bitter cackle that ended with a cough. 'You westerners think you can control the weather, that time can be measured by mathematical units, that light travels at the same speed everywhere, and that all that you see in these four dimensions is palpable and finite. It has woken you up, this Pharaonic toy. I had taken you to be a bigger man, Oliver.'

'I prefer a world based on solid understanding, if that's what you're suggesting.'

'Then go back to England, to grey skies and red brick, to the godless monotony of commercial enterprise, and leave the astrarium to others.' He took a sip of his coffee and winced. 'Usta! The coffee is not strong enough!' he yelled, then turned back to me. 'The astrarium has given you your death date, has it not?'

I found myself not wanting to answer him. Somehow, the fewer people I told, the less of a hold I felt the mechanism had over me. Hermes watched my face with interest.

'Oliver, you must understand that the astrarium is a fascinating weapon for those who wish to control the events around them.' He sighed. 'But you have been foolish. In your desire to keep everything logical, you have challenged the mechanism's power.'

'Perhaps,' I replied curtly, still not willing to reveal the extent of my involvement.

'The scientist's Achilles heel: nothing is real until proven. Newtonian empiricism will undo the world. Oliver, the astrarium is real, whether you can prove it or not, and it will pass judgement on you. In your dry scientific terms, the Ancient Egyptians believed that certain raw materials contained the essence of a soul — what you would call electromagnetic vibrations, force fields. They constructed sacred objects out of these materials and then brought them to life through incantations. How long has the machine given you?'

The seriousness of his tone, his total belief in the authenticity of the astrarium, was now beginning to alarm me.

'The second hand has come up — but it means nothing, and if you want to get literal, the dates could be over two thousand years out anyway.'

'How long?' he persisted.

'Eight days.'

'I can stop it, Oliver.'

'Isabella couldn't stop it.'

'By the time she discovered the mechanism, it was too late. You know that yourself.'

'All I know is that the information I'm being presented with is so bizarre and unfamiliar that I fear I'm losing my reason.'

'The moment you, the staunch rationalist, so adamant about the bricks and mortar of the known world, turned the dial to your own birth date, you revealed your hidden doubts. You have tinkered with the magic of others and now the machine is committed to your fate. I can save you. Give it to me.'

His voice had slipped into a hypnotic rhythm: blues shifting in halftones bumping gently against soft violets. The room had warmed up and bands of sunlight now illuminated the low glass coffee table; a large fly buzzed blindly against the window. Leaning back against the cushions, I closed my eyes. The jarring exhaustion of the past few days floated like a luminescent throbbing mass to the top of my skull. How easy it would be: give up the astrarium, fly back to Abu Rudeis to search for an investor to partner with, return to my normal life. The luminescent mass shifted from blinding white to a deep red, then began to bleed; long languid droplets that solidified into the image of Isabella's heart, then into the crimson of Rachel's lips. Sitting upright, I forced my eyelids open.

'What happened to Nectanebo at the end of his reign?' I asked.

'So you are finally using your intuition, Oliver.'

'Am I?'

Hermes smiled indulgently. 'Officially, Nectanebo's rule ended in 343 BC when the Persian general, Ochus, attacked Pelusium. According to Diodorus, a series of massacres and other atrocities followed and the Pharaoh reluctantly abandoned the granite palace he'd built at Behbeit el-Hagar, his birthplace—'

'So Nectanebo disappeared?'

'Unofficially, he fled, supposedly to southern Egypt and possibly to Ethiopia. Interestingly, his empty tomb was never raided, almost as if it was left pristine while awaiting his return, for all those thousands of years.'

'But how does this relate to the astrarium?'

'As a weapon of prediction it failed him, as it is failing you now.'

'But what happened to him? Didn't the astrarium predict his death?'

'This is the great mystery. There is no record of his death, and there are some who claim he still walks amongst us.'

Hugh Wollington's comment, 'Some say he still lives to this day,' echoed in my memory. It was an absurd hypothesis, but, nevertheless fascinating that both men had voiced it.

'You know that's not possible,' I retorted. 'And besides, if you're right, wouldn't that mean he finally conquered the power of the astrarium?'

'Or learned to work with it,' Hermes said with a smile.

I stood up to leave, irritated by the fact that I was now more frightened by the potential of the astrarium than I had been before.

'If you are so convinced the device has no power, there is nothing to worry about, is there?' Hermes concluded. 'Give the device to me for safekeeping, or at least let me be your guide. What do you have to lose?'

I hesitated. Should I trust the Egyptologist? I remembered Francesca blaming Amelia for her husband's belief in the old ways, not Hermes. Was it possible Hermes had truly cared for Isabella? If so he would have protected her as a child, as any sane person surely would have. No, I couldn't afford to trust him, not yet.

I walked to the front door. Hung above it was a papyrus scroll with a hieroglyph painted on it. The image showed the four-legged creature I'd seen twice in the last two days. Hermes followed my gaze.

'That is Seth, god of thunder, chaos and revenge — once the ruler of Ancient Egypt, after he murdered his brother Osiris and overthrew his nephew Horus.'

'I've seen him before.'

'Of course you have. The Christians bastardised him into the lesser form of Satan.'

\* \* \*

I locked the door of my hideaway above the barber's shop and unpacked the astrarium again. Almost too terrified to check I forced myself to peer into the mechanism, my reluctant gaze found the small death pointer — the date was unchanged. The low ticking of the magnets' movement now sounded like an inevitable acceleration towards my own death.

I reached for the reference book I'd asked Ibrihim to pack with my clothes and looked up Seth.

> *Names: Seth, Sutech, Setekh, Seti, Sutekh, Setech … god of destruction, thunder, storm, hostility, chaos and evil. Manifestations: sometimes as a crocodile; sometimes as a four-legged beast with a curved beak, two upright ears and a forked tail. Referred to as the lord of the northern sky in the Book of the Dead, Seth was considered responsible for seizing the souls of the unprepared in the underworld. Son of Nut and Geb, or Nut and Ra, brother of Isis, Osiris and Nephthys, Seth battled with Horus, his nephew, after he murdered Osiris … According to one myth, every month Seth attacks and consumes the moon, considered the sanctuary of Ausar and the gathering place of the souls of the recently dead … In the Old Testament, Seth was the third brother of Cain and Abel; he also appears in the suppressed gospels recovered in Egypt in 1945 at Nag Hammadi, in which he is Sethian, the gnostic god who rules over the thirteenth realm of the cosmos and carries out the will of the stars on mankind, regardless of how much havoc that might wreak …*

Why had Seth's shadow appeared on the wall of the catacombs during the ritual, I pondered. Was it meant to frighten me into believing Isabella's soul had been taken by the devil? And why had the other players seemed so terrified?

I couldn't come up with an answer. Instead, my mind filled with the unsettling sense that the astrarium had begun to control not just me, but also the events around me.

# 36

Rachel hung the bag of fruit and food over the hook on the door then swung around. She looked exhausted; the events of the past two days were taking their toll.

'Why didn't you send a message last night?' she asked. 'I was worried.'

I walked over and held her, hoping the embrace might dispel some of her obvious anxiety. 'I went to the catacombs at Kom el-Shugafa,' I told her. 'I was enticed there, by someone I thought was Isabella — madness, I know.'

'Oh, Oliver …'

'It gets worse. I stumbled across some kind of crazy re-enactment, and the lunatics conducting this little performance injected me with drugs …' I pulled my shirt from my shoulder; the puncture mark had bloomed into a small purple bruise. 'It was an Ancient Egyptian funerary rite called the weighing of the heart. I couldn't tell you whether they were Egyptologists, a local cult or just some unemployed actors hired for the occasion, but they were deadly serious and in full costume.' I held back the gruesome detail of the heart itself.

'And you think this is somehow connected to the death of your wife and the astrarium?' Rachel asked.

'They were trying to pressure me into giving them the astrarium. I suspect they were the same group Isabella's grandfather was involved with — apparently he dragged Isabella into it as well.'

We both sat down on the rickety bed and Rachel pulled my eyelids wide and stared into my pupils. 'Oh, baby, you're still wasted. I'd have thought strong hallucinogens would be difficult to get here in Egypt — unless you have military connections. The US Defense Department experimented with extreme hallucinogens in Korea — I wrote a piece on it once. Scary stuff.'

'Any long-term effects?'

'Flashbacks, paranoia, delusions.'

'Great, I was having those already.'

'There's something else you should know.' She moved closer to me. 'I spent the best part of today interviewing various members of Sadat's family for *Time* magazine.'

'So?'

'Well, just as I was leaving an aunt of his told me that another journalist had visited them the day before asking all kinds of weird questions about Sadat's date of birth — whether the official date was correct, the hour exact to the minute, that kind of thing. She obviously didn't believe he was really a journalist, and she was doubly suspicious because, although he spoke English and claimed he was writing for an American magazine, he looked Arabic — like a Saudi, she said. She gave me his card and wanted to know whether I'd heard of him or the magazine.'

'Had you?'

'No, it doesn't exist. Besides, I know every journalist covering this part of the world — the guy's a fake. I'm beginning to believe Majeed *is* after the astrarium. Why else go to so much trouble to get Sadat's birth date?'

'They must really believe it is capable of killing.'

'You mean it can kill? How do you know?'

'I've used it. Only in my case, it passed judgement, and spontaneously gave me my death date.'

She stared at me. 'Oliver, you're a scientist, you know that isn't possible.'

It was a question rather than a statement. I didn't answer her.

'Come here.' Rachel pulled me into her arms.

My tension evaporated as I inhaled the sweet smell of her. Burying my face in the mist of her hair, I fell back onto the bed with her, our limbs winding around each other, searching for release. My brain emptying until my death date floated back into my mind.

\* \* \*

I woke the next morning to the sight of Rachel, already dressed, clutching a newspaper.

'I went out to find some decent coffee and saw this — it's a day old.' She handed me a copy of *The New York Times*. 'Isn't GeoConsultancy the company you work for?'

I nodded and sat up, still bleary-eyed from sleep.

'You might want to turn to page five.'

The article was headlined: 'Oil chief dies mid-flight'. I read down the page:

*Last night Johannes Du Voor, sixty, the CEO of GeoConsultancy, the oil industry's largest independent geophysics consultancy, died of a suspected heart attack during a helicopter flight north of Cape Town. Shares in*

> *the company fell overnight due to uncertainty about future ownership and leadership of the company. Du Voor left no heirs ...*

Shock ripped through me. 'This happened the night of the explosion?'

'Pure coincidence, Oliver, nothing else. Okay?'

I sat there stunned. Johannes was such a large personality it was hard to imagine he'd actually died.

I began pulling my clothes on. 'I have to find a phone.'

'You can't go out there!' She grabbed my arm, 'It's not safe!'

I held up my cassock. 'I've been lucky so far.'

'They're going to catch up with you sooner or later. You've got to get out of town.'

Downstairs, the shop suddenly filled with the sound of men shouting. One voice was raised above the others — gruff, deep and aggressive. Both of us recognised it.

Rachel looked at me, her eyes wide with fear. I indicated she should stay quiet and, after grabbing the bag the astrarium was in, rushed over to the window. Outside stretched a panorama of rooftops and terraces interspersed with squares of colourful laundry.

I helped Rachel up and we both climbed out, dropping the blind back as we left. Crouching, we scuttled across the tiled roof of the shop next to us, then onto the next, never looking behind. We arrived at the top of a fire escape precariously attached to an old brick wall; its steps led down to the busy market street below. We raced down them and onto the ground, and were instantly engulfed by a wedding procession that had turned into the narrow lane we were standing in. A deafening cacophony of drumming and horns filled the air, the guests dancing madly around the veiled bride and bridegroom who were being carried above them on golden painted thrones.

I was in jeans and a T-shirt while Rachel wore a kaftan, her blonde hair wild around her head. We both stood out in the jostling crowd. Glancing around I got my bearings. 'This way!' I said, grabbing her arm.

We pushed our way through the crowd to finally emerge at the other end of the lane, our shoulders and heads covered with flower petals and confetti. From there I knew my way to the only place of sanctuary left to me.

\* \* \*

Father Carlotto, not in the slightest bit surprised by our sudden appearance, ushered us deep under the cathedral and to a hidden room at the back of the crypt. We could hear the boys choir practising upstairs, the thin voices floating down in muffled soprano. The room was situated beneath stone arches that were obviously support structures for the building, and I had to bend my head to walk down the three stone steps into the small chamber. It stank of pipe tobacco and candle wax and the white paint had begun to flake off the stone walls. By the light of the one lamp burning, I could see it contained a plain wooden desk with church records stacked behind it, from floor to ceiling.

Father Carlotto switched on another lamp, his soft features transforming into sculptural planes as he leaned over it. 'You are sure you weren't followed?' he asked.

'We lost them back at the barber's shop,' I answered. 'I think I know who they are.'

The priest held his hand up. 'I have promised you sanctuary; I do not wish to know anything else. Personally, I have always prized survival over martyrdom, but I have no immediate desire to be confronted with the choice.'

I noticed a large old-fashioned Bakelite telephone on the desk and wondered if it worked. Father Carlotto opened a drawer in the desk and, to my surprise, pulled out a bottle of Benedictine and three small glasses.

'A Christmas present from Saint Benedictus,' he joked, but neither Rachel nor I laughed. I reached out and took her hand, the heat of her fingers burning into my own.

Father Carlotto filled the three glasses. 'For fortitude. I suspect we will all need it.'

The liquor burned a path from the back of my throat to my eyes, reviving me instantly.

'So now, down to business,' he said. 'How long do you want disappear for? A month, two months?'

I exchanged glances with Rachel. 'I haven't much time — I was thinking a week at the most.'

'Easily achieved — as long as we agree that no questions are asked and no answers given. My Coptic brothers are closely watched; I do not wish to endanger them more than necessary. And if anyone comes asking, Mr Warnock, I do not know you.'

'How can I thank you?'

I meant it sincerely; it seemed remarkable to me that this man I hardly knew would risk his life helping me.

'I do it for Isabella, for the confession I did not act upon, that is all. Although I pray that one day you might return to your faith.'

I grimaced. 'I'm afraid I will disappoint you, Father.'

He chuckled and poured himself another glass of Benedictine. 'We shall see.'

I glanced at the telephone again. 'One last request — I need to make two phone calls. I can reverse the charges.'

He pushed the telephone towards me. 'Be my guest. I promise this one is not tapped. The operator is one of my congregation.'

While Father Carlotto gave Rachel a tour of the crypt, I called the operator and finally got a connection to New York, to Ruben Katz, the chief financial officer for GeoConsultancy.

'Ruben, it's Oliver. I'm phoning from Egypt. I just heard the news — I'm so sorry.'

I meant it. As much as I'd disliked Johannes Du Voor, he didn't deserve such a death.

'Yeah, yeah, it's chaos here. Clients are ringing in left, right and centre.' Ruben was a pragmatic individual, completely loyal to Du Voor. 'I'm afraid the news is a lot worse than what's been reported.'

I steeled myself. 'Tell me.'

'I finally accessed some subsidiary accounts Johannes had been stalling me on for months. Turns out they had huge borrowings — all guaranteed by the parent and signed by Johannes. The company's in debt to the tune of twenty million, and most of it falls due in the next few months. We're seriously considering filing for bankruptcy — Chapter 11.'

'What about the Abu Rudeis project?'

'You can carry on for now, but don't make any long-term plans. Meanwhile, I suggest you start to think about your own future. But hey, you're the best in the business, so I wouldn't worry too much.'

'What about the clients, the company's goodwill?'

'The clients care about the people in the field, Oliver. You know that. You want to go independent, you just holler. There are plenty of people here looking for a raft to jump on. Meanwhile, I have to figure out what I'm gonna tell the shareholders tomorrow morning. I tell you this much, it ain't gonna be easy. I'm so sorry, Oliver. I should have seen this coming — Johannes had been acting pretty weird the last couple of months. Some of his recent business decisions have been ... well, plainly ... suicidal.' I could hear another phone ringing in the background. 'I have to go,' he said. '*Wall Street Journal* has just rung in ...' The line clicked off.

Next I dialled Moustafa's sat phone out in the oilfield. Just when I was about to give up, he answered.

'Moustafa?'

There was a silence; I suspected he was checking the office was empty.

'Oliver,' he whispered, 'are you okay, my friend? Head office said you have gone missing. Mr Fartime is most concerned.'

'Well, I'm alive, which I guess is good. Seems I've got something a lot of people want.'

'Nothing is worth getting killed over, my friend.'

'Do I sound dead to you?'

Moustafa laughed. 'It's good you still have your gallows sense of humour. But I need you here. The findings for the new oilfield look very promising. When can you come out and confirm them?'

'Give me a week or so, but in the meantime, are you able to visit me in a couple of days?'

'Where are you?'

'Let me contact you. I'll get a way of getting a message to you.'

'I will wait with anticipation.'

It was great just to hear his voice; the familiar realities of the oilfield sounding out beneath it. I put the telephone down with great reluctance. Without the structure of GeoConsultancy behind me, it was going to be a lot harder to find the finance for the licence and to back any new exploration. How would I tell Moustafa our plans may not be workable? Again it felt as if I was in free-fall, another reality imploded. Was it possible Johannes's death might be linked to my setting of the astrarium, after all his fortune had been tied to mine.

Father Carlotto came back into the room, followed by Rachel. 'I have spoken with the abbot at Deir Al Anba Bishoy,' he said. 'You can leave with a group of pilgrims heading to Wadi El-Natrun this afternoon, as long as you are willing to play the part of a monk,' he joked.

I thanked him then turned to Rachel. 'It's only a couple of hours' drive. It should be easy enough to get a message to me if you need to — right, Father?'

'Certainly.'

'Stay safe,' she said. 'I'll contact you in a couple of days, okay?'

We embraced and, momentarily, the ground beneath me felt solid.

# 37

The open-top army truck hurtled down the desert road to Wadi El-Natrun. There were ten of us huddled together in the back: a family obviously travelling to the monastery for a christening, the wailing baby held tightly in the crook of his father's arm; five earnest novice monks who looked frighteningly solemn, their beards barely covering their chins; and myself. We shared the space with one terrified goat and four trussed chickens, including a cockerel that, with every pothole in the road, emitted a loud shriek. It was an exhausting four-hour drive from Alexandria, with only a tarpaulin sheltering us from the afternoon sun and no stops, not even for water.

I'd spoken to no one, in case my accent and my blue eyes would betray me. As I was older, the novices treated me with respect and mistook my silence for religious reverie. I held the astrarium in a hessian bag between my feet and stared out at the passing landscape, analysing over and over the sequence of bizarre events that had happened since my return to Alexandria. Finally, the swaying of the truck sent me to sleep. The sensation of it pulling up woke me with a jolt.

The monastery of Saint Bishoy loomed out of the night sky — the towers with their distinctive domed roofs, the four-way crosses on top, the high walls and the single tower originally built to warn of attacks from the nearby Berbers. Birds circled the tower, attracted by the insects that danced in the beams of light illuminating the keep; they looked as if they were in the grip of some invisible force.

The truck pulled up beside the gate set into the north-facing wall. A couple of monks pushed open the gate from inside and we all climbed down wearily. An older man dressed in slightly more ornate robes came out after the first two monks and approached me, hand outstretched. His wide full face broadened into a smile. 'Please, come with me, Monsieur Warnock.'

He took me to a monk's cell with curved sandstone walls, a narrow high window, a mattress rolled out on the ground, a prayer rug and a kerosene lamp on the floor at the head of the mattress. A washing stand with a jug of water stood in the corner with a small cupboard beneath it. Incongruously, there was a large tin ashtray beside the lamp — a concession to guests, I imagined. On the opposite wall was an alcove that held a large wooden crucifix, its tortured Christ's carved eyes turned upwards.

The abbot lit the kerosene lamp; it ignited in a small white glow, throwing out long shadows against the domed ceiling.

'Morning prayers are at four-thirty, breakfast is at seven in the refectory. It is humble fare — bread, olives, cheese, fruit. You will join us then.'

'And if I need to get a message to anyone?' I asked.

'We have messengers coming and going all the time. The Bedouin will also carry letters for us.'

'I have to contact someone at Abu Rudeis, in the Sinai.'

'I believe there may be a caravan passing through tomorrow. In the meanwhile, may I suggest you get some sleep and gather your strength, both spiritually and physically. Father Carlotto told me you would be with us for a week, is that correct?'

'Perhaps even less if I can work out a way of making myself invisible,' I joked.

'A week it is then,' he replied. 'Any longer could be difficult for us. These are tense times, Monsieur Warnock; even out here in the desert we feel the ripples of President Sadat's ambition, may God protect him.'

\* \* \*

After the abbot left, I wrote a letter to Moustafa asking him to visit me at the monastery, then carefully unpacked the astrarium. The faint click of its bronze teeth sounded out: the mechanism was still working, the death date pointer as fixed as sunrise. Theoretically, once this night had passed, I had six days left to live.

Frustrated, I smashed my fist into the hard mattress. As I did, the tin ashtray beside the lamp slid across the cement floor and attached itself firmly to the side of the astrarium. Amazed, I pulled a safety pin out of my cassock and put it on the mattress. It too glided to the astrarium and stuck. The magnetic force of the mechanism appeared to be strengthening.

I packed the astrarium away and placed it on the floor of the alcove. Then, without bothering to undress, I lay down on the hard mattress and stared at the domed roof. Again, I debated the scientific alternatives of measuring the change in the device's magnetic qualities. I turned the concept over in my mind, forming a mental diagram of all the elements of the mechanism I'd seen so far. Within minutes, I was asleep.

\* \* \*

The next morning I woke and realised I'd missed breakfast. After rinsing my face in the washbowl, I hid the astrarium in the cupboard beneath the stand. Then I made my way through the cool arched corridors out into the blinding white light of the courtyard. The Church of Saint Bishoy stood directly in front of me: an impressive series of sand-coloured domes, with a high arched entrance flanked to the right by four smaller arches, each with a stained-glass window from ground to roof. I walked around the church to the main courtyard area on its other side, passing the remains of a mill, a dovecote and a well. Opposite the church was the garden: rows of pomegranate bushes, some olive trees, and various vegetables. Several young monks were busy hoeing and planting. I asked one of them where I could get some breakfast and he plucked a pomegranate and threw it to me, grinning. Then, in a heavy rural accent, he suggested I try the refectory as sometimes they fed the very old monks later.

In the refectory, I sat down at a low long table bathed in light filtering in through a skylight set in the top of the cupola. A young peasant woman with a wide, curiously blank face, placed a bowl of rice pudding in front of me. Across the table, an ancient monk sat eating very slowly from his bowl; he paused, holding his heavy pewter spoon in midair, and stared hard at me. I tried smiling and he guffawed — a sound between indignation and a cough — then continued his painfully slow meal. I spooned the pudding into my mouth; it was surprisingly salty. I spat the spoonful out. The monk burst into laughter, I turned to the peasant woman and asked her in Arabic for some honey, but she ignored me, carrying on with her task of stacking plates.

The monk pushed his bowl away with a clatter and nodded towards the woman. 'She has no ears — deaf!' His wrinkled hands flapped at the side of his head. 'You, Englishman?' he went on in heavily accented English.

'That's right.'

He sat back and examined my face intently, his raisin black eyes, buried in crevices of wrinkles and creases, empty of emotion. Suddenly he reached across the table and ran his hand over my cheeks and beard. I froze, astounded.

'It is okay, you are good man.'

'I am?'

'You are.' He spoke with such absolute conviction that, to my surprise, I found myself filled with irrational gratitude. 'My name is Father Mina,' he went on. 'Yours?'

'Oliver ... Oliver Warnock.'

'Come, Oliver, I am librarian, chief librarian, our library. It is one of the most famous in our order. Many treasures. You must see it. Or perhaps you are here to take a vow of silence?' He grinned, and I realised he was joking.

'No, no vow of silence and, in any case, I would still be able to read,' I replied, smiling.

'Indeed, to read is to fly over the walls but perhaps you are here to hide?'

I chose not to reply, and, in response, the monk patted my hand.

'You keep your secrets and I keep my books. Come, my friend, I show you rest of monastery.'

\* \* \*

We walked across the courtyard. Father Mina was tiny — I doubted he was more than five feet tall — and so rotund it was a miracle he could walk at all. He stopped by the large circular well outside the Church of Saint Bishoy.

'Here Berbers washed their swords after killing the forty-nine martyrs. They threw martyrs in the well then locked them up in Saint Marcarius Monastery. This is why it is called Well of the Martyrs.'

I stared down into the well. It looked deep, the water just a silver glint at the bottom.

'Always we get fresh water here, always. This is Christ's miracle. But now to library, it is very special.' Father Mina tugged at my arm.

'First I have a letter that has to get to the Sinai by tomorrow,' I told him. 'The abbot said there may be a caravan of Bedouin passing through?'

Father Mina nodded then gave a quick, sharp whistle. Immediately a skinny fellah boy of about ten appeared from the shadows and ran towards us — a flash of thin legs and grinning white teeth.

'You are right, give me letter, please?' Father Mina commanded. I handed him the letter to Moustafa. He squinted at the address short-sightedly then gave it on to the boy, barking an order in Arabic. The youth disappeared. The priest read my incredulous expression.

'Do not worry. It will be with Bedouin by nightfall and in Sinai by tomorrow's sunset. But now to more important matters.'

The library was situated at the far southeast corner of the compound, next to an ancient mill where the monks had once ground their own flour. It was a narrow room running along the monastery's outer defensive wall, which had been built in the ninth century and stood over ten metres high and two wide. The library was lit from above through openings at the centre of each cupola and was lined with ornate reading stands and floor-to-ceiling eighteenth-century glass cabinets filled with manuscripts.

Father Mina walked me around proudly describing the historical and religious significance of the texts kept in the cabinets, finally arriving at a small oak chest tucked away in a corner. With a dramatic flourish the priest pulled out a small key from a pocket in his cassock and opened the chest. He lifted out a hand-bound leather notebook and laid it out on a table. Its stained and yellowed pages were filled with elaborate erratic handwriting that travelled across the page as if being chased — all of it archaic French.

'This is one of library's great treasures,' the old man said, 'a notebook of Sonnini de Manoncour, the French naturalist and explorer who was part of Napoleon's expedition in 1777.'

My heart began to race. Sonnini de Manoncour — I recognised the name. Instantly I was transported back to the bar in Goa, to Isabella as I first met her, the passion in her face and voice as she told me about a letter that proved the existence of the astrarium; a letter shown to her by the mystic Ahmos Khafre. Hugh Wollington had mentioned the historian too, and told me that Khafre had bequeathed the letter to the British Museum. I'd seen a copy of it myself, and now recalled the ornate script that matched the hand that had inscribed the pages of this notebook.

Mina's wrinkled fingertip ran down the page. 'You see here there are notes and little drawings. They are of a naos he found.'

He pointed to a column of tiny ink sketches, each showing a side of a naos that had been inscribed in a language I didn't recognise — something later than hieroglyphs.

'The naos tell of occasion when Queen Cleopatra receive a present of a ...' Father Mina looked at me as he searched for the right word, ' ... a star teller? An instrument that speaks of the skies? I do not know the word.'

'Astrarium,' I said, hoping my voice didn't betray my excitement.

'This astrarium is wedding gift for Cleopatra's wedding to younger brother Ptolemy XIII from eunuch priest Pothinus,' the monk continued then carefully turned a page. 'Sonnini de

Manoncour wrote of this machine in letter to Napoleon. We had letter here too, but it was stolen by visitor to our monastery in 1943. Some have never forgiven him.'

'Ahmos Khafre,' I breathed.

The monk glanced at me sharply, his black eyes surprised. 'You know Khafre?'

'I've heard of him,' I said. 'My wife was an archaeologist, she spoke of him.' I kept my voice low and controlled, not wanting to betray my surprise and shock at the astonishing coincidence of the library housing the letter that set Isabella on a journey; one that had led to her death. Again, I had the suffocating sensation that the astrarium might be controlling my life — had it somehow lured me here?

The old monk pulled me towards him, his breath pungent against my cheek. 'The letter was written but never delivered. Sonnini de Manoncour stayed here in 1778 — we have records of visit. They speak of a great excitement, a great discovery he was about to make. A hundred and sixty-five years later, 1943, just before the end of the war, when all was chaos, Ahmos Khafre came here to research Sonnini's visit, but something made him very frightened. He stole the letter and ran. Maybe you know why?'

I shook my head, wondering if this was some kind of set-up; a trap to make me reveal the whereabouts of the astrarium.

'I spend five years translating this notebook after Khafre left,' Father Mina went on, turning the pages carefully. 'I was sure it contain reason for Khafre's betrayal. We were good friends, so for me a double betrayal. I found the notebook after he was gone, hidden in almanac of botanical plants. This naos Sonnini write about, it must be linked to letter to Napoleon. But this is most interesting of all ...' He pointed to a sentence on the last page of the notebook. 'This means "poisoned chalice". I have a theory about this. Pothinus the eunuch priest who gave the astrarium to Queen Cleopatra, also attempted to have Cleopatra assassinated and to take over the throne himself, with twelve-year-old Ptolemy XIII — Cleopatra's brother — as puppet prince. The astrarium mentioned could have been the "poisoned chalice".'

\* \* \*

I retired early that evening, after watching the sun descend behind the ancient Keep — debating whether I, like hundreds of monks must have wondered before me, shouldn't be standing guard at the top scanning the desert for attackers.

The air was now cooling, and a dry desert breeze brought smells from the nearby village; sounds of children playing, a sudden car horn, a distant radio, yet here, within the walls of the oblong enclosure it felt as if time itself was suspended, hovering above a far grimmer contemporary world.

Back in my cell I left the astrarium packed and hidden; if the dials were still moving inevitably towards my death it could wait until tomorrow. I rolled out my mattress and collapsed onto it, to sleep, again, without dreaming.

# 38

I spent the next two days arduously trying to read Father Mina's French translation of Sonnini's notebook. I was hoping for some further insight into the astrarium — but the work also helped to distract me from a growing sense of panic as each day moved me closer to my supposed death date. There was little new information in the notebooks — apart from Sonnini guessing at the mechanics of the device — however, there was one footnote that caught my attention. *Ame* and *Ombre* — the French words for Soul and Shadow — were written together beside the five elements Ancient Egyptians believed made up a human soul. Sonnini had drawn a box — a little like a prison — around the two French words: as if they were trapped together. It looked like a whimsical doodle and it was bizarre to imagine the French naturalist bent over the page, quill in hand, drawing as he half-thought, half-imagined. But the small scribble disturbed me; the drawing of the box had an inked spiky malice that was haunting.

My study was interrupted by a shy young priest who informed me that my guest Moustafa Saheer had arrived at the monastery. I went to meet him at the gates, and helped him haul the magnetometer I'd asked him to bring into my cell.

Moustafa wiped his sweating brow with the hem of his jellaba then grinned broadly. 'I knew you were a crazy Englishman but I didn't think this crazy. You make a very convincing Copt. I would never have recognised you with this beard and robe.'

'And you make a very convincing fellah.'

I had only ever seen Moustafa in western clothes or overalls. Despite his ethnicity, the Cambridge graduate looked amusingly uncomfortable in his jellaba.

'At least this is my traditional dress, whereas you …' he faltered. 'My God, the excuses I've had to make to the company. They think you have gone a little crazy with grief. Lucky your reputation is so sterling.'

'Just don't ask me any questions,' I warned. 'I only need the magnetometer for a day. You can take it back with you tomorrow. Are you sure you weren't followed?'

'Followed? Don't be ridiculous — who is going to follow a man who is going to trek across the desert to get to his aunt's funeral? Besides, I am unimportant in the big scheme of things. I like to keep it this way; unlike you, my friend, who must always be in the eye of the storm. But I have already promised — no questions. I had to see you anyway — I have wonderful news.' He closed the cell door; now only the faint sunlight filtering in through the narrow window lit us. 'The geophysics have come in.'

'And?'

'They confirm the structure is huge — at least a billion barrels, almost all in the adjoining block.'

I didn't reply. All I could think about was the astrarium; it was as if it was playing a bad joke on me — showing me where to find great treasure yet at the same time removing the resources to dig it up, as well as leaving me, theoretically, with only days to live. If the device did have a soul, what kind of morality lesson was this?

Moustafa, misinterpreting my muted reaction, put his hand on my shoulder. 'My brother, I understand your ambivalence. The news about GeoConsultancy's bankruptcy was in the financial papers this morning. But fear not, good fortune has smiled upon us twice.'

I glanced sharply at him. Was it possible he knew something about the astrarium? 'What do you mean?' I failed to keep the paranoia out of my voice.

Hurt, Moustafa stepped back. 'Oliver, please, I am your partner, am I not?'

I put my hand out to reassure him. 'I'm sorry. Lately I've been finding it hard to trust anyone. Tell me about the field. I am excited, really.'

'Firstly, I have spoken to friends at the ministry. The government will lease the block to us for a reasonable percentage, and we can use whatever company we choose, so long as we can post a bond. Secondly, I have found an investor — a private individual who doesn't want to be involved directly but will put up all the finance required for the project.'

'All of it?' I was shocked; it was virtually unheard of for one individual to fund an exploration. There simply weren't that many people around with that kind of money. 'Even without GeoConsultancy's infrastructure behind us?'

'He knows of your reputation, Oliver, and thinks very highly of you.'

'How does he know of me? Is he already in oil?'

'No, he's a private businessman, an Egyptian, originally from Behbeit el-Hagar, but he's lived most of his life abroad.'

I recognised the name of the dig site where the photograph with Giovanni Brambilla, Amelia Lynhurst, Hermes Hemiedes,

Hugh Wollington and Isabella had been taken all those years ago; Behbeit el-Hagar was the place where Nectanebo II had been born, and where Amelia had found the key to the astrarium.

'Wasn't that the site of an ancient city?' I asked, struggling to keep my voice neutral.

'It's just a village now. This man, Mr Imenand, has immense wealth. He will fund us and ask no questions. He is well known in certain business circles within the Arab world. Oliver, he will put up all the finance for the first stage of exploration and he wants only forty per cent of the licence.'

Stunned, I walked to the window. The church bells had begun to peal and I could see the monks crossing the courtyard with calm, measured paces, intent yet tranquil. In here, we were engaged in a whole other realm. What kind of man would contribute millions of dollars to a commercial undertaking without expecting a decent return? This was hardly a philanthropic venture.

I swung back to Moustafa. 'I'm very suspicious of people when I don't understand their motives.'

He laughed. 'Mr Imenand is an eccentric individual who wants to see this country developed. He is very enigmatic, not many people have met him, but he has the reputation of great wisdom and experience. We are fortunate that he wants to back us. Trust me, this is an amazing deal.'

He unrolled several survey maps and laid them flat on the mattress. 'We executed the tests you wanted along the points you'd marked. Your intuition was right, except for one thing …'

'Which was?'

'You can see the large structure we had already identified here, but we also found anomalies at these two points, which suggests—'

'A further reservoir below,' I finished for him.

'Exactly. Again, my friend, you have shown yourself to have the Midas touch.'

I scanned the new maps: two cross-sections drawn up from the seismic data, and a landsat image. The change in geology was obvious; the anticline that indicated oil and gas trapped between rock strata was clearly visible. It was extraordinary that the potential oilfield hadn't been discovered until now. But what was even more extraordinary was that there were two reservoirs. I didn't know if I would have the luxury of time to pursue this project, but I knew I had to get back to the site nevertheless. If the oilfield's discovery was linked to the astrarium, perhaps something further would be revealed about the device if I took it there. Perhaps it would even stop working? It was worth the risk.

'I want to meet the man before I agree to trust him,' I told Moustafa.

'I can arrange a meeting in Alexandria, just give me a few days.'

'It will have to be in the next three days, at a safe house, and I'll have to travel there in disguise.'

Moustafa's dark face was alight with excitement. 'We'll keep the people down to the bare minimum — Mr Waalif from the Egyptian Government Oil Agency, ourselves, and Mr Imenand. Waalif is discretion itself, and we need the EGOA involved — after all, we will be leasing their land.'

'Agreed. But don't say anything to Waalif about where I am. Keep it vague, and choose a safe house for the meeting at the last possible minute.'

'I understand.'

'In the meantime, I want you to discreetly find out which rigs are available and look for some decent tool pushers. If we move with Imenand, I want everything in place to begin the exploration immediately. I'll leave the hiring of the roughnecks up to you.'

'No problem.'

'Excellent. Tomorrow we'll drive to the site.'

'Tomorrow?'

'Moustafa, I'm running out of time as it is,' I finished grimly.

\* \* \*

I showed Moustafa to the guest quarters of the monastery, made sure he knew where to go for the evening meal, and informed the abbot that I would be leaving with my visitor the next morning. By the time I returned to my cell it was nightfall and I was grateful for the respite the small, silent room provided. I closed my door, unpacked the astrarium and lifted it out onto the floor.

It seemed to squat there malevolently, staring up at me. Again I had the impulse to destroy it, to kick it to hell. But how would that help? For all I knew, my death date would continue to exist after the destruction of the mechanism.

I switched on the magnetometer, curious about the strength of the astrarium's magnetic field, then hesitated with my hand on the lever. The possibility of proving the device had extraordinary physical properties disturbed me, especially as I still had no idea of the precise materials used in its construction. The scientist in me desperately wanted an empirical explanation: perhaps the device worked at a quantum level to achieve non-local effects? But even if I proved the machine affected its environment, how would that help me to stop it?

I pointed the magnetometer at the astrarium. The detector bleeped wildly and the needle swung off the dial. I'd never seen such a strong reading. Whatever the alloys in the mechanism, I was certain they were unlike anything I'd seen before. The magnetic field seemed to have gained hugely in strength since London. I reflected on what could have affected it — was it something in the surrounding stone? Whatever the reason, the machine was increasing in power — it seemed more alive than even before. It wasn't a consoling observation.

I unwrapped the Was, the metal cool against my sweating palm. I hesitated then made my decision. I would try again. I inserted the key into the mechanism and tried to change the dates on the dials. The pointer wouldn't shift, and if I pushed any further the key would snap. I gave up, irrational fear pounding in my gut. The pointer indicated that I had just over three days to live. I sat down, trying not to panic.

A tentative knock came at the door. I ignored it, still paralysed by fear. A young monk shouted outside: 'Mr Warnock, you have another visitor. A woman. We cannot let her into the sleeping quarters — you must come out to see her.'

\* \* \*

Rachel sat on the edge of the Well of the Martyrs, wearing a simple white dress; she looked like a young girl despite the air of apprehension about her. I was secretly shocked at how happy I was to see her.

She stood up when she saw me. We didn't kiss, both of us cautious about intimate contact in front of the monks. Instead, I took her hand and led her into a smaller enclosed courtyard, secretly surprised at how elated I was to see her.

'Mr Warnock, we cannot allow women to stay within the compound,' called the monk who had told me Rachel was here.

Rachel squeezed my hand. 'It's okay, I have accommodation at the village.'

'Half an hour of privacy is all I ask,' I called back, and the cleric withdrew.

'I came because I had to see you,' Rachel said. 'I also have a letter from your housekeeper, Ibrihim. He brought it to me at the Cecil Hotel.' She handed me the sealed envelope.

'Bad news?' Rachel asked, reading my face.

'There are still men looking for me. The villa was broken into again, despite the extra security. They even dug up the garden,' I replied, scanning the letter.

'Does he say who it was?'

'No, just that he didn't think they were Egyptians. He says they sounded like Saudis — thugs, he calls them, professional soldiers. Also, Hermes Hemiedes' assistant came looking for me — Hermes has been arrested and he wants me to try to influence his release. Apparently Hermes has dual citizenship and he wants me to go to the British consul on his behalf.'

'From what you've told me about this guy, it sounds as if he's playing on your fears, manipulating you,' Rachael interjected.

'But why would he bother? He's the one in prison, not me.'

'Maybe he's still trying to get the astrarium.'

'At the moment he just wants to get released. I don't like the idea of helping him, not after the way he treated Isabella.'

I stared up at the moon. The crater-marked crescent was now rising over the wall.

'Rachel, my death date's unchanged. I have three days to go from dawn tomorrow, and the terrifying thing is that I'm beginning to really believe it.'

'Don't. Hang on to your rationality. You have to.'

'Too late — I don't know what's rational any more.'

'Oliver, you're not going to die. At least, not in three days.'

I heard her but I wasn't convinced.

'Listen, I have to leave Egypt myself. That's another reason why I came to see you.' Rachel's voice seemed to hang on the still air.

I tried to cover my dismay with staged casualness. 'Well, thanks for making the trip out.' I hated the way I sounded so defensive.

'You don't understand — I've been given a major break. Scoop of the century, I *have* to go.'

'What is it?'

She looked out at the courtyard. 'I've been asked to witness a secret meeting between Sadat and Begin, to record it for posterity.' Now she swung around and took my hand. 'It'll take place in the desert while Sadat's en route to Damascus. There's a rumour Sadat will visit the Knesset in person if the initial meeting goes well.' Her excitement was apparent even in her lowered voice.

'Are you serious — Sadat in the Knesset? Do you realise how revolutionary that would be? Neither Syria nor Saudi Arabia would tolerate such a visit.'

'I'm telling you, it's going to happen and I'm going to be there. Fifteen years I've waited for an opportunity like this. Fifteen years, Oliver.'

'You've worked hard for it. You deserve it.'

'I do, don't I?' She grinned.

There's always the point when an encounter segues into a relationship. When I was younger, this happened so seamlessly I wouldn't notice; I'd just find myself waking up next to the same woman a month after the first night. In those days, there wasn't the self-examining, self-flagellating furore of sexual politics that exists now. Or was it just the naïve courage of youth? I couldn't tell you. All I knew was that standing there, staring at this diminutive woman in the moonlight, her face alive with an emotional intensity that was familiar and yet not familiar, only one thing was important: that I wanted her; perhaps — and this was extraordinarily difficult to admit at the time — even needed her.

'Tomorrow I have to go with my assistant Moustafa back to Abu Rudeis to check out a prospective new field,' I said. 'Come with us. You can see some of my world — before you leave it.' I tried, unsuccessfully, to sound light-hearted.

'I'm not leaving it, Oliver. Is that the Eastern Sinai?'

I nodded.

'I have to be in Port Tawfiq by Tuesday — it sounds like it's en route anyhow. But will it be safe?'

'Moustafa's an expert on back roads and military roadblocks. By the time we hit the camp itself, it'll be night and no one's expecting me.'

Rachel pulled me into a sudden embrace and, like teenagers we became a mad fumbling of lips, fingers and legs. From somewhere in the shadows came a polite cough, and the fellah boy who had taken my letter to Moustafa appeared. We broke apart smiling.

'We leave early, around five,' I told her.

'I'll be here.'

I watched her and the boy walk away towards the village that lay beyond the monastery's walls.

# 39

To our left stretched the Mediterranean in a flat, pale blue monotone — infinity, a place I'd now like to escape to. To the right yawned the desert, the coastal track we were driving along the dividing line. Between the dirt road and the beach were several villas — beach retreats for the wealthy, but at this time of year deserted. White sand and scrubland ran right to the edge of the sea — the lip of the ancient world, its desolate beauty captivating.

Moustafa swerved the company jeep around the potholes and rubble. I bounced in the seat next to him, in my Coptic monk guise and sunglasses, while Rachel sat in the back with the surveying equipment. We made a bizarre group but I wasn't willing to take any chances of being recognised. Moustafa had been diplomatic enough not to ask any direct questions but I could see that the stress had begun to affect him. Although we'd taken the back roads via Ismailia then across the Suez Canal and down towards Port Tawfiq, with the heightened military tension, Moustafa was still worried about encountering army blockades. So far we'd seen only a few farmers, a couple of tankers and a tourist bus.

The astrarium was in my rucksack hidden underneath the back seat. There were now less than three days to go until my supposed death and I was acutely aware that I'd begun to resort to desperate measures.

A roadblock loomed up suddenly as the road curved around a sand dune. A soldier ran out onto the dirt track and flagged us down. As we drew nearer an army tank became visible, partially concealed behind a clump of palms.

'What now, my friend?' Moustafa asked me grimly as he pulled up beside the trees.

'You are driving me to visit a Coptic family with a dying son,' I said. 'Rachel's a missionary from America working with the church. Understand, Rachel?'

She nodded and I turned back to Moustafa. 'Think you can handle this?' I noticed that his hands, still around the steering wheel, were clenched.

'This is the last time, understand, Oliver?' he sounded unhappy. 'I am getting tired of playing this game. I have asked no questions so far, but there is a limit even to my patience.'

The soldier was now almost at the window. I touched Moustafa's hand reassuringly. 'Thanks, friend.'

After a tense glance at me, Moustafa got out of the jeep and started smiling and talking to the soldier, his arm on his shoulder — a strategy to guide him away from the vehicle and hopefully avoid a search. From the severe expression on the young soldier's face it didn't look as if he was buying Moustafa's story. To my dismay, he called over two other soldiers who were lounging against the tank watching. They put out their cigarettes and sauntered towards us.

One of them, an officer, circled the jeep slowly, staring in at Rachel and me through the windows. We both kept looking straight ahead.

He stopped outside my door and my heart jumped into my

throat. I tried to look as relaxed as possible. Abruptly he pulled open my door. 'You, out!' he demanded in Arabic — to my relief, for it meant he thought I was local.

'What monastery?' he demanded.

'Deir Al Anba Bishoy,' I answered, praying he wouldn't notice my English accent.

He stepped closer, peering into my face. I noticed the glint of a fine gold chain at the neck of his open shirt. Suddenly I understood why he was so curious.

'I work with Father Mina, in the library,' I elaborated, hoping my hunch was correct.

The officer smiled slightly then leaned forward so the others couldn't hear him. 'Father Mina baptised me.' He swung around, again bristling with machismo, and shouted, 'Let them go!'

The two other soldiers and Moustafa looked surprised. 'But, sir …' the younger soldier began.

'I tell you, they're nobodies! Let the jeep through!'

Before they had time to argue amongst themselves, Moustafa and I had climbed back into the jeep and accelerated out of there. None of us spoke for several miles.

When the tank was well out of sight, Moustafa started shouting at me. 'Oliver, this has to stop! I am sorry that you are in trouble, but if you are serious about this new exploration I have to have your assurance that it will all be over in a few weeks. You understand?'

'A few days at the most, I promise you, Moustafa, then all will be normal.'

'Normal? What is normal? We were almost arrested back there, or worse!' The jeep sped along the desert track.

'The guy let us go! Moustafa, calm down, you're driving like a crazy man. You'll get us all killed!' I tried to steady the steering wheel.

Moustafa slowed down then looked at me. I'd never seen him so grim. 'You don't understand. That third man, he wasn't a soldier.'

'But he was wearing a uniform.'

'That's just it — his uniform wasn't right. I know the soldiers around here, Oliver, I even served myself. That third guy, the young one, I swear he wasn't working for the government.'

'So who does he work for?'

'Secret police, government, maybe even higher up. Whoever it is, I don't like them.'

\* \* \*

'Is that it?' Rachel asked, leaning out of the jeep window.

The mound loomed up to the left of the track. The area had already been fenced off, and the shothole scars where Moustafa's seismic crew had inserted explosives to get the required seismic measurements were visible.

'If you could read the land, you would hear it sing!' Moustafa yelled as he revved the engine over the rocky ground. 'Tell her, Oliver! Tell her how we are driving over a miracle. How this land will make us both very rich!'

He pulled up beside a boulder and I jumped out. Rachel followed while Moustafa started unpacking the surveying equipment. Opening the back door, I pulled out a shovel and pick. Sensing Rachel's ambivalence, I turned, swatting the flies away from my face. 'You disapprove, don't you?'

'I just think perhaps natural resources should stay that way,' she said. 'In nature, untouched.'

'Rachel, it won't just be Moustafa and me or our investors who'll make a profit from this. Money will go to the government and in turn to the people. There will be employment for the locals.'

She looked around ironically. 'The locals are Bedouin — shepherds and traders. Do you think they'll be interested in working on an oilfield?'

Ignoring her, I hauled the rucksack from under the back seat and, with the pick and shovel under one arm, strode off towards the far end of the ridge.

'Where are you going?' she asked.

"I've decided not to let my life be dictated by ridiculous superstitions any longer!'

Rachel struggled up the mound behind me, while Moustafa, politely ignoring our argument, set up the surveying equipment. His industrious figure disappeared behind me as I clambered over the crest of the ridge.

Rachel, running, caught up with me. 'So you drill, you dig up the land, pump the oil out, make a load of money, then what? This whole area will be ruined.'

'It's not a nature reserve, and anyway it won't be ruined!'

In the distance I could see the same Bedouin shepherd I'd met before, his headscarf with its distinctive pattern. He sat watching his scraggly herd of goats picking their way around a few clumps of long grass. I waved, but this time he didn't wave back.

'Maybe you have sold your soul,' Rachel said.

Her disapproval made me snap. 'Rachel, this is my industry, just as propping up a whole lot of western propaganda is yours!'

'That's unfair!' She stopped in her tracks, shaking with anger.

I put down the rucksack on a small flat area behind a boulder and slammed the pick into the stony ground.

'What are you doing?' she asked.

'Digging.'

'Why?'

I pulled the astrarium out of the rucksack.

'Oliver, you can't bury that, it's a priceless antiquity.'

'So let someone else find it in a hundred years and have it screw up their life!'

Fuming, Rachel marched off back to the jeep. I glared down at the rocky earth, furious with her obstinacy, furious with myself, furious with the stony ground. A tiny scorpion stared back at me. Poised with stinger erect, it was David waiting to take on Goliath. I didn't have the heart to kill it. A second later it scuttled sideways under a rock. Resigned to my labour, I drove the pick into the ground, the reverberation running up my arm.

After packing the sand back over the astrarium, now at least two metres below the surface, I joined Moustafa and helped him with the surveying. Rachel took photographs of the landscape. The sun — a great red orb like a huge omnipresent eye — hung on the horizon.

'Have you forgiven me?' I ventured and tentatively slipped my arm around her waist. To my relief she didn't remove it but continued to stare out towards the Sinai Peninsula.

'It's timeless, isn't it? Elemental,' she said finally, avoiding our previous debate.

'The desert isn't timeless. The changes are more subtle but they're there.'

'But without any evidence of human activity you can almost see history reaching back. You could almost believe time wasn't linear.'

'Maybe it isn't,' I replied, momentarily believing it.

'Oliver, do you really think that by burying the astrarium you can destroy its influence?'

'Let's hope so. Otherwise it will be you writing my obituary.'

A breeze blew across the plain, foreshadowing the night and the uneasy truce between us.

'We should get back before it is dark!' Moustafa yelled from beside the jeep where he'd begun repacking the equipment. Dusting the desert from my hands, I ran over to help him.

\* \* \*

It was already night by the time we drove into the Abu Rudeis camp. Out at sea, flares from the offshore rigs formed yellow smudges shooting up from a glittering black mirror. Already I felt better, more in control in this known terrain. I parked the jeep outside my hut and jumped down from the driver's seat, the familiarity of the camp enveloping me. The air was filled with the distinctive smell of burning fuel and the fecund odours drifting off the top of the mud-logging bins — the signature scents of the oilfield. Rachel grimaced as she breathed it all in. I laughed watching her.

'It's rough, but you're probably used to that. The other drawback is that you'll be sharing a single bed with me.'

'Believe me, I've had worse,' Rachel replied, deadpan.

Behind us Moustafa guffawed.

\* \* \*

'How many more days do we have?' Rachel asked.

'Two, after dawn tomorrow. But it's over, remember? The astrarium is dead and buried.'

We were lying on the bed; Rachel's hands wrapped around the iron rails of the bedhead.

'Still, who knows, this might be the shortest relationship I've ever had,' I joked, but failed to keep the concern out of my voice.

'I once fell in love with a man who got killed by a landmine three days later.'

'Rachel, you're not making me feel any better.'

I opened a beer and tossed the bottle cap onto the floor, together with the bottle opener. Immediately they slid across the room and stuck firmly against the side of the chair in the corner. In the same instant the electricity went out, plunging us into darkness, and the door flew inwards, revealing the scrubland outside, beyond a horizon broken only by the flares of the offshore rigs. Rachel screamed. I jumped off the bed and ran for the doorway, thinking we might be experiencing an earthquake. Naked, Rachel cowered.

'What was that?'

'Another earth tremor, I think. A shift in tectonic plates ... Christ, I'm not sure.'

A metal ashtray began to slide across the floor, first slowly, then accelerating as it neared the chair.

'What do you mean you don't know? You're a geophysicist! You're meant to know!' Rachel pulled the bedspread over herself, terrified.

I found a torch, switched it on and left it balanced on the side table, then tried to shut the door. It wouldn't move.

'It's become jammed somehow,'

'Just shut it!'

The metal doorknob seemed governed by an invisible force: as I pushed the door closed, it seemed to push against me. Staring into the gloom of the room I noticed that the beam of the torchlight had lit something up in the chair, something that hadn't been there before. To my amazement, it was my dusty rucksack. I picked it up. The astrarium was packed inside.

Horrified, I lifted it out and placed it on the table. The metal objects in the room moved with it.

'What's that doing here?' Rachel said. 'Didn't you bury it?'

'I did, I swear.'

'What's happening?!'

'It has some physical properties I don't understand — magnetism is just one of them. It seems to be growing stronger.'

'But how did it get here in the hut?'

'I have no idea.'

I sat down on the chair and stared at the mechanism, thinking over the details of the afternoon. The hole I'd dug was deep. No one had witnessed the burial, at least as far as I could remember. Moustafa had been on the other side of the ridge the whole time. But there had been someone there when we'd arrived, someone at a distance. Was it possible the Bedouin shepherd had seen me bury the astrarium and had then dug it up and brought it back here to the camp? But why?

Desperate to find some concrete explanation, I didn't dare examine the terrifying thought that the device might actually have moved itself.

'Okay, so now I'm a complete believer.'

Rachel's voice broke into my thoughts. Leaving the astrarium on the table, I joined her and held her, trying to think of something to say that might be reassuring. Something pinned to a reality that could defuse my fear. There was nothing.

'We'll drive to Cairo, talk to other Egyptologists, see what can be done,' she murmured into my chest.

'You know it isn't that simple.' I tried to sound rational, unafraid.

The door slammed shut again, the torch light flickered, then died, the battery dead. Rachel whimpered. I felt along the edge of the bedside table for the drawer, found a box of matches and a candle I knew were inside, and lit it. For the first time since I'd told Rachel about the astrarium, I saw real fear in her eyes.

'Isabella knew when she was going to die,' I told her. 'That was the real reason she was so desperate to find the astrarium, so she could change the date of her death. Call it a self-fulfilling prophecy, but she drowned on the exact date predicted in her horoscope. Maybe I could have saved her, but I just didn't know how.'

I was unable to meet Rachel's gaze. A large moth threw itself against the window with a dull thud and we both jumped then laughed out of sheer nervousness.

Rachel ran her hands through my hair, her fingers tracing my cheekbones, my mouth, then pulled me down to her.

# 40

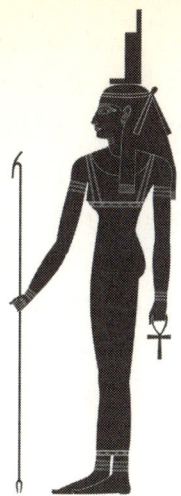

I lay there staring up at the ceiling. Rachel was curled up against my side, her face pressed against my shoulder, her breath hot against my skin. She was snoring slightly; the musk of sex drifted up from under the sheet. This time the lovemaking hadn't felt like a betrayal and that both pleased and disturbed me. Had I begun to forget Isabella? I didn't want another relationship but I'd started to feel the familiar twisting of involvement hauling me in. But I didn't want to run either, not yet.

The cry of a bird broke into my thoughts. It sounded again: ke-ke-ke-ke … The plaintive cry of a sparrowhawk. Careful not to wake Rachel, I slipped on my jeans and stepped out into the night.

A cloud of insects and moths swarmed around the lanterns. Over to the east, the pale glow of dawn had begun to creep over the horizon. The sparrowhawk cried again, somewhere high above me. I scanned the sky but saw nothing. I sat down on the wooden step of the hut and watched stars so bright they made me imagine a brilliant cosmos hanging behind a curtain of night.

'Isabella ...' My voice sounded naked and pathetically human. How does one talk to a ghost? I cleared my throat. 'Show me how to stop the mechanism, to save myself ...' The utterance felt uncomfortably close to a prayer.

It was then that I became aware of the sensation of being watched — that distinctive prickling at the back of the scalp. Careful not to make any sharp movements, I looked over at the pool of light thrown by the nearest lantern. Just beyond its edge, two yellow eyes stared back. I froze thinking it must be a jackal, or even a hyena. It was hard to see the animal's body. We stared at each other for only seconds but fear stretched time.

The beast jolted into movement, its haunches lowering in a blur as if readying itself to spring at me. Terrified, I scraped up a handful of stones and threw them. The creature spun and leaped back into the receding night — a swirl of tawny fur and slender legs — and I saw the tip of its forked tail sweep across the sand.

\* \* \*

Before the others woke, I drove back to the site where I'd buried the astrarium. It was mid-morning by the time I reached the dune and the sun was radiating waves of heat that pushed against my eyes and dried my throat and nostrils. As I began to climb the ridge, I tried to distract myself from the fear of finding something supernatural or extraordinary by visualising the sedimentary structure I was walking over, the consoling thought of all that black gold beneath my feet. It didn't work and by the time I could see the gaping hole where I'd buried the rucksack my whole body thudded along with my heart.

Rubble lay strewn around the hole, as if whoever or whatever had dug up the astrarium had done so in a frenetic manner. I kneeled down. Bird prints ran in a hectic pattern around the edges of the vacant grave, the unmistakable claw marks of the sparrowhawk. I looked up at the sky. It was a void of blue.

When I got back to camp, the hut was empty. Rachel had gone, no doubt to Port Tawfiq to join President Sadat's motorcade before it left for its great historical expedition. Pinned to the pillow was a note on Cecil Hotel letterhead. I lifted the pillow to my face; it still smelled of her hair.

*We are both crazy in our own ways, having abandoned caution and logic for greater truths. Maybe that's why I wanted you in the first place, because years ago I recognised your blind courage as being my own. Stay safe. Rachel (212 657 1086)*

It was a Manhattan number. Oh God, another departure, I thought, crushing the pillow against my body, cradling all the women I had ever known and all those who had abandoned me. It was then that I remembered why I felt so filled with dread — according to the astrarium I only had two days to live.

\* \* \*

Later that day, with me disguised once more as a Coptic monk, Moustafa and I left for the safe house he'd organised in Alexandria. The drive took twelve hours and we arrived not long before dawn. Our meeting with Mr Imenand was scheduled for that morning. Judging by the crowing roosters and braying donkeys I could hear as we approached the safe house, I suspected it was situated near or above a livestock market.

It was a neoclassical apartment that had seen grander days. Decorated in a glitzy mock Louis XVI style, it looked like the kind of place a government official would procure for his downtown mistress. Moustafa assured me we had the apartment for the whole day, after which he'd drive me back to Wadi El-Natrun. I hadn't told him that it was possible I had only twenty-four hours to live.

At 9 am, four of us gathered around the long glass-topped dining table below a large black and silver glass chandelier. Mr Waalif, the official representing the Egyptian Government Oil Agency, sat opposite Moustafa and myself, staring at the spreadsheets and surveillance maps Moustafa had supplied. A cadaverous man in his late fifties, whose flat features were covered in an inordinate number of large sunspots, he had mentioned nothing about the clandestine nature of the meeting, but that didn't really surprise me. Waalif was famous for two things — discretion and his own clandestine deals. His approval was essential if we were to get the licensing agreement.

Sitting at the other end of the table was Mr Eminites, Mr Imenand's representative, a short Jordanian dressed in a pale blue jellaba with an expensive tie and shirt underneath. Large black-framed glasses wrapped themselves around his wide face. Initially he'd seemed friendly, but had frosted up when I demanded an explanation as to why Mr Imenand wasn't there himself. My insistence had shocked my companions, but after Moustafa had murmured something into Mr Eminites' ear, the representative had assured me that Mr Imenand would be at the meeting, but in his own time and that we should begin without him. None of which I had found reassuring.

Waalif cleared his throat. 'So, Mr Warnock, I understand that you and Moustafa Saheer, in partnership with Mr Imenand, wish to lease the land for an initial exploration period of three years, followed by a production period of twenty-five years at our standard terms. That will mean an annual land fee as set out in schedule 4, production bonuses as set out in schedule 5, a government royalty as set out in schedule 6, and a share of production as set out in schedule 7. I gather the initial work program is already agreed.'

Mr Eminites glanced at the draft contract in front of him. I found his expression impossible to interpret and without the presence of our enigmatic benefactor it all felt very risky.

'We obviously can't predict the eventual production,' I said, 'but we are confident the reservoir is there and that we can get the best from it.'

'And who will be the other oil company partnering us?' Waalif went on.

Moustafa and I exchanged glances. Mr Eminites adjusted his tie-knot before speaking in polite but heavily accented English.

'There will be no other partners. This is one of the conditions of Mr Imenand's commitment, which, as you can see, is considerable. He also insists that the exploration program begin within the month.'

'That quickly?' I interjected, silently wondering if I would, myself, live long enough to see the work begin.

'Mr Imenand is not a young man and he is keen to see the fruits of his investment.'

'This is unusual,' Waalif said, 'but the Egyptian government is respectful of Mr Imenand's eminence and the significant capital he is offering this project, and we trust our friend Mr Warnock. So we are happy to proceed on this basis.'

Waalif, a pedantic negotiator famous for exhausting his colleagues with endless minutiae, was smiling; his usual arrogance replaced by what I could only describe as reverence. I sat back trying to conceal my amazement. Who exactly was this Mr Imenand? The only information I'd gleaned from

Moustafa was that he had extensive investments across the Mediterranean, from Spain to Turkey, and in North Africa, and that he'd had been based in Greece for most of his working life. His holdings were complete and, more interestingly, he had no heirs. It wasn't much to go on, but without the backing of GeoConsultancy I knew it would be hard to raise the funds ourselves for even the most basic exploration, and never on the terms he was offering. I had no choice but to trust him.

Suddenly I was aware of a change of atmosphere in the room. Mr Eminites had risen to his feet, bowing his head reverently. The others followed. I swung around. Behind me, silhouetted in the doorway, was a thin figure.

'Oliver Warnock. It is a delight to meet such a legendary individual in person.'

His voice was resonant; the bass notes seemed to reverberate right down into my feet. He stepped out of the sunlight and I could see him properly. Lean and around five feet eight inches in height, he was dark-skinned, almost Libyan in appearance, with a finely honed face with high cheekbones and a long curved nose. He was hard to age; I estimated he was somewhere between fifty and seventy — his skin had the well-preserved sheen of wealth. His posture was upright and regal, and he exuded a charisma I had witnessed only once before — on the one occasion I had met Prince Faisal. He was immaculately dressed in what looked like a Savile Row black suit, with a lavishly patterned cravat and matching handkerchief. The cravat was held in place by a gold tiepin modelled in the shape of an ostrich feather; it was an eccentric detail that suggested a man capable of unconventional behaviour.

Mr Eminites pulled a chair out for the new arrival. 'Mr Warnock, it is my honour to introduce you to Mr Imenand,' he said.

The entrepreneur held his hand out and I shook it. To my astonishment, although the skin on his hand appeared youthful, its touch was that of a far older man.

'Nice to put a face to the enigma, Mr Imenand,' I said.

'And for I to meet the Diviner. Your reputation precedes you — I have been following your career for a while now. You have a very successful exploration record, one of the most impressive on the globe.'

'You exaggerate,' I replied modestly. To my surprise, he seemed to take offence.

'I never exaggerate. Perhaps you are unaware of the full extent of your powers. At your age, that is not merely foolhardy, it is also culpable.'

'I am a scientist, Mr Imenand, no more, no less. I am thorough in my research.'

'We shall see. But I must extend my condolences for the loss of your wife. She was a great archaeologist.'

'You knew of her too?'

'I have read several of her papers. There was one in particular, on a dig at Behbeit el-Hagar — a fascinating read. I was particularly captivated as Behbeit el-Hagar was my birthplace. Of course it is nothing now, a mere village, but once it was a beautiful city. I am a collector of antiquities and, one could say, a little of an archaeologist myself — amateur, of course.' He laughed, and the others followed politely. 'But now, to business. You are satisfied with the terms of the contract?'

Cornered, I became flustered. 'Of course. They are more advantageous to us than to your corporation. The terms are generous, perhaps too generous.'

'I shall be the judge of that. Do not be deceived, Mr Warnock — or may I call you Oliver?'

I nodded.

'Oliver, I shall be taking a strong personal interest in the exploration. I have decided to make you my hobby.'

Again, he laughed, and again, like a chorus, the others followed. I didn't join in; something in me wanted to resist the allure of that charisma spreading like perfume throughout the room.

'So we have a deal?' I said bluntly, determined to resist his charm. Immediately the laughter was cut short.

Moustafa glanced at me, his expression pensive as if I had overstepped the mark. Mr Eminites coughed, while Waalif adjusted his wide silk tie. The tension built until finally Mr Imenand broke into a smile, to the others' visible relief.

'We have a deal, and now I have a plane to catch. But we will be seeing a lot of each other in the future, Oliver — that much is certain.'

We shook hands again, and again I felt the rough, wrinkled skin of a much older man.

Mr Eminites gathered up our presentation material and placed it into his briefcase. As he moved to open the door, I noticed that he manoeuvred himself so his back was never presented to his employer.

Mr Imenand paused in the doorway. 'Oliver, I believe your mother's maiden name was McDermott.'

'How did you know that?' I blurted, astonished.

'I too am thorough in my research. The McDermotts are direct descendants of Milesius of Spain, chief of the Gaels and father of the first Irish king, Heremon. As we know, the Gaels migrated from the Black Sea but originated from Libya. The very same Milesius was a general in the army of the last great Pharaoh of Egypt and for his efforts he was awarded the Pharaoh's daughter, Scota, in marriage. They left Egypt for Spain and then eventually Ireland.'

'The last Pharaoh of Egypt, you mean Nectanebo II?' I ventured, my heart banging violently against my chest. The sense of being encircled was overwhelming and I now wondered about the remarkable fact of the entrepreneur's birthplace being the same as Nectanebo.

'Milesius worked for both the uncle and the nephew — Nectanebo I and Nectanebo II. In fact, it was Milesius who assisted Nectanebo II in the building of his temples. So you see, I am perhaps more of an archaeologist than you imagined.'

To my astonishment, he winked at me before walking out the door.

# 41

While Moustafa was out buying supplies for the long drive back to the monastery, I unwrapped the astrarium. Nothing had changed: the mechanism was still whirring away and the tiny pointer with the head of Seth was now only one degree away from my death date.

Carefully I wrapped it up again. The meeting with Mr Imenand had disturbed me. Was he just interested in the exploration or did he have other intentions? I knew Nectanebo II was a well-known Pharaoh but it seemed a fairly large coincidence that the entrepreneur had brought him up — particularly in relation to my own family history. I recalled my father's face as he told me about Connor McDermott, my mother's great-grandfather, the diviner. It seemed unbelievable that he could have been a direct descendant of a man who had worked for the Pharaoh. Again, that sensation of being overwhelmed by events beyond my control, beyond my lifetime even, washed over me. I needed to get out of Alexandria as soon as possible — but there was one encounter I had to have before leaving.

I waited until Moustafa returned. After asking him to guard the bag containing the astrarium, I stepped once more onto the streets disguised as a Coptic priest.

* * *

The prison guard slipped the fifty Egyptian pounds into the back pocket of his uniform and beckoned me into a narrow corridor reeking of urine and disinfectant.

'Mr Hermes, he special friend, maybe?'

Ignoring his grin, I followed him, fighting disorientation and fear as I recognised the peeling plaster and old metal doors from my own interrogation only a week before. We walked past cell after cell — some of them empty and unlit; some with men curled in the corners, abandoned knots of despairing humanity. Some called out for help; others chanted in prayer, rocking themselves backwards and forwards.

At the end of the corridor was a slightly larger cell with a wooden bench and a latrine bucket in the corner. Hermes Hemiedes lay on the bench wrapped in a grey blanket that he had pulled over his face too, almost as if in shame. His old man's legs — pale, with twisting veins encircling the thin ankles — stuck out from underneath, the feet, gnarled with bunions, thrust into a pair of battered oversized sandals.

'Thirty minutes,' the prison guard informed me, unlocking the barred door with a large iron key. 'Normally fifteen, but for you …' he tapped the money in his back pocket, 'thirty.'

He left, locking me in behind him.

'Oliver?' Hermes threw the blanket off his head and sat up. I was relieved to notice that his face didn't appear to be bruised. 'Thank God you've come. I cannot stay here — I will not come out alive!'

'Hermes, please, let's not panic. Tell me first, what have they charged you with?'

'I have been charged with conspiracy to undermine the state. It is a trumped-up lie. They have attacked me.'

'The prison guards?'

'Don't be ridiculous, the prisoners! They ambushed me in the yard and ... humiliated me.'

'Really? You look unmarked.'

'You don't understand. For an individual such as myself, with differences ...'

'Your sexual orientation?'

'My sexual orientation?' He laughed bitterly. 'If only it were that simple.'

Suddenly all of the oddities I'd noticed about the Egyptologist made sense: the hairlessness of his skin, the narrow shoulders, the wide hips, the curiously wavering tone of his voice, which now reminded me of the alto voice of an older woman. Noticing my expression, Hermes slowly lifted his stained prison shirt to reveal pendulous shrivelled breasts — female breasts.

'You're a hermaphrodite?'

He covered himself up. 'In this life I have chosen to live as a man.'

'I don't understand ...'

'I was born over seventy years ago in a small village in the Sudan. We did not have the technology or the medical staff to correct such "abnormality". My parents were horrified. They gave me to the *darwish* who brought me up as his apprentice. That was Ahmos Khafre, the mystic I sent Isabella to visit in Goa all those years ago. So you see, the circle is even tighter than you might have imagined, Oliver.'

I stared at him, a sense of vertigo hitting me as I wondered exactly how much of both Isabella's life and my own had been manipulated from a distance, as though we were marionette puppets jerking at the end of strings.

'How did you survive?' I asked.

'I started to research the history of people like me, whom the Ancient Egyptians had once considered sacred. The perfect blend of the masculine and feminine, we were often chosen to be the high priests and even to play the gods themselves in the ceremonies.'

As he spoke his voice seemed to be getting higher, as if he was finally relaxing into his natural ambiguity. My memory jolted me straight back to the catacombs, to the painted features of the goddess Isis shimmering unnaturally, the voice behind the wooden mask. I leaned against the wall, sickened by the realisation. I'd been on the wrong trail the whole time — it had not been Amelia Lynhurst leading the worshippers, but Hermes.

He reached out and grabbed my wrist. 'Oliver, we need each other. No one else can save you. No one else knows how to stop the astrarium.'

I pushed his hand off. 'You lied to me. You took her heart, you violated her!'

I banged against the bars to get the attention of the guard.

'Wait, I'll tell you everything!' he said.

I stopped rattling the bars. Hermes settled himself on the bench and patted the space next to him. I ignored him, preferring to stand.

'Giovanni Brambilla ran a small salon that attracted individuals interested in mysticism and the occult. I'm talking over forty years ago, in 1936, when the world we knew was beginning to fragment. None of us wanted to lose power. We were a disparate group — academics, businessmen, archaeologists — but we all had a passion for Egyptology. And they were desperate times in a desperate city. At first the re-enactments were innocent, a naïve attempt to experience some kind of authenticity. But as the years passed I wanted to go further. I was convinced that if the rituals were carried out correctly, real sorcery would occur. One day, unknown to the others, I replaced the sheep's heart we'd been using in the weighing of the heart ritual with a human heart.'

'Whose heart?'

'A criminal's — I stole it from the mortuary.'

'You're lying again! You had a man murdered, didn't you? Ashraf heard screaming.'

'It was a noble sacrifice! Besides, the man was condemned anyway. What is important is how that little detail changed everything. That night we conjured Seth, his very being. It was phenomenal — suddenly we had the power of gods.'

'That's not possible.'

'Isn't it? Oliver, you've seen it for yourself.'

I shivered, remembering the long shadow falling across the walls of the catacombs. Hermes watched my face with a kind of objective curiosity; a whole other personality seemed to be materialising under his veneer of obsequiousness.

'After that, dissent broke out in the group,' he went on. 'But this was not the debate of a bunch of academic archaeologists. This argument had much broader implications.'

'Giovanni wanted to use the rituals to destroy his political enemies?'

He nodded. 'For a while, it worked. I couldn't tell you whether it was the power of all those people believing together or whether it was real sorcery. Then Amelia broke the circle and ruined it all. She took some of the others with her, to pursue their own interests.'

'And Isabella?'

'She did whatever her grandfather wanted, anything. It was Giovanni who first came across the astrarium in his research;

research he was foolish enough to share with Amelia Lynhurst.'

'And the excavation at Behbeit el-Hagar?'

'Giovanni organised it. We were all convinced we would find the astrarium there. Instead, Amelia found the Was key and fled with it, betraying us. Giovanni persuaded Isabella to dedicate her studies to the mechanism and to search out Ahmos Khafre, who would be able to direct her towards its discovery.'

'What about Isabella's death date?'

'Ahmos Khafre was the greatest astrologer the world has ever known. The death date was real.'

'She was just a child, Hermes.'

'Childhood is such a modern concept.'

At that, I couldn't contain my anger any longer. I lifted my fist; only the fear in his eyes stopped me from striking the blow. Relieved, Hermes wiped his sweaty face with a filthy sleeve.

'I was deceived by Mosry. He infiltrated our group. It was I who arranged for his man to be on that boat when Isabella drowned. I didn't know he was working for Prince Majeed. It was he who murdered your Australian friend — an interrogation gone wrong.'

'I could kill you now,' I said thickly.

'I am ready to die anyway.'

He bared his scrawny neck, as if waiting for me to strangle him. I kept my arms stiffly by my sides. He pulled his collar back up.

'The astrarium has a reputation amongst the military elite, both in Saudi Arabia and Egypt. They believe in its powers. After all, it is known that Alexander of Macedonia wanted it, and Napoleon sent troops to look for it. If Prince Majeed gets hold of the device, it will be bedlam for this region — tribal anarchy. He will use it to help create the kind of political chaos he thrives on. All I wanted was immortality.' He smiled cynically. 'No use to me now. They will kill me in here.'

'What about Hugh Wollington? Why does he want the astrarium?'

Hermes' face turned ashen; I'd never seen him look more frightened.

'How do you know about Hugh Wollington?' he asked.

'He was the voice of Horus, wasn't he?' I shook him furiously. 'He was behind all of this from the beginning!'

'He is the high priest. He rules us all.' Petrified, Hermes could barely speak.

'You're talking nonsense. He's just a man like the rest of us. Just give me the facts!'

'If he gets hold of the astrarium, he will release Seth, the god of confusion,' Hermes whispered. 'Then may the gods help us all.'

Horrified and angry at myself for finding this latest revelation terrifying, I turned to call for the guard again. Hermes clutched at my arm.

'Please, you have to understand. I stopped them from sacrificing you in the ceremony. You are Osiris. You are the deliverer. You must be allowed to complete your task.'

'The deliverer — what are you talking about?'

'At Behbeit el-Hagar we discovered a prophecy which said that if the astrarium was ever lost, the only person who would be able to restore it to the mummy of Nectanebo would be a priest of the underworld, a follower of Osiris, someone who brought forth the subterranean treasures of the earth. It was no accident Isabella chose to marry you,' he concluded with relish.

Again, I had to restrain myself from lashing out at him. How dare he suggest that Isabella had married me because she was instructed to! Yet despite my fury, I couldn't contain the tsunami of doubt now roaring up inside me, undermining all I'd ever believed in.

'You wanted me to take responsibility for the astrarium because of some archaic prophecy?' I said, incredulous.

'You have no choice. Please, please help me, Oliver.' Again he reached out.

I pushed him away now, wanting just to escape. I shouted for the guard. My calls ignited a chorus of wailing from the other prisoners until the whole corridor was transformed into a cacophony of misery. When finally I stumbled out into the courtyard, Hermes' entreaties still rang in my ears.

# 42

The iron gates of the prison shut with a clang. I walked towards the main street, distracted by the various scenarios that swirled around my brain. It was still before noon and the pavements were thronged with people: women on the way back from market, men sauntering to the midday meal, schoolgirls linked arm in arm. Isabella loved me, I told myself. But the prism of our marriage was now collapsing into a complexity of shards I didn't understand. Had my profession been the single factor in her decision to marry me? Had it had some kind of mythical symbolism for her? Everything I had known to be solid, to be real, was evaporating around me. Isabella had been my anchor, the continuity that gave my life foundation, for the last five years. To imagine our shared years of intimacy, of lovemaking, of believing in the life we had, that she loved me for who I was not what I did, was nothing but mere simulacra — was devastating.

And if my marriage hadn't been real, what else was false in my life? I'd assumed myself in control of where I worked and who for, but now I had to ask just how much of those decisions had been my free will? Had I been unwittingly following a path dictated by an unseen master? The idea that parts of my life might have been preordained was suffocating. It was an affront to all of my personal philosophies: my atheism, my belief in free will, the notion that a person had control over their destiny.

At least there was Rachel, I thought. She seemed to hover just in front of me — a reality with solid, concrete possibilities; nothing to do with this terrifying labyrinth of archaic gods and disturbing coincidences. I had to hold onto her regardless of whatever lay ahead.

Panic travelled over me in waves, I was painfully aware of time passing.

Light seemed to bounce off everything — car mirrors, glass shopfronts, even the metal stirrups of the horses. I needed to get back to the apartment and then to the monastery. But then what?

Behind me there was the roar of a car engine. I turned; a black Mercedes was trailing me. I could see Mosry at the wheel, Omar beside him. I darted into a side street. The car followed, swerving onto the pavement towards me. People scattered, women screamed, fruit spilled over the street as the car headed straight for me — but just before it hit me, someone pulled me into a doorway, inches clear of the front bumper.

It was Faakhir.

'Down here!' he said, and bundled me into a side alley and then into a darkened building entrance.

\* \* \*

'I suppose you imagined I was the anti-Christ incarnate,' Amelia Lynhurst stood at her desk, a vast Victorian construction covered with maps and papers. An elegant cabinet stood against one wall, covered in framed photographs; several showed Amelia in uniform, one of her sitting atop a tank flanked by a couple of grinning British soldiers. *Sinai, 1944* was scrawled across the bottom.

'A sort of a demon goddess in tweed?' she continued, beginning to stride around the room.

It was a rectangular chamber on the top floor of offices belonging to the British Archaeological Society — an organisation that had been in Alexandria since the 1850s. The walls were lined from ceiling to floor with shelves crammed with papers and books. One whole wall was dedicated to Jung: I spied *Man and His Symbols*, *The Archetypes and the Collective Unconscious*, *Psychology and Alchemy*, *The Structure and Dynamics of the Psyche* amongst others. Another shelf contained books on physics, including several on the latest developments in quantum physics.

'Just tell me again why I should trust you,' I responded warily.

'Because she allowed you to keep the astrarium,' Faakhir interrupted. He sat down and pulled a cigarette out of his pocket. 'She could have told me to keep it.'

'And how do you fit into all of this?' I asked him, still amazed to see the two of them together.

Amelia put her hand on the youth's shoulder. 'I had to make sure there was someone close to Isabella who could protect her.'

'But you failed.' I couldn't keep the fury out of my voice.

'This was my tragedy as well as yours.' Faakhir's face was grave with emotion.

'Just tell me who you are!' I slammed my fist on the desk but Faakhir didn't even flinch. It was obvious his previous naïvety had been a façade.

My patience had finally snapped. I was horribly aware of the clock hanging over Amelia's desk, the fine black second hand ticking notch by notch. I'd had enough of enigmas, of people who weren't what they seemed.

Faakhir exhaled slowly. 'Let's just say I was trained by the Israeli navy.'

'Mossad?' I persisted.

He chose not to answer.

'None of us predicted the earthquake,' Amelia said. 'We all thought Isabella would reach the astrarium in time. When, a few weeks before her final dive, Isabella discovered what Hermes intended to use the astrarium for, she came to me. We made plans for every eventuality we could anticipate.'

'How do I fit into those plans? Why did I inherit the astrarium?'

'You are the diviner, you embody Osiris. It must be you who reunites the astrarium with the Pharaoh. This is the only way we can avoid Maat — political and emotional chaos — and the era of Seth.'

She pointed at a black-and-white television in the corner. The sound was turned down but I recognised the footage: Sadat meeting with Assad — the president's last stop before his secret meeting with Begin, the meeting that Rachel would be attending.

'Is that what the era of Seth is — a failed peace initiative?' I asked incredulously.

'Don't play the idiot, it doesn't suit you,' Amelia snapped. 'You sense what chaos could be unleashed, but your fear keeps you holding onto the small, known world you're more comfortable functioning in.'

Faakhir interjected. 'Enough, Amelia, we're running out of time. Do you have the Was, Oliver, the key to the mechanism?'

'Thanks to Amelia's old friend, Professor Silvio — but then you stole it in the first place, didn't you, Amelia?'

'I had to put it out of reach of the others. I was frightened they would abuse the power of the mechanism — turns out I was right.' She stopped, reading the ill-concealed anxiety in my face. 'So you have used the machine. That was very foolish, Oliver. Very bloody arrogant.'

I collapsed into a chair, shattered by the barrage of recent events. 'The sin of hubris,' I volunteered.

'It usually is with scientists. So when is your death date?'

'Can you help me?' I asked. 'I know you were part of the original sect.'

'I left after the first manifestation of Seth. I wish Isabella had too. From that moment, her whole career was directed by Giovanni — in some ways, even after his death. Then she fell under the influence of Hermes Hemiedes.'

'And he sent her to Goa.'

'When I got that teaching position at Oxford, and once I felt I'd gained her trust, I explained some of the terrible things her grandfather had done, the events he had manipulated. She wouldn't believe me, couldn't believe me. Then, when you both returned to Egypt, Hermes heard that Isabella was close to finding the instrument. He persuaded her to attend a few of the rituals and, naïvely, she agreed.'

'I had no idea. If only she'd told me.'

'Would you have believed her?'

I didn't need to answer.

Her expression was one of sympathy. 'I'm afraid, Oliver, that you have a part to play, no matter how reluctant you are. As I tried to tell you at the opera, this is a great love story. You see, the astrarium was commissioned by Banafrit, chief consort and sister of Nectanebo himself. It was common practice for the pharaohs to marry their sisters — a way of keeping power within the family. You already know about the assassination plot; I believe she might have died trying to save her lover. What I know for certain is that the assassination attempt was organised by a religious cult that worshipped the god Seth; a cult both Hugh Wollington and Hermes Hemiedes wished to re-create. Their manifestation of the god is one that thrives on chaos; the personification of amoral evil, the fascistic shadow self.'

'And the manifestation I saw in the catacombs — how was that staged?'

'What makes you think it was staged?'

I didn't answer. The idea that the manifestation might have been real was profoundly disturbing.

'You have to remember that when a group of followers come together,' Amelia continued, 'their desire and will unite. That in itself is a hugely powerful force, an energy many charismatic political leaders have exploited. Think of Hitler, Stalin, Mao — individuals capable of galvanising hundreds of thousands of people at a time. Jung also believed in the idea of mass hypnosis, alchemy of faith. There, Oliver, I have given you a psychological explanation you may feel more comfortable adopting.'

'I'm due to die in ...' I glanced at the clock hanging on the wall, '... sixteen and a half hours. It's hard to find anything comforting at the moment.'

I laughed cynically but the others stayed grimly silent.

'What about Hugh Wollington?' I asked. 'Who's he working for?' Was he involved in the ritual designed to terrify me?'

'I'm sure he was one of them, the rest — followers of Hermes Hemiedes. Wollington has been associated with the Saudis. I believe Prince Majeed might have contacted him to glean more information about the astrarium, but then our friend Wollington got greedy.'

There was a knock on the door, which startled us all. After a nod from Amelia, Faakhir went to answer it. We could hear him conversing in Arabic. A moment later he came back.

'Hermes Hemiedes has committed suicide. He hanged himself in his cell.'

I buried my face in my hands. 'Jesus Christ.'

Amelia put her hand on my arm, her cool touch was somehow reassuring. 'Oliver, concentrate. We have to move fast.'

# 43

I sent Faakhir to the apartment with a letter for Moustafa. What seemed like minutes later he'd returned with the astrarium. Amelia lifted it from its wrapping and I witnessed the same reverence in her face that I'd seen in Hermes' when he first saw the device; an expression of religious rapture. But in seconds she switched back from worshipper to scientist. Using what looked like a dentist's stylus, she pushed at the base from one end. To my amazement, it shifted and slid outwards. She carefully removed it and picked up a magnifying glass to peer at its surface.

'As I thought.'

She offered the magnifying glass to me. A set of hieroglyphs and a line drawing were clearly visible on the tiny panel: I recognised the symbols for Osiris, the Sun god Ra, and Thoth, but that was all.

'This is an Amduat,' she explained, 'a map of the afterlife to help the deceased become an Akh Aper, a prepared spirit. It describes how the spirit must travel to the mansion of Osiris — an early prototype of Hades — and to the Field of Hetep in a twelve-hour journey that mirrors the journey of Ra, or the Sun, in the hours between dusk and dawn. The map shows us how the spirit of the deceased must travel from east to west along a blue waterway across the inner sky. Then back again, from west to east, on a black land path across the outer sky. Finally the spirit becomes a star in the sky next to the god Thoth. However, this particular map is more than allegorical; it is a deliberate smokescreen.'

She reached over and pulled a cigarette lighter from Faakhir's shirt pocket. Flicking it open, she ran the flame over the metal surface. Shocked, I grabbed her wrist.

'I hope you know what you're doing …'

Smiling, she shook my hand off. 'My dear man, of course I don't! It's always ten per cent fact and ninety per cent guesswork. But the flame can't hurt it.'

As the surface of the metal blackened, the lines of another map appeared. The distinctive shape of the Nile, like the delicate branches of a wayward tree, was instantly recognisable. At the bottom, Aswan; with the ancient city of Memphis near the top; and the cities of Luxor and Thebes in between, small pale dots on the tiny illustration. A route was etched into the metal, from Alexandria along the coastline to Marsa Matruh, then swinging inland to the southwest near the Libyan border.

'This is the true map, added later I suspect, after Nectanebo's murder — a cartogram describing the route the Pharaoh's mummy was taken along before being placed in a secret tomb. The assassins would never have left him unburied without some ceremony — the danger of angering the gods was too great.'

'And how will following this map help me?'

'Your role is to return the astrarium to its rightful owner, to place it into the arms of Nectanebo's mummy. The astrarium's soul will unite with that of Nectanebo and the device will cease to function, maybe even to exist. Therein lies your redemption, Oliver.'

I peered down at the small soot-laden map — it looked terrifyingly tenuous to me, the silvery etchings of a smoky dream. I still found it difficult to believe completely in the powers of the astrarium, but, as I noted bitterly, my disbelief hadn't prevented me from becoming embroiled in the events surrounding it. I could still even be killed over it. My own ambivalence aside, it was clear that Amelia believed in the power of the astrarium and I had nothing to lose by trusting her. It was a calculated gamble: go with her plan, which might switch off the mechanism; or not. I couldn't dismiss the fear that I had only hours to live.

'According to this map,' Amelia continued, 'Nectanebo's mummy lies somewhere in the Oasis of Siwah near the Libyan border. The inscribed instructions aren't only to show the route the Pharaoh's mummified corpse travelled; they are also our guide through the twelve stages of the journey to the afterworld.'

I raised my eyebrows and glanced at Faakhir. Reading my expression, he stubbed out his cigarette and said, 'My friend, Egypt is riddled with mysteries. Here, the divide between the inanimate and the animate is not the same as in the West. Our land has its own spirits. This is not a new story.'

'If I agree to go, will you be coming with me?' I asked.

Faakhir looked at Amelia, who spoke for him.

'Faakhir has been called away to another mission, equally important. I will be your guide and protector.'

Faakhir put his hand on my arm to reassure me. 'She knows the area better than anyone, and she is more of a soldier than I, believe it or not.'

I must have looked apprehensive but Amelia ignored me. Carefully she slid the base of the mechanism back into position.

'It's important that you understand the symbolism of the journey before we leave,' she told me.

'Isn't it the soul of the deceased overcoming moral trials and tribulations as he attempts to pass into the afterworld? A little like a day of reckoning?'

'In the first hour, Ra, the Sun god, enters Akhet, the eastern horizon, a place that lies between day and night. The spirit of the deceased accompanies him. In the second and third hours, Ra and the spirit travel through the Waters of Osiris, a realm also known as Wernes. Hours four and five are passed in the world of the desert, Sokar. In the fifth hour, the spirit finds the tomb of Osiris, recognisable by the pyramid mound built over it, a hidden lake of fire beneath the interior enclosure.'

'And will we really be travelling through a desert?'

'Both physically and psychologically. The New Testament also contains a version of this—'

'The temptation of Christ?'

'For an atheist you know your Bible.'

'I blame my mother. What happens next?'

'The sixth hour of the journey is the most crucial. This is when the Ba of the sun god has to unite with his body. If this does not happen, the sun will not rise the next day and such an event symbolises the end of the world. On a smaller scale, the spirit accompanying the god will not pass into the afterlife. There is no worse destiny according to the Ancient Egyptians. The unification of Ba and form traditionally happens within a celestial circle made by the mehen serpent — the snake biting its own tail — which is a symbol of infinity in many cultures. Hour seven leads us into an even more difficult transition. The nemesis of Ra and of renewal — the huge serpent god Apophis — will be waiting to attack and destroy Ra and his spirit companion. Isis is called upon to protect and defend both Ra and the deceased. You will be most vulnerable in this hour. But there is no one who knows Isis's spells from the Book of the Dead as well as I do — except Hermes Hemiedes, which now, of course, is irrelevant.'

'And how does this metaphysical journey conclude?'

'At the eighth hour, the tomb gates open to allow the spirit to depart from Sokar. The ninth hour is spent returning back over the waters. Hour ten sees the regeneration of the spirit through immersion in the waters.'

'How dangerous is this going to be?'

Amelia and Faakhir glanced at each other. Amelia answered.

'Oliver, we can't guarantee we won't be pursued, and we can't guarantee your survival. But I will endeavour to protect you to the best of my abilities.'

'And if I stay in Alexandria?'

'Mosry will kill you anyway,' Faakhir answered bluntly.

I turned to Amelia. She shrugged then began packing away the astrarium.

'According to the map, by the eleventh hour you will be on an island in Lake Arachie and the god's eyes — and those of the accompanying spirit — are fully restored. In the twelfth and final hour, Ra enters the eastern horizon as the dawning of a new day, while the deceased's soul ascends to become a star in the sky.'

'Meaning I emerge having reunited the astrarium with Nectanebo and my death date has slipped somewhere to the distant future?' I said. 'I wasn't planning on becoming a star in the sky.'

Neither of them laughed.

'If the gods will it, Oliver,' Amelia said seriously. 'I am of the view that there are many life paths all running in parallel. Free will lies in the choices we make, which paths we step onto at any given moment — but those life paths are already written.

Isabella knew it was likely she would die that day in the water. She also knew that you would inherit her task. The question is: do you have the strength of character to complete it?'

Again, I found myself thinking about my marriage — the idea that Isabella had married me because of some prophecy she believed was haunting. Had she really been that obsessed?

I looked at the astrarium, an ancient mesh of cogs and prophecy, and remembered how frustrated I'd been with Isabella's focus on finding it; how absent she had been when working, as if incapable of registering anything outside that circle of intent. I'd begun to view that absence as a rival. Perhaps my instinct had been right.

And what about Rachel? She offered a chance to escape this labyrinth that had suddenly redefined my marriage. Would I lose her if I committed to this extraordinary quest Amelia was proposing? And my father and Gareth — would I ever see them again? Now it really seemed my life was dictated by the wants of this ancient machine.

I glanced at the clock. I'd already been here for an hour — one precious hour of the few I supposedly had left. I went to the window and looked down at the site of the old Roman amphitheatre. The site was a Napoleonic army barracks in the eighteenth century, that was taken over by the British in the nineteenth-century — Alexandria was so full of layers of history and conquest, remnants of the old superstitions emerging in more contemporary rituals. And here I was — irredeemably trapped in the great swirling miasma.

'What have I got to lose if I don't go?' I asked.

'Only your life, if you believe the prediction — or if you believe in Mosry!'

Faakhir indicated the television. It now showed Sadat's convoy crossing the Syrian border before it wound its way across the desert; the same convoy Rachel was in.

'There's something else you should know,' Faakhir went on, 'we believe Mosry has details of the secret meeting between Sadat and Begin, right down to the hour. Prince Majeed wants the astrarium now, Oliver. He wants to destroy any possibility of an accord any way he can.'

Amelia put her hand over mine. 'We leave in an hour.'

# 44

The sheikh wore a traditional Berber striped jellaba and sat cross-legged on the rug on the floor of the mud-brick house. He looked about seventy, and had a large scar that ran in a zigzag across one cheek and over his nose. He paused mid-sentence to stare at me dismissively, then swung back to Amelia — who, he'd been in deep conversation with since we'd arrived in the ancient city of Siwah. Although most of their exchange was incomprehensible to me — they were speaking in a dialect I couldn't follow — occasionally I recognised the word 'sister', which made me curious about the nature of their relationship.

I took a sip of the black tea I'd been offered, heavily flavoured with rose syrup, and waited for Amelia to tell me what was going on. Eventually, she turned to me.

'Sheikh Suleiman is an old friend and a Berber. This community dates back to 10,000 BC. They, and a few Bedouin traders, are the only people who really live in Siwah.'

The sheikh interjected and they both laughed.

'He tells me to warn you about walking amongst the date pickers,' she said.

I was perplexed and it must have shown.

'There is an ancient law here that the date pickers, who are male, must remain virgins until they are forty years old. He thinks your blue eyes might turn their heads.'

Slightly insulted, I glanced at the sheikh who smiled back sardonically.

'Shouldn't we be on our way by now?' I asked Amelia, conscious of the astrarium in my rucksack and the insidious hum of a large electric clock that sat, rather incongruously, next to an ornate hookah. I was running out of time — literally and it was hard not to feel panicked.

Amelia put her hand on my knee. 'Patience. The sheikh has a gift we should take with us.'

The sheikh nodded, then stood and left the room.

'Why does he keep addressing you as sister?' I couldn't help asking.

'Because I am his sister.' She went over to a low chest that stood in an alcove. 'This once belonged to my husband.'

She opened it and took out a photo to show me. It looked as if it dated from the 1940s. Standing in front of a pool surrounded by palms was a young woman in army camouflage, beside her a young Berber holding a rifle. They were smiling at the camera and his arm was wrapped around her waist, but there was tension in their faces, as if this moment was a respite.

'The man I loved is buried here,' she went on. 'He was a local sheikh. This was taken in 1943 — we'd been married for two weeks, fighting Rommel for ten. The German troops were notorious in Siwah for desecrating this pool, Cleopatra's bath, by bathing naked in it. The people claimed this contributed to their defeat.'

She touched the photograph, almost a caress. 'He was the love of my life.'

I now realised why, when we'd walked through the streets of the ancient white-clay town with its huts made of palm fronds and its braying donkeys, many of the older tribesmen had greeted Amelia as if she were an honorary male. It was the legacy of her military service in the region during the Second World War.

'He was killed only days after this was taken,' she said, replacing the photograph in the chest.

'I'm sorry.'

'Love while you can. Nothing is certain in life, only this — nothing is certain in life. Old Arabic proverb.'

The sheikh returned carrying a couple of objects wrapped in muslin. He sat on the rug and unwrapped them to reveal two handguns, which he pushed towards Amelia. She picked one up. I went for the other, but she stopped me.

'You can't be armed.'

'But it could get dangerous, right?' I insisted, my hand still on the gun.

'For goodness' sake, stop looking so worried. I'm a crack shot.'

She handed the second gun back to the sheikh before tucking the other into her belt.

The sheikh chuckled and put his hand on my shoulder.

'Believe me, my friend, she is.'

It was the first English he'd uttered since we'd arrived.

\* \* \*

We stood at the base of the bleached ruins of the Temple of the Oracle, staring out over the valley of thick green date palms swaying like seaweed below us. Despite my intense anxiety, it was hard not to find the place beautiful. Siwah or Sekht-am, an oasis of mainly date palms and olives, it looked as if it had remained unchanged since Biblical times.

Now dressed in khaki trousers, shirt and a headscarf, the Egyptologist brushed the flies away and gestured towards the waters of Birket Siwah. 'Behold — the oasis as seen by the gods ...'

The terrain had been spectacular, as we'd flown west from Alexandria. The small plane, flying low, had turned inland heading southwest across the Qattara depression, then over the sudden emerald of the Qara Oasis before flying onto Siwah. Now the huge salt water lake, Birket Siwah, shimmered in the sunlight, broken only by the mountains that loomed up like breasts beyond which stretched the dramatic landscape of the Western Desert — the Great Sand Sea, a swathe of white cut only by the zigzagging trail or Masrabs — as they were known.

'This is where our journey begins,' Amelia said and gestured to the temple. Its plain exterior wall loomed above us, an occasional square window breaking the fortress-like façade. 'In Alexander's time, the oracle of Siwah was one of the six most famous oracles of the ancient world. This was the first place Alexander came upon landing on Egyptian soil, to gain the blessing of the oracle both as Ammon's son and son of Nectanebo II — in other words, the son of God. It was a popular motif amongst ambitious men at that time. This temple is the first clue. According to the astrarium's map, it's where the Pharaoh's journey into the afterworld began.'

She pulled a sheet of paper from her shoulder bag and rolled it flat on a piece of fallen masonry. I recognised the map from the astrarium.

'Here is the ancient town of Aghurmi, and there's Lake Zeitan — a little differently shaped in antiquity. Here, on the opposite side, are the various mountains — Gebel al-Dakrur,

Gebel al-Mawta and the twin mountains of Gebel Hamra and Gebel Baydai. But the one that concerns us is this one ...' She pointed at the hieroglyph of Anubis, the jackal god and protector of the desert necropolis. 'Gebel al-Mawta, the mountain of the dead. But first we need to get to the temple of Amun-Re, built by Nectanebo II himself. Unfortunately there's only one wall left standing, after some Ottoman general blew it up in 1896 to use the stone to build himself a mansion. But the hieroglyphs we need still exist. Is the astrarium secure?'

I nodded, indicating the rucksack strapped tightly over my shoulders. It was difficult to repress the growing knot of anxiety in my gut as dusk approached. Too late to back out now, I reminded myself.

'You mustn't let anyone or anything take this from you, Oliver, do you understand? No matter what you see, or what you think you see.'

I scanned the plateau of waving date palms, then looked further, to the edge of the dunes. The only other individuals I could see were a few Berber boys collecting dates. Beyond, on the great sea of sand itself, a black serpent of Bedouins wound its way towards the mediaeval city of Shali. If Mosry or Hugh Wollington had followed us, they were well hidden.

Amelia checked her watch, then, with her hand shading her eyes, gazed at the sun, a crimson disk starting to dip towards the tops of the palms. 'We have twenty minutes before the journey begins. We should get started.'

I gazed at the horizon; was this to be my last night alive? I had the uneasy and now familiar sensation that we were being watched; not just by unseen enemies, but by the mountains themselves.

I followed Amelia up the mound of earth and rubble towards the base of the temple. Surprisingly small, the temple stood high on a hill, obviously positioned to impress an audience standing below and looking up at the priests conducting their ceremonies at the entrance — a smoke and mirror show designed to inspire and intimidate. I tried to rationalise that what I was about to experience would be similar — phantoms plucked from my subconscious. They can't hurt you, I told myself, but a childhood memory of being terrified by the images of hell in my schoolbook Bible floated into my mind. I looked at Amelia's broad back ahead of me, her grey hair reassuringly real and maternal. She would be my anchor.

She paused to catch her breath. 'You know, most worshippers never actually entered the temple. Can you imagine what it must have been like for visiting military leaders seeking religious legitimacy? Climbing up here alone, dusty, exhausted, sweating into ceremonial armour, already humbled by the climb, to confront a half-demented seer whose blessing could either make or break your strategies? I came up here myself with my husband in April 1943 to pray to the gods for a victory.' She smiled ironically. 'I suppose it worked, but my prayers had a price.'

The temple's classical portico, flanked by columns, had been eroded by wind and sand; only a few alcoves remained, which must once have held icons or statues. Inside, it was a series of small rooms, no doubt designed to maximise an air of mystery through the use of light and shadow. It reminded me of a De Chirico painting, and I half-expected Isabella or some Grecian goddess to step into the dream-like interior.

Amelia crouched in the doorway and pulled a flask from her backpack, followed by a small brown envelope. She unscrewed the top of the flask and filled the cup with what looked like wine, then opened the envelope and crumbled a bluish powder into the cup.

'This is for you, the ceremonial cup that will give you the sight of the gods.' She held it out to me. 'You lucky man.'

I eyed the concoction warily, hesitant after my recent experience in the catacombs.

'Oliver, take it. You've got no choice — you must open yourself to other ways of seeing.'

'I have no intention of making myself that vulnerable again. What if we're attacked?'

'I'll protect you.'

I eyed her. Even armed and with her military training, it was hard to imagine her fighting off seasoned killers.

'Oliver, I have the element of surprise on my side, and besides, I know the terrain a lot better than Mosry or Wollington.'

I shook my head. 'I was lucky to survive the last time. It's too dangerous.'

'Listen, do you think Faakhir's friends would have left us to do this alone if they didn't think I was capable of protecting you? You have to see what the priests saw, you have to recognise the symbols when they appear. Please … it's too late to stop trusting me now.'

She thrust the cup under my nose; the rich, pungent smell of red wine and a finer perfume, like that of a flower, drifted up.

'This is wine mixed with a bouquet garni of mandrake and blue lotus — you've probably seen them painted in reliefs in the tombs. The Egyptian priests would drink the concoction to attain a state of heightened spirituality. You need to drink it too.'

'I've told you, no.'

Suddenly enraged, Amelia rose to her feet. 'Okay then, I'll leave and you can work out what you want to do next! You can risk your life on the gamble that all of this is some elaborate charade put on solely for your entertainment. Or you can decide to actually commit fully to something for the first time in your life!'

She packed the flask away. I glanced up at the sun; my heart really pounding now. I had to drink it, I knew. My fear had pushed me kicking and screaming over to the side of belief; and besides, there was the undeniable fact of Isabella's drowning and its dreadful timing. Amelia was walking away with a determined stride. 'Wait!' I yelled out.

She still had the cup in her hand. She held it out and I drank the bitter contents.

# 45

As we sat there, our backs resting against the stone that was warm from the day's sun, I found my mind clearing. My memory erased itself into a white blankness. It was as if I had been pushed into the present tense in a way that was infinitely more vivid than I'd ever experienced before. The grain of the stone magnified, the pale mauve of the sky intensified, and the heroics of a large ant carrying a grain of sand across the rock wall by my knee became absolutely fascinating — an allegory for my own struggles.

Something moved at the perimeter of my vision. I lifted my head. Through the stone opening I could see the silhouette of a large ram standing proudly on a boulder just beyond the temple. The sunlight painted his fleece gold and the noble length of his curling horns and his beard marked him as the patriarch of his herd.

'Amun-Re the divine is here,' Amelia whispered.

'Can you see the animal? Is it real?'

'I see the animal, but I also see the god behind the creature. I learned from the Berbers how to see without the aid of the drug.'

The animal stepped closer. Now I could see the vertical slant of its pupils, the green-golden irises. It stared directly at us, then cocked its head in the direction of the desert and took a step backwards.

'You must follow.'

The tone of Amelia's voice gave me no choice. The animal turned and began to nimbly leap over the ruins towards the remnants of the Temple of Amun-Re. I followed, abandoning any attempt to make a rational analysis of my actions.

As we climbed, I began to see the temple better: a pile of toppled columns with one standing wall, one side patched up with modern bricks. The ram stopped beneath a mural of hieroglyphs clearly visible on the inside section. Amelia scrambled to join me about a yard away from the ram. I stood transfixed by the animal's stare; it was of a piercing intelligence, neither malevolent nor benign.

'What do we do now?' I found myself whispering as if in church.

'Kneel,' Amelia said, and dropped to the ground.

Rather self-consciously I joined her. The ram disappeared around the wall and down the hill as silently as it had appeared.

Amelia pointed to the characters carved into the reddish sandstone. 'The top row indicates the higher deities.'

I could see the line of gods. In the middle, flanked by the other deities in profile, stood a figure with both hands outstretched, his headdress adorned with the horns of the ram.

'The central figure is that of Amun-Re himself,' Amelia explained, 'with Isis on one side, Nephthys on the other, and on either side of them Horus and Osiris. But concentrate on the figure of Amun-Re — he is the key.'

The sun's rays formed a perfect half-circle above the top of the wall, directly above the figure of the god. The light grew brighter and brighter until the figure was surrounded by a magenta halo. He seemed to become three-dimensional, suspended in the air before me, and I was filled with an intense sense of wellbeing and invincibility.

Then a shadow crossed the crescent of the sun. It was a bird, a falcon. It landed on the wall, arched its neck and let out one piercing cry.

'We are entering the second hour.' Amelia's voice had taken on an echoing, reverberating quality. 'Horus is upon us. He will lead you into the Waters of Osiris.'

This time I didn't doubt her.

She grabbed my arm and together we clambered down the rocky slope on the other side of the temple, following the falcon as it plunged into the tops of the palm trees that bordered a lake. We reached the thicket of palms and stumbled through the undergrowth, over dead palm fronds and desiccated dates. Finally, the skyline cleared again as we reached the edge of the salt-encrusted lake. The falcon, swooping like a black arrow, was still above, guiding us. My boots squelched in the marshy ground and were soon covered with the snakeweed and algae that floated in the shallow waters.

A crash sounded behind us and I swung around. 'Is someone following?' I whispered to Amelia.

We stood still and watched. At a far distance, set against the dusk sky two torch beams swung across the foreshore, their passage broken by the lattice of palm trunks and low bushes. Terror swept over me.

'Let's go, as quickly and silently as you can,' Amelia commanded, gripping my arm again and hurrying me towards a vessel moored to a log. It was a traditional felucca, made of reeds with a primitive sail hanging limp from a single mast and an oil lantern on a pole at its other end. With a flurry, the falcon landed on the side of the boat, its head cocked, waiting.

Night was falling quickly, as it does in the desert. Only the distant glow of the mediaeval town of Shali — a scattered shower of pinpricks glowing from those buildings still occupied — lit the horizon. I clambered into the boat after Amelia. She cast off the rope, then lit the wick inside the lantern. It spluttered into flame and within minutes a dancing cloud of insects had gathered around the shimmering yellow light.

I touched the straps across my shoulders that held the astrarium securely on my back, aware that my senses had become distorted. My imagination elaborated shade and shadow into fantastical creatures; my heightened hearing made it impossible to discern what was close by and what was distant. Above us, the moon, a three-quarter, crater-pocked orb, was now visible. It was as if it was beckoning me — a thousand white arms bending and glowing.

Amelia followed my gaze. 'The Ancient Egyptians believed the moon was the midpoint for ascending souls,' she murmured.

What had I abandoned myself to? I settled lower into the boat, horribly aware that we were clearly visible from the foreshore.

Amelia pushed the boat off, the falcon took wing, and we floated away from the shore and out onto the shimmering water. Apprehensively, I glanced at Amelia. Her figure seemed to have grown in height and authority and I could see a radiance dancing about her features. She hoisted the sail and announced, 'We are now entering the Waters of Osiris.'

The limp sail swelled and filled like the white wing of an ibis. With a creak, the boat gathered speed, the insects trailing behind the lantern as the prow cut a ripple into the huge white spectre of the moon that undulated across the water's surface.

I looked into the pool of light, thrown by the lantern, that travelled across the lake with us. The sound of water lapping against the sides of the boat grew louder until it built into the crashing sound of huge waves against rocks. Despite the noise, I couldn't see anything except gentle ripples on the lake's surface. Fear began to churn my guts again. Irrationally I kept expecting a tidal wave to appear on the horizon, a massive wall of water. My perception of the boundaries of matter had begun to blur, as if the very laws of physics had altered and the molecular structure of all that I knew had been transformed. I huddled lower in the boat and forced myself to match sound with vision; gradually the roar of the crashing waves subsided. You can control this, I told myself, you can control the demons. I reminded myself I was doing this for Isabella. I would finish her journey, even if it killed me. The reality of that thought shot through my mind and dissolved into the core of my being.

Then, just as I was congratulating myself at having regained control of my senses, a pale flash of bluish-white broke the surface of the water then submerged again. I heard the distinctive thud of something bumping against the wooden hull of the felucca. As I forced myself to look over the edge, a body floated into view: white legs, the split peach of a naked vulva at their apex, small breasts barely breaking the surface, long hair streaming over the face. I recognised her immediately — Isabella. The current dragged the hair away from her face and her eyes opened and stared at me.

I shouted her name and leaped to my feet, determined this time to rescue her, to put right the tragedy of her death. This time our lives would play out in the way they had been meant to — our long future together, children, old age. This time she would not have to die. The boat rocked dangerously as I reached out towards those white drifting legs.

'Isabella, here!' I shouted.

Amelia wrestled me back down. 'She isn't real! Oliver!'

I fought her, openly weeping now, wanting to pull my wife's body to mine, wanting to stop her growing cold. I leaned back over the side; she was still there, white skin flashing like the underbelly of a dead fish. Her lips opened and she mouthed, 'Help me.'

I struggled to suppress every instinct that told me to dive in. I shut my eyes. When I opened them again, her white thighs were caught in a spiral of churning water, the ripple of a crocodile's tail cutting the surface in a ridge of jagged scales.

'This isn't happening, this isn't real,' I repeated as the wind pushed the felucca across the water to the distant shore.

We were now almost at the centre of the huge pale reflection of the moon. To me, it seemed the planet had reached its loudest vibration, buzzing like a thousand cicadas. It was then I noticed a mist rising off the water at the middle of the glinting mirage. It began to twist like a miniature tornado, gathering shape above the lake as if the moon's reflection itself was gaining form. The wind blew us straight into the thickening fog and suddenly there was the beating of a million wings all around me, tiny insects that smashed blindly against my face, in my hair, up my nostrils, suffocating me. They were moths, large white creatures that twisted and swirled into a single massive cloud. The very air seemed to be raining a soft smothering powder as my hands bashed frantically against the velvety bodies, trying to make space in the cloud to breathe. I felt my lungs squeezing against my ribcage, then Amelia's arms were around my own, pinning them to my sides.

'Surrender,' she said, and the shape of the word descended on me like the moth powder coating my tongue, the inside of my nostrils, my burning eyelids.

We sat there in the strangest of embraces, Amelia behind me, her legs wrapped around my hips, her arms holding my arms, the astrarium between us, while the felucca moved through the frenetic mass of dazed insects flying in chaotic circles as if they, themselves, were bewildered by their own predicament.

As I made out the shape of the approaching shore, the wings of the insects surrounding us transformed into a harder, brilliant cascade of hues that glittered in the lantern light. I focused my gaze on the creatures hovering just before my nose, their heavy bodies clumsily defying gravity like bumblebees, their translucent wings a whirl of air, and, with a shock, recognised them — scarab beetles, the sacred manifestation of Ra, signifying rebirth.

The cloud thinned into a column that spiralled and curved in a path to the shoreline. The boat followed and soon its wooden bottom was scraping along the shallow bank of salt crystal.

At that moment the lantern blew out, plunging us into a lunarscape of sand, dunes and the distant outline of a mountain squatting on the horizon like a giant in repose. Time stretched like taut wire in the darkness until Amelia's voice cut the silence like a bell.

'We are now entering the sandy world of Sokar.'

I couldn't believe that time had passed so quickly — the distortion of the drugs, I guessed. Just then the sound of an approaching speedboat echoed across the water

'Quick!' Amelia said, and she grabbed the extinguished lantern and stepped out of the boat.

I followed, my feet hitting a beach made uneven by the drying rock salt and tangled vegetation. The only illumination came from the moonlight and the glistening wings of the scarab beetles as they flew in a zigzagging black-purple snake into the hushed, expectant desert.

Amelia pulled me down behind the cover of some bushes and we watched the dark outline of the approaching boat cut across the lake. As we crouched there it was as if the sound of that boat engine was my fear curdling at the base of my spine, threatening to burst any minute, into sheer blank terror.

The boat drew up to the bank and I could just make out the faces of the two men sitting by the motor. One looked Arabic, the other European. Turning they sighted our felucca on the beach.

'Wait here!' Amelia whispered.

Keeping low, still holding the lantern, she ran from bush to bush towards the boat. The sound of a twig breaking made one of the men look over. My stomach tightened in fear. Amelia cupped her hands to her mouth and made the call of a marsh bird — a perfect imitation. Now I could see the guerrilla fighter emerging from this middle-aged woman and realised the years of experience she'd had fighting in this terrain. The man dropped his gaze and got out of the boat to pull it up onto the crusty salt bank.

I turned back to Amelia; she was holding a lighter to the wick of the lantern. In a second it was alight. Silently but accurately, she hurled it into the speedboat. It smashed against the wood and the spilled oil burst into flames, which spread quickly across the boat. In that flash of light I recognised Hugh Wollington.

Shouting, both men leaped into the lake. Amelia bolted back to me. The boat's diesel tank exploded and shattered wood rained down around us.

'Run!' she ordered.

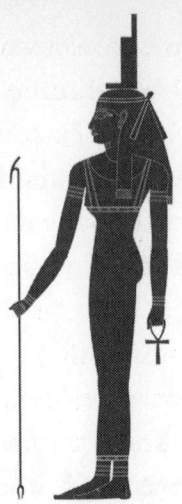

# 46

We sprinted up the beach and into a thicket of thorny shrubs that tore at our skin, Amelia propelling me forward while bullets flew blindly over our heads. It felt like several minutes of battling the dense foliage before a path opened before us. Amelia pointed upwards: etched against the night sky was the column of glistening scarabs. Following them, we climbed higher and higher until finally we reached a moon-drenched plateau surrounded by majestic rocks that looked like chess pieces abandoned by a reckless colossus. Above us, the scarab beetles hovered a moment, then disappeared into the night sky.

In the centre of this clearing stood a huge antelope, its twisting horns piercing the low moon. A falcon perched on its back.

'Seth in his antelope form and Horus,' Amelia whispered reverently.

Her voice seemed distorted and when I turned towards her she was unrecognisable. She had grown to over six feet in height, her skin had turned to copper, and her grey hair was now thick, black and reached beyond her shoulders. She wore a headdress of cow horns between which hung a golden disk. I stumbled back, terrified. She had become the goddess Isis. A moment later she switched back to the form I was familiar with, then she was the goddess again. My hallucinatory state kept her flickering between the two. She caught my arm just before I fell from dizziness.

'Oliver, stay with me. Stay in the moment.'

We heard our pursuers crashing through the shrubs behind us. Bending its head, the antelope pawed the ground, then turned and cantered up the mountain slope in front of us. The falcon flew ahead.

'Come on!' Amelia was instantly after the antelope, clambering up the rocky incline.

I climbed blindly after her, hauling myself higher and higher, tearing the palms of my hands on the jagged stone. Each new plateau accelerated the sense of infinity stretching above and behind me — the huge, open cosmos — and I got closer and closer to the ground as I climbed, terrified of falling into that void.

As I pulled myself up onto yet another ledge, my foot slipped, dislodging an avalanche of sand. I froze, both hands gripping the rock above me, my right foot on solid rock but my left hanging in midair.

'Haul yourself up — you have to!' Amelia peered over the ledge, one arm extended, ready to help.

I made the mistake of looking over my shoulder. Far below, at the foot of the mountain, the moonlight reflected off the tiled roofs and mud-brick walls of Shali Ghali and I realised we'd climbed far higher than I had imagined. The rush of vertigo almost made me let go. I shut my eyes and prayed, still frozen in the same precarious position.

'There is no reversal of fortune. You have to get yourself up here!' Amelia insisted.

With a supreme effort, I pushed down on my right foot and hauled myself up, scrambling and clawing to pull all of my body onto the ledge. I lay there panting in the darkness, my heart banging wildly against my chest. I could just make out openings cut into the mountain — burial tunnels. We were climbing Gebel al-Mawta — the mountain of the dead — and we were near the top.

Below us, I could hear the two men scrambling up the rock face. My limbs felt as if they were moving through treacle, a thousand repetitions of a thousand muscles exploding in effort. My fear had almost transmuted into something else — an ecstasy? Yet part of me was still aware that I was in great danger. I gazed transfixed into the vast cosmos. Could I die now? In some ways it felt as if I had already.

In that second, a bullet whistled past my ear. Amelia pulled me violently behind a boulder. Lying on her stomach, she exchanged fire; bullets ricocheted against the rock like flint, thudding down into the sand. There was a scream as one of the men was hit.

'Move!' Amelia grabbed my arm and pushed me towards one of the burial tunnels. I crouched against the stone as two more bullets struck near the entrance.

'Help me!' Amelia called. 'We haven't got long — they'll be here in seconds!'

She indicated a pile of rocks that looked as if they'd been deliberately stacked on a length of wood beneath. Together we levered the wood until the rocks fell across the entrance, completely blocking access. Exhausted, I leaned against the cool rock; it smelled faintly of lime. The astrarium was a lead weight across my shoulders.

'How do we get out?' I asked.

'We don't need to.'

'But we'll die in here!'

'Trust me.' Amelia dusted off her hands, 'Come on, we have to keep moving. It's now hour five — the timing is precise.'

She pulled out a torch and switched it on. The walls and ceilings of the tunnel were covered in brightly coloured murals that, in my drugged state, appeared to be moving. Hieroglyphs and drawings telling of the life of Osiris: here, his marriage to Isis; there, Seth murdering him. On the opposite wall was the story of Isis magically piecing together the fourteen parts of her husband's dismembered body.

Amelia walked before me, shining the torch ahead. As I followed her, I could feel the blue lotus pounding through my veins, rippling through my perception. Light glinted off the burnished disk of her headdress and blossoms — poppies, lotuses, lilies — sprang from her feet as she led me deeper into the mountain. Fascinated, I glanced down at my own arms and wondered if I too had metamorphosed. I held my hand up and my fingers danced before me, five, ten, a hundred of them, all moving slowly, as if the air itself had become gelatinous.

We arrived at a thick wooden door carved with a relief of monstrous animals. In front of it sat an old man, his back to us, huddled over.

'The gatekeeper,' Amelia murmured, unable to keep the fascination out of her voice.

The old man turned around. To my horror, it was my father, naked, his thin, aged body bent, the wrinkled pouch of his sex hanging from his sagging flesh.

Amelia pressed her gun into my hand. 'You must kill him.'

'I can't,' I said, terrified.

'He is not what he appears to be.'

My father whimpered when he saw the gun in my hand. I couldn't drag my eyes away from him. Memories ran through me: the first time we flew a kite together on the Fens, my father showing me how to unreel the string and let the kite catch the wind, his pride as I managed to haul it up high into the air; my astonishment and joy at my graduation when I caught sight of my father's figure from the podium after he'd sworn he'd sooner see Carlisle United lose than walk into any university; the last time I'd seen him, only weeks ago, standing at his front door, shrunken and vulnerable, wearing my mother's pink cardigan over his undershirt. I knew the image before me now was an illusion, but it felt utterly real as I lifted the gun.

He cowered, petrified, the whites of his eyes peering out of his dust-covered face. Pleading, he began to claw at my legs, but the sounds that came from his mouth were not human, rather the grunts of an animal.

Still I couldn't bring myself to squeeze the trigger.

'Shoot!' Amelia ordered me.

Instead, arm shaking, I lowered the gun. The creature lunged at me, his hands now reptilian claws, the skin on his wrists darkening and congealing into scales. I smashed the gun against his head, knocking him to the ground, then reeled around, expecting another attack from behind.

Nothing came; just the sound of Amelia chanting what I assumed was a spell from the Book of the Dead. The creature's legs began to shrivel and his distorted face flattened into the snout of a hippopotamus as he convulsed and writhed on the ground. Then his jaw stretched wide, cavernous and red, and a sparrowhawk burst out of his mouth and began to fly wildly around my head.

'It's Isabella's Ba,' Amelia whispered. 'You will carry her to the end — you must help her spirit reach the afterlife.'

Awed, I reached out to the bird. The fluttering of its wings formed a thousand after-images that enveloped me in Isabella's scent, in the soft whispering of her voice. Finally it landed on my shoulder.

Amelia took the gun from me and tucked it back into her belt. As she did, we heard an explosion in the distance — the tunnel's entrance being unblocked.

\* \* \*

We ran along the narrow passage for what, to my tired limbs, seemed like hours. When I was sure I could go no further, we emerged into a massive underground limestone cavern deep within the mountain — a vast temple with multi-faceted crystal stalactites glistening like hundreds of diamonds.

'This is where you will meet your Ka, your spiritual twin,' Amelia said.

In the middle of the huge stone floor flickered a large lake of flames that illuminated the ceiling that arched over us like the sweep of a cathedral roof.

'Walk towards the fire,' Amelia told me, and pushed me forward.

Tentatively I moved towards the blazing lake. Curiously, the nearer I got, the less heat I felt on my skin. Encouraged that the flames too were an illusion, I moved quickly closer and stopped about a foot from the edge.

The flames became iridescent and reflective at the same time, winding around themselves to fuse into the smooth surface of a mirror. Reflected in it was an image of myself. I stared at the tousled, bearded man with scratches covering his forehead and cheeks, barely recognising the dirt-stained face, the bewildered blue eyes staring through the red dust. I lifted my hand and he lifted his too. Then, to my amazement, he extended his hand towards me, the flesh becoming real as it extended out of the swirling reflective surface.

I stumbled back and my double stepped out and steadied me. His touch burned, and as his fingers closed around my arm he began to merge into my body. I blacked out.

When I regained consciousness, I seemed to be hovering high above the ground, next to the glistening limestone ceiling. I looked down. Amelia stood below me — an aerial perspective, her figure foreshortened against the stone floor. Shocked, I plummeted downward for a second then regained my balance. As I did, feathered tips came into my peripheral vision. I had wings! I had transformed into my own Ba! Sensing a presence behind me, I turned my head and saw a sparrowhawk swooping towards me. Isabella.

We flew together, twisting around each other like acrobats, swerving and swooping and narrowly missing the rock walls of the cave. I chased her, revelling in the power of flight, wanting to catch up with her, wanting to feel her spirit engulf me as if we were one being. Memories of our marriage streamed through me: our first night together; her first visit to an oilfield and her amazed expression as she watched me reading the ground, the way we laughed together at an unspoken joke; how we fell asleep in each other's arms. And I knew then that despite all I'd learned since her death, all that Hermes had told me about our marriage being arranged by others, our union had been true, her love for me was genuine. Isabella might have married me to fulfil the prophecy, but she had loved me above and beyond that — I was certain of it now. All of these certainties seemed to tumble with us as we plummeted down to climb again in blind joy. Then, in the grip of my epiphany, I crashed into the cave wall.

I opened my eyes to find myself lying on the sandy ground. The sparrowhawk, perched on my outstretched arm, cocked its head quizzically at me. I tried to sit up. My whole body ached. It felt as if the hallucinogen pumping through my blood was receding.

The sparrowhawk hopped down onto the sand and pushed against my leg with its beak, as if to make me stand. All around me the sand started to undulate.

'Oliver!' Amelia shouted. 'The mehen serpent!'

Two glistening eyes emerged, then a reptilian snout blowing grains of sand. The mottled head of a huge rock python followed, its smooth, scaly body now stretched in a huge circle around me. The sparrowhawk dived at the snake with claws outstretched and the snake hissed and lunged back.

I struggled to my feet. The serpent reared up, sand cascading either side of its patterned skin. It stared at me with indifference, as if I were little more than a fly. I held my ground, determined not to show fear. Then, almost as suddenly as it had appeared, the serpent collapsed into dust and I realised I was standing on a vast mosaic, its design a serpent holding its tail in its mouth.

The last of the blue lotus left my body and I became aware of the cold dampness of the stone tiles, the straps of the rucksack cutting into my shoulders, the sharp throbbing of the scratches on my arms and legs. Uncontrollable shivering gripped my limbs. I looked at Amelia. Her solid figure was also dusty and scratched and very definitely human.

Above us, the sparrowhawk screeched.

There was a whoosh of air as a bullet flew past me, narrowly missing my left shoulder. I ducked, the crack of gunfire horribly real. We bolted to the far side of the cavern as Hugh Wollington, dressed in army fatigues, ran into the huge space, gun raised.

Amelia had her pistol in her hand and squeezed off two quick shots, forcing Wollington to take cover.

'Over there, Oliver, behind that stalactite lies the entrance to the final chamber of the tomb. The doors will open as you reach them.'

'What about you?'

'This is my fate. Who am I to question it?' she answered, smiling.

Wollington fired again and the bullet caught her in the left shoulder, flinging her body back with the impact.

'Go! Go now!' she told me. 'I'll cover you!'

Blood was seeping through her jacket. I reached out to help her, but she urged me on. Lying on her side, she kept firing as I darted from one rock to another. As I reached the low archway, barely visible in the shadows, a bullet caught me in the foot. Falling to the ground I cried out in shock and pain.

I rolled over and looked behind me. Wollington was running towards me across the cavern as Amelia worked furiously to snap a new clip of ammunition into her pistol. I watched in horror as he stopped and raised his pistol directly at me, taking careful aim. His eyes locked onto mine — just a dozen paces and the gun barrel between us.

At the edge of my vision, I saw Amelia pull back the slide of her pistol, heard the click of the breach.

A gunshot rang out. My heart jolted. I stared at Wollington, astonished I was still seeing anything at all, and as I watched, Amelia's bullet took him squarely in the stomach. Her second hit his temple — spinning him around and dropping him to the floor in a spray of blood.

A scream welled up inside me but I felt and heard it as if I were outside of myself. I gasped for breath, hyperventilating with shock, but as Amelia turned towards me, concerned but calm, I felt the hysteria recede.

I raised my hand and called, 'I'm okay,' though I could feel my boot filling with blood.

'Can you move?' she called back.

I levered myself up onto my good foot. Pain shot up my leg. Just then, another shot rang out, the sharp, loud crack of a pistol from the very back of the cavern. Amelia's face had just begun to open into a smile, but it had suddenly frozen. I expected her to turn and fire back, but instead she pitched backwards, her arms akimbo, her pistol clattering on the stone floor.

In the silence that followed, I heard a pair of heavy boots running across the cavern towards me. I was horrified at the loss of Amelia, but there was no time to grieve. Dragging myself through the lichen-covered archway, I prayed my pursuer wouldn't find the trail of blood I was leaving behind. I looked around for a ready weapon. Reaching for a heavy rock, I lifted it and waited, desperately trying to control my breathing. His footsteps seemed to be coming nearer, but before they reached me a space opened up in the cave wall behind me and I was pulled backwards into it.

# 47

An old man helped me to my feet and supported me as we made our way to a small rowing boat that appeared to be floating on an underground river. He lowered me into it and I collapsed onto the bottom. Murmuring in a dialect I didn't understand, he drew a rug over me. As he bent down I noticed that his eyes were white with cataracts.

He cast off and the boat, lit only by a single lantern, began its journey along the dark water, to where I didn't know. The stalactites passing above us dazzling as the crystals reflected back thousands of shards of light. I felt the blood draining away from my body.

\* \* \*

A luminous orange shape pressed against the darker red of my eyelids as external sound and light sucked me back into consciousness. I heard the sound of dripping water, and smelled the acrid odour of manure and damp straw and the distinctive apple-scented tobacco of the hookah. I opened my eyes and realised I was grasping something in my hand. I looked down. I was holding a feather — a brown sparrowhawk's feather.

I was on a low divan covered in goatskins. The old man was sitting beside me with a bowl of water on his lap, smiling, his toothless mouth sunk into his wrinkled face. Chanting what sounded like a prayer, he lifted a cup and poured the cold water over my head. Shocked, I spluttered and gasped.

My head ached, but I was aware that, despite a strange feeling of dislocation and a heightened sense of colour, I was now entirely lucid. 'I don't understand you,' I said in Arabic.

'That is because I was using an ancient language,' he replied, also in Arabic. 'Aramaic, the old tongue. Forgive me, the immersion had to be done. It is the tenth hour.'

I sunk back against the cushions as he bent down to examine the wound to my foot, now covered with a brown-green poultice of moss. Shocked, I pulled back my foot. The poultice went flying. He scolded me and replaced the moss.

At that moment I remembered the astrarium. My hands flew up to my shoulders; my rucksack was gone. I looked around wildly. Reading my expression, the old man reached for a small woven basket at his feet and pulled out the astrarium, now wrapped in an oiled goatskin.

'Fear not, my friend, the treasure is safe. This is the last hour of your journey and I have restored your health and your sight.' He touched my eyelids in turn, his fingertips pungent with the musk of the poultice. 'I am Yedaniah bar-Ishmael. For centuries my family have protected the secret tomb of Nectanebo II, since the time my ancestor was hired as a personal bodyguard by the Pharaoh at Elephantine, long before the living memory of this epoch.'

'You are a Jew?'

'My family chose not to leave with Moshe ben Amram ha-Levi across the divided sea; our hearts were wedded to this land. I was born here and I will die here.' His fingers scraped at the earth floor of the cave, crumbling the soil. 'I am sorry for the death of your companion. The Berbers will collect the shell of her body and they will bury her next to her husband.'

The vision of Amelia's crumpled form swept bleakly through me. Battling sudden panic, I tried to calculate how many minutes I had left of my own life — not many.

I looked around. The room appeared to open onto a courtyard, a mat of woven rushes covering the entrance. The bluish dawn light filtered through the gaps between the rushes and I could just make out a couple of goats tethered to a post outside and the outline of a metal water pump.

The cave itself had obviously once been a tomb: murals of the gods hunting and feasting covered the walls. There was a huge stone oven carved into the back of the cave, large enough for a man to crouch in; a blackened copper pot sat atop it. Against the wall was a set of shelves made of wood from a shipping carton — the stickers advertising Siwah Dates were still visible — filled with tinned food, condensed milk and one lonely jar of Nescafé instant coffee. I noticed a radio propped up against a low table that held a backgammon board, the pieces poised mid-game. The prosaic nature of the setting was reassuring.

I looked back at the old man. His skin hung in folds below his chin and his face was a map of moles and uneven pigment. Again, I saw the clouds of cataracts in his eyes. It was impossible to say how old he was — over ninety, I imagined.

'Where am I?' I asked.

'On the island of Arachie, in the cave of Horus. But we must hurry. Ra has almost risen and you must place the skybox into the Pharaoh's arms before then. You know the parable: a king is sacrificed for the greater good of his people, entombed for a time, then rises again to join his father in the sky. This is the universal story, one that is told again and again.'

He reached up to his neck and, with a jerk, broke the leather thong of the pendant hanging there. He pressed it into my hand. It was a large gold coin embossed with a rearing horse.

'The coin of Nectanebo,' he said. 'This was the first payment made to my ancestor. It will protect you.'

From outside, at some distance, came the sound of running feet. My fear, which had ebbed in this man's care, returned instantly.

'They'll kill us,' I said. 'They'll kill us both.'

Yedaniah put his hand on my arm to reassure me. 'Have faith. Come now, it is time you faced your own death.'

I swung my legs around to the mud floor and he helped me stand. Gingerly, I placed my weight on my injured foot, then slipped the coin into my pocket. Outside, a cockerel crowed, followed by shouting.

'We must hurry,' Yedaniah said. He picked up the astrarium and bowed his head ceremoniously as he placed it into my arms. 'For you and Nectanebo, my king. May the gods bless you both.'

He led me to the oven at the back of the cave, guided me over the cooling coals and pushed against the soot-covered back wall. To my amazement, it opened, revealing a large cavern beyond.

'Quickly.' He bundled me through.

Feeling panicked, I looked around the chamber; there was nothing but the stone walls, dirt floor and an ancient mural illuminated by two lanterns hanging from the ceiling.

'But where's the coffin?' I asked.

'You were chosen. The gift of Osiris will guide you,' Yedaniah told me, and stepped back into the outer cave. 'May Amun-Re and my God protect you.'

His voice echoed against the walls as he pulled closed the hidden door, leaving me alone in the tomb.

* * *

The air was dry and smelled faintly of paraffin. The mural painting showed Seth spearing Osiris; an allegorical declaration of victory by Nectanebo's assassins, I assumed. I put down the astrarium and limped slowly across the dirt floor, my left foot trailing blood. Closing my eyes, I concentrated on the ground beneath my naked feet and, for the first time in my life completely unassisted by science and technology, attempted to read the subterranean geology.

I thought I could hear the distant rattle of gunfire, but I pushed it and my fear to the back of my mind as I concentrated on the earth, sensing its very resonance as it spoke to me. It was as if any distrust of my gift that had impeded me in the past had finally evaporated and I could see the strata in the rock around me as clear as day.

I walked into the centre of the chamber. My eyes closed, I pushed my naked right sole back and forth across the dirt. I could feel a ridge in the surface.

I kneeled down and with my fingernails dug wildly at the layers of impacted sand and earth. There was a marked line underneath — it looked like a rectangular corner. I cleared more dirt away and soon I had revealed the full outline: about seven feet by four — the size of a coffin. I brushed away a section in the middle and found a cartouche, one I'd now seen several times: the ostrich feather — Nectanebo II's insignia. But as I kneeled there, my hands flat on the ground, I sensed nothing; the area felt as dense as the rest of the floor.

I stood up and stepped out of the rectangle, moving several feet to the left, closer to the wall. I felt a tingling under my soles.

Here the structure changed radically — I could sense it as clearly as I could see the lights above me. The cartouche was a false lead — a trap to entice tomb raiders to dig in the wrong place.

I kneeled again, running my hands over the floor. Beneath the layers of dried mud and compacted stone dust I could feel a slight bump — the raised indentation of a circle. Scraping with my nails, I unearthed a metal ring and, with all my strength, hauled on it. With a great grinding of stone and metal, a door opened in the floor, revealing a wide, deep grave with a single wooden coffin laid in it.

I jumped in and walked around the simple coffin: its wood was decaying at the corners, the grain eaten by time. The only ornamentation was the painted door for the occupant's Ba to escape. The rest of the coffin was starkly bare, as if Nectanebo's buriers had given him the minimum possible for his journey into the afterlife. I stood over the wooden lid, my legs shaking in nervous anticipation, my body racked with a terrible fear and tremendous excitement. What was I afraid of? Dying? Or seeing the great Nectanebo himself?

I climbed out of the grave and fetched the astrarium. The date of my death was unchanged. The two pointers had almost fused into one, announcing that my final moments were imminent. I had no time to waste — even if the astrarium's power proved fictitious, Mosry would probably kill me anyway. My only hope was to complete the task and then hide or try to run.

I stepped back into the grave and used a rock to break the lid of the coffin; the ancient wood splintered dramatically. Reaching into my pocket, I pulled out the feather from Isabella's Ba and placed it into the coffin. If I was to die I could at least try to ensure that she found peace.

I could hear shouting coming from Yedaniah's cave, then gunfire and the sound of furniture being broken. Frantically, I tore off the rest of the lid. There was a mummy inside, a gold mask over the face. To my amazement I recognised the features despite the curl of the royal beard. It was the moulded face of a beautiful woman — I'd seen it on the sphinx that had toppled down onto Isabella, causing her to drown, in the shadow cast by the astrarium, and again in Amelia's thesis, and once more in Gareth's drawing: Banafrit, Nectanebo's high priestess and lover. I lifted the mask off and underneath — desiccated, skin blacked like leather but still beautiful — was the face of the woman herself. Now I noticed the outline of breasts under the brownish linen bandages that ran in long lines down the body, a filigree of beaded string stretched over the torso.

Despair washed over me, and I leaned against the side of the grave for support. Had this whole journey been in vain? I'd failed to unite the astrarium with its rightful owner, Nectanebo — did that mean I was about to die?

Suddenly there was banging from the direction of the secret door to the chamber. I had no time left. I stared at the dial of the astrarium, waiting for the setting to change. To my horror, the black pointer continued ticking towards the moment of my death. I had no choice. I had to take the gamble.

I lifted the astrarium, ready to place it on Banafrit's torso.

Just then the door of the cavern was kicked open. 'Don't move!' a man shouted in heavily accented English.

I froze.

Mosry stood above the grave, his gun pointed directly at me. I looked at the astrarium and the death hand — and in that moment I surrendered completely to belief in the device. Expecting to feel a bullet pass through my body, expecting to die, I placed the astrarium onto the mummy. In the same instant a shot was fired.

I shut my eyes, waiting for pain to shoot through me. Nothing happened.

Incredulous, I turned to see Mosry sprawled on the chamber floor, blood seeping from a fatal head wound. Behind him in the doorway was Yedaniah, injured on his hands and knees, cradling an ancient Uzi.

There was a click from the astrarium and I looked down at it. The small black hand with its Seth figurehead disappeared from view. My death date no longer existed. As I watched, both the astrarium and Banafrit's youthful face began to oxygenise and crumble until there was nothing of the mechanism or the mummy but a fine reddish dust.

I ran back and crouched by Yedaniah's side. Blood was now pooling beneath him.

'Such is God's will.' He groaned in pain. 'You must go, you have succeeded in your task.'

I hesitated, staring back into the cavern, at the plain wooden casket, Mosry's broken body, and the allegory of Seth spearing Osiris.

'Go …' Yedaniah fell back as his spirit finally left him.

\* \* \*

Outside, the new day was breaking. I collapsed against a rock and stared out over the valley.

Despite the two dead men in the cave behind me and the deaths of both Hugh Wollington and Amelia, I felt a great sense of completion. I had succeeded; I had returned the astrarium to its proper place and fulfilled my promise to Isabella.

A sparrowhawk flew out of the cave behind me. She circled above me, then sailed out over the shimmering lake below, its salt-encrusted surface a mass of sparkling diamonds.

I watched the bird for as long as I could, until I lost her in the sunlight.

* * *

I sat on the veranda of a café looking out over the tiny runway at Siwah Oasis. The exhilaration had faded and I was exhausted; physically, emotionally, existentially drained. Now the real grieving had begun.

Sipping my mint tea, I stared past a plane to the sea of desert that yawned beyond, the horizon with its wavering bands of heat, and reflected on what my future held. I'd emerged from an odyssey that was already beginning to feel like an extended dream.

Inside the café, someone turned up the sound of the television. I thought I heard the word 'Knesset', the Israeli parliament, and then shouts of disbelief from my fellow diners made me swing around. To my surprise, the screen was showing live footage of Sadat in the Knesset, one Arab within a mass of Israeli politicians. He glanced almost shyly from under his thick black-rimmed glasses then began to read in a clear and confident voice.

'In the name of God, Mr Speaker of the Knesset, ladies and gentlemen, allow me first to thank deeply the Speaker of the Knesset for affording me this opportunity to address you … I come to you today on solid ground to shape a new life and to establish peace. We all love this land, the land of God, we all, Moslems, Christians and Jews, worship God. I do not blame all those who received my decision when I announced it to the entire world before the Egyptian People's Assembly. I do not blame all those who received my decision with surprise even with amazement, some gripped even by violent surprise …'

So the convoy and Rachel had arrived safely in Jerusalem and the peace initiative continued, I thought, as my fellow diners fell into a stunned silence.

I leaned back in my chair and felt something in my pocket — the gold coin Yedaniah had given me. I pulled it out and examined the noble profile of Nectanebo II. I tossed the coin into the air then caught it face up.

# Epilogue

**21 December 1978**

An illuminous blue broke into foaming waves as the water rushed under the bow of the speedboat; I watched hypnotised. It was over a year since I left Egypt and even now that time felt as if it happened to another man — as if my memory and the need to make things logical had started to mythologise those extraordinary events.

In the near distance the outline of Dokos, the Greek island home of Mr Imenand loomed up; following instructions from his assistant I caught a plane to Athens, then a boat out to the home of the entrepreneur. Although he had shaped my life and career over the past twelve months I hadn't seen Mr Imenand since Alexandria and I now wondered why suddenly the recluse had demanded to see me.

A dolphin appeared by the boat, its distinctive fin rising and falling in joyful abandon as it raced alongside. The water was a brilliant turquoise — a marine cosmos that seemed to promise both mystery and release.

As the speedboat cut through the Agean Sea I couldn't help remembering that last day I spent with Isabella, before her death; her face when she emerged from the water wildly excited about discovering the astrarium, her frantic panic the night before, her nightmares.

I hadn't dreamt of her for months, I knew I would always hold her within me but a sense of her had finally left me; if there was a soul, hers was at rest.

After returning to London, I moved to New York and into Rachel's loft in Chelsea. It was a tumultuous relationship; neither of us was good at compromise and both of us were away working most of the time. But somehow that suited us. The separations gave us the intellectual and emotional space we both needed. I didn't know whether I was going to marry her but nowadays I tended to live for the moment and that was something Rachel and I both excelled at.

I'd moved Gareth into my flat in London, and he was busy recording his first album with Stiff records; more importantly, he seemed healthy. Back in Egypt, Moustafa was happily managing the new oilfield full time. Faakhir had disappeared, but I received the occasional postcard from him from politically interesting places, such as Algiers, Guatemala, Sri Lanka; I never did find out whom he was actually working for. Francesca had retired to the Casa di Reposa — the retirement home for all the European diaspora — having now completely retreated into senility. The Brambilla villa was now leased, although I had given Aadeel ownership of the flat within the complex; it was the least I could do for his services to the family. President Sadat and Prime Minister Begin shared the Nobel Prize for peace the end of that year, and finally it felt as if there might be a whole new climate of optimism. Life had moved on and I should have been happier.

But my drive to find oil had changed irreversibly. When the second well on the new lease tested at eighteen thousand barrels per day, I was pleased, of course, but not excited in the way I once would have been. I'd discovered in myself a need to use my divining ability for more egalitarian purposes. Perhaps Mr Imenand, who had made a commitment to back any ventures my newly formed company may be interested in, had intuited my change of heart. After all, it was he who had arranged this meeting, not I.

When I was shown into the room where he was waiting for me, it took my eyes awhile to adapt to the dimness after the dazzling light outside. I was shocked to realise that despite the size of the space — almost like an art gallery, with its white walls — and the magnificent Persian rug that covered the marble floor, this was a sick room. The figure propped up against the pillows was bent and old, his face hollowed by illness, dark shadows under his eyes.

'Oliver, welcome.' His voice was impossibly frail.

'Mr Imenand, you are unwell.'

I faltered. Words seemed superfluous to one obviously so close to death. In the silence that followed, his laboured breathing seemed to grow in volume, scratching at the walls like a caged bird.

'Unwell?' he said drily and laughed. 'I am dying, finally, thank the gods.'

He beckoned me forward. A lamp clicked on, as if my movement had triggered the switch. I could see the room more clearly now. Apart from the bed with its surrounding medical apparatus, the only other object was a large stone sculpture of a sphinx. A third presence in the room, it sat against the wall, its face still in shadow.

There was a leather seat at the foot of the bed, angled I noticed, in a way that meant Mr Imenand did not need to turn any part of his body to see me. A tube ran from under one pyjama sleeve up into a clear glass container hanging off a steel frame. A single pomegranate, half-peeled, sat on a white plate on a side table, the red seeds spilling onto the china.

'I chose you, you know, because you were like me, another Orpheus ...' he whispered, his voice as pale as parchment.

'Chose me for what?'

'You will be my heir. And my legacy is far greater than just material possessions.'

I tried to contain the wild uncomfortable excitement that rattled through me and concentrated on the long veined hands lying like old leather gloves against the sheets. They looked abandoned, as if he had already started to vacate his body.

Mr Imenand spoke again, his voice growing in confidence and volume. 'I never thanked you for returning the astrarium.'

Startled, I glanced at his face. For a minute I thought I had misheard.

'What are you talking about?' Shock made me discourteous. I had the disorientating sensation of all the strands of my life converging at this one juncture — this moment right now. The old man pulled himself up with great effort.

'Oliver, we have no time for games,' he croaked, his fingers twitching. 'Whether you believe me or not is irrelevant but I owe you an explanation of at least the last few pieces of a jigsaw puzzle that stretches far beyond our limited human comprehension. You see there is another truth hidden behind the astrarium. Please, for now, Oliver, put aside your scepticism. Indulge a dying man.'

Spent, he sank back against the pillows. Anxious I might possibly hasten his death by further questioning I took his hand into mine.

'I'm listening.'

He sighed with profound weariness then began his story.

'Nectanebo had many women, many wives, but there was one he loved beyond all the others, his sister and Queen —

Banafrit. She was not only his high priestess but also a skilled astronomer and astrologer who consulted with the greatest engineers of her day — from Greece to Babylon. Over there is a statue made in her honour — a sphinx that has survived to this day. I believe you have seen the companion piece, at the bottom of Alexandria's harbour, among the ruins of what was once a magnificent city.'

I swung back to the statue of the sphinx. Now I recognised the patrician arch of the nose, the high-heekbones, the distinctive shape of the face — Banafrit. It was the mirror image of the stone features of the sphinx that had loomed at me underwater, and that had essentially killed my wife. But the statue before me bore no marks of erosion; it was as if it had been carved yesterday; the features of the face clear and precise. I turned back to the figure in the bed. With a shock I suddenly saw how these features were repeated in the man before me — his a masculine heavier version but the resemblance was unmistakable. A shiver ran through my body. Watching me Mr Imenand smiled thinly, then with renewed effort continued talking.

'It was so long ago and yet it is still as clear as yesterday to me. I tell you the pharaoh loved this priestess of Isis more than his own life, more than his divine right as a God incarnate. But there was mutiny; the priests, the ministers, even some of the army, were secretly aligning themselves with the Persians. And there was a plot, a plot of assassination. Banafrit heard rumour of this, and unknown to Nectanebo, she posed as his double that day, hiding her own features beneath the Pharaoh's golden mask.'

His voice cracked with emotion and he paused before finding the strength to go on.

'Banafrit was killed in the assassination attack not Nectanebo. That evening the Pharaoh waited for his lover, instead, her servant came to tell him Banafrit had been poisoned by his enemies and was lying in a coma. Mad with grief, Nectanebo went to his lover and, in the hope of saving her set the astrarium to her birth date. He did not know that she was its creator and that by using the machine to attempt to save her, he was instead enabling it to steal her soul. The astrarium passed judgement on the Pharaoh, condemning her to suffer for eternity, denying him the release of death. And so it was that Banafrit and Nectanebo could never be reunited in the afterlife — until now.' His breath had become a terrible wheezing sound as if his very lungs were hollow, but he was determined to finish his tale.

'And so you see, Oliver, you and I have both played Orpheus. I have been doomed for thousands of years to a lingering half-life, a living hell, unable to enter Tuat — heaven — to join my Queen until you placed the astrarium into her grave and reunited her body and soul.'

I stared at him, convinced that his impending death had brought with it some kind of a semi-lucid senility. Reading my expression he smiled.

'I said before, Oliver, whether you believe me or not is unimportant. Nevertheless, you have been my saviour; thanks to you, the sorcery was broken. As you see, I am ageing again, rapidly, but I am grateful I had enough time to find an heir, a talented man who will make his own mark.'

With a supreme effort he reached for my hand — his own hand little more than a bony claw covered with skin. 'Thank you,' his head fell back against the pillow. Then, with his hand still in mine, he spoke again in the faintest of whispers. I recognised his tone was one of blessing, even though the language was one I had never heard in all my travels, euphoria sweeping across his face as his eyes focused on a point beyond me — 'Banafrit,' he whispered before exhaling for the last time.

\* \* \*

I stepped into the bright hallway, closing the bedroom door quietly behind me.

A servant — a young Greek girl — sat sewing in a cane chair beside an open window. She looked up and smiled. 'You must forgive the old man, he is crazy, completely crazy,' she announced then bent to her work again.

The faint jangle of goats' bells floated in from outside, and for a moment I thought I heard the sound of a woman's laughter.

# BIBLIOGRAPHY

Awad, Mohamed and Hamouda, Sahar (editors), *Voices from Cosmopolitan Egypt*, The Alexandrian and Mediterranean Research Center, Bibliotheca Alexandrina, 2006.

Callender, Gae, *The Eye of Horus: A History of Ancient Egypt*, Melbourne: Longman Cheshire, 1993.

Foreman, Laura, *Cleopatra's Palace: In Search of a Legend*, New York: Discovery Books, 1999.

Goddio, Franck and Bernand, André, *Sunken Egypt: Alexandria*, Periplus Publishing, 2004.

Haag, Michael, *Alexandria Illustrated*, American University in Cairo Press, 2004.

La Riche, William, *Alexandria: The Sunken City*, London: Weidenfeld & Nicolson, 1996.

Maspero, Gaston, *The Struggle of Nations: Egypt, Syria and Assyria*, London: Society for Promoting Christian Knowledge, 1896.

Yergin, Daniel, *The Prize: The Epic Quest for Oil, Money, and Power*, New York: Simon & Schuster, 1990.

**For further information on the Antikythera Mechanism:**
www.nature.com/nature/videoarchive/antikythera

**Recommended related fiction:**
Durrell, Lawerence, *The Alexandria Quartet*, Penguin, 1991.
Kharrat, Edwar Al, *Girls of Alexandria*, Quartet Books, 1993.
Sattin, Anthony, *In the Pharaoh's Shadow*, Indigo, 2001.
Sole, Robert, *The Photographer's Wife*, London: Harvill Press, 1999.

# Historical Notes

THE SUEZ CRISIS:  On 29 October 1956, Britain, France and Israel began an unsuccessful military attack to secure the Suez canal after Nasser's decision to nationalise the Suez Canal in reaction to a withdrawal of an offer by Britain and the United States to fund the building of the Aswan Dam.

THE EGYPTIAN REVOLUTION: In 1952 there was a military coup d'état that lead to the overthrow of King Farouk I and to the establishment of a republic, initially run on loosely socialist principles.  Many of the old colonial structures and elite were stripped of their assets and many fled.

THE EUROPEAN DISAPORA IN ALEXANDRIA: There were up to fifty-two nationalities living and working together until Nasser's revolution. The nationalities included Italians, Greeks, Syrians, Jews, Armenians, British, French, and Lebanese.

PRESIDENT SADAT'S PEACE INITATIVES: The Egyptian president Sadat surprised the world and Egypt by visiting the Israeli Parliament – the Knesset – on 20 November 1977 in a gesture of peace and conciliation after being at war with Israel twice, once in 1966 and one in 1973. A year later both President Anwar El Sadat and Israeli Prime Minister Menachem Begin shared the

Nobel Peace Prize; within decades they were assassinated by their own people. Both heads of state, witnessed by President Carter, signed the Camp David Accords at the White House on 17 September 1978. The Accords led directly to the 1979 Israel-Egypt Peace Treaty.

NECTANEBO II – Ruled Egypt 359/358 – 342/341: The last independent Egyptian pharaoh, Nectanebo spent much of his reign fighting off Persians, finally fleeing and mysteriously disappeared – probably to perish in Nubia. His tomb always lay empty; a fact that has been the inspiration behind many myths and stories. During that era many Egyptians believed Nectanebo, who had expanded Egyptian territory into Syria and Cyprus, would return as the great liberator and free them from Persian occupation. As it turned out it was Alexander the Great who liberated the Egyptians from the Persians, leading to the legend that Alexander himself was not the son of Philip of Macedonia but of Nectanebo. Nectanebo himself was known as the Great Magician and was famous for the vast number of temples he had built during his reign in an attempt to rebuild Egyptian self-esteem and resurrect the spiritual and mystical glory of earlier Egyptian dynasties.

ANTIKYTHERA MECHANISM: Discovered off the coast of Rhodes in 1901, the Antikythera mechanism dates from the 1st century and is the most mechanically sophisticated artefact from classical antiquity ever discovered. Contained within a box-like frame it is assumed to have been able to calculate the movement of the Sun, Moon and the five planets as well as display the actual orbits of these celestial spheres. It contains at least thirty gear wheels and there is nothing remotely as sophisticated until medieval times. The extent of its functions are still being analysed to this day. As far I know, no predecessors of the mechanism have yet been discovered.

# Acknowledgements

I am indebted to my partner, Jeremy Asher, without whose support and editorial input this book would not have been possible. I'd also like to thank the following individuals for their invaluable contributions. For geological and oil information: Tom O'Connor, Ian Francis, Jonathan Green, Mike Lakin. With regard to Egyptology, archaeology and local culture: Rosalind Park, Gae Callender, Dr Jean Yves Empereur (French Centre for Alexandrian Studies), Dr Mohamed Awad (Alexandria Preservation Trust), Dr Grzegorz Majcherek, Angus Jackson OBE, Heba Tadrios, Farida El Reedy, Victor Politis, Nino Magy, Captain Mohsen El-Gohary, Dr Emad Khalil, Mr Joe 'Giusy' Barda, Mrs Racheline Barda, Dr Ashraf Sabri, David Thomas, Mr M Rashidy (Cine Egypt), Dr Zahir Hawass (Supreme Council of Antiquities, Egypt), Nina Learner, Rachel Skinner, Paul Schütze. Thanks also goes to the Press Office of the Harbour of Alexandria and to the Windsor Palace Hotel and its staff. Finally, thanks to my editors, Linda Funnell, Sarah Golding, Nicola O'Shea, Lydia Papandrea; and agents, Rick Raftos, Julian Alexander and Catherine Drayton; with special thanks to Rosalind Park whose insight and feedback got me through the more esoteric aspects of the narrative.